Deep in the Earth's crust beneat
site likely to be the birthplace of

MW00564628

And a portal into unimaginable forces and incredible wealth . . .

A place where large ships mysteriously disappear, including the vessel carrying Jack Strider's goddaughter, Katie . . .

A greedy energy baron risks everything to pursue vast supplies of power trapped deep in the Pacific Ocean seabed off the Oregon coast. But the man's psychopathic scheme is about to launch a terrifying tsunami that will destroy the entire west coast of the United States. Strider's beautiful, brilliant partner in law and love joins the fight, and Jack leads a desperate attack on the largest offshore platform ever built. Jack Strider may be the only man who can stop the disaster that is already underway . . . or maybe no one can.

Dedication

Dedicated to Lisa Turner: Calming, stimulating, and a fountain of happiness. My writing mentor, critic, and cheerleader.

And with deep gratitude to:

Deb Smith - my editor who sees the big picture, asks the right questions, and provides sound advice

Dr. Brian Todd - geophysicist whose expertise draws him to the oceans

Ed Gardner - expert on deep sea platforms and those who go to sea

Jeanette Roycraft - for her many insights

Kelly Brother - illustrator and map maker with boundless curiosity

Deb Dixon - publisher and astute counselor

Pam Ireland and Linda Orsburn - who always believed

V. K. Holtzendorf - for her information on gene sequencing

Linda Kichline - publisher/editor/friend - in memoriam

Bart Shea - schooner sailor extraordinaire/friend - in memoriam

And my thanks to the generous and courageous readers who critiqued my manuscript in its early, most ungainly stages: Dr. Ann Livingston, Eric Murphy, Marq de Villiers and Frank Williams

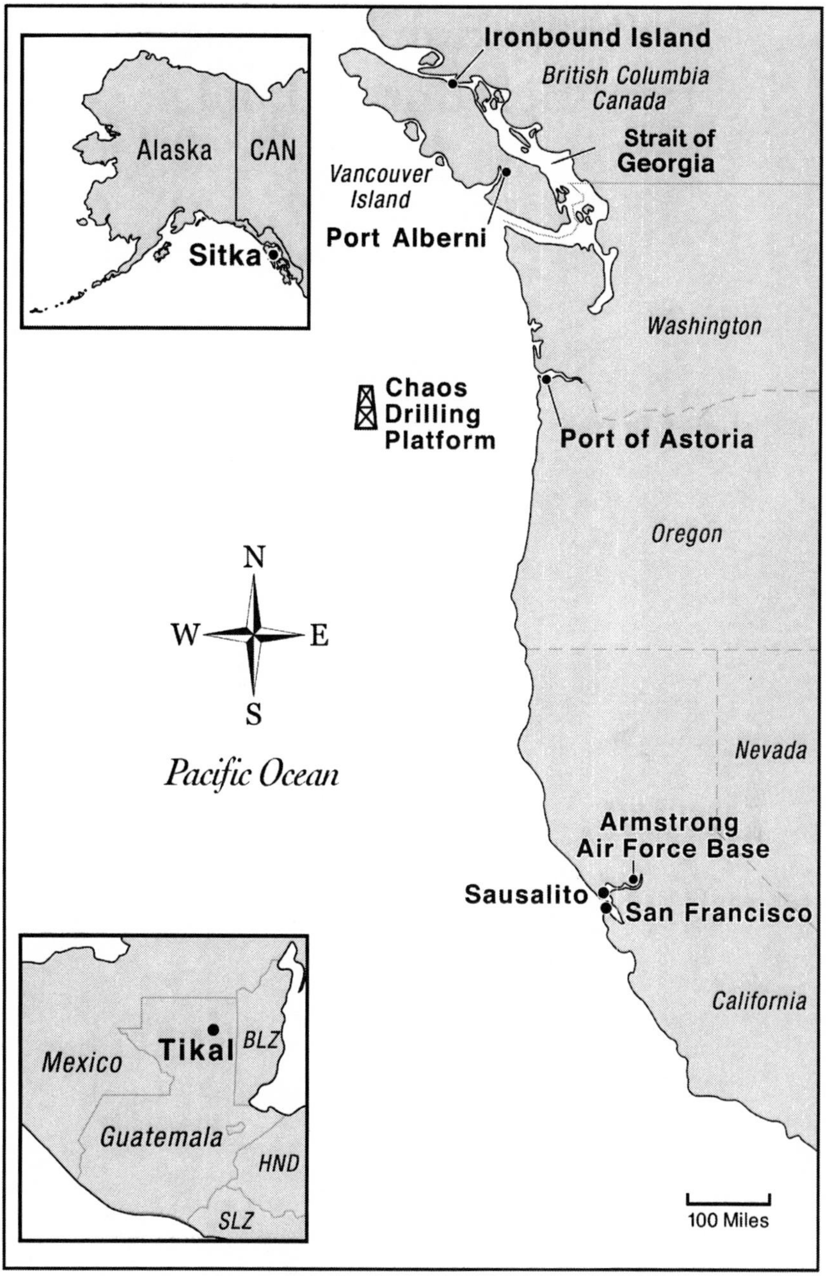
Ironbound Island
British Columbia
Canada
Strait of
Georgia
Vancouver
Island
Port Alberni
Alaska
CAN
Sitka
Washington
Chaos
Drilling
Platform
Port of Astoria
Oregon
N
W
E
S
Pacific Ocean
Nevada
Armstrong
Air Force Base
Sausalito
San Francisco
California
Mexico
Tikal
BLZ
Guatemala
HND
SLZ
100 Miles

Also by Rob Sangster from Bell Bridge Books

Ground Truth
A Jack Strider Thriller

Deep Time

A Jack Strider Thriller
Book 2

by

Rob Sangster

Bell Bridge Books

This is a work of fiction. Names, characters, places and incidents are either the products of the author's imagination or are used fictitiously. Any resemblance to actual persons (living or dead), events, or locations is entirely coincidental.

Bell Bridge Books
PO BOX 300921
Memphis, TN 38130
Print ISBN: 978-1-61194-632-1

Bell Bridge Books is an Imprint of BelleBooks, Inc.

Published in the United States of America.

We at BelleBooks enjoy hearing from readers.
Visit our websites:
BelleBooks.com
BellBridgeBooks.com
ImaJinnBooks.com

10 9 8 7 6 5 4 3 2 1

Cover design: Debra Dixon
Interior design: Hank Smith
Photo/Art credits:
Ship/ocean (manipulated) © Maxirf | Dreamstime.com
Oil rig (manipulated) © 1971yes | Dreamstime.com

Map design: Kelly Brother

Author photo: Hal Jaffe

:Ltdc:01:

Chapter 1

July 6
7:30 p.m.
Northeast Pacific Ocean

"ALL HANDS TAKE cover," Captain Turner shouted into the microphone that reached every space on his ship, *Aleutian.* "Rocket-propelled grenades incoming. Helmsman, hard to starboard. Engine Room, get us out of here."

Turner dove for shelter behind a steel bulkhead on the bridge as a rocket-propelled grenade whistled past and threw up a geyser beyond his ship. A second RPG slammed into the hull just forward of the deckhouse and exploded.

He'd had *Aleutian* circling *Nikita Maru* since dawn, loudspeakers citing the international laws the whaling ship was violating. His crew had dropped small explosives and noise-making devices into the water to scare off any whales in the neighborhood.

To him, *Nikita Maru* was far more than a seaborne factory butchering whales its high-tech hunting boats had killed. It represented insatiable corporate greed driving its prey to extinction. He had committed himself to fighting them every way he could. Damn them to hell.

Very aware that a sister Greenpeace vessel had been rammed and sunk by a similar Japanese ship, he'd felt like a matador engaging a maddened bull, but with no weapon that could kill it. Now the bull had turned on him. He had to flee to save the crew and the ship.

He kept *Aleutian* turning until she presented only her stern to the whaler, heavy seas making her an erratic target. The next two RPG shells splashed harmlessly short. Just as he thought *Aleutian* was out of range, a Hail Mary shot crashed squarely into the fantail.

"All hands, man your stations. Damage Control, see whether that last shot hit the rudder or steering gear. Communications, tell our Vancouver office what happened, and that we're running for Seattle." He looked over his shoulder at his navigator. "How far to the nearest land?"

"Two hundred ten miles to the Oregon coast, Skipper."

The Japanese captain had already been so aggressive he might decide to come after them. If he did, he had the speed to run them down. It would be dark soon, and that also favored the whaler, because its electronic equipment was far superior to *Aleutian's* thirty-year-old systems.

"Jenkins, have the lifeboats made ready. Katie, keep close watch on the radar. Tell me immediately if *Nikita Maru* is catching up to us."

He wiped sweat from his forehead. *This is going to be a very long night.*

A FEW MINUTES after midnight, the ship entered a pocket of cold air. Captain Turner shivered and said to the helmsman, "Holding up okay, Tommy?"

"Heavy seas. Doin' my damnedest to keep on course, sir."

For the hundredth time, he stared over Katie's shoulder at the radar screen. More than once he'd seen ghostly blips that faded away. Must be nerves from worrying that the son of a bitch might run right over his ship. Katie had been aboard only a week, but had already proved smart and strong-minded. She'd kept her attention riveted on the radar screen for hours without a break. He knew if anything real showed up, he could count on Katie to spot it.

He braced himself against a steel bulkhead while his eyes scanned the darkness. Almost immediately, he saw something unexpected. He squinted. *Good God, it isn't possible.*

"Skipper," the helmsman shouted, "tell me what—"

Before he could answer, it was too late.

Chapter 2

July 7
5:00 p.m.
Tikal, Guatemala

JACK STRIDER pressed his long frame against a nearly vertical rock face hundreds of feet above the Guatemalan jungle tree canopy.

His weight rested on his left toes wedged into a crack and his right foot on a slightly higher, angled shelf. He'd jammed his left hand into a shallow crevice above his shoulder, but his right hand was useless, unable to reach any handhold. His muscles quivered from fatigue, ready to let go. He could hang on for only a few more seconds. He'd taken one chance too many.

Trying to back down blind would be suicide. His only chance was an unprotected leap for a hold above. If he missed, he'd be dead in however many seconds it would take to plunge into the tree tops far below. The humid stillness was broken by buzzing insects strafing his head.

Son of a bitch. I was insane to try this climb alone.

He sucked in a deep breath. Time was up. He had to try.

Desperate for lift, he shifted more weight to his right foot. As he lunged upward, top layers of rock scaled off, and the shelf collapsed. He hooked his right hand, fingers like talons, over the edge of an impossibly out-of-reach hold. Dangling from his hands, he jerked his left knee up and flattened his climbing shoe against a crease in a column. His stability would only last for a few heartbeats. A one-arm pull-up gained him a higher connection with his left hand. His foot found a niche.

Adrenaline, skill, and urgency all kicked in, and he moved fluidly from point to point, defying gravity, until he hauled himself across the summit outcrop.

Muscles burning, he rolled onto his back and tossed his Petzi helmet to the side. After several looping spins across the rock, it dropped out of sight over the lip of the cliff. *Damn.* There was a spot a few hundred yards away where he could rappel down, but now he'd have to descend with his head unprotected against falling rocks.

Something that had seemed so important when he'd stood at the bottom of the cliff looking up had vanished a couple of minutes ago when he'd felt trapped. Now it filled his mind again. His old friend, Zalman Amos, fascinated by the ancient Maya civilization, had proposed months ago that they attempt to scale this peak in Guatemala's Tikal National Park. They both knew the climb would be tough, but the panoramic view of Tikal, seat of power of the Maya empire, was said to be unsurpassed. When Zalman later developed health problems, he'd made climbing to this place the only entry on his bucket list. Then he became too weak to make the trip.

Thinking the climb was too risky to attempt solo, Jack had invited Debra Vanderberg, his law partner and very significant other, to join him. She was an experienced climber who could hold her own. She was also the love of his life. He remembered how days under a tropical sun and nights wrapped in sultry breezes had stoked their intimacy in the past.

She had accepted, but had been very reserved on their flight down, keeping busy and avoiding eye contact with him. Not long after they'd reached their room at the Tikal Inn, her frustration had burst out.

"You keep hiring more lawyers—sure, they're hotshots, but they're all expensive, and they need desks and paralegals and. . . . The point is that the firm's revenues haven't been keeping up. We're close to going on the rocks. And you've been acting like a stress-bomb because you're way behind schedule finishing your brief for the make-or-break appearance in federal court coming up. That lawsuit against Armstrong Air Force Base is the most important this firm has ever handled for our clients, for the firm, and for you."

Her flashing eyes and flushed cheeks told him that her frustration had transformed into anger—at him.

"I care about helping people too," she'd said, "but we can't keep turning away paying clients. We're on the edge, and I'm fed up."

Caught by surprise, he'd been defensive. That had upset her so much she'd packed up and hired a van to catch a plane to Guatemala City and back to San Francisco.

The intensity of her feelings had shaken him, but he'd still felt committed to the mission he'd accepted from Zalman. It was about respect. Okay, maybe some of his decision had been a testosterone-fuelled need to prove something to Debra. Taking on this wicked technical climb solo had been nuts, but he hadn't thought it would almost kill him.

Giving his nerves a few moments to unclench, he sat crossed-legged at the edge of the cliff, looking down at monumental stone structures built in the fourth century BC, hundreds of years before London was even a settlement on the Thames. Fierce Mayan kings had ruled from Tikal's palaces until the whole region was mysteriously abandoned in the tenth century. Since then, the grip of the rain forest had taken over. Temples poked above Spanish cedars and mahogany giants laced together by spiny lianas. He couldn't see the jaguars, ocelots, and coatimundis in the dense forest, but knew they were there. A brilliant red and gold toucan tilted to inspect him as it blazed past far below.

He reached into his fanny pack and pulled out the cell phone he'd brought to photograph the landscape so important to Zalman. Moving carefully along the ledge, he took the shots and emailed them.

The ringtone startled him. He hoped it was Debra calling from Guatemala City to say she was coming back to Tikal to work it out. Then he saw Hank Thompson's name on the screen.

An instant of disappointment, then pleasure. He and Hank had been good friends since sophomore year of college. They'd rowed on the Stanford crew, double-dated, even bought an old Ford convertible together for $500. Even though they lived hundreds of miles apart and led hectic lives, they found time to get together for some small adventure at least once a year.

Hank's job at Greenpeace had led to Jack doing *pro bono* work for the non-profit. When Hank had asked him to be godfather to his only daughter, Katie, he'd been delighted to accept. With his own parents dead, and having no siblings, it was his chance to become part of a family.

Katie was no distant goddaughter. Last summer, she'd put her blond hair up in a bun and worked for Debra as an intern. She'd also crewed for him in Saturday sailing races, sure-footed on deck and able to read the wind as well as any seagull. He and Debra thought of her as almost their shared child.

He'd sworn to himself that as a surrogate father, he'd do a damned sight better job than his own father had. That brought a flash-memory of his father to whom he'd been no more than an extension of ego. He'd been too young then to understand why that hurt. Now he did. He brushed the dark thought back into its cave.

"Hey, Hank, what's up?"

"Katie's in bad trouble. I need your help." His voice was raw.

"Of course. What's the problem?"

"*Aleutian*, our ship in the northeast Pacific, was attacked. Katie is aboard as radar operator."

"My God, no. Tell me what happened."

Hank told him about the RPG attack by *Nikita Maru* and *Aleutian*'s attempt to escape. "Captain Turner said *Aleutian* was taking on some water but seemed seaworthy. No one was hurt. He thought he could make Seattle unless the whaling ship tracked them down. Using the VHF emergency channel, he hailed what he thought was a fleet of fishing boats a few miles south of him, but they didn't respond."

"Damn them. As soon as *Aleutian* makes port in Seattle, get depositions from Turner and his crew. We'll file a complaint against *Nikita Maru* and track down the fishermen who refused to help."

"*Aleutian* never made it to port, and Captain Turner never contacted us again. That's why I'm freaked out. We tried to reach him. No answer. We also tried to communicate with ships and aircraft that might be in the area, including the fishing fleet he saw. Nothing."

"Then you have no idea where *Aleutian* is." *Or even if she's afloat,* he didn't say. "You must have a search going."

"Coast Guard Air-Sea Rescue, but they've found nothing, not even debris or an oil slick. She's disappeared."

He pictured Katie and the rest of the crew clinging to lifeboats somewhere in the vast northeast Pacific.

"I know someone who can help search. Give me the coordinates of *Aleutian*'s last position." Seconds ticked away. "Hank? Hank, are you there?" *Damn it.* Some mindless satellite had dropped the call. He tried again. No signal.

He heard fluttering overhead. Surprised, he turned just as a king vulture—bald head, hooked orange beak, and white shoulders—dropped to the rock a dozen yards away.

"Get away!" He shouted and waved both arms. Flapping heavy wings, it hopped on its talons but didn't go far. Others would be on the way, lured by the possibility of a big meal. He hurled a stone. The vulture ignored it.

He was damn glad Debra wasn't with him now. He fitted the harness, got the line in his hand, and backed over the side, hanging in space. If he got stuck as he rappelled down and hung motionless against the cliff, he'd have to fight off the vultures. That didn't matter. Katie needed his help.

"WELCOME BACK, Sr. Strider," the clerk at the desk of the Tikal Inn called softly to him as he hurried past the open window of the rustic hotel's office. "You had a pleasant afternoon I hope," she said with a tentative smile.

"I'd call it . . . memorable. Listen, an emergency has come up. I need your help to get back to San Francisco right away."

Her eyes opened wider and the corners of her mouth turned down, meaning she knew Debra had left abruptly and alone. Then a smile returned as she assumed that he was doing the right thing, going after his maiden.

After giving her instructions about lining up transportation and airline tickets, he walked to his thatched-roof bungalow. Distracted by his thoughts, he banged his head on a doorway not designed for someone his height.

He slumped into an armchair and punched the stored phone number for Frank Williams, president of Google Maps which had exclusive use of the GeoEye satellite. If GeoEye didn't cover the section of the northeast Pacific where *Aleutian* had last checked in, he'd know who had a bird that did. The signal was back, so he impressed on Frank the urgent need for satellite reports.

"I'll get right on it. If *Aleutian* is afloat, GeoEye will spot her," Frank said.

Jack told him how to contact Hank to get the last coordinates they had for *Aleutian.*

"I'll get them. Problem is, GeoEye is blind until after dawn. I'll call you as soon as I have something to report."

He couldn't accept that Katie might be lost. If the satellite didn't find her, then what? The Coast Guard was doing what it could with limited resources, but had found nothing. Maybe an airplane that could fly low, slow patterns over the area like an airborne bloodhound could do better. He wondered how fast he could charter a plane and pilot. *Wait a minute!* He already knew the perfect pilot for the job. He tapped in a number in Mexico and listened to it ring over and over. No answer. No invitation to leave a message.

He was about to break the connection when he heard, "What's up, Mr. Justice Jack? You headin' back down here to Copper Canyon, maybe for some high-flying target practice out the airplane window like that Sarah Palin woman? If you do, bring that fireball partner of yours along, you hear?"

The syrupy sound of Gano LeMoyne's voice always reminded Jack of a New Orleans pool hustler.

"I'll tell Debra what you said." He wasn't about to tell Gano that Debra had stormed out with smoke shooting out of her ears. "Gano, there's an emergency, so I'll get right to why I called. A Greenpeace ship has disappeared somewhere off the Oregon coast." He repeated what Hank Thompson had told him, but left Katie out. It hurt too much to repeat that part. "If we don't find the ship or the crew fast . . . well, we just have to."

"That's some damn mystery, son. So I suppose you want me to crank up my ol' Cessna Skylane turbo-banger and fly those wave tips like some drunk crop duster. Well, I'm afraid that's not in the cards. Lookin' for poor souls lost at sea just ain't my kind of gig. Here's the thing, you got this picture of me stoned and bored, feet up on the railing of this rickety ol' hotel of mine in Divisadero, right?"

That was exactly how he pictured Gano—lanky, tan, bold mustache, cowboy hat shading his eyes as he stared across Copper Canyon, some kind of firearm within reach, willing to work on either side of the law.

"Fact is," Gano went on, "there are a lot of fine ladies down here, within arm's reach you might say, and well-heeled clients who pay for my services in cash. *Comprende*?"

He had to have Gano, so he had to tell him the rest, "My goddaughter Katie is in that crew. She could be in a lifeboat or a life jacket. I need your help. You're the only—"

"Why are you still talking? I'll be airborne in an hour. With my extra tank, I have a range of fifteen hundred miles. All I need are the search coordinates."

He gave Gano the contact information for Greenpeace.

"I hate to sound mercenary at a time like this," Gano said, "but the motto on my business card reads, 'If the money's right, I'll get it done.' These Greenpeace folks are always raising funds from rich whale huggers and the like, so they must be loaded. No sweat them financing this excitement, right?"

"Damn it, Gano, it's a non-profit, not that you'd know what that is. If they don't have enough, I'll make up the rest."

"I'm pulling my stuff together as we speak."

"Good man." He hung up.

Gano was unpredictable, hot-headed, and far too quick to draw and shoot. But when Jack had needed someone to protect his back in the past, even step out front, Gano had been rock solid. If Katie and the crew of *Aleutian* could be found, Gano would do it.

He called Hank to give him a status report, but was routed to his voice mail.

He had a few minutes before the van would show up, so he got out of his sweaty climbing clothes and turned on the shower. The water was tepid and the pressure low, but he came out feeling better. He pulled on a navy blue shirt and faded Levi's, ran a comb through his black hair, and stuffed his clothes and climbing gear into his duffel bag.

Plate of nachos and cold bottle of Moza Bock beer in hand, he sat on a small verandah to wait for the van. Staring across a clearing into a dense stand of cedars, he remembered how he'd thought this evening would end. He'd planned to find a park guard who didn't mind taking a few *quetzales* to break the rules and let a crazy *gringo* and his lady back into the park. He and Debra would climb the steep wood ladders attached to the side of Temple IV, the tallest structure in all of pre-Columbian America. They'd sleep up there so they could watch the glorious sun rise together. He'd thought it would be pretty romantic.

He'd met Debra when she was a student in one of his advanced seminars. From the moment she'd walked in, her beauty had filled the space. He'd learned later that her Balinese mother had provided the genes that gave her high cheek-bones, golden coloring, and long, glossy black hair. Her eyes were slightly almond shaped, tilting up infinitesimally at the outer corners. But it wasn't how her eyes looked that reached him. It was how her eyes looked at him. Her height of five feet nine had been inherited from her Dutch father. There was something in her enigmatic smile, composed demeanor, and the tilt of her head that made him sure that in her childhood she'd been admired, even adored. By the end of the third class session, it was also clear she was the smartest student in the room.

He'd been a professor long enough to know better than to give in to his strong temptation to get to know her on a personal level. That had changed when they'd been thrown together in Mexico three years ago. She'd been sent to spy on him, but soon joined him in a battle that involved nuclear waste and contamination of an aquifer that millions depended on. Afterward, romance had bloomed.

His cell phone signaled a call. Hank. He delivered the news that Google GeoEye and Gano would be on the job and would report back.

"That means a lot," Hank said, but his voice was as glum as it had been earlier.

"Hank, ships as big as *Aleutian* just don't suddenly disappear, so what could have happened? If there had been a tsunami or violent weather, you would have mentioned it, right?

"Of course."

"If *Nikita Maru* had been catching up, *Aleutian* would have picked her up on radar miles away. Even if she had started to sink, *Aleutian* wouldn't have gone down instantly. Same for a collision with some other vessel."

"We heard nothing."

"Pirates?"

"Not in the northeast Pacific. Besides, the whaling ship would have been a much better target for ransom."

"Terrorists?"

"No one has claimed responsibility. In any of those situations, *Aleutian* would have fired out a distress call. Whatever happened, they had no time to call for help."

Jack agreed to stay in touch and clicked off. He took a swig of the Moza Bock. It tasted sour. He couldn't make himself bite into the congealed nachos.

The tension on the cliff face followed by the horrible news about Katie and *Aleutian* had drained him, but something nagged deep in his brain. He, Hank, and everyone else were approaching this in a rational way. What if the answer wasn't rational or was beyond their experience? He'd read for years about strange phenomena at sea, but had given the stories no credibility because they usually pointed fingers at aliens or Greek gods. But maybe something really weird was going on in that part of the Pacific Ocean.

Chapter 3

July 8
8:00 a.m.
San Francisco, California

DEBRA VANDERBERG strode through the front door of Strider & Vanderberg and down the hall toward her office. As she passed the desk of Jack's assistant, Mei, she saw the surprised look on her face. Mei obviously wasn't expecting her back from Guatemala ahead of schedule. No doubt Mei wanted an explanation, but, seeing Debra's expression, she immediately looked back at her computer.

After closing her door behind her, Debra bent her knees slightly and delivered a side snap kick to her office bookcase. Then another, and a third, fourth, and fifth. Light and lightning-fast—she didn't intend to destroy anything, just vent some of her frustration boiling inside. She'd calmed down a little since storming out of the Tikal Inn and flying back to San Francisco, but her sleep had been fitful. Points she wished she had made kept flashing through her mind. They'd argued about business decisions once in a while, but this was the first time a disagreement had been left unresolved.

She would have gone to Tikal simply because Jack had made his commitment to Zalman and needed her as a climbing partner, but she'd jumped at the chance for a romantic trip together. She'd been stressed about the firm's financial condition but thought she could suppress it until they got back. That hadn't worked.

She'd thought Jack would call while she was waiting in the Guatemala City airport for the onward flight. She wanted him to beseech, plead, or whatever, to get her to come back to Tikal. But he hadn't called, so neither had she.

He could have admitted she was right to be worried that their firm was plunging into the red. Instead, he'd been self-righteous and lectured her on the importance of practicing public interest law as though she'd had some mysterious lapse of conscience.

She knew his passion for helping people came from his core. That had been a powerful magnet that had drawn her to him in the first place. Not nearly so attractive was that she sometimes had to be a portal into the real world for him. How could he ignore the fact that their offices had gotten so crowded that two lawyers had to work at desks set up in a hallway, or that others had to scurry to vacate the conference room when it was needed for a client meeting? And what about the guy who sometimes took his laptop and sat in a chair at the end of the wharf just to get some quiet?

Damn it! He had no right. He was the one who had so overextended himself that he'd fallen badly behind schedule on their lawsuit against Armstrong Air Force Base.

There was a discreet knock on her door, then again louder. She was about to tell the knocker to come back later when the door opened halfway. Her paralegal's head poked in. Seeing her face, his eyes widened, and he withdrew without a word and closed the door quickly.

She looked out a window in the direction of the stone building on the next pier but didn't see it. She resented having to keep bringing up the business side of their practice. It made her sound like she was obsessed with money. She didn't deserve that. She wasn't a student in Jack's law school class anymore, and she wasn't his bookkeeper. She was a named partner in the firm.

She couldn't resist a small smile, remembering the law seminar she'd taken from him at Stanford. It had drawn the cream of the third-year crop and each of them wanted to show how smart he or she was. They often did that by challenging Jack, throwing a complicated legal conundrum or obscure case at him. He handled them with ease and always kept his cool. On the rare occasions he was bested, he would smile and offer a nod of approval. He liked to give examples of lawyers who showed high ethical standards in tough situations, but usually balanced that with a small joke or something self-deprecating. Within a week, everyone talked about him as the kind of lawyer they wanted to be. For her, it hadn't hurt that he was ruggedly handsome, athletic, six feet four, and seemed to enjoy engaging her in debates. He'd kept a distance because he was a professor, but she'd wished the situation had been different.

After clerking for a 9th Circuit court judge for a year, she'd joined Sinclair & Simms, a high-powered San Francisco law firm, and immersed herself in the law and The City.

At the time she took his seminar in law school, Jack had been a rising star with an unlimited future. That had changed dramatically several years later after his father, a prominent San Francisco judge, was involved in a nasty scandal and committed suicide. Jack had no knowledge of what his father had been doing, but his name had been tarnished by association. When the dean pressured him out of the law school, he'd joined Sinclair & Simms as a partner. Because the scandal kept making headlines, Stan Simms had demanded that Jack be fired. Instead, Justin Sinclair, the firm's managing partner, had exiled Jack to work in the firm's Mexico City office.

A couple of months later, Sinclair had become furious about Jack's investigation of one of the firm's clients and sent her to Mexico City to spy on him. She'd quickly realized that, unless Jack could stop him, the firm's client was about to cause catastrophes on both sides of the border. She'd dumped her sure-thing partnership at Sinclair & Simms, thrown in with Jack, and, fighting side-by-side with him, had stopped the bad guys.

Her reminiscence was interrupted by buzzing that meant her assistant was trying to reach her. She noticed three lights flashing—indicating calls on hold—and, for the first time, the stack of memos and notes that had piled up during the brief trip to Guatemala that had left her exhausted, all for nothing. *To hell with them all. They'll have to wait.*

She and Jack had returned to the U.S. from Mexico wrapped up in a high-energy, loving relationship, and he had asked her to be his partner in his new public interest law firm. She'd thought marriage was coming up, but it hadn't turned out that way. They still spent most of their private time together, but neither one of them had even made a move toward living together.

He was far different now from the man she'd met in his classroom. Some of that was the result of the drama that followed the death of his father, and part of it came from his battles in Mexico. The ivory-tower intellectual had transformed into a man who'd had his boots in the dust and learned the meaning of "ground truth." He'd also dumped the life goal of serving on the U.S. Supreme Court drilled into him by his father and replaced it with his own. She'd been attracted to him in law school, but she loved the man he'd grown to be—well, most of the time.

She picked up the notes and rifled through them without paying attention.

She wanted two big things to happen. They *had* to win the Armstrong case, and they *had* to bring the firm back from the edge of the financial cliff. But that wasn't enough. She needed back the intense relationship they'd had. Their blowup at Tikal had made her understand that she was caught in a bargain with the Devil. To win the lawsuit and save the firm, she'd been behaving like a grumpy accountant. It wouldn't be long before that drove Jack away. If that happened, well, that was a world she didn't want to think about.

Her paralegal knocked and entered, looking determined to say his piece. "I just had a call that two people representing the plaintiffs in the Armstrong lawsuit will be here at three thirty to meet with you and Mr. Strider. The guy who called seemed pretty upset. It's not on your calendar, so I thought I'd better mention it. You do have that time slot free."

"Jack is still out of the country, so I'll handle those clients by myself." They were forcing a meeting, and that meant they were stressed. She understood, and her heart was with them, but it was going to be a tough meeting.

Chapter 4

July 9
3:30 p.m.
San Francisco

"THE FARE IS thirty dollars, Mac, plus the extra ten you promised if I beat fifteen minutes from SFO. Got you here in fourteen minutes flat." The cabbie reached out for the cash.

Jack paid and stood for a minute, duffel bag at his side, looking down Pier 9 toward his office. He'd barely survived the stupidest climbing blunder he'd ever made, including dangling from a rope while a half-dozen buzzards patrolled his back. Much worse, Katie was missing, and he'd have to give that news to Debra. It would break her heart. Despite his weariness, he had to go inside.

Good afternoon, sir," Mei said. "It's a good thing you called from the airport. Ms. Vanderberg has been sitting with the representatives of the Armstrong plaintiffs group waiting for you for quite a while."

"Don't tell them I'm here yet. I need a couple of minutes to get my head straight." He went into his office and closed the door. He'd already heard that many of the plaintiffs, suffering from the stress of severe health troubles, were losing faith in the legal process. Some, out of money for health care, were close to despair. There had already been two suicides.

As he saw it, his job was to give them hope. That would be hard because he also owed them absolute honesty. Even if he were at the top of his game, which he certainly wasn't right now, it would be a rough meeting.

The plaintiffs were a group known as Victims of Armstrong, thirty fearful and angry men and women. Dozens more would join them later. They were active duty military and civilian employees of Armstrong Air Force Base. Along with family members and retirees, they all lived in the area of the base. Most were sick, some were dying, and others represented those already dead.

Before he took the case, he'd had no idea that Armstrong was such a massive military presence. The eleven thousand men and women in uniform and four thousand civilians who worked there handled more passenger and cargo traffic than any other military terminal in America. He and Debra quickly realized there were two types of culprits. Most obvious were the mammoth military cargo planes—the C-5 Galaxy, C-17A Globemaster, and KC-10 Extender—that generated thousands of tons of toxic emissions around-the-clock, as well as daily dumps of oil and jet fuel. In his mind, the greater culprits were the series of commanding officers who had a duty not to harm people on and around the base. Instead, they'd ignored the damage so they could protect their careers and keep from sending waves up the chain of command. He looked forward to making them defend that behavior in a court room.

Thinking about all those who had suffered made his emotional temperature rise. He looked at a desk drawer by his knee where he'd tacked a list of their names.

He'd memorized the list of appalling health problems around the base: bleeding disorders, cancer, dementia, depression, diabetes, GI troubles, heart attacks, high blood pressure, kidney failure, miscarriages, Parkinson's disease—it went on. Some of the cases were so rare they baffled the docs.

He suddenly felt a touch of claustrophobia. Compared to the wide- open spaces he'd just left, his office felt stuffy and dark. He stood and raised the blinds Mei had lowered. He opened the door onto the deck outside his second-floor office. A few deep breaths and the familiar sounds of the waterfront made him feel a little better.

But his clients at Armstrong *never* felt better. It had taken them a long time to sense the connection between those pollutants and the damage to their health. When they did, they demanded help from the city council, but its members were not about to take on the Air Force, the Pentagon, and, as one of them put it, "the whole damned federal government." Their state legislators had also brushed them off, except for one who had pushed back hard, questioning his clients' loyalty. Debra later got a tip that the man was on the secret payroll of one of the largest manufacturers of military aviation parts in the world.

They'd come to Strider & Vanderberg with no money to pay legal fees, so that would have to come from winning the case. If his clients didn't win, the firm would get nothing. Now, six months later, interviews, investigations, and experts had cost the firm more than $100,000 out of pocket.

He reminded himself of what he wanted to accomplish. First, get enough money to compensate the clients for their expenses and suffering. Second, require the Air Force to cut far back on the contamination. His third goal was even more ambitious: set a precedent that would stop similar practices at other U.S. military bases. That would also decrease the massive volume of greenhouse gasses the military pumped into the atmosphere 24/7, unrestrained by the laws that regulated most industries. He'd taken this case to seek justice for these plaintiffs but, as he dug into the facts, he saw how much more was at stake. He wished he were about to confront the base commanding officer instead of meeting with wounded plaintiffs.

He opened a folder that held photographs of every plaintiff and stared at the wan faces and resigned expressions. He rubbed his eyes, knowing that some of them would not live long enough to be awarded money for better health care.

Mei's voice came through the speaker. "While you were at Tikal, you had a call from a man who wanted to meet with you day after tomorrow morning. I told him you were working on a major case and weren't accepting any new appointments."

"Exactly right. Thanks."

"But then he said, 'Eight a.m., Sausalito Yacht Club aboard the schooner *Excalibur.* Give Mr. Strider my name and tell him to bring Ms. Vanderberg with him.' Then he hung up. He wasn't rude, just very sure of himself. His name is Petros Barbas."

That got his attention. Petros Barbas's empire included tankers and container ships, a collection of ultra-luxury resorts in remote outposts, and much more, all under the umbrella of Odyssey Properties, a privately-held Greek holding company. It was possible that in the past decade not one person had declined a meeting with Barbas.

"Tell him I'll be there." Then he remembered the other part of the message. "And Ms. Vanderberg too, if she's available."

"I don't think he expects a confirmation."

I'll bet he doesn't. Then a thought drifted past. Why had Barbas specified that he wanted Debra present?

"Sir," Mei spoke up again. "Also, Ms. Vanderberg wants me to remind you that she and the representatives of the plaintiffs' group are still waiting in the conference room. I'm afraid she might be in a bad mood."

She had every right to be. She'd been honest in raising the red flag about financial survival for the firm when she knew he didn't want to hear that. And he'd been a jerk to be defensive rather than give her a rah-rah and promise to share that load.

As he entered the conference room, a young man wearing clean but worn Levi's and a California Bears T-shirt stood up, nodded, and then quickly sat. He looked about twenty, perhaps ten years younger than the woman who remained seated. She had short-cropped blond hair that had the look of a wig. Her eyes were unusually deep-set with a haunted look. Debra sat across the table from them.

"I'd like to introduce Mrs. Jane Rose and Mr. Tom Barlow," Debra said.

He was very aware that she hadn't said his name, hadn't even looked at him. When she finished the introduction, she pursed her lips tightly in the way she did when she was very ticked off but determined not to vent.

He'd read the briefing on their histories. Mrs. Rose was married to a lieutenant whose squadron was stationed at Armstrong. They had lived in officers' quarters on the base for five years and had two daughters. Mrs. Rose was working as a civilian CPA for the Air Force when diagnosed with aggressive metaplastic breast cancer, a type found in less than one percent of women who have breast cancer. The surgery, radiation, and chemotherapy she had received would not save her.

Tom Barlow, a physics student at UC Berkeley, had grown up in housing one block beyond the base perimeter. His father had been an aircraft maintenance specialist on the base for twenty-three years. Tom's mother had died ten years ago from a heart attack of unknown cause. His father had died four months ago from extensive small cell lung cancer, the kind usually caused by smoking. Because his father had been a non-smoker, Tom joined Victims of Armstrong and started probing into the cause of his father's cancer. He'd quickly discovered that the percentages of people around Armstrong who were afflicted with various diseases were far higher than in the general population. Since genetics and lifestyle did not come close to accounting for the higher percentages, he became an outspoken leader who raged against the base commander's refusal to undertake an unbiased investigation. He'd been quoted as saying that the Air Force didn't *want* to know the answers.

Jack shook their hands and sat at the head of the table. "I'll begin by telling you about our strategy in your case. First, we have to prove that military activities at Armstrong generate vast amounts of pollution. Second, we have to show that those emissions are carcinogenic and otherwise hazardous to health. We've identified the ingredients of the fuel that are harmful, but the Pentagon has refused to release data to us on how much fuel is consumed at Armstrong. Third, we must demonstrate that a significantly above-average number of people on the base and in its vicinity got sick, and many died. After that, the highest hurdle will be proving that this pollution *caused* the illnesses and deaths. We'll be working on that right up until the trial."

"My dad told me," Tom said, "that one of those giant Stratocruisers burns more than thirty thousand gallons of fuel an *hour*. That's six times what an average driver uses in a whole *year*."

"We can prove," Debra said, "that the types of aviation fuel they use are super-polluting, generating three times as much CO_2 as gasoline does. That exhaust also includes nitrous oxide, sulfur dioxide, and soot—more pollutants."

"Are you guys going to bring up the damage a big fire or explosion on that base would cause?" Tom asked. "Or an earthquake? That place is loaded with radioactive materials. Throw that stuff into the air, and the wind direction will decide whether San Francisco gets wiped out."

Debra looked taken aback. Several seconds passed before she said, "We have to focus on actual damage done to these plaintiffs. We've lined up medical experts to testify that the toxicity created can cause the illnesses and deaths suffered by people on and near the base. Then we have to prove that it *did* cause that harm in a number of cases large enough to convince a jury to conclude that pollution was the culprit. Results so far are very supportive, but we have a long way to go. Suing the government is a steep mountain to climb, but the facts should knock the jurors out of their socks."

"You should know," Jack said, "that we're going to be navigating through minefields in this trial. If we come off as broadly anti-military, we'll lose sympathy from some on the jury. That's ironic since most of the people we're trying to protect are the airmen themselves. They're soaking in the poison day and night."

He wouldn't tell them that this high-profile lawsuit could be a disaster for his firm. Being stereotyped as anti-military or anti-government would cost him clients. Something he'd never mentioned to Debra was that if the lawsuit got really nasty, some vigilante might come after him with an AR-15.

"Just a minute," Tom blurted. "Civilian kids grow up knowing the make and model of every hot car. Not me. I can give you the specs of any U.S. military aircraft. We're military families. Air Force blue and silver run in my veins. At least it used to. Do you know about McClellan Air Force Base, which isn't far from Armstrong? Spills and leaks of fuel and all sorts of caustic crap contaminated the groundwater so badly EPA had to put it on the Superfund cleanup list. Think how many people got sick and died at McClellan without ever knowing why."

Before Jack could tell him they would be using the McClellan example, Tom kept going. "When a hose breaks loose and dumps jet fuel on the ground, it migrates down to where our drinking water comes from. Exhaust from a huge cargo jet taking off doesn't poison just the airmen standing on the tarmac. It's also sucked into the lungs of kids playing Little League baseball miles away. When people join the military, they know they might have to face danger to defend their country, but they didn't agree to be killed by their own people. So if Victims of Armstrong is 'broadly antimilitary' now it's because those bastards killed my father, they're killing Jane, and they're killing God knows how many others."

Jack knew the firm's research showed that children from infants through teenagers had been hit especially hard at Armstrong. That cut deep.

"Tom." Jane put her hand on his forearm to calm him.

"I won't shut up. The military is the largest user of energy, including petroleum, in the U.S. With five percent of the world's population, the U.S. generates more than thirty percent of all global warming gasses, and a lot of that comes from its military. Overall, global military operations use more energy than any other activity on Earth. How screwed up is that?"

Jack already knew those numbers but wasn't about to cut Tom off. He wondered whether Tom knew that the Pentagon spent an amazingly high percent of its budget not on buying oil but on assuring *access* to oil. That was part of its justification for maintaining more than a thousand military outposts inside 140 countries around the world. He'd like the jury to know all that, but some of the jurors might think that was just fine, so he couldn't indulge himself.

"Jane, Tom, you need to report back to the other plaintiffs where your lawsuit stands, so we have to be candid. This lawsuit is so full of uncertainties and difficulties that winning is a long shot."

They glanced at one another. Tom didn't look nearly as defiant now. He straightened and said, "Representing us is costing your firm a fortune, and you're telling us that we probably won't win. Why did you take our case?"

"Because what's being done to you, and others like you, has to be stopped, and you had nowhere else to turn. We didn't get into this to make a point. We got in it to win for you. As we go forward, the government lawyers may move for continuances over and over to try to outlast us. Law students are taught the maxim that 'justice delayed is justice denied.' In this case, if our plaintiffs don't get prompt justice, some won't get any justice because—" He cut himself off. He didn't want to say more in front of Jane.

"Or," Debra said, "they could switch strategy and demand an early trial date.

They would do that because this is such a complex case. They know we have limited resources and haven't had time to complete our research and preparation."

"And they will definitely try to get our complaint thrown out of court," Jack said. "I'm afraid they're going to demand dismissal at a crucial hearing that's coming up very soon."

He paused, wanting to tell them that they might be better off marching in the streets and beating down the doors of their legislators. And that he wanted to, but couldn't, go into the courtroom and blast the generals who turned away from the suffering and death. Just once he'd like to let it all out. He couldn't remember the last time he'd done that. He restrained himself as he always did, remaining the voice of reason.

"We're doing everything we can to win," Debra said. "You already know that the Pentagon refused to give us records on how much of each kind of fuel they burn at Armstrong. They did it to force us to spend time and money to come after them. Well, we did. I got word this morning that our Freedom of Information Act request has been granted. Being required to release that information to us could turn the tide in our favor." Debra wore a pleased smile.

"Oh my God," Jane said.

"So you're not giving up." Tom's voice was stronger.

"Not unless hell freezes over," Jack said. But he felt a chill in his bones.

TOM BARLOW AND Jane Rose were gone, but neither he nor Debra had made a move to leave the conference room. He knew that was because each had things to say to the other. She was making notes, still avoiding eye contact, so he broke the ice.

"Good thing we both got back from Tikal early, or we wouldn't have been here when those two showed up without notice." That was a clumsy start, reminding her of the scrap they'd had. *Try again.* "You did really good work on that FOIA request. It gave Jane and Tom some good news to report to the group."

She glanced at him, seeming surprised by the compliment. "We're still a long way from winning," she said evenly.

No response to his flattery. "True, but if we do pull it off, our firm's share of the recovery will be in the seven figures."

"Jack, I stand by what I said in Tikal." She put down her pen. "But I do apologize for one thing. I was airborne on the Taca flight home when I realized that my leaving meant you couldn't keep your promise to Zalman and make the climb. I'm sorry about that."

Without thinking, he said, "I made the climb anyway." Oops, that answer was likely to derail any possible reconciliation.

She did an almost comical double take. He felt her thoughts: *risking your life—future of our firm—impact on me—how stupid can you get?* Before she could verbalize, he said, "I made it up and down without a scratch. I know it wasn't smart, but my brain was a little scrambled. To tell you the truth, I was thinking about what you said just before you . . . left."

That was true enough, but there had been another reason he'd made that climb. It was because of the demon he carried inside, the one he made sure no one knew about. His father had instilled in him the message that he wasn't "good enough" so deeply that he was driven to prove himself in some way every single day. On the day of the climb, his cowardly, long-dead father had whispered that he couldn't make it to the top, so he had to try. It hadn't been until a couple of years ago that he'd realized he almost always raced his sailboat, very seldom took her for a leisurely sail. He was always competing. In situations where others weren't competing, he competed more subtly. He was ashamed of that.

He knew her mind so well. She was outraged by the risks he'd taken. She felt a little guilt that her absence led to that, but not much, because it was up to him not to be dumb. And since he was sitting in front of her safe there was no point in holding on to fear he might get hurt.

So he said, "I heard the points you made. We'll freeze hiring. We'll figure out how to cut expenses. We won't take any more *pro bono* clients for a while. Well, unless we absolutely have to. And I'll get more involved in the firm's finances."

Some of the tension left her face. "Glad to hear that."

Not much of a reconciliation, but he had to move on to what he'd been dreading. He hadn't called her from Tikal to tell her about Katie, because he'd hoped to be able to report that Katie had had a rough time but was safely back home. But he'd heard nothing from Hank. He moved over to sit in the chair next to her. She looked puzzled.

"I had a call from Hank Thompson. *Aleutian*, a Greenpeace ship, was attacked and damaged while on an anti-whaling mission. It seemed able to reach Seattle but, somewhere along the way, fell out of contact. Hank got an Air-Rescue search started right away. They haven't found *Aleutian* or any lifeboats. The ship has disappeared."

"That's terrible. Hank and the others must be beside themselves worrying about the crew. Do you know how many—"

"Thirty-two on board." He took both her hands. "Katie was one of them."

"No! I knew she—that's not—there must be a mistake." Tears filled her eyes. "What can we—"

"No mistake. I got GeoEye to scan the entire area right after dawn this morning. Their techs reviewed the film carefully. No *Aleutian*. No wreckage. I also got Gano to fly up there to search at low altitude. So far, nothing from him either."

She buried her face in his chest and cried uncontrollably. He held her in his arms until her sobbing slowly ebbed.

She finally looked up. "Could there be any . . . survivors?"

"No one can last long in that water before hypothermia paralyzes them. Maybe we'll hear something from Air-Sea Rescue, GeoEye, or Gano before dark." He was fighting against losing hope.

Debra leaned back, but continued holding his hands. They exchanged stories about Katie dashing around the office, at the helm of the sailboat, sampling everything on a Chinese buffet, telling corny jokes, and being wise far beyond her age. Looking into each other's eyes, they understood that their shared grief was a big step toward rebuilding their bond.

He lowered his eyes so she couldn't see and interpret the doubt he felt. He'd keep digging, trying to find out what happened to *Aleutian*, but his feeling that something very strange had happened in that northeast corner of the Pacific Ocean was stronger than ever.

Chapter 5

July 10
10:00 a.m.
San Francisco

"MR. STRIDER, THERE'S a . . . gentleman . . . here who says he has a contract on your life that he's come to execute." Mei, usually totally poised, sounded shaky.

"He's leaning over your desk trying to look down your blouse, and you think I should call the cops, right?"

"Yes, sir."

She had been spooked by a master. "Tell Mr. LeMoyne to check his weapons at your desk. He won't do it, but send him in anyway. After that, go to our bar and bring in a bottle of rum."

"But it's only 10:00 a.m."

"Mei."

"Yes, sir."

Gano would have been in the air almost the whole time since he cranked the Cessna and left Mexico. He must be nearly out on his feet. Nevertheless, he wanted Gano to stroll in with a big smile and good news about *Aleutian*. Or, worst case, something about the lifeboats. Anything hopeful. But that wasn't going to happen. If Gano had good news, he would have called immediately. He'd come in person to deliver very bad news.

Jack had gotten the first jolt when Frank Williams had reported that GeoEye had found nothing. Hoping Gano would call with something better, he hadn't passed that on to Debra or Hank. That hope was about to crash.

His office door opened. Gano's black cowboy hat was oversized in the Mexican style. His mustache, almost obscuring his nostrils, was as dense as the business end of a tar brush. He wore Western-cut tailored denims, a green-and-red striped shirt, and a calfskin vest. Jack knew the vest concealed a handgun, maybe two. Overall, he looked like a caricature of Hunter S. Thompson, the Gonzo journalist.

Wiry and no more than five feet ten, his size wouldn't intimidate anyone, but his self-possessed manner and keen eyes radiated danger. Even in the office of a friend, he seemed watchful and moved as though ready to defend himself.

They clasped hands and exchanged shoulder slaps.

Mei came in with a tray holding a bottle of rum, ice, and lemon. She set it on the desk, keeping wary eyes on Gano.

"What kind of rotgut you got here, Jacko? Hmmm. Twelve-year-old Cuban." He poured a glassful and took a long drink. "Not bad. I stayed dry during that whole damn flight. Well, not from Mexico to Seattle but all the time I was searching at sea." He took another long drink. "Even I couldn't stand the way I smelled after all those hours in the cockpit, so I checked into the Hyatt Regency down the road for a hot shower. They'll send you the bill."

Jack grimaced. No matter the situation, Gano always passed him the check. Then something unusual caught his eye. "You weren't wearing that wristband last time I saw you. I've never seen one like it. Must be three inches wide, no decoration. Where did you buy it?"

Gano didn't even glance at his right wrist. "Made to my specs by an old Mexican shaman who died the day after he handed it to me."

Jack looked more closely. "There's no clasp, not even a seam. How do you get it off?"

"When it comes off, that will mean I'm dead."

Jack didn't want to go there. "Looks like silver, only brighter."

"It's made of mithril. I paid twenty thousand an ounce." Gano took a drink and looked away.

There was a story behind that wristband, but Gano wasn't going to tell it. This was not something to pry into. Besides, there was something much more urgent to talk about.

Gano set his glass down, cleared his throat, and looked straight at Jack. "Arghhh, matey, I flew every search and rescue pattern in the Coast Guard play book, crisscrossed the whole area. Used my best Bausch & Lomb long glasses. *Semper paratus*, you know. *Aleutian* is not there. Not even a life jacket. I'm sorry, man."

He'd known that was coming, but it still hit hard. He had no words.

"There was a moment, about two hours in," Gano said, "when I thought I spotted the crew in the water. Turned out to be about a dozen dolphins floating close together—dead."

Jovial shouts from deliverymen working on the wharf suddenly seemed loud and annoying.

"It was weird about those dolphins, you know. There was no slick, so it wasn't oil that killed them. And even the slowest dolphin can avoid getting hit by a ship. They'll be in sharks' bellies long before anyone can get out there for an autopsy. Another mystery."

Jack had hoped Gano would come through, that there would be a happy ending for *Aleutian* and Katie. But now . . . he swallowed hard and said, "*Aleutian* on the bottom. I can't get used to that."

"Look, I'll turn around and go right back out there."

"No point. Air-Sea Rescue has flown its own patterns. And my friend at Google Maps said its satellite struck out too. No ship, no lifeboats, no debris. No one could survive in that water for three hours, let alone days. I'll let Hank Thompson at Greenpeace know."

Gano sat quietly, eyes averted. When he looked back, he said, "Is there any chance *Aleutian* was up to something Greenpeace didn't tell you about?"

"No. Katie was on that ship. Hank would have told me anything that might help find her. The mystery is what made it disappear without calling for help. But you sound like you think there's something more to it."

"Don't see any connection, but a helicopter staked me out the entire time I was on the western side of the search area. It stayed out near the horizon but didn't try to hide. That pilot wanted me to know he was there. I tried to hail him on the Homeland Security channels. No joy. I don't like being messed with, so I was tempted to go bump up against the bozo. Then I figured that wasn't why I was there, so I headed back." He reached toward his glass and then let his hand fall away.

"I'm sorry I couldn't find her, Jack."

"MEI, PLEASE GET Hank Thompson on the line."

When Hank came on, Jack said, "I don't have good news. The GeoEye looked at the whole area and came up empty. Not even a 'maybe.'"

"And your pilot friend?"

"He crisscrossed the search area, first at high altitude to pick up a wake or reflections of sunlight, then at three hundred feet off the deck looking for . . . small things. He spotted nothing."

"Air-Sea Rescue just notified me they've called off the search." Hank's voice was solemn. "It's like our ship dropped into a hole in the ocean and," his voice choked, "took Katie with it. I'm so torn up I can't think straight. If I'd thought she—"

"Working on *Aleutian* was her dream job, doing what she believed in. Like you do every day. Like I do. I'll come up to Seattle if you—"

"Thanks, but I have to notify the other families. They'll be devastated, and not knowing what happened and why makes it even worse. Right now, we need some time alone."

After he hung up, Jack pulled a thick legal memo out of his in-box—something a young associate had probably worked on most of the night to impress his boss. He scanned three pages of analysis of complex laws on insider trading but couldn't concentrate.

He tossed the memo back on top of the stack, leaned his elbows on his desk, rested his chin on interlaced fingers, and tried to let some of the tension drain away. His heart ached over the fact he'd never see Katie again. His relationship with her had been a rebirth for him of a long-lost emotion. Even though he had been only a godfather, he'd felt parental love.

He thought his own mother might have loved him, probably did. He didn't know. She had been a striking, silent figure who wilted in the shade of her domineering husband. After she died, Jack had thought of her as a photo in a frame more than as a flesh-and-blood mother.

He had no doubt about his father's love for him. There had been none. His father's single-minded goal had been to extend his own persona through his son Jack. He'd groomed his only offspring like a thoroughbred racehorse. Nothing but the best of everything: schools, tutors, coaches— everything except even one shred of love. His price for that had been total control of all of Jack's behavior, every decision that might affect his future.

When an algebra teacher had praised Jack to Peck, his father had just nodded, accepting the compliment for himself. When Jack had looked up at his father and put his hand on his shoulder, Peck had stepped away. Remembering those days made his throat tighten. He reached for water and drank deeply.

He'd never been allowed to take a risk or make a single mistake that might deflect him from serving on the U.S. Supreme Court. His father, as a prominent lawyer, prosperous businessman, and then judge on the influential Circuit Court of Appeals, had come close to getting that appointment for himself. After he fell short, he announced to his peers that, "By God, a Strider will sit on that bench. Bet on it."

Some kids got very little of their father's attention. He'd gotten way too much, and, as soon as he understood what was going on, it hurt him to the core. To his father, he was just a project under construction. The problem had been the non-stop, never-spoken message that his father didn't trust his son's ability to manage his own life.

After leaving home for university, he'd taken stubborn pride in keeping his low self-esteem secret from the wider world. People saw him as a scholar, a member of an Olympic crew, and a professor at a top law school. They sought his opinions and friendship. For quite a while, his life and career had kept speeding along on the track laid down by his father.

All that had ended after six girls died in the hold of an old freighter and ownership had been traced to his father. It was soon discovered that the dishonorable Judge H. Peckford Strider had been buying Mexican girls, many barely in their teens, and shipping them to Northern California in that freighter to work as prostitutes. Rather than face disgrace and prison, Peck had blown his brains out in front of Jack. That horror would always be seared in his emotions. Later, Jack had been shown grisly photographs of girls who had died because of his father and mug shots of those who had lived. He'd never forget either. Since then, he'd felt driven to make up to society for what his father had done. One way to prove he was not his father's son was to stop what was being done to kids at Armstrong.

He'd kept his deep-rooted feeling of unworthiness secret from Debra—or hoped he had. But he couldn't shake his skepticism that someone as talented, beautiful, and centered as she was could really love him. When women had said they loved him in the past, he hadn't known how to respond. It had felt dangerous, because he didn't want to let himself depend on anyone ever again. He had secrets to keep.

Because they had been powerful women, each had, in her own best interests, moved on. That had underscored his feeling of being unworthy. And maybe it explained why he hadn't moved forward with Debra to marriage.

The phone buzzed. He glanced at his watch. Thinking back to his conversation with Hank, he wondered whether he'd been wrong not to tell him what he planned to do next.

Chapter 6

July 10
11:15 a.m.
San Francisco

CAPTAIN TURNER hadn't been able to save *Aleutian.* Attempts to rescue the crew had failed. All Jack could do now for Katie and the grieving families was find out what had happened. The best way to do that was to inspect the ship where she lay on the bottom.

His research had convinced him that the person most able to locate *Aleutian* was Dr. Stephen Drake, renowned for his explorations of the deep sea, who was based at Scripps Institution of Oceanography near San Diego. His research vessel, *Challenger*, was temporarily tied up at a berth in Alameda, just across the Bay from Jack's office. Drake's underwater robot, cameras, and other search gear would be aboard.

The problem was: why would Drake agree to try? There were no survivors to rescue, no treasure to claim. *Aleutian* had no historic merit, and her salvage value wasn't enough to make her worth bringing up. Jack had to find a way to talk him into it.

He called Drake, did his best to sound legit and, talking fast, related the facts about *Aleutian.*

Drake listened without interrupting and then said, "I donate to Greenpeace every year. I support what they do, but I just can't fit this in." His voice was raspy, as if he'd spent too many hours shouting into the sea wind. "Maybe you could try—"

"Dr. Drake, this disappearance is a huge mystery, maybe tougher than finding *Titanic.*" He intended the reference to Robert Ballard's famous discovery to stir Drake's competitive juices. "You're the only person who can solve it. The area you'll be searching is just off the Oregon coast, not far from where *Challenger* is right now. Here's the thing: You'd be doing a huge service for a lot of good people."

He'd appealed to ego and guilt. What was left? He racked his brain. He had to make this sale.

"People call me Steve," Drake said. "How far off the Oregon coast?"

"Hundred and fifty, maybe two hundred miles."

Jack heard what sounded like Drake leafing through papers. "Give me the exact coordinates of *Aleutian*'s last known position again and the heading she was on to Seattle."

Jack checked his notes and told him.

After a long silence Drake said, "Repeat those coordinates."

Puzzled, he read off the numbers again.

Drake said, "I'll have to shuffle my schedule, but I'll take the job."

Drake was in. "That's great. What kind of search equipment will you use?"

"Same as usual, calculations based on information, sensors, and, near the bottom, a very advanced robot. Why do you ask?"

"I was wondering whether you ever use a submarine. I remember reading that the Russians have developed a small titanium sub. They're using it in the Arctic Ocean trying to prove that an underwater ridge is part of the Russian land mass. If they can prove that, they'll claim the whole Siberian Sea area for themselves when the continental shelf up there is divided by the UN Law of the Sea treaty."

"I have my own eighteen-foot, two-man sub that's better than theirs," Drake growled. "It has—" He cut himself off. "Doesn't matter. Forget it."

Jack didn't actually care what equipment Drake might use. He was stalling for time to figure out how to ask how much Drake would charge. "Maybe we should talk about your fee."

"My fee is $25,000."

"That's a lot, but this is so important they'll find a way to pay it."

"You understand that's $25,000 *per day*."

Jack's heart sank. No way Greenpeace could pay that.

"But in this case I'll make the search if Greenpeace will cover my out-of-pocket expenses up to $50,000."

"That's very fair."

"We need to be clear on one thing: I'm in command. Not Greenpeace and not you."

"Agreed. What's your timing?"

"I'll fly up to SFO this afternoon."

"I'm in the city. I could pick you up or—"

"My people will do that. Just courier $25,000 to get this rodeo started."

He wanted to meet Drake but knew a brush-off when he heard one. "Let me know if there's anything you need," he said, but there was no longer anyone on the other end of the line. He wondered what caused Drake to reverse his decision. Tax deduction? Publicity? He'd asked twice about the coordinates. Was it something about the location that made him willing to shuffle his schedule? Or maybe he saw potential for a documentary.

He called Greenpeace.

"Hank, we have a chance to find out why *Aleutian* sank. I need that closure. Do you and the others at Greenpeace feel the same?"

"Every one of us. But I don't know how—"

"I just talked with Steve Drake down at Scripps. He's agreed to search for

Aleutian for reimbursement of expenses up to $50,000. Will Greenpeace pay for that?"

"For someone with Steve Drake's reputation, of course we'll come up with the money." He was silent for a few seconds. "It means admitting no one survived."

"We can still hope someone made it, but we know the ship is gone. Drake will start his search as soon as he can get here."

"I'll fly down to meet him, so we can set up a search plan."

"He made it clear he works solo. If you even offer to give him a tide chart, he will probably bail. I think he's interested in finding *Aleutian*, but I suspect he has his own agenda as well. I'll keep you posted." He hung up.

Glancing at his calendar, he realized that he'd never told Debra about the call from Petros Barbas. That meeting was scheduled for tomorrow morning. He walked to Debra's office to tell her about the upcoming meeting and to see if she knew why Barbas wanted her present.

"I'll be darned," she said. "About a week ago, I was a volunteer at the McLaughlin Gallery art auction for Doctors Without Borders. I was recording purchases when a handsome man wearing a silk suit came to my table. There was a beautiful, much younger woman trailing along behind him, her hair piled up like a golden helmet. She stayed several feet away while he started chatting with me about the gallery, then about a particular piece of sculpture, and then—"

"Yeah, I know all about that kind of 'chat.' And then he asked you for your name and phone number, right?"

"No. He handed me his card and said, 'Call and I'll take you for a sail. I'll be in town for a week or so.' It was Petros Barbas. He walked away, then came back. That's when he asked for my name and phone number."

"So you . . ."

"So I what?" She raised her eyebrows. "Of course I told him my name, but I gave him our firm name and number rather than my home. I mean, he does have quite a reputation with the ladies. I read somewhere that he often runs his conglomerate from his yacht."

"That was all?"

"Not quite. After he looked at the card, he said, 'Would that be Jack Strider who taught at Stanford?' After I said 'yes', he smiled and said, 'I'll be seeing you again.' He left a while later, blond in tow. A few minutes after that, another volunteer brought a check to me to record. Barbas had bought a small Beniamino Bufano sculpture of a polar bear for $30,000."

"Doctors without Borders should send you a thank-you note. So I guess you're free for the meeting tomorrow morning."

"If I'm not, I will be." She grinned. "Maybe *you* owe me a thank-you note."

"Depends on what the meeting is about." Now he had a good idea why Barbas had invited Debra. "Listen, I have to tell you that Gano was here earlier this morning."

"I thought he was going to call if he. . . . . Oh my God. He came here to tell you in person . . . because he couldn't find *Aleutian*. Is that right?"

He nodded. "That was our last chance. The ship's gone. No one survived. The search is over."

She sighed deeply. "I knew it. I'll always miss her. I wish we knew what happened."

"I just got Steve Drake to agree to search for *Aleutian* on the bottom. Maybe he'll find the answer."

"We need that. And if Petros Barbas wants legal representation, we need that too."

Tomorrow's meeting is going to be interesting, on several levels.

Chapter 7

July 11
8:00 a.m.
Sausalito, California

JACK POINTED AT *Excalibur*, a classic black-hulled wooden schooner tied up at Pier 3 of the Sausalito Yacht Club. "What a beauty," he said to Debra. "At least seventy-five feet at the water line. I wouldn't mind a turn at the helm."

"First we have to get past those Secret Service lookalikes," Debra replied, nodding toward two men standing shoulder to shoulder, blocking the gate leading to Pier 3. "With those black suits and mirrored Ray-Bans, I'm guessing they're not members here. Looks like Mr. Barbas has his own palace guard."

As Jack and Debra approached, the guard on the right said, "Sir?" in a gruff voice. Neither moved aside.

"We're here for a meeting with Mr. Barbas."

"And you are?"

Jack didn't like being interrogated, but he went along. "Jack Strider."

"Of course, Mr. Strider. And she would be Ms. Vanderberg. Mr. Barbas is expecting you." He was trying to sound cordial, but his lips were tight. "Please go right down, sir." Without looking away, he spoke into a concealed microphone and the two gatekeepers stepped apart.

As they walked down the ramp, Jack saw a solid-looking man about six feet tall standing on deck at the top of the gangway. Beneath tight black curls he had heavy eyebrows, deep-set eyes, and an arched nose imbedded in a full beard. Jack knew Barbas was in his mid-fifties, but he looked closer to his own age of thirty-seven.

"Welcome aboard." His broad smile seemed genuine.

Jack gestured toward Debra. "This is Ms. Debra Vanderberg, my law partner. You two have met."

He watched Barbas take in Debra's long, shiny black hair falling from beneath her wide-brimmed sun hat and scanned her body down to her toes. Her tailored khaki shirt and twill trousers neither concealed nor accentuated her shape. He knew she was aware of Barbas's inspection and would ignore it unless it became annoying, then watch out.

Barbas bowed slightly. "Ms. Vanderberg, I've been looking forward to seeing you again. I had some research done to learn more about you. As it happens, I already knew about Mr. Strider. Since you're his partner, you, too, must be one of the best lawyers in this country."

Research? He wondered why Barbas had already known about him and what he'd learned about Debra.

During the next couple of minutes of pleasantries, he detected only a trace of Greek accent, the rest probably polished away in prep schools and by world travel.

"Nice day for a short sail," Barbas said. "Not much breeze today, Jack—I'll call you Jack. You might be able to handle the helm yourself."

He started to tell Barbas that by the time he was sixteen he could handle a schooner in a gale, thank you, but held his tongue.

"But," Barbas continued, "we have business to talk about, so I'll put Stefan on the helm. He'll take us across Raccoon Strait to Angel Island and then back to Sausalito."

So this is about business. Great.

White sails snapped crisply as they were winched up the two masts into place. "Spring lines off. Cast off the bow line," Barbas called, "then let the stern line go."

As soon as they were well underway, Barbas led them toward the bow. Two women in their early twenties lay back languidly against the forward cabin. As Barbas approached, the women pulled bikini tops into place and scrambled to their feet. Jack guessed that the one with the pile of blond hair was the one Debra had seen at the gallery. As she walked past them, her eyes were downcast, as if she were ashamed.

Morning fog was burning off, revealing the Golden Gate Bridge, the San Francisco skyline, and even Mt. Tamalpais rising northwest of Sausalito. As they drew closer to Angel Island, he thought of the many times it had been one of the course turning points for races out of San Francisco Yacht Club, of which he'd won more than his share.

Barbas explained that *Excalibur* was a "loaner" from a friend who'd brought her up from Cabo San Lucas. "Mine is still in the Adriatic Sea. At least I think that's where she is." As they relaxed leaning against the cabin, he dominated the conversation in an engaging way. Lots of eye contact, expansive gestures, and occasional touches. He was a gracious, almost courtly, host going out of his way to make his guests feel comfortable.

Stefan tacked into Angel Island's Ayala Cove and ordered the sails lowered and the hook dropped a hundred yards offshore. This must be where the mysterious Petros Barbas was about to make a business proposition.

A crewman arrived with a bottle in a bucket of ice and a platter loaded with fruit, cheeses, and a variety of other *hors d'oeuvres.*

"Please set that up in the cabin, Arne." To Jack and Debra he said, "There's someone I want you to meet."

They followed Barbas down the ladder into the cabin. The man waiting for them wore a white lab coat with a yellow orchid pinned to the lapel, white trousers, and white Reeboks. He was very slender and had no visible hair, not even eyebrows, and an unusually prominent Adam's apple. Jack couldn't gauge his age but sensed he was younger than he appeared.

"This is my science expert, Dr. Renatus Roux. He answers only to 'Renatus.'"

The thin man nodded, remaining silent and expressionless.

"Don't take that personally," Barbas said. "Renatus suffers from Moebius Syndrome. It has already caused facial paralysis, and it's spreading. He can speak in a whisper but can't form expressions, and his irises move only up and down. He's bitter that Moebius will kill him—yes, we speak openly about it—and because it's so rare, there's no research being done to find a cure. Perhaps as a result, he has a personality like a thorn bush." His glance at Renatus said there was some history there. "There's his way and no other way. Doesn't care whether people approve or not. If you remember Howard Roark in *Fountainhead*, you know what I mean. I'm paying him a fortune because he's a genius. Knows more about the oceanic seabed than anyone else."

Arne removed the bottle from the bucket and popped the cork without a sound.

Damn, that's Armand de Brignac champagne, $500 a bottle. The snobs who lived in Pacific Heights called it A de B. He was impressed. Yachts, women, fine wines. For Barbas this was clearly about enjoying life, not impressing Jack Strider. He noticed Barbas watching him.

"Yes, I live very, very well," Barbas said. "You'd enjoy it."

He was afraid Barbas might be right. With a small gesture, he waved Arne away, turning down the champagne. Not a good idea before nine in the morning.

"Make yourselves comfortable"—Barbas pointed to leather captain's chairs on the far side of a rosewood table bolted to the deck—"and I'll tell you why we're here." As soon as they were settled, he said, "We know a lot more about our brains, inner space, and outer space, than we do about our own oceans. For example, we didn't figure out how tectonic plates work, one of the most important mechanisms on our planet, until a half century ago. And we're just now learning anything useful about the ocean depths and the seabed." He leaned toward Jack. "Do you know what hydrothermal vents are?"

The question caught him off guard, but *National Geographic* had taught him something to work with. "They're vents in the seabed that emit very hot fluids, often located near underwater cracks in the Earth's crust, especially where tectonic plates are moving apart. On land they're called *geo*thermal vents, like the geysers at Yellowstone. That's about it." Then he thought of another fact. "And I've read there are similar vents on Europa, a moon of Jupiter."

"I don't give a damn about Europa," Barbas replied, "at least not yet. But the interface between the ocean and Earth's crust is vitally important to the future of mankind. That's why I put a research vessel and a team of oceanographic experts to work ten years ago. Tell him, Renatus."

Renatus was ready for the cue. "They discovered that around hydrothermal vents there were lumps of minerals about the size of potatoes lying on the seafloor."

He and Debra had to lean closer to hear him.

"Initially they found manganese, copper, nickel, cobalt, iron, and zinc, but then they found polymetallic sulphides and ferromanganese crusts. All very valuable."

Barbas broke in. "So-called mining experts tried to figure out how to get these minerals up from the deep seabed at costs that worked. But they were old farts who grew up digging shafts miles into the ground then building a huge infrastructure to drill and blast ore loose and transport it aboveground, all of which requires a large workforce. They haven't adapted to mining the sea. When I got involved, undersea technology was primitive, so I brought new brains to the problem and came up with new solutions. All my life people have told me what I can't do. Then I do it."

Jack was struck by the excitement showing in Barbas's eyes and his more rapid speech. Debra, too, was paying close attention. The façade of suave Greek billionaire playboy had given way to an entrepreneur turned on by a new venture with huge potential profits.

"Are you going to enlighten us about your 'new solutions'?" Jack asked.

"Of course. After all," he glanced at Debra, "we're going to be working very closely together. My solutions are already in operation. First, I put a floating platform in place 7,200 feet above a hydrothermal vent. Next, I built a complex infrastructure on the seabed and used state-of-the-art technology to collect the minerals. I bring them up in conduits with a suction pump system. It's like using a vacuum cleaner on the seabed. On the platform, we separate the minerals from seawater and transport them to our smelter on the mainland. There's much more to it, but that's the general idea."

"Sounds very expensive. Is it profitable?" Debra asked.

"As you already know, I donate to charities, but this isn't one. Front-end costs have been enormous, but now revenues are coming in. I'm counting on mineral prices doubling within a year, and then I'll really cash in."

"What about competition?" Debra asked. "I read about a company operating in the Bismarck Archipelago north of New Guinea that's already going after the minerals you described. And there's another operation a few hundred miles northeast of New Zealand."

"Oh, there are a few of them out there, but the pitiful handfuls of nodules they dredge up won't make a blip in meeting market demand. In this business, like many others, location is everything. And no other location is as rich in polymetallic sulphides and ferromanganese crusts—which carry a lot of gold and silver—as the one I've staked out. But that's all you need to know for now."

"Fair enough," Jack said. "So tell me why you invited us here. Are your mining operations causing some sort of environmental damage?"

Barbas tugged on his beard, then refilled his glass. "Our equipment stirs up sediment from the seafloor that might affect some filter-feeding organisms nearby. Nothing I worry about."

Jack had occasionally dealt with CEOs who rationalized or denied the damage their operations did to the environment. Barbas sounded like he was one of them. Time to test him with a dose of reality.

"When the government wanted to build the Tellico Dam on the Little Tennessee

River," he said, "construction was held up for years to protect the snail darter, a kind of minnow. In other words, it doesn't take much damage to get the regulators on your back."

"I won't let that happen to me." He made a chopping motion with his left hand. "Too much at stake. Besides, my platform is located where U.S. regulators can't touch me. No, the issues I want you to handle are land-based. The minerals are shipped to my processing plant in Oregon. In getting that permit, I crossed every technical 't' and dotted every damned regulatory 'i'. No objections from the locals. They'd turf their own mothers to get a job at my plant. But there is one potential problem. The volume of ore I'm processing is a lot higher than I projected for the bureaucrats. Your job will be to do whatever it takes to make sure nothing interrupts my operations."

Jack had heard that song before. When violations turned out to be horrendous, the client expected him to act like some Mafia *consigliore* to make the regulators disappear. He liked this part of a conversation with a prospective client where he stuck his spear in the ground and challenged him or her to walk away. Only two had left in a huff, but several had thought they could hire him and still find ways to cheat. Those relationships had turned out badly.

"I can advise you about laws and regulations and how to comply. What I *won't* do is help you get around them."

Barbas didn't miss a beat. "Listen to me, Jack. I'm not going to waste time trying to evade some penny-ante rules. I intend to follow the law. That's why I identified you months ago as the best lawyer to guide me on this. When I met Debra it was a sign it was time for me to make a move. Now you know what kind of legal work I expect from you, so I'll tell you what you can expect from me. High fees, of course, and you also get a chance to share in my lifestyle." He glanced at Debra. "After you've been with me for a while, first-class results, no mistakes, and my mining and refining operations are in full swing, there's no end to what I can do for you. I can put you on the boards of banks like Credit Suisse or Deutsche Bank. Maybe you'd prefer the Senate or Supreme Court. Whatever you decide, my friends and I can provide the money it takes to get there. Now let's get this done. I'm ready to hire your firm."

Barbas was putting on a full-court press. Jack took a harder look at the self-assured smiling man. Could he really deliver all of that? Or any of it? Barbas couldn't know how deeply his casual reference to the Supreme Court struck home. Until the tumultuous events three years ago had stood his career on its head, he'd bought into his father's obsession that his son be appointed to the court. He shook off those thoughts. He had to respond to Barbas's immediate offer, not to pie in the sky.

He'd been at this kind of crossroads before. He could wait until the processing plant did its damage and then sue Barbas on behalf of claimants, or he could step in now and prove to Barbas it was in his best interest to obey the laws in the first place. The truth was, he preferred the latter, and legal fees would start immediately. But there was a major roadblock. The Armstrong case had priority.

"I'll represent you, but I can't start for several months. I'm committed to another major client."

Barbas frowned. Then he bared very white teeth and ran his tongue across them. He was clearly used to getting what he wanted, and a delay of several months wasn't it.

"All right. I have the solution. I'll call on you only rarely, for very special problems. Debra will manage the day-to-day work on my account. I'm sure you're both okay with that."

Deadpan, Debra looked at Jack and waited.

He hated to take any of her time away from the Armstrong suit, but for the firm and their relationship there was no way he could turn this down. He looked at Debra and nodded. She nodded back in agreement. Then he saw Barbas taking another swallow of Armand de Brignac champagne and breathed in the lifestyle. For the first time in his life, he felt a prick of envy.

"You have a deal, but we'd like to go out to your platform."

"I'm afraid that's not allowed."

"We can do a better job after we see your business in operation." He might be right about that, but knew he was pushing the point mainly because he was curious. And maybe this was a small forerunner of what their relationship would be like.

Barbas smiled benevolently, swallowed the rest of his champagne, and said, "As long as you're not making that a condition to signing on, you can come aboard for a short look-around." He climbed the ladder back to the cockpit. "Stefan, take us back to the barn."

Jack noticed the scientist, who had remained standing off to one side, watching him. Nothing challenging, just paying close attention.

"Doctor Roux," he said, then perceived an infinitesimal frown, "I mean, Renatus. What does your work actually consist of?"

"I advise Barbas on mining operations." His voice was slightly louder than a sigh. "I'm also an expert on hydrothermal vents. Using my calculations, I discovered our present site."

Because of the stiffness of Renatus's face, the normal clues that conveyed complex meanings in speech were nonexistent, but Jack noticed he referred to his employer as "Barbas," not Mister or Petros. Lack of respect? Some distance between them?

"Since the platform is already operating, what are you working on now?"

"My work is in the Earth's crust, which means the thin shell from the seabed down three to six miles. At its upper surface, what we call the seabed, the temperature is near freezing. At its deepest levels, it rises to 750 degrees," Renatus answered. "Below the crust are thirty-eight hundred miles of mantle and core. The inner core is nearly at hot as the surface of the sun, but it is gradually cooling. That will cause the electromagnetic field that shields the Earth from the sun to fail in the future. Life as we think of it will end. You can understand why all this is fascinating to a serious scientist." Renatus paused as if something had sidetracked his train of thought.

Jack wanted to keep him talking so he said, "I know that many more people have walked on the moon than have gotten to the bottom of the deepest oceans, but I read that Craig Venter and Richard Branson are spending fortunes on exploring the deeps. And James Cameron actually did it in 2012. Are you working on something like that?"

Renatus's pupils flicked up and down several times like the spooling symbol that indicates a computer is "thinking," then he turned and climbed the ladder to the main deck.

"Interesting," Jack said to Debra, "almost as though he sees those guys as rivals. I wonder why."

Jack and Debra followed Barbas up on deck. Watching Stefan at the helm, Jack wished he would steer off the wind a few points and let the sails fill to pick up the pace. To take his mind off the sails, he asked Barbas, "Where in Oregon is your processing plant?"

"Up the Columbia River from the port of Astoria."

"I sailed into Astoria for supplies a few years ago. I remember a visitors' information sign on the pier that called it the 'Graveyard of the Pacific' because there have been so many shipwrecks there. It was also the end of the trail for Lewis and Clark."

Barbas looked surprised at Jack's knowledge. "Before it lost out to Portland and Seattle, Astoria was a boomtown. It's still a nice little port with deep water access and plenty of people desperate for jobs. But there was another reason I chose it. In 1810, John Jacob Astor sent a crew there to set up a fur trading business. When he died, he was the richest man in America, worth over $100 billion in today's dollars. I thought that was a good omen for me."

"How far is your site from Astoria?"

"About twenty miles upriver. I bought a tract of land from Trans-Continental Iron and Steel Company. The blast furnace, crucible, metal refinery, and even a rock crusher were still there. The equipment isn't all that 'clean,' but the locals don't complain." Barbas looked at Debra. "I want your help with that. We'll get together and decide on a strategy."

As *Excalibur* approached Sausalito, the crew started the engine, dropped the sails, and hung the fenders over the side to protect the hull from scraping on the timbers of the pier. Even before the crew had finished making lines fast to the cleats, Barbas jumped to the pier. He turned back to face Jack with a crooked smile that seemed to say, "You'll love being around my kind of life."

Chapter 8

July 13
6:30 p.m.
Northeast Pacific Ocean

EIGHT TIMES IN THE past six hours, *Challenger*'s instruments had reported contacts. On closer examination, none had been *Aleutian*. Steve Drake's eyes burned, and his mind played tricks, believing it saw what he wanted to see. He didn't care. He'd go through this a thousand times rather than glide past a target without seeing it. And *Aleutian* wasn't his only target.

He thought of himself as a surgeon using a robotic scalpel to perform a delicate operation. He sent signals down through thousands of feet of salt water to an autonomous robot the size of a golf cart. Two bulbous pods attached to its cylindrical body with V-shaped struts made it resemble a miniature starship *Enterprise*. Three months ago, using its state-of-the-art lights, cameras, and sensors, he'd mapped a mid-ocean ridge and discovered a small hydrothermal vent.

With a start, he realized he'd been daydreaming. He peered closely at his monitors and saw an indistinct echo and noticed a vague shape out of context.

"Mark this spot!" he shouted, letting his crew know that he saw something special on the screen. He felt the energy level in the room shoot up. Finding the prize was why they were all on board.

Alex Andrews, tall and taciturn, and Lou Potter, whose eyes had a permanent squint from decades at sea, were his experts in operating the tools used to search for targets. Alex called instructions to the bridge, and the helmsman immediately brought *Challenger* into a slow pirouette around the blip on the GPS and guided her into a search pattern. Even if the instruments sending gigabytes of data to *Challenger*'s computers detected what appeared to be the target, she'd continue until she completed this sequence.

Lou took manual control of the multiple lights and cameras. Steve grasped the joysticks that manipulated the "arms" and "hands" extending from the robot probe. By the time the probe had made its second pass over the target, feedback from sensors and video images made it clear they were looking at a sizable ship resting upright, keel wedged into the mucky seabed.

"Lou, I'm sending the probe in closer for a sweep up the starboard side. Get those lights focused on her stern and move them slowly up and down. Take plenty of photos." He felt like a cheetah who had been chasing his prey and was about to leap onto its haunches and claw it to the ground.

The camera lens immediately showed him what he wanted to see. "Bull's-eye, boys." His analysis of *Aleutian*'s most likely track and his calculations of the effect of current during her long descent had been dead on.

"Now we'll poke around and figure out why she's on the bottom." He had the robot slowed to a crawl along the 160-foot hull and saw the effects of maintenance done on the cheap. There were patches of hull paint that didn't match and more rust than he would have permitted on any vessel he owned. But he saw no sign of any breach in her watertight integrity.

"Look at that," he said, pointing at the fifty-foot long Greenpeace placard painted on the hull. It told him that the captain of *Nikita Maru* knew exactly who he was attacking.

During a slow journey along the hull on the port side, the lights picked out a ragged puncture an RPG had made forward of the deckhouse.

"That one might have knocked out a refrigerator in the galley," Alex said, "but otherwise, no big deal."

Steve knew *Aleutian*'s crew had reported an RPG hit on the fantail, so he made the probe hover aft of the stern while he took a closer look. There was enough twisted metal that *Aleutian*'s captain must have worried about damage to the rudder or steering gear, but he'd reported no difficulty in maintaining course.

He pulled the robot back a few more yards for one last slow pass. "Lou, shine the lights on deck and on the superstructure." He pointed to the monitor. "Look at the lifeboats, boys, still locked in their davits. This ship is so old it must have required manual action by the crew to release them, and they never had time. She went down fast, and that wasn't caused by those RPGs. No sign of having been hit by anything big like a missile. No damage from a collision, and there's no debris field."

"Even if someone deliberately opened all her seacocks," Lou said, "the crew would have had time to put out a Mayday." He shook his head. "I don't get it."

"All right, boys, time to move on to our next task. Set the course I laid out, then write up the notes on *Aleutian*."

The crew could bring up the probe without him, so he hurried to his stateroom and closed the door. His heart was beating faster already. *Challenger* was finally bringing him closer to his dream.

Years ago, he'd read a long report of a deep sea exploration undertaken in 1960. Jacques Piccard and Don Walsh had piloted the bathyscaphe *Trieste* seven miles down into the Mariana Trench near Guam. He'd admired their courage, but since they couldn't maneuver *Trieste* they'd come right back up, having traveled only a vertical column of water, not the seabed. Mostly because of pathetic lack of curiosity, *Trieste* had not had a successor during more than half a century.

Before reading that report, he'd been satisfied being an expert at finding sunken treasures. But Piccard and Walsh had inspired him to do three things: Explore much deeper. Do it in person. And serve his curiosity about the vast ocean depths rather than merely retrieving objects from the seabed. He'd decided right then to have a sub built that could reach the sea bed thirty-six thousand feet beneath the surface.

He sighed, remembering how, year after year, other projects had taken his time, and he hadn't gotten the sub started. Then, a few years ago Sir Richard Branson had announced that he intended to dive to the deepest points in five oceans. Branson's Virgin Oceanic Expedition had built an eighteen-foot long submarine out of carbon fiber composite and titanium with a quartz dome. Branson claimed that its thrusters and stubby wings enabled it to "fly" like a manta ray through the ocean. Branson's announcement had made Steve feel like he was being choked. Someone was already *doing* what he promised himself he would do.

Since Branson made no secret of the specifications and components of his submarine, Drake had let his engineers copy them. He'd felt bad about that, but it was a shortcut that got his project underway. Like Branson's sub, his could dive about four hundred feet per minute and navigate across five to ten miles of ocean floor. Perfect for what he wanted to do. All of the work had been done in a nondescript hangar on the Strait of Juan de Fuca near Seattle.

During the building process, he'd come to terms with the difference between sitting on the surface aboard *Challenger* and diving to depths himself. In the latter case, rescue was impossible.

He glanced at the three framed photos screwed to the wall of his stateroom. They had been taken by one of his robots in the course of another underwater project eight thousand feet down near the Galapagos Islands. They showed his unexpected discovery of a hydrothermal vent. What made it such an awesome find were the six-foot tall tube worms around the vent that were thriving despite total darkness, no photosynthesis, and no standard nutrients. Most explorers would have missed the significance, but his training in science signaled him that what he was seeing might rewrite chemistry and biology textbooks.

While still at sea on that exploration, his mind had raced ahead. Searches for signs of life on other planets and beyond had been based on the assumption that conditions necessary for life had to be the same as those on Earth. But since he was seeing life flourish in the seemingly harsh conditions in and around a hydrothermal vent, it might flourish in similar conditions beyond our planet. That thought had grabbed him. He had to learn more. Back in the States, he'd become obsessed with those tube worms. How had they originated? How did they interact with the hydrothermal vent? Were there other new life forms in and around such vents? He remembered the Friday night during a party at the Hotel del Coronado near San Diego when he'd reached the conclusion that learning the secrets of HTVs and new life forms would be his legacy to humankind.

He'd spent countless hours calculating where he'd be likely to find hydrothermal vents, finally concluding that one of the most promising areas was the northeast Pacific Ocean off the coasts of Oregon, Washington, and British Columbia. He'd just decided to visit that area when the call came from Jack Strider. He had agreed to help because *Aleutian* was somewhere in his HTV search area. Now he *felt* a vent, a big one, somewhere nearby. His feelings about his quest were so intense he thought he might be infected by the same madness that drove

Captain Ahab. He shook his head to clear it and called Jack Strider.

"Steve Drake here. My search is over. I think you understood that the chances of my locating *Aleutian* were worse than finding an honest money changer in Morocco."

"I did, but I still hoped—"

"Well, I beat the odds. *Aleutian* wasn't where your information said she should be, so I applied the variables that could have affected her, and that's where I went. My robot probe and video cameras finally found her at forty-eight hundred feet. She had *Aleutian* painted on her bow and a fifty-foot Greenpeace placard on each side. I'll email the photos to you and Greenpeace."

Strider didn't reply. Steve knew he must be thinking about the crew, maybe even knew some of them, so he continued. "That ship went down a hell of a long way from land, and if it carried any survival gear it was probably ancient. There can't be any survivors."

"I understand. You have our thanks." A long pause. "Look, could you tell why she sank?"

"With no holes below the waterline, I'm sure she *wasn't* sunk by *Nikita Maru*. What *did* cause it is a damned mystery."

Strider was silent for another few moments. "We're grateful to you for stepping up so fast. Let me know how much Greenpeace owes you."

He thought about that. "I don't want any more of their money. As soon as we switch the gear we're using, I'm taking *Challenger* on a search of my own." He looked again at the photos on his wall.

"Very interesting. Tell me about it."

"You're a lawyer. Can I trust you not to talk about it, even to Greenpeace?"

"I'm not *your* lawyer so there's no attorney-client privilege, but I give you my word."

"I got rich finding sunken treasures. My new passion is hunting hydrothermal vents. Until now, people who found an HTV acted like Stone Age savages picking up nuts that fell from a tree. I'm going to change that by figuring out what the role of HTVs has been on this planet. From what I've already found, I've catalogued terabytes of data."

"So you're hunting for another one?"

"Not just 'another one.' I believe there's a granddaddy HTV that's hundreds of thousands of years old and dwarfs the others. I'm going to find it."

"Why do you think you can find it when no one else has?"

"Because I know where to look, and I have a secret weapon: my own two-man submarine loaded with sophisticated instruments."

"Good luck with your hunt, and thanks again."

He broke the connection. There was already a perpetual knot in his stomach over the possibility that someone else might find the granddaddy hydrothermal vent before he did. So why had he told Strider about it? Maybe because he admired the way Strider had pulled out all the stops to find *Aleutian*. Or maybe because he had an odd premonition that Strider could be of use to him in the future.

Chapter 9

July 14
8:30 a.m.
Astoria, Oregon/platform

AT THE ASTORIA airport, the pilot of Barbas's helicopter nodded at Jack and Debra as they approached. Then he squinted at Gano who was dressed like a yacht captain, including white boat shoes and a billed cap whose emblem read El Paso Yacht Club. The pilot turned to Jack. "I make a run in from the platform and back every other day, and I can tell you no one makes this trip without Mr. Barbas's say so. I was told to expect you two, but not . . . him."

Jack wasn't surprised. To avoid a hassle, he hadn't mentioned Gano to Barbas in advance. "Call Mr. Barbas. Tell him Ms. Vanderberg and I are bringing an assistant. We'll wait in the car for five minutes."

After they walked back to the car and got in, Gano said, "If I had my .38 I'd make that egg-sucking coyote do a little dance."

"Not cool," Jack said. "If we're going to represent Barbas, I want to see what he's doing out there. Roughing up his pilot would really piss him off. I'll handle this my way."

A few minutes later, seeing the pilot ambling over, Gano started the engine. The pilot broke into a run.

"Mr. Barbas said it's okay, but he ain't happy about it." His surly tone meant Barbas must have taken his annoyance out on him. "Now hand over your cell phones or cameras. Pick them up when we get back. No one takes a cell phone to the platform and there's no Internet for the crew. Out there you're out of contact with the world. That's the way Mr. Barbas wants it." He stuck his jaw out, expecting another hassle, but confident Barbas would back him on this one.

They handed over their phones. Jack knew Gano had a miniature Nikon in his jacket pocket that shot photos through what looked like a button hole.

As they approached the helicopter, Gano whispered, "When I was searching for *Aleutian*, this is the helo that played long-range tag with me."

"Are you sure?"

"Hey, if you spot a cool chick at a cocktail party, then see her somewhere else a couple of days later, you're likely to recognize her, right? I'm a pilot, so these birds don't all look alike to me. This is the one."

Why was Barbas having his platform's perimeter patrolled?

The helicopter lifted off to the southwest. Out a starboard window, Jack saw the bridge spanning the Columbia River in the distance and the light blue shallow water over the deadly "Graveyard" bar. Then they were over the featureless Pacific with no way to measure progress besides a watch. Finally, the platform appeared on the horizon.

"Platform, dead ahead," the pilot said.

Jack had researched deepwater platforms, mostly oil drilling rigs, so he was amazed by the massive size of this one. It was a rectangle, wider than a football field and more than three times as long, resting on twelve hollow tubes.

"Those tubes run down to horizontal pontoons about fifty feet underwater that hold fuel or seawater as ballast," Jack told the others. "In rough water, a floating structure like that one is much safer than one resting on fixed legs or tethered to the bottom."

Debra pointed at a narrow structure three stories tall running along one side of the platform. "That reminds me of the superstructure of an aircraft carrier."

"It probably contains the bridge, navigation, communications and the computer center," Jack said.

Two sturdy hoists stood on the centerline of the platform with a box-girder structure between them. Beyond them he saw a couple of heavy- duty pedestal cranes. More than two dozen modular metal buildings were located around the deck. As the helo drew closer, workers stared up. None waved.

Gano nudged Jack. "That Barbas dude thinks big. Must have some Texas blood in his veins."

Pretty much what Jack was thinking. He'd badly underestimated the scale of Barbas's operation and felt . . . not intimidated exactly, but impressed and a shade cautious. That was a damned big deal down there.

Two red circles at one end of the main deck marked chopper landing areas. Near them, three more choppers were secured to the deck with chain tie-downs. One was a twin of the one they were aboard. The other two, partially covered by tarps, were twice as big.

Their chopper came in hot and dropped to the deck. Barbas was nowhere in sight.

"No surprise," Jack said. "He's reminding me he didn't want me aboard."

"I'M JORGENSON," said a man in his fifties who had the rough-hewn look of a lumberjack. "Mr. Barbas told me to show you around our floating palace. Follow me."

He took them straight to the deck below, the counterpart to the hanger deck of a carrier, and started talking and pointing. "Down there is the accommodation block of 140 double cabins, all of them better than on any platform I've worked before. Plus a damn good galley and dining room. Food as good as anything in Astoria." Then he showed them a game room, library, fully-equipped gym with sauna, and a basic hospital. "Back down that way"—more pointing—"are offices, laboratories, and storage spaces." He didn't offer to take them there.

Next stops were mechanical spaces, including the engines driving the twelve thrusters capable of moving the platform. There were generators, tool sheds, and a warehouse with racks of parts. They stopped at the base of the drill tower where the drill string passed through the moon pool straight down to the waves far below.

"One of the lads got careless and tripped into the moon pool. Sixty feet down. Hit the water spread-eagled. Flattened him like a pancake. Could happen to anyone," he said with a sly grin, "especially when they first come aboard." Next he pointed out huge containers filled with ore waiting to be offloaded onto conveyor belts through a thirty-foot wide hatch to where a cargo ship would be waiting below.

Back on the main deck, Jorgenson talked about multibeam sonar, sub-bottom echo sounders, electrohydraulic control systems, and fiber optics for downhole monitoring, as if they all understood. Jack got more and more restless as they walked. It was obvious they were being showed only what Barbas wanted them to see. It was a dog-and-pony show, but he'd stick with it to see where the pony stopped.

Out of curiosity or boredom, Gano wandered off from time to time. Jorgenson didn't bother to call him back because every door that wasn't on the tour was locked.

Near one end of the main deck of the platform, Jorgenson showed them a structure whose walls were translucent panels. "That's a greenhouse where Renatus grows orchids . . . something about fiddling with genetics. Someone told me he's trying to create the perfect orchid, whatever that means. They say he's going to name it *Esperanza*. He may be a genius, but he's a world-class weirdo for sure. When he's working on one of his personal projects he wouldn't take down his 'Do Not Disturb' sign even if the platform was sinking." He pointed again. "And over there is where we store remotely operated vehicles when we bring them to the surface for maintenance. One of my mates told me Renatus had an ROV modified to bring microbes and other small creatures up from the depths. Now what has that got to do with mining, I ask you?"

"Well, that's it, Jack." Walking up from behind them, Barbas cut Jorgenson off and waved him away. "I'm sure Jorgenson showed you how my Chaos Project operates."

"No doubt Mr. Jorgenson did exactly what you told him to do," Jack said, keeping sarcasm out of his voice. He waited while Barbas took Debra's hand in his. "And this is our colleague, Mr. Gano LeMoyne." Barbas's mouth tightened, and he didn't offer to shake.

Gano lifted his yacht cap and smiled broadly as if they were old friends. "You called this your 'Chaos Project,'" he said. "That's an unusual name."

"My inside joke," Barbas said to Debra rather than Gano. "It's the name of the Greek goddess of the gap between Heaven and Earth. She's the air humans breathe."

"And she's also called the Mother of Darkness," Debra said, drawing a frown from Barbas. Unfazed, she pointed at an eight-wheel contraption. "What's that? Looks like an undersized Caterpillar backhoe."

"Hardly. That's one of my ROVs that work under immense pressure seventy-two hundred feet down, scooping up chunks of seabed and transporting them to a processing plant on the ocean floor. Japan, China, Russia, and the U.S. have nothing anywhere near as sophisticated."

Barbas eyed Debra, ran his fingers through one side of his beard, and seemed to make a decision. "All right, since you're going to be working for me, I'll explain a little about what's going on down there. Seawater at just above freezing percolates downward through the seafloor into the Earth's crust, getting much hotter as it goes deeper. At very high temperatures, it reacts chemically with rocks and picks up minerals from them. When that hot water rises, it comes out the chimney of the HTV and collides with icy seawater. Presto! The metals precipitate out and rain down onto the seabed. That's why I target my mining to the vicinity of this HTV while my so-called competitors are ripping up miles of ocean floor."

Jack watched Barbas closely. He wasn't the same champagne-drinking playboy figure he'd been aboard *Excalibur*. Here, he still had his swagger, but he was much more intense.

"Those guys are like the old wildcatters who had to *see* oil pooled on the ground to know where to drill." Barbas's tone was contemptuous. "On Chaos, I have reverse MRI technology that measures the magnetic resonance of hydrocarbon atoms, and we send out robot scouts with instructions about what to look for. When they find it, they notify other equipment to come get it. The minerals are brought up here to the platform in insulated tubes run by a row of suction pumps in that building over there. The end of each tube is equipped with lights and cameras and has small water jets to direct the mouth of the tube where we want it."

"It must take incredible suction to bring all that rock to the surface," Gano said.

"It would, so we don't do that. We built a totally automated primary processing plant that rests on the seabed. As we collect mineral nodules, they're fired into the processor where they're crushed and run through water jets that flush mud and sand back into the ocean. The slurry that remains is much easier to suck to the surface. After more processing aboard this platform, we dump about eighty percent of that material back into the water. The valuable minerals are offloaded to ore carriers to be delivered upriver from Astoria."

"Doesn't all that dumping screw up the ocean big-time?" Gano asked.

Barbas scowled. He'd clearly developed a dislike for Gano. "To the contrary, Mr. LeMoyne, we're very careful about that. What we release from the platform is highly diluted and disperses quickly. When we finish with an area on the bottom, our machines are programmed to level the site and leave it pretty much as we found it."

To Jack, Barbas sounded like a West Virginia coal mine owner who tears off a mountain top, dumps the toxic debris into the water supply, and then explains how good it is for the economy. Jack pointed to the tall box-girder structure between the two hoists. "That looks like an oil drilling rig."

"We're not drilling for oil or anything else," Barbas snapped. "I use that tower to send mechanical eyes and hands to the seafloor that can repair anything down there."

When Barbas turned aside to answer a question from a foreman, Gano spoke softly in Jack's ear. Jack nodded. He'd been thinking about the same thing. When Barbas finished with the worker, Jack said, "I've been wondering about the buildings on this deck and the spaces in the superstructure we didn't visit. What are they for?" He was prying, so he watched carefully to see how Barbas would react. He didn't, not even a twitch at the corner of an eye.

"I allow no visitors inside the superstructure. Most of the top level is my suite. I keep it private except for special invited guests." His expression was somewhere between a smile and a leer. "The 02 level, that's the middle one, is full of proprietary equipment and what I call Command Central. From there I control all underwater operations. On this deck, I built lots of extra space for expansion. Nothing to see."

Total brush-off. He was about to explore that when he noticed that Barbas's fists were clenched.

"Jack, come with me to the bridge. I have something important to tell you."

Chapter 10

July 14
1:30 p.m.
Chaos platform

BARBAS UNLOCKED the door and preceded Jack into a space that ran the full width of the third level of the superstructure.

"This is a replica of the admiral's bridge on the nuclear carrier *USS John F. Kennedy*, CVN-79. I would love to be in command of that baby. She carries more firepower than was expended by *all* sides during WWII."

"Very impressive."

Barbas slid into the admiral's pivoting chair. "I never could have built this bridge the way I wanted it if I'd had to conform to government specs." He picked up a pair of binoculars and twisted the focus rings repeatedly without looking at them. "Thunder Horse, the largest semi-submersible oil drilling platform in the world at the time, was built to government specs. It got knocked silly by Hurricane Dennis. Then Ocean Ranger, a platform as tall as a thirty-five-story building, sank in a storm off Newfoundland, taking eighty-four crewmen to the bottom. Piper Alpha, a gas production platform in the North Sea, blew up, killing 167 men. Both of them were built to government specs."

Barbas's nostrils were flaring in outrage. His Greek accent was stronger. "This platform is more than two hundred miles offshore, so the U.S. government had no control over how I built it. Because of that, it's a technological marvel that laughs at storms. It's the safest rig ever built."

The captain of the "unsinkable" Titanic couldn't have said it better.

Barbas paused, thick eyebrows raised as though daring Jack to contradict him. "I'm a gambler. Have been all my life. The silver spoon in my mouth was my first stake, and I've been on a winning streak ever since— until now. I've sunk more than a billion dollars into this project, and I'm on the hook for a hell of a lot more. From seabed to processing plant, this operation is costing me $250,000 a *day*, seven days a week, and we're not even breaking even. When Wall Street imploded, the world economy locked up and my home country turned out to be built of straw. My international shipping business went on the rocks. Occupancy in my resorts is under thirty percent. This project will break me unless it pays off big—and soon. I can't let any goddamn bureaucrats interfere."

Jack had heard many of the people who walked into his office go off on "goddamn bureaucrats" within the first five minutes.

"So far," Barbas went on, "my platform operations have been free from interference from the Law of the Sea treaty and the International Seabed Authority. I assume you're familiar with both."

He should be. He'd taught international law courses for five years. "U.S. regulations can't touch you," Jack replied, "because you're in the *Mare Liberum*, international waters. And you're not subject to rules of the 1982 UN Convention on Law of the Sea because the U.S. hasn't ratified it. The U.S. also refuses to recognize the ISA as having any power over seabed drilling outside territorial waters."

"If the sons of bitches at the ISA ever get their hooks into me, they'd steal my secrets and blackmail me to keep them from shutting me down. I discovered this site, and no one, *no one*, is going to tell me what I can or can't do here."

Jack was struck by the passion, almost hate, in Barbas voice. "So far at least, you're unregulated. What's the problem?"

"I'll tell you what the damn problem is. In the past, whenever the Law of the Sea was about to come up for ratification, a group of senators announced ahead of time they would vote against it, so the majority leader didn't bring it up. But now, if that group loses even one member, they can't stop it. That treaty is scheduled to be brought up again in three weeks. If it's ratified, the ISA will shut my platform down for years while it conducts studies on whether my mining business might theoretically threaten some deepwater shrimp."

Jack thought of the Tennessee snail darter that Barbas had dismissed so coolly. "Have you talked with anyone about this?

"Of course I have. I know how the system works." He twisted the focus knobs faster. "I talked with Ed Cargill, legislative director for the Senate majority leader, and explained that I need to make sure his boss never brings up the treaty for ratification. He said the majority leader appreciated my past contributions, but he wouldn't commit. I've sent notes to him for five months and haven't gotten one damned response." He stood, strode to the window, and watched the activity on the main deck thirty feet below. He seemed no less agitated when he sat back in his pivoting chair. "When I call the UN Secretary General, I get a call back the same day, but that pipsqueak Cargill is jerking me around. I'll make him pay for that, but right now he's a dead end. I have to find another way to keep that treaty in the deep freeze."

Barbas tilted his head back, maybe fantasizing he was a real admiral. His eyes popped open and he said, "My best shot is to get President Gorton to stop it, but I backed the guy who ran against him so I have no line of communication. In asking around, I heard that Gorton wanted you to be his White House legal counsel a few years ago. So it seems reasonable that you can ask him to do a favor for a big client."

Jack looked across the compass bolted to the deck and out the fortified window of the imaginary admiral's bridge. *Of course!* That's why Barbas had perked up when Debra told him the name of her firm. Barbas had already had him in his sights. That "strong connection" and the "favor" were the real reasons Barbas had invited them for a sail aboard *Excalibur*. Now he'd finally delivered the punch line.

"And that favor," Jack said, "would be getting the president to explain to the majority leader that the Law of the Sea treaty and the ISA are contrary to the security interests of the United States and should not be ratified . . . ever."

Barbas beamed. "Exactly. And if he's reluctant, tell him I'll donate five percent of the profits I make from selling minerals, except for gold, to him. Like a tithe, you might call it. How soon can you get that done?"

That was blunt. Barbas called it a tithe, but he was proposing a bribe. Being asked to take advantage of his relationship with the president had happened three times before, and each had made him feel like a lottery winner being hit up for a handout. But he'd brought it on himself. Just before he'd opened the doors of Strider & Vanderberg, he'd asked Gorton to very publicly offer him the prestigious job of White House legal counsel, assuring him that he would not accept. That was at a time when Gorton very much wanted Jack's good will, so he'd done so immediately. That announcement had pushed the Peck Strider scandal into the shadows, and clients had come pouring in.

Gorton's offer had been a charade that served both of them, but it did not mean there was any special relationship between them. In fact, because he knew things that could hurt Gorton politically, he was sure the president would always be wary of him.

He noticed Barbas pick up the binoculars again and start fiddling with them, waiting for an answer. Tricky moment. Not the right time to deny the relationship and give away the leverage Barbas thought he had. He decided to waffle. "It's not a matter of how soon. I haven't agreed to contact him at all."

"This is about money, isn't it?" Barbas's smirk reeked of condescension. "I showed a little vulnerability, so now you want more than legal fees. Maybe a piece of the action? Listen, I'm Greek. I bargain for a living. I'll give you one percent of the net from the minerals for three years. That's not all. When you're in a deal with me, I'll introduce you to world-class CEOs, every one of them a potential client."

Big money, more than he'd ever make practicing public interest law.

Barbas transformed his serious look into a social smile. "Then there are side benefits like access to private jets, my yacht, my clubs, and some beautiful . . . companions. All you have to do is get a commitment from Gorton within, say, a week."

All that money. Side benefits. Hire more lawyers. Sounded great. Just a couple of problems. The Chaos project was hemorrhaging money and so was the rest of Barbas's empire. One percent of nothing was nothing. Barbas couldn't deliver on any of his promises, including the grand delusions he'd spun back on *Excalibur* when he'd been pressing hard to hire Strider & Vanderberg. The other problem was that, having escaped the path his father had dictated for him, there was no way he'd get back in harness for anyone, least of all Petros Barbas.

"What I do for you"—he heard the stiff self-righteousness in his voice—"will be billed at my rate as a lawyer. Save you a lot of money."

"That's chump change. You insisted on coming to Chaos to see what I'm doing. Now you understand what's at stake. I'm your client, a very big client, and I'm telling you to kill this ratification, whatever it takes."

Jack looked out at the Pacific—choppy, as if agitated from below. Barbas had created a serious dilemma. He very much wanted—needed—to keep Barbas as a client. But the tour had raised questions. So had Barbas's intensity about the treaty. What was Barbas so worried about? He played political poker at an international level, so he knew he would be taking a risk by twisting arms in the Senate. Since blocking the ratification was worth that risk, something was going on beyond sucking up nodules through a seventy-two-hundred-foot-long straw.

"Understand this," Barbas said, standing. "If you won't do what I need, or can't get it done, by God, I'll find someone who will. Now it's time to get you in the chopper."

The playboy surrounded by a harem and luxurious toys had left the building. They walked down to the main deck in silence.

As they approached the helo, Barbas walked directly to Debra, took her elbow, drew her a few feet away, and turned his back to Jack and Gano. Jack couldn't hear what he said, but when Debra replied, he heard her clearly.

"I'll talk with Jack about it, Petros. We'll all benefit if we can reach agreement."

Barbas turned back, face inscrutable, then stepped closer to Jack. "Don't screw with me. As soon as I get back to San Francisco, I'll send word, and we'll meet at the Pacific-Union club. You know what I expect."

Arrogant bastard. The moment of truth was coming. He turned away without a word.

Just before they climbed into the helo, he turned back to face Barbas and said, "Nine days ago, a Greenpeace ship named *Aleutian* sank in this area." He looked away and inhaled deeply. "We've located the ship on the bottom, but we don't know why she went down. In one of his last messages to Greenpeace, her captain reported trying to make contact with other vessels to provide assistance. He thought he saw the lights of a fleet of fishing boats, but that could have been the lights on this platform. Did you hear his communication? Do you know what might have caused *Aleutian* to sink?"

The corners of Barbas's mouth turned down. "I got a report when that communication came in, but it wasn't a Mayday or SOS and we're not the Coast Guard." He turned and stalked off.

Jack flashed on the small framed photo of Katie on his desk. He knew damn well that Barbas wouldn't have sent his helos to help even if it *had* been an SOS. "You son of a bitch," he muttered and started after Barbas.

Gano grabbed him by the back of his jacket. "Cool your jets. Not the time or place."

ON THE RETURN trip, he gave Debra and Gano the whole story about Barbas's demand. "Since that was his objective from day one, he played it very well, got me watching the wrong target and sucked me right in— almost."

"He pushed me hard to pressure you to do what he wants," Debra said.

"That's because I was evasive up on the bridge. I have to make a decision. If I don't help him block that treaty, he'll fire us for sure."

For the rest of the flight, he and Debra talked about business while Gano caught a nap. The helo landed in Astoria, where they retrieved their cell phones and stepped out. They watched the pilot take off and gain altitude fast.

"I think that weasel got the picture that we're not on Barbas's A-list," Gano said. "You know, for a guy who's famous for throwing wild parties, Barbas wasn't very hospitable. I've had warmer receptions as a *gringo* gatecrasher at a *narcotraficante* hideout in Juarez. He acted like shaking my hand would send him to a leper colony."

"I could use a drink," Debra said.

As they walked into the Bridgewater Tavern on the waterfront, the bartender motioned toward a table across from the bar. Jack chose one next to the rear wall instead.

"Now you want to sit where the bartender can't listen in," Gano said as he slid into a chair that put his back to the wall. "You've come a long way since I met you in Mexico. Back then, you were as green as a field of shamrocks." He waved for a server to come over.

"I may be less green, but I still didn't get what I wanted on this trip."

"Which was?"

"To persuade myself Barbas has been telling us the truth and come away with a better relationship to keep him as a client. I also wanted to find out what he knew about *Aleutian*. Instead, well, you heard it all. What's your take on it, Debra?"

"Obviously he came to us for more than legal advice. And I'm furious that he ignored *Aleutian*—and Katie." Her face flushed. "I don't see how we can make this work out."

Wow. She's made a U-turn.

"So you're going to dump him," Gano said.

"I'm convinced that Barbas had been conning us, and the Chaos Project is an iceberg of which we've seen only the tip. Now I'm making up my mind about how to play it."

"Then there's something you should know about those helicopters. He needs one for routine passenger trips and to transport spare parts, maybe a backup for a medical emergency. But I got close enough to the two birds partly covered by tarps that I can tell you those babies are Russian-made Kamov Ka-52 gunships, cream of the crop. They hit 250 miles per hour when they swoop down on a target. They carry twelve air-to-ground missiles that can take out armored vehicles, and their underbelly cannon can shoot down other aircraft. They also have a couple of 23mm guns, eight 80mm rocket pods, and four thousand-pound bombs. They're flying battleships, not the kind of thing you keep around in case you come across the great white whale. Like we say down in bayou country, a man carrying a shotgun probably ain't huntin' a mouse."

Chapter 11

July 15
4:00 p.m.
San Francisco

MEI TURNED ON her heel and stalked out of Jack's office. He didn't blame her. The tension he felt had put a day-long strain on their friendly relationship. If his office wall wasn't made of wide-plank redwood, he'd have tried to put his fist through it.

His mind had been racing, careening thoughts trying to grasp a wisp of something and connect it to a clump of something else.

On the world atlas map of the northeast Pacific Ocean spread across his desk, he'd marked several *X*s. One was the last reported position of *Aleutian*. From it, he'd drawn a line depicting the course it had been on. A second *X* was where Drake had located *Aleutian* on the bottom. The third was Gano's location when he spotted the floating carcasses of mysteriously dead dolphins and where he been bird-dogged by a helo patrol. Connected, those three *X*s formed a relatively small triangle.

From a large-scale hazards-to-navigation map he'd downloaded, he'd gotten the exact location of Barbas's platform. That was the fourth *X*, and it was only a few miles from the triangle formed by the other *X*s. He wanted to enter a fifth *X* for the location of the super-HTV that Drake was certain was in the same area, but he didn't have enough information—yet.

What did his triangle plus one tell him? That Gano was right. The helo he'd seen must have come from Barbas's platform. Barbas clearly felt justified in using force to protect his monopoly. If he'd thought *Aleutian* had been a threat, maybe he'd had some role in its demise. The *Xs* could even mean that Barbas had already found the HTV Drake had been searching for. If so, a collision was coming up fast between those two powerful, headstrong men.

He got nothing more from staring at the very small area in the vast Pacific, so he tried looking at the situation from an angle, hoping to open up his right brain. If more answers were there, he still couldn't see them.

It was much easier to understand what his confrontation with Barbas had been about. Barbas had wanted him to do something and tried to make it appear that doing it would be in Jack's best interests. He'd kept throwing out incentives, expecting one of them to hook Jack.

Barbas's attempt at manipulation made him think of his father, who had played puppet master, maneuvering his son into position to win appointment to the U.S. Supreme Court. The realization that had changed his life was that the goal had been his father's, never his own.

He'd set up his law firm to represent ordinary people such as those damaged by Wall Street, banks, insurers, and corrupt officials at all levels. Trouble was, his eagerness to fight those battles had put his firm in danger and stressed his relationship with Debra.

Now he had to take on Barbas. The man could be charming, but he had a dark side and felt the best way to get what he wanted was to dominate everyone else. *That's never going to happen to me again, by God.* The question was: how would Barbas retaliate if he didn't get what he wanted? It would be ugly.

Chapter 12

July 16
8:30 a.m.
San Francisco

DEBRA STRODE INTO Jack's office, fresh from a quick shower after teaching her early morning karate class. She often used karate to center her thoughts in preparation for a hectic day, but this time it hadn't worked worth a damn. She dropped into a chair across the desk from him, very aware that a cloud of tension had trailed her into the room. Since she could always read his mood, she could tell how worried he was about his confrontation with Barbas on Chaos. She felt tense about potentially losing Barbas as a revenue source and gaining him as an enemy. She wished she weren't bringing more bad news—but she was. She had another reason for coming and hoped that might turn out better.

As soon as he looked up, she said, "There's a new problem with Barbas." A grimace flicked on and off Jack's face. "When I got back to my office after our trip to the platform, I found that Barbas had left a message inviting me to return to Chaos to join him for the weekend."

Jack's face reddened. "Damn him. Who the hell does he think he is?" His scowl was fierce. "That's a very bad idea. You should never go back there."

"I wasn't asking for permission. The fact is that I don't have time for two men dead set on getting their own way. One is trouble enough." She hoped being a little flippant might get him to lighten up. "When I called back and turned him down, he was furious. He called me a name I didn't appreciate, so I hung up. That could complicate the meeting you have coming up with him."

He nodded. "Don't worry about it. You did the right thing."

Since he seemed reassured, she decided to press ahead with the second reason she was there. "Jack, it's been more than a week since we had that blow-up at Tikal. We were under a lot of pressure, so I don't think either of us heard the other very well. The point is, we still haven't straightened it out. Our firm is important to me, and so are our clients. But my highest priority is the relationship between us, and I'm worried."

She had brought this up tentatively before and let it pass when he ducked. But the anxiety was disrupting her work, her whole life. They had to resolve it.

Jack's face looked like a fox with his foot in a trap—but a cunning fox. He knew better than to try to flee, knew better than to bite. She knew alternatives were flashing through his brain.

"Nothing to worry about," he said. "You know I love you. We'll get through all this crap and everything will . . . this isn't the best time—"

A rap on the door was followed by Gano strolling in. She could tell by his broad smile he was about to crank up his Louisiana charm machine. This time, she wasn't in the mood to hear it.

Jack cut him off. "Sit down, and tell Debra about the Bermuda Triangle."

Gano put on a mock studious face and smoothed both sides of his mustache. "Picture a triangle in the Caribbean northeast of Cuba. Its points are Miami, Bermuda, and San Juan, Puerto Rico. It's also called the Devil's Triangle because many boats, and a few planes, have vanished there. Every time a boat disappears when there's no foul weather or collision, media hounds fire off sensational explanations involving extraterrestrial beings, UFOs, and columns full of paranormal crap."

"Give her the example you gave me."

"Well, there I was a few months ago in the Carib making a delivery for some fellows from Singapore. I was hangin' out in this sweet little back-street bar with—well, her name doesn't matter—when folks started talking about one of them fancy Ferretti 500 motor yachts out on charter. Sumbitch vanished just north of the Bahamas. No hurricane and no Mayday. Turned out I knew the skipper. Now, that guy—"

"My guess," Debra cut in, knowing he liked to tell stories that only occasionally intersected with reality, "is that you have a theory about what happened."

"What I have is a reasonable alternative to the mumbo jumbo stuff, and it's a lot more than a theory. The sediment on the seabed and the crust underneath parts of the Triangle are loaded with methane hydrate."

"Which means what?"

"I won't go into exactly what methane hydrate is right now because, well, I'm not quite sure. But I do know that when something disturbs methane hydrate, methane gas under pressure shoots to the surface like a giant burp. The density of the seawater in a fairly small area suddenly decreases, making the water frothy and much less buoyant. A boat caught in a burp would sink like an anchor. The Aussies know a lot more about this than we do. While we're still blaming mysterious disappearances on ET, they've done tests that prove a methane burp can sink a ship. In fact—"

"Hold on," she said, "are you suggesting that a methane burp—"

"Could explain what happened to *Aleutian*? Damn right I am."

"But she was much bigger than the charter yacht," she said. "Could there be a burp big enough to sink it?"

"For damn sure. Deepwater Horizon," Gano answered, "a BP drill rig in the Gulf of Mexico, blew up in 2010. Killed eleven people. A year before that, reports say that geologists told BP that its rig was located over a reservoir of compressed methane gas that could blow if BP drilled into it. They were talking about a 'bubble' twenty miles across. No safety equipment can contain gas pressurized to a hundred thousand pounds per square inch, but they say that didn't stop BP from going ahead."

"What happened?" she asked.

"The robotic submersibles they sent down photographed cracks in the seafloor where plumes of methane were seeping out. If BP tapped into methane far below the seabed, some experts say it would blow like a volcano and rip through the seal on the blowout preventer. That would send gas, oil, and mud up the pipe at over six hundred miles per hour. It would explode when it hit fire, even a spark, on the drilling platform. So while the 'drill, baby, drill' crowd preaches about ending U.S. dependence on foreign oil, it's really about their own profits, and damn the risks to mere human beings."

"Here's where I think we are," Jack said. "Gano is correct that there's a lot of methane hydrate in the seabed within the Bermuda Triangle. Maybe that is what's causing boats to sink. Maybe not. He's also correct that there's a huge volume of methane hydrate in the Gulf of Mexico, and it may have caused the BP disaster. Then there's the Australian research. We have more work to do, but it looks like sudden release of methane, a methane burp, might be the culprit. We know Barbas is mining near a hydrothermal vent and that they emit methane, so the next question is whether there was enough methane hydrate to produce a major burp in *Aleutian*'s path. Methane might also have killed the dolphins Gano saw."

The idea that a methane burp could sink *Aleutian* was so new to her that she didn't know how she felt about it. And how would the families of *Aleutian*'s crew feel? Some would want to keep believing that *Nikita Maru* sank her even though the facts didn't support that. Others had to be worried that the tragedy was caused by something the crew did. If a methane burp might be the culprit, they'd be greatly relieved to know that.

"Jack, I'm going to assign two of our new lawyers to find out about methane hydrate in *Aleutian's* area. You okay with that?"

"Of course."

She didn't feel like chatting, so she stood, nodded at both of them, and walked back to her office.

It was what *hadn't* happened in Jack's office that had her emotions jangling. He had brushed off the chance to take an honest look at the friction in their relationship, and this was the third time he'd done that. It really got to her that he wouldn't look her in the eyes while he was doing his evasive tap dance. That was so unlike him. Of course it hadn't been the best time to get in to a touchy subject, but it didn't feel like the best time was coming up.

As a partner in the firm, she had more thorny challenges to deal with than ever before in her career. They woke her up in the middle of the night and too often made her short-tempered, but she felt strong enough to face everything head-on. Another question bothered her almost as much. Where would she be if the firm did survive? Would she wind up being one of those rich, workaholic lawyers with no love in her life?

In the beginning, three years ago, their relationship had been red-hot. He still told her he felt the same way about her, so, because he was an honest man, he must believe that was true. But if it were, they'd have blown away this friction between them in a heartbeat. In her heart, she knew it wasn't true, and that was tearing her up every day.

What was the truth?

She had a good idea what had caused their relationship to get stuck on a plateau. Even if Jack understood those reasons, she wasn't sure he had the emotional tools to deal with them. His issues ran deep, deep, deep, all the way back to his childhood.

A plateau could be a resting point where you get a second wind and the will to keep climbing for the summit. What was eating at her was knowing that two people on a plateau might not keep climbing together. One might fall off. She had the aching feeling she was losing him. She couldn't fix that by herself. She loved him, but that wasn't going to be enough this time. And this was the only time that mattered

Chapter 13

July 20
1:30 p.m.
San Francisco

JACK HAD JUST finished an expensive lunch with a client at the Mark Hopkins Hotel, but he had a hollow feeling in the pit of his stomach. He stopped at the corner, waiting to cross California Street to meet Petros Barbas at the Pacific-Union Club.

Some thought the Club's four-story brownstone building at the crest of Nob Hill was majestic. Far more, including Jack, thought it was just plain ugly. Either way, it was one of the oldest and most exclusive private clubs in America. The membership roster included names from William Randolph Hearst to, more recently, McNamara, Packard, and Schwab. Even though his father had been a member, and even if Peck's scandal hadn't made acceptance unlikely, Jack had no interest in joining.

Waiting for the light to change, he thought about the upcoming meeting. Since returning from Chaos, he'd thought carefully about the pros and cons of Barbas's demand that he get President Gorton's help. Of several "cons", the biggest was giving a high-rolling profiteer a blank check to operate however he wanted to, damn the consequences. He barely knew the man and had only a sketchy idea of what he was doing. It made no sense to help someone he didn't trust.

But there was a "pro" the size of an elephant. Barbas had made Gorton's help a condition of remaining a client. Well, today he had to get Barbas to understand that he needed Strider & Vanderberg regardless of Gorton.

He crossed on the green light, climbed the front steps, and entered.

An elderly man in a starched white uniform with dark blue epaulettes was waiting just inside.

"Mr. Strider?

"Yes."

"Mr. Barbas is expecting you. He's in the card room. I'll show you the way, sir."

Barbas, the only person in the hushed, dimly lighted room, waved him to a seat across from him at a chess table. Barbas scanned a document, signed it, and pushed it aside.

"Good to see you, Jack. Hope you enjoyed your visit to Chaos. How about a gin and tonic? This button will bring the steward."

"I'm fine, thanks," he said as he sat. This was a relief. He'd been concerned that Barbas would show up as agitated and aggressive as he'd been on the platform. Instead, he seemed to have chosen the role of urbane host. More likely a tactic to get something he wanted badly.

"Been a member here long?" Jack asked to break the ice.

"Don't know whether I'm a member or not. I think this place," he said with a dismissive wave as if referring to a local YMCA, "is affiliated with The Jockey Club in Paris where I've been a member for decades. Now, let's get right to it."

"I agree." He'd already decided to take the initiative. "You asked my firm to help you obey all laws applying to your mining operation. Based on what you told me about Chaos and your processing plant on the Columbia River, we can do that. Our firm's expertise goes beyond Debra and me. We have three associates who specialize in—"

"No doubt you'd be very helpful, but right now I want to know that Gorton is going to make sure the Law of the Sea treaty isn't ratified."

"I don't know his position."

Barbas's smile disappeared. "Have you contacted him about what I want?"

A bald man pushed through the tall door into the game room. Leaning on an ebony cane, he started across the room toward the fireplace.

"I reserved this room," Barbas snapped.

The man straightened as if he might make a fight of it. As a member, he must have been a mover and shaker in his time. He stared at Barbas for several seconds, decided against trying to assert himself, and shuffled out.

With a snort, Barbas turned back. "I want you as my lawyer, so your answer to my next question is important." Barbas's voice was husky, as though holding back strong emotion. "Do you *intend* to get Gorton's support for me?"

If he answered honestly, he'd lose any chance he had to stop Barbas from damaging the Columbia River and maybe the northeast Pacific Ocean. Time for ambiguity.

"I'll say this. You have to rely on your lawyer to give you honest advice, even if you don't want to hear it. You can trust me to do that. My advice is that seeking Gorton's help is premature. Even if that treaty were ratified, you have no need to be concerned. If anything should come up in the future, I can advise you how to deal with it. If, down the road, you think we ought to talk with President Gorton, we can discuss that then."

That's the bait. Hook the client. Then show him what's in his best interests.

"No one gets away with playing me for a fool." Barbas made his left-handed chopping motion. "No one." Black eyes flashing, he stood up and pointed across the table. "You're fired!"

Jack hadn't expected that, not so fast, not so final. He stood, willing himself to be calm. "Let's take a break and talk it over in a couple of days. My firm—" Barbas's smile, a nasty mix of condescension and smugness, stopped him.

"I didn't get rich by being stupid." Barbas leaned forward. "I knew from your reaction on Chaos that you wouldn't come through for me, so I've already interviewed Stan Simms at Sinclair & Simms. When I told him I might replace you with him, he almost cheered. I think his words were, 'I owe that bastard a big one.'"

Jack felt his temperature soar toward the flashpoint. Barbas firing him was very bad. Replacing him with Simms was rubbing salt in the wound. "You two will make a great pair, and I'll tell you this. If Gorton finds out Simms is your lawyer, he won't let you in the White House even on a tour."

"I don't know about that. What I *do* know is that if you continue being such a pain in the ass, I'll really turn Simms loose on you, Debra, and your whole damned firm. Hell, I won't even have to pay him for that. After you left Chaos, I made a deal to buy all the buildings on Pier 9. I figured that if you did what I needed, I'd make you a sweet deal. If you didn't, I could kick your ass out." He nodded in satisfaction. "By the way, be sure to tell Debra she'll be in my thoughts."

"Barbas, you and I will meet again. Count on it."

"You better hope not. I play for keeps. A few people have tried to cross me the way you did. They're dead—every one of them." He grabbed his papers and stomped out.

Jack dropped into his chair, heart pounding, fists clenched. He'd tried to persuade Barbas with reason. Now he wished he'd shouted, punched him in the teeth. Barbas had run a power trip on him. He felt humiliated. The fees the firm needed were gone. That was bad, but the situation was likely to get worse. He had a suspicion that Simms blamed him for the disappearance three years ago of his partner, Justin Sinclair. Simms knew Sinclair had gone to Washington, DC—maybe even that it was for a showdown with Jack Strider—and never been seen again. That disappearance had cost his firm millions. Now that Simms had Barbas's backing and encouragement, he would be an even more formidable enemy.

His left brain shouted a warning. Barbas had been suspicious of him. That was understandable. But he had acted on that and made the effort to set an ambush. When he hadn't gotten what he wanted, he'd pulled the trigger without hesitation. Two lessons in that. First, for whatever reason, that treaty was damned important to him. Second, Barbas was a tougher enemy than he'd realized.

He returned to thinking about Barbas's threats. He wasn't bluffing about Pier 9. He'd obviously learned that Jack's office lease provided that if the buildings on Pier 9 were sold, the new owner could terminate all leases on thirty days' notice. Jack had objected to that provision in the lease, but one family had owned the buildings for three generations, and the current patriarch had assured him the family would never sell. Weighing that, he'd considered the risk to be minimal. Barbas had turned the highly unlikely into reality.

He'd chosen his office space with care, knowing it would be a second home. At his desk, he could contemplate legal issues while watching comings and goings on the Bay and savor the smells of international trade along the wharves. If Barbas thought he could flick him away like a fly on his sleeve, he'd damn sure show him otherwise.

BACK IN HIS OWN office, he wrapped up a disclosure he had very much not wanted to make.

"So that's it," he said to Debra and Gano. "Barbas is now our enemy."

Debra was silent, tight-mouthed, staring into the corner of the room.

He tried to put himself in her place. She'd been a star at Sinclair & Simms, but that future had crashed after she sided with him against Sinclair. She'd been happy to become Jack's partner in the new firm, but now that was on the verge of collapse. No wonder she was mad at him.

Her face was stern when she finally said, "I'm not going to waste my breath giving you a sermon on what Barbas could have meant to our firm, but his threats worry me."

They should worry her. "Barbas told me his game plan, and that will help us protect ourselves. And he sent more of a message than he intended." He used a deeper tone of voice to sound more confident than he felt.

"Hey, he's Greek," Gano said. "He got excited. What's the big message in that?"

"Keeping the ISA from supervising his mining business might save him some money, but his reaction was way over the top. There's some other reason he's desperate to keep the ISA away. I'm going to find out what that is."

"Damn it, Jack, get your head back in the game," Debra said. "Think Armstrong. Think overhead. Think Simms. Oh, for God's sake!"

A CHILL WIND swept under the Golden Gate Bridge and swirled around the Bay. Jack zipped up his windbreaker and eased the tiller to take advantage of a gust coming across the water. His boat was designed for speed, and he was pushing her hard. After an hour, he'd burned up some of the stress, so he turned more into the wind, slowed, and let more tension flow out through his fingertips. Now he could consider his confrontation with Barbas more rationally.

He was troubled, even apprehensive. Barbas was a shark hardwired to behave in certain patterns. He was skilled at concealing his shark nature for a while but would always revert to genetic commands. When Barbas hadn't gotten what he wanted, he'd bitten down hard. And he'd do it again and again.

If he interfered with Barbas in any way, Barbas would declare all-out war that could harm more than just Jack Strider. That was bad, because interfering with Barbas was exactly what he intended to do.

Chapter 14

July 21
5:30 p.m.
Chaos platform

HE WAS PETROS Barbas, by God.

They envied his wealth, admired his flamboyant life, and feared his take-no-prisoners business style. But they'd seen nothing compared to the Chaos Project that would be his greatest triumph.

Feet resting on a leather foot stool made of premium hides taken from a *hacienda* he owned in Argentina, he gazed idly through the bulletproof glass of his suite in the top level of the superstructure of the Chaos platform. Far from shipping lanes and commercial flight paths, with no land within two hundred miles, all he saw were the restless swells of the Pacific Ocean.

He thought back to the morning in his Athens office years ago when his administrative assistant had advised him that a very strange-looking man named Dr. Renatus Roux was in the outer office. He claimed to have a plan that would make Mr. Barbas rich. Amused by the claim, and knowing the guard in the lobby had searched the man, he'd had him sent in.

On first meeting Renatus, he'd felt put off by the man's immobile face. Within fifteen minutes, his excitement was building almost as it had the day he'd launched his first cargo ship. With no idle conversation, Renatus had started to outline the characteristics of hydrothermal vents.

"Very interesting," he'd said to the strange man, "but I was told you had a plan that would make me rich. So tell me what that is, or get out." Renatus had ticked the index finger of his right hand. "First, my calculations show it is theoretically possible for an HTV to exist that is more than thirty times larger than any yet discovered. Second,"—he ticked his middle finger—"if such a vent exists, I can find it. And finally,"—the fourth finger—"in the field surrounding it, such a vent will have produced very large deposits of valuable minerals, including gold and silver."

"For the sake of discussion, let's assume all of that is true. What would you want out of it?"

"If I'm right, you pay me five million U.S. dollars a year for as long as you continue mining. You also pay for my research on the HTV itself. If I can't find that HTV, or the minerals aren't there, you owe me nothing. I report only to you."

For what Renatus promised, he'd have paid far more, even given him a tiny percentage, but he'd quickly realized Renatus wasn't motivated by money. As soon as they made the deal, Renatus had dropped out of contact.

Petros looked around but couldn't find the cigar he craved. He called to the steward who was, he knew, hovering outside the door. "Bring me a cigar." The man returned in seconds with a Montecristo on a silver tray. "I'm tired of the Cuban stuff. Toss them all over the side, and bring me a Davidoff Nicaraguan Toro." After the steward lighted it for him, he savored the complex floral and coffee tastes. He recalled that he'd waited impatiently for Renatus to resurface, had even considered having him tracked down.

When Renatus showed up several months later, he said he'd identified an area most likely to contain a giant HTV and specified the equipment needed to find it. After listening to Renatus explain his calculations, he'd called in his own scientists. To ensure confidentiality, he gave each a separate section of the calculations and challenged them to refute Renatus's work. None made a dent in it. After that, his holding company made its first big investment in the enterprise.

While conducting the search of the target zone in the northeast Pacific Ocean, Renatus had personally controlled the submerged remotely operated vehicles with their multiple cameras and sensors. He allowed no one else to review the images. At the end of the third week of crisscrossing the seabed, Renatus had announced, "I found the vent. It's"—for the first time, his whispery voice had contained emotion—"enormous."

Because he had no interest in the HTV itself, he'd said, "What about gold and silver?"

"According to my calculations, the minerals will be there."

Using robots to bring up samples from almost a mile and a half down had been more expensive than he'd expected, but it was tolerable because they'd immediately found manganese, copper, and amazing veins of silver. There had been almost no gold, but Renatus had been unruffled. "Silver is on the seabed. Gold deposits are in the crust. Finding and extracting gold will be more difficult, but it will be there."

"Then I'll buy a drill ship and go after it. I can get a decent one for under $200 million."

Renatus had rejected that approach. "We're not after oil, so a drill ship won't work. My system requires a semi-submersible platform that will cost at least $500 million. The entire project could run one billion dollars."

Petros took a long draw on his cigar. That number had been a shocker. Anything close to that amount would strain his entire corporate cash flow before he saw the first dollar in revenues. He shook his head, remembering how little he'd understood of what the scientist was saying. Being in that position had made him so uncomfortable that he'd begun calculating the considerable investment he'd have to write off. He was a high roller but not a fool, so he'd turned Renatus down.

Finally convinced that Odyssey Properties was not going to fund the mineral mining project, Renatus had switched to a radically expanded business proposition, repeating key points as he would to a dim-witted student. In the end, Renatus had spun an incredible vision.

Petros stood and paced, puffing more often. If he'd called it off right then, there would be no platform and none of the wild swings of exhilaration and depression he was going through, the depression coming too often now. But he hadn't called it off. He remembered how his brain had started free-wheeling with possibilities far beyond what Renatus imagined. If he could pull off Renatus's new business proposition, he could transform geopolitics. It was worth risking every *drachma* he had.

That conversation had changed everything. Indifferent to his cash flow and ignoring objections raised by his accountants, he'd taken the biggest gamble of his life. He cut a deal with Daewoo Shipbuilding to give his project the highest priority in its shipyard in Okpo, South Korea. He hired the best naval architects away from Hyundai Samho Heavy Industries to use the latest block construction techniques. His giant platform had been assembled using prefabricated multi-deck segments with built-in pipes, electrical cables, and equipment. In record time, the platform, which he privately christened Chaos, was towed to the northeast Pacific.

He paused in front of a window on the north side of his suite overlooking the main deck. He felt a glow of pride. This wasn't just another tanker or hotel. This was the crown jewel of his kingdom, floating above an unimaginable treasure thousands of feet down. Getting that treasure to the surface rested solely on the shoulders of Renatus, a man who was a genius and, certainly, a sociopath.

He heard the low hum of the powerful engines that meant robotic equipment was pulverizing the seabed near the HTV, and suction pumps were bringing the mineral slurry to the platform. Making all this happen had been an incredible high, far better than the finest hashish, dried mescaline, and various psychedelics he kept in the Chinese lacquer chest across the suite from him. He exhaled a funnel of smoke toward the ceiling.

The huge system was working as planned—except that it was failing. The gold being collected wasn't generating enough income to offset the cost of building and operating the massive platform. At the same time, his businesses around the world were hemorrhaging red ink. Pleas for cash were pouring in from every corner of his empire. The global recession combined with Chinese competition was strangling his shipping business. The only people vacationing at his luxury resorts were those who'd lost so much money they had to spend big to keep up appearances. The financial nut-crusher was getting worse. Only Renatus's vision could save his company now, and that project was dead in the water.

He'd thoroughly investigated Renatus's reputation and gotten five-star reviews, but the man hadn't been able to solve the problem preventing his vision from going into operation. When Renatus's most recent experiment misfired, he'd calmly explained that it had been a valuable learning experience. But as far as meeting financial needs, it had been a total failure.

Because he'd planted hidden cameras and listening devices in Renatus's lab, he knew he was working twenty-hour days. What he resented was that some of that time was spent on research into the mysteries of the HTV. He couldn't bully or threaten Renatus, because he was in too deep to do without him.

If Renatus succeeded, so much money would pour in that he could steamroll over anything in his way. But every day that passed without success, the knot in his stomach got more painful. If the Law of the Sea Treaty was ratified and the ISA shut him down, he could never recover.

He'd depended on persuading Strider to get Gorton to pressure a few senators. How big a deal was that? In most countries where he did business, that would take just a phone call followed by an envelope. He'd tried to be nice to the guy, hiring his law firm even though he had no intention of being transformed into some sort of environmental angel. How dare that stiff-necked bastard refuse his simple request?

Strider should have been able to see this situation from Odyssey Properties' point of view. He employed thousands around the world. His tankers were a key factor in international commerce. His success with this project could mean huge benefits for world economies. Instead of confronting him, Strider should have cheered him on.

He clenched his fists and wished Strider would walk through the door.

Now he'd have to use a far more risky strategy. There were senators he could exploit if he could identify them in time. He still had enough cash to stuff a few pockets. He'd pay or he'd play rough, whichever was necessary. From running a shipping and construction empire, he knew when to break bread and when to break heads.

He pressed a button to connect with his communications office. "Get Simms."

Simms had the temperament of a Rhodesian Ridgeback with a score to settle, so he'd snap at the assignment he was about to get.

In seconds, his handset pinged. "Simms, have Strider's firm thrown out of their offices as soon as the law allows. Between now and then, raise hell on Pier 9. Make it impossible for them to practice law."

He hated not having gotten Debra Vanderberg to Chaos for a couple of days. He was sure Strider had fouled that up too. Firing and evicting him weren't even close to enough. He'd screwed women for a lot of reasons, but doing it to emasculate their men was always sweet. If he got another shot at Debra, he wouldn't miss.

Chapter 15

July 21
6:30 p.m.
Astoria, Oregon

KILLING TIME IN the Columbia River Maritime Museum, Jack had watched a video of forty-foot storm waves pounding the infamous Columbia River Bar called the "Graveyard of the Pacific" at the entrance to the port of Astoria. Exhibits of steamboats, cannery operations, and sailing vessels had held his attention for a while. He'd even looked at the photographic history of maritime tattoos. Now, standing next to a simulated tugboat, he was fed up. *Where the hell is Gano?*

He couldn't help thinking about his law firm under attack and his failure to meet his commitment to the Armstrong plaintiffs. And Barbas's mining operations were a serious threat to the Columbia River downstream from it. But what worried him most was his gut feeling that Barbas was also engaged in some much more malevolent enterprise. His brain felt like a gerbil running on a wheel as it recycled those thoughts.

His plan had been for Gano to stake out the Astoria airport until Barbas came in from the platform on his helo, and then track him from there without being spotted. If they were lucky, Barbas would meet someone or go somewhere that would shed light on what was really going on at the platform.

Gano had agreed to meet Jack at the museum at half past five to report. He was already an hour late. Could Barbas's men have grabbed him?

"Ahoy there, Captain America," Gano called across the exhibit room. "Come on outside. There's a place by the river where we can talk."

They were barely seated on a concrete bench when Gano said, "Your plan fell apart right after the tip-off. I rented a truck and staked out the airport. Boring, boring, boring until Barbas's whirlybird dropped in, the same one that took us out to the platform. The pilot got out and had the bird loaded with fuel. I was ready to get on Barbas's trail as he drove away from the airport. Then, instead of Barbas getting out, the helo went airborne. I sprinted over to my Cessna, powered up, and headed north up the coast in pursuit. He had a head start, but I was much faster, so I caught up. I stayed above him in his visual blind spot and kept clouds between us.

"He flew across Washington State and over Vancouver Island, British Columbia. Then he veered east over the Strait of Georgia toward the Canadian mainland. Suddenly, through a broken cloud layer, I saw him dropping out of the sky like a goose full of buckshot. I couldn't see where he went, but I noticed on my map that a village called Powell River had an airport. I figured that was my only choice. I couldn't land right after he did without being obvious, so I circled a few times above the clouds before I went down. As I was on final approach, too late to stay airborne, I saw there was no helo on the tarmac or in the air.

"No one was around the airstrip except two guys working under an airplane engine about fifty yards away. Both slid halfway out, looked at me kind of sideways. I asked if a helo had just landed there. One of the fellows said, 'Yep.' I asked whether a man had gotten out. 'Yep,' and both of them started sliding back under the engine. I said, 'Hold on,' and gave him fifty dollars, your money of course, and asked, 'You know where he went?' If he had said 'Yep' again I was going to stomp on his neck, but he must have seen that coming. He said, 'He drove off in a Land Rover. Always leaves it down on the waterfront next to Jake's Bar and heads for somewhere out there.' He jerked his head toward the strait and rolled back under the truck. Those two northern rednecks figured I'd used up your fifty bucks."

"That's weird. You know anything about the Strait of Georgia?" Jack asked.

"I do now. It's about 150 miles long with a few big islands in it and lots of small ones. It's a magnet for the scuba-diving, whale-watching crowd. Anyway, the waterfront wasn't far so I got there fast."

"What did you find?"

"The Land Rover but no Barbas. So there I was, sucking my thumb. Nothing to do but go into Jake's Bar to do some, you know, research. Place was empty except for a hunched-over old geezer wearing a gray fisherman's sweater. He looked up and smiled. No teeth. I knew he was my man. After I loosened him up with two shots of rum, he started rambling about bizarre cults and secret societies up and down the banks of the strait. He said one island, named Ironbound, is so hexed locals are afraid to go there. Then he started in on all the drugs, guns, and murder in the villages along the strait. But Barbas was getting farther away, so I cut him off and asked about the guy in the Land Rover. His mouth snapped shut like a clam. He turned away and started talking with the bartender. If he knew the answer he wasn't going to give it to me. I guess it's their code that outsiders are lower than whale shit, maybe tolerated but never trusted.

"I got out my electronic magic carpet and checked out the Internet. There are a lot of homes on the big islands, but I figure Barbas wants privacy so he wouldn't go to any of them. In the little port villages along the mainland everybody knows everybody, so he'd stand out like Bigfoot. That left the small islands, but most of them are inaccessible. I wanted to take a look, but that would mean going lower and slower than I can in my Cessna."

"Barbas must have left by boat, so you got a boat, right? Did you rent one or steal it?"

Gano flashed a look of fake offense. "Neither. I was too far behind to use a boat. But there was a rack of tourist brochures next to the door. One had an ultralight on the cover, and there were some for rent on a big island called Texada. I hitched a ride over there and mounted up."

"You know how to fly one of those things?"

"I can fly anything. One time in Nepal near Annapurna—never mind, I'll tell you about that some other time. Anyway, it was a great way to look for Barbas in a boat and cruise past the small islands within reasonable range. Problem was, nothing lit me up, so I decided to check out the place that rumpot fisherman mentioned where no one goes. Ironbound is a few miles north from Powell River and about a mile offshore. It's totally forested with a center ridge running its length. Pleasure boats stay away, because it's surrounded by jagged granite ledges and the current screams past.

"I figured if anyone was watching and saw me gliding by they wouldn't feel threatened. I spotted a big ol' shingle-covered lodge. Verandas, gazebo, even a tennis court that looked like it hadn't been played on since F. Scott Fitzgerald's time. Classy place, except for three long metal buildings in a line off to one side. And I saw twin generators big enough to power a cruise ship. If the Hole-in-the-Wall Gang had a hideout like that, they'd still be in business."

Jack thought about that. "So whatever is going on in those buildings requires a lot of juice, a lot more than a vacation cottage. Anything else?"

"Damn right. There's a concertina wire fence around most of the compound. Barbas doesn't want visitors. But since there's a lodge, there must be a path through the rocks and maybe a concealed boathouse."

"Any sign of life?"

"Lights on in the lodge, so our raptor might be in his nest. I was thinking what to do next when the little lawn mower motor on the ultralight started cutting on and off, so I decided to get my ass back to Texada."

"Anything else important you can think of?"

"Not really important, but on my way back to Texada the motor conked out. I had to ditch it in the strait. Talk about cold water. I got pulled out right quick by a salmon fisherman on his way back to Powell River. If the rental place hassles you about the ultralight, tell them I'll sue them for nearly killing me. Hell, that thing can't be worth much anyway. It was just a go-cart hanging under a kite. I wouldn't have minded warming up in Jake's Bar, but since I was still on the clock I fired up the Cessna and headed back here. Just another fun-filled day in the Gano LeMoyne Mission Impossible series."

Jack admired, even envied, Gano's damn-the-torpedoes attitude about life. He responded to danger as though it were high octane fuel.

"Glad you're okay. Now let's see what we know for sure. Barbas's helo flies to Powell River and drops a passenger on a regular basis. The passenger leaves Powell River and may or may not go to the hexed island. If he does, we don't know why. In other words, we're still at the starting line."

"Well damn, I busted my butt all day. Thought I did better than that, and I know I earned a quart of black rum."

"I'm fine with that. A bar could be a good place to get information from the locals about what kind of work they do on Chaos and at the processing plant."

"If they're like the folks I dealt with today, what makes you think they'll even tell us what time it is?"

"Because I'll tell them I represent out-of-state investors who are considering building a hotel. No, starting a grocery, or buying an existing one and expanding it, so I need to find out about the local economy."

"Are lawyers allowed to lie like that?"

THEY STROLLED along a row of canneries between them and the waterfront. On their left beyond the small business district, the Victorian architecture of the homes gave character to the hillside. After a few minutes, they spotted the Bridgewater Tavern and walked in. It was packed. The biggest flat screen showed a NASCAR race, another featured a truck destruction derby, and a third showed pro football. Country music filled the main room as background for loud, jovial conversations.

Gano nudged him. "Take a look at that gorgeous bartender."

Her white blouse would have looked at home on an eighteenth century pirate ship. Her auburn hair was gathered in a loose braid over her shoulder. She was holding a bottle of red wine up to the light to appraise its color and clarity.

All bar stools were taken, so Gano pounced on a table in the middle of the room just as it was vacated.

"I'll have a 'Dark 'n Stormy,'" Jack told the server.

"Your best dark rum, my man, and bring the bottle," Gano ordered.

The server's eyes widened, and she headed for the bar without comment.

Jack looked around. Mostly men, maybe a half-dozen women, no kids. Mustaches, beards, or several-day stubble were the norm. He saw a sea of real or knock-off Pendleton products: tartans and plaids, dark blues and greens, peacoats, pullovers, and knit seaman's caps. Not a button-down or polo shirt in the place. Faces were weathered and rough, the kind seen aboard trawlers, in saw mills, and on lumberjack crews. He and Gano had walked in on a tribe. No one was openly paying attention to them, but he knew they were being thoroughly scanned. Verdicts were pending.

"Pardon me, gentlemen."

A woman's voice came from close behind Jack, but the look in Gano's eyes told him the speaker was the beautiful bartender. She came around and stood by the side of the table between them.

Looking at Gano with a smile, she said, "Sorry. We can't serve a bottle at a table. And before you argue with me"—although Gano seemed to have lost the power of speech—"that's state law. Besides, I know from experience that nothing good happens when there's a bottle on a table in a bar." Gano scrambled to his feet, but she walked away, stopping to chat with people at several tables.

Gano watched her until she returned behind the bar, and then he signaled for their server, a college-age blond.

"Pardon me, miss. May I ask you a question about the bartender?"

"If you want to know if she's married, I'm not allowed to say. But she's not a bartender. She owns the tavern. She grew up in Astoria, went away to college, and then taught at Oregon State until a year ago when her father got sick and needed her here. After he died, she stayed to keep this place going, keep people employed. She's a wonderful boss. Sorry, I have to go."

"But wait," Jack said. "We're from out of town and thinking about making an investment here. We need to talk with local business people. Will you ask her to come over and talk with us, please?"

He watched the server deliver the message, saw both women look over at them, then grin at each other. The owner walked from behind the bar and through a door in the back wall of the tavern.

"Damn, Mr. Charm School, you should have let me handle it. I've been around this track before. I'd have said—"

The auburn-haired woman re-appeared and walked across the room to their table. "Name's Molly McCoy. I understand you're thinking of doing business in Astoria."

Gano was first to his feet. "I'm Gano LeMoyne. That's Jack Strider. Please join us."

"For just a moment. So, where are you fellows from?"

"San Francisco," Jack said and casually laid out his cover story and why they needed to get a sense of the local economy. At the first opportunity, Gano jumped in with his tale of having to ditch the ultralight. At least he had enough good sense to leave out anything about the reason for the flight.

While Gano, acting like a teenager in heat, continued to banter with Molly, Jack took a closer look at her. Emerald eyes, built-in smile, skin radiantly healthy. She looked like someone who guided kayak trips down the whitewater rapids of the Rogue River. She appeared to be in early to mid-thirties, but there was a sense of self, a calmness that suggested she might look pretty much the same at seventy.

He glanced at her left hand. No wedding ring. When he looked up, she was watching.

"No, Jack, not married. My boyfriend, at least a guy who wants to be my boyfriend, works on a big offshore platform."

The ideal lead-in. "Do many people from Astoria work out there?"

"Just about every plumber, welder, electrician, and everyone with a strong back got sucked right out to sea or upriver at a processing plant. We call it 'the mill' because that's what it used to be. When our walk-in cooler broke down last week, I had to get someone to come all the way from Portland to fix it. But I'm not complaining. This town was dying before Mr. Barbas showed up. All those jobs are like the Holy Grail."

"So everyone's happy that he's here?"

Her smile left her eyes. "You won't hear anyone in Astoria say a bad word about Mr. Barbas."

"What sort of work does your boyfriend do on the platform?" He noticed that Molly had said "platform" not "Chaos" so he did the same. Maybe Barbas didn't use that name with his workers.

"He's an electronics technician, but he doesn't talk about what he does." Her voice had changed just enough to tell him she was suddenly stressed. She looked at Gano. "My gosh, you still don't have your rum." She signaled to the server, who quickly returned with what looked like a triple shot.

"I need to get opinions about the local economy," Jack said, "and whether there's a need for a new grocery store. The more I learn about the local employment situation, the better I can project what's needed. Think I could talk with some of Barbas's workers?"

"I'm afraid not," she said firmly. "Everyone who works for Mr. Barbas has to sign a paper agreeing to pay a big fine if they shoot off their mouth about their work. When they come back from a six month shift on the platform, they won't say a word about it, not even in bed. That's the way Mr. Barbas wants it, and that's all we need to know. Those jobs saved this town . . . at least for now."

Gano spoke up. "So your, uh, boyfriend is gone for months, or does he come in for a weekend now and then?"

Gano was as subtle as a dump truck.

"Six months straight on the platform. No exceptions unless, well, a couple of guys died."

"What about 'the mill?'" Jack asked. "Can't be any secrets there."

"Of course not."

"So we could go up there," Jack said, "and do some market research about what they might want in a new or bigger grocery store? We could talk to people on their breaks or lunch hour."

She frowned. "There's so much valuable stuff on the site that security is extremely tight. They even search the workers when they leave. Since they don't know you, there's no chance you'd get in."

Jack looked around at the men at other tables. "Some of the men here tonight work there?"

"A lot of them. When the mill started back up, there was one eight-hour shift a day. Now there are three shifts, twenty-four-seven. The whole thing is much bigger than they said it would be when they got city council to approve it. Anyway, the economy is doing much better. It's just that some of us worry." She stopped and looked over at the bar.

Jack saw she'd become more uncomfortable and was about to leave the table. He decided he better probe quickly. "A big operation like that must wind up with a lot of waste material after they've finished refining what comes in from the platform. What do they do with that?"

"Well, there is a lot more than they told us there would be. Some people worry about that, but . . ." Her voice trailed off.

"What I'd be worried about," Gano said, "is the chemicals they use getting into the river or the groundwater."

"Wait a minute," she said. "What does that have to do with a grocery store?"

Suddenly a stocky man wearing a Pittsburgh Steelers cap walked up, stood squarely behind Gano's chair, and laid a heavy hand on his left shoulder.

"Me and some of the other boys have been listening," he growled across the table at Jack and nodded to three men sitting at the next table. "We think you're spying. Maybe you got something against Mr. Barbas. Well, that don't go in our town. Stand up!" He grabbed a handful of Gano's shirt.

"Clem, back off," Molly ordered.

"Take . . . your . . . hand . . . off . . . me." Gano didn't turn around or raise his voice.

The man didn't move his hand. Everyone in the tavern had stopped talking. Hank Williams singing *Your Cheating Heart* seemed much louder.

"Don't want any trouble," Jack said.

"You *got* trouble," the man in the cap said. "Now get up and get out, or we'll throw you out." He jerked hard on Gano's shirt.

Gano's right hand stretched forward, palm flat on the table. Jack saw it form a fist.

"Gano, don't—" but he was too late.

Gano rotated his upper body slightly to his left, then swung back and drove his right elbow like a pile driver straight back into Clem's crotch.

"*Yeeowww!*" was followed by agonized moans as Pittsburgh hunched over, grabbed his balls, and collapsed, crashing into the table behind. Glasses shattered, followed by cries of outrage.

Chairs scraped back around the room as men started toward Gano.

Gano jumped to his feet and reached behind his back under his shirt. "Listen up!" he shouted. "I got a Glock 23 in my belt. Thirteen shots. And a Beretta in my ankle holster. Which one of you wants to go first?"

No one moved.

"Everybody calm down. I don't plan on shootin' nobody tonight." He locked eyes with the men at the nearest table who'd been eavesdropping. "I don't plan on gettin' beaten up either. So let's not be spillin' blood all over Molly's furniture. We'll just walk out peaceful." A few men raised both hands high, others backed away.

"Sorry for the disturbance, Molly."

She crossed her arms and frowned. Gano stepped closer and held out his business card. She looked away, so he set it on the table in front of her.

Jack didn't walk out backward, but didn't quite turn his back to the room either. After they were a block away, he asked Gano, "Ever see *Bad Day at Black Rock*?"

Gano, vibrating with repressed energy, maintained his surface cool. "Nope."

"Spencer Tracy, who has only one arm, shows up in this small town and asks a lot of questions. The locals threaten him, because they have a community secret they're ashamed of. The sheriff throws him out of town, and someone runs him off the road."

"Why are you telling me this?"

"It'll come to you. Right now we better get the hell out to the airport before your airplane gets torched."

After a high-speed ride to the airport, they saw that the Cessna looked okay—no fire, no damage yet. Gano checked to make sure the motors hadn't been tampered with. "Good time to advance to the rear. Let's get airborne ASAP."

"Can't do that. I set up a meeting with Steve Drake here for tomorrow morning."

"Cool. That's one dude I'd like to meet." Gano smiled at the thought, but kept glancing around the tarmac watching for visitors.

"Sorry, I need him to do something he's not going to want to do. He's very prickly, so this is a solo."

Gano looked disappointed. "Yeah, well, what do you want from him?"

"Drake is taking *Challenger* out again. He thinks he knows where his super-HTV is located. If he's right, it will be a very big deal for him."

Gano got it instantly. "My God, you think he's after the same HTV that's under Chaos, the same one Barbas is working."

"I do, and I also think he'll use a two-man sub he has to explore it. I have to persuade him to take me along."

"Why is that a problem?"

"He'll want to keep the location of the HTV secret."

"Since you hate tight spaces, which would include a midget sub"—he tugged on his mustache—"this must be about Barbas."

"It's about Barbas and Renatus, and what we saw and didn't see on Chaos. It all tells me Barbas is about to do something that could have very bad consequences for a lot of people. He'll never let me back on Chaos, and I have no other source of information. The only thing I can do is go down deep, inspect his seabed operations, and figure it out from there."

Gano stopped looking around the landing strip and stared at Jack. "You are a genuine lunatic."

Jack chuckled. Gano had no idea how worried he was about Barbas. "I need the camera you used aboard Chaos. How many images did you take?"

"Maybe fifty, but I ain't Ansell Adams, you know."

"Doesn't matter. I want you to divide the images in the camera. Put ten shots that show various machines in one file and all the rest in another so I can access them separately."

"I'll get 'er done." He patted the wing of his plane. "But since we're staying in Astoria overnight, I'll have to stay aboard and keep an eye on my baby."

"We'll both stay, sleep in shifts."

"Won't be so bad. There's one thing I never leave home without and that's good rum. And I have a bag of Lance cheese crackers, a can of cashews, crunchy peanut butter—plenty of stuff for a well-rounded meal. Did I mention the rum?"

After Gano had pulled his emergency rations together, they sat side by side in the plane. "Time to invite Patsy Cline to join us for dinner." He turned up the volume of his iPod stereo. Then he poured Captain Morgan dark rum and offered a toast: "To life, love, and loot."

Before long, rum circulating through his brain, Gano began to muse about the nature of life. That soon brought him to recalling an adventure in a faraway place.

"And there I was . . ."

With Gano's tall tale and Patsy's love laments in the background, Jack's eyes kept scanning the tarmac for townies sneaking up in the dark. He'd hoped Gano's trip to Ironbound would help him see inside the Chaos Project, but it hadn't. Unless he could dig out more information, he was defeated. If Drake turned him down, he had nowhere else to go.

Chapter 16

July 22
8:00 a.m.
Astoria

JACK PAUSED ON the Astoria wharf about fifty yards away from where *Challenger* was tied up, gently rolling with the swells. *Challenger* looked like a powerful working boat, maybe eighty feet long at the water line, her gray steel hull built to survive pounding storms. The large number of antennae, radars, and several electronic devices he couldn't identify also gave her the air of a research vessel. A rugged Zodiac with a hefty silver Honda outboard engine was lashed to the cabin top. A compact helicopter landing platform was cantilevered about fifteen feet beyond the deck aft. *Challenger* was shipshape in every respect.

Steve Drake stood on deck in twill shorts, a navy blue shirt with a *Challenger* logo, and a broad-brimmed hat with a chin cord. Wiry, not more than five and a half feet tall, he pulled off his wraparound sunglasses and squinted in Jack's direction.

"Jack Strider requesting permission to come aboard." He liked using the Navy terminology.

"Strider. Hell, man, permission granted. Come on up here."

As they shook hands, Jack noticed Drake's knobby knuckles, then his bright blue eyes, and skin that looked like tanned leather. "I want to thank you in person for finding *Aleutian*. Now the families of the crewmembers know where the ship is and that a methane burp was likely what sank her. They can handle that a lot better than the other possibilities."

"It's a damn shame. I admire people who take on causes like Greenpeace. Glad I could help. Now, what can I do for you?"

"It's serious."

"I got that from your tone on the phone. Let's sit out here on deck. Hey, Jeff," he shouted to a man at work nearby, "bring us coffee, then give us some space."

With coffee in hand, and having talked about weather and sea conditions for a couple of minutes, Jack said, "When I asked you to search for *Aleutian* you said you couldn't because of other commitments. But as soon as you focused on the latitude and longitude where she was last reported, you changed your mind and accepted. Then you made a second search at no charge to Greenpeace, because you intended to combine it with a search for a giant HTV. I assume you were searching not far from *Aleutian*, but you didn't say exactly where."

"That's true."

"Did you find what you were looking for?"

Instead of answering, Drake picked up a short length of cord from the deck and swiftly tied the ends together. He untied it and did it again using a more intricate knot.

"It's no coincidence," Jack went on, "that you brought *Challenger* here to Astoria instead of going back to San Francisco. That tells me you think you're close to finding the HTV you've been looking for."

"What's that to you? Just being nosy?"

"It's much more than that. In a moment I'm going to make you a proposal, but first I have one question. What do you know about the mining platform owned by Petros Barbas?"

"I know I'll kick his butt if I ever see him."

Jack wondered whether the diminutive Drake knew how burly Barbas was.

"I have good reason," Drake continued. "*Challenger* was about ten miles from Barbas's platform when our sensors picked up signals that might indicate the presence of a big HTV. Right then, this big-ass helicopter showed up. Couldn't have come from anywhere but that platform. On its loudspeaker some donkey-brain ordered me to get my ass out of there. I had no intention of getting run off, so I flipped him the finger and kept steaming ahead. About a minute later, the SOB fired a machine gun salvo dead ahead of us and then another one so close it threw spray on our bow. I have enough weapons aboard *Challenger* to fend off a few pirates, but that was a fight I couldn't win. I did a slow U-turn."

"Good thing. That was a Kamov Ka-52 attack helicopter. It can sink a Navy destroyer."

Drake glared. "How do you know what it was?"

"I was on that platform about a week ago because Barbas was a client of mine. That's where I saw it."

Anger flared in Drake's eyes.

"Relax. I said he *was* a client. No longer. In fact, I'd call him an enemy. Now, will you get me a map of the northeast Pacific, say from the California-Oregon line up to Vancouver?" Drake handed it to him within minutes. "Do you mind if I make a few marks on it?" Drake nodded assent. "This first *X* is where you located *Aleutian* on the bottom. This second *X* is where my associate, Gano LeMoyne, was flying when he was bird-dogged by a helicopter on patrol. And this last *X* is the location of Barbas's platform. Connected, those three *X*s form a small triangle." He looked from the map to Drake. "I believe you have a mark on another map that shows where you think your super-HTV is located, and I'll bet you $10,000 it's in or near my triangle."

Jack continued before Drake could interrupt. "Now here's the piece of the puzzle I have that you don't. Barbas *told* me there's a hydrothermal vent beneath that platform. And since it generates the massive volume of minerals Barbas is extracting, it must be enormous."

Drake's attention was riveted on him.

"So I put together what I know about Barbas and the HTV he's exploiting for his mining operation, and your calculations about the location of the HTV you're hunting. My conclusion is that Barbas's HTV and the one you're looking for are the same. That's why I'm here."

This was the crucial moment. Knowing there was a giant HTV beneath Barbas's platform should definitely motivate Drake to get there fast. He'd expected Drake to be elated that his search was over; his prize was within reach. But something in Drake's face gave him a dark premonition it might not work out that way.

"You could have told me this on the phone." Drake's voice was controlled, no joy, no gratitude, nothing.

"I told you I had a proposal. I came here to make it in person." The sun had risen enough that Drake's eyes, under the broad brim, were shaded and unreadable. "Now that I've told you where that HTV is, you'll go there as soon as you can. I want to go there with you."

"Go with me? I don't know what you're talking about."

"The first time we talked on the phone, you mentioned the two-man submarine you own. That's probably it hanging under canvas from the starboard davits." He pointed. "It's the right dimensions: cylindrical, about eighteen feet long."

Drake's mouth tightened. He'd probably regretted telling Jack about the sub as soon as he hung up. Now he was wondering whether he could get away with denying there was a sub under the canvas.

Listen," Jack said, "you and I have a common interest. We both need to see what Barbas is doing down there on the seabed."

"What difference does that make to you?" Drake looked suspicious. "You said he's an *ex*-client."

"I'm sure he's doing more down there than mining minerals. I have to go down, inspect what he's doing, and figure it out. My research and my gut tell me it's very dangerous,"—he decided to stick the needle in—"including to the hydrothermal vent. That should concern you because you think it's so special."

"It *is* special. Emissions from an HTV are very faint, easy to miss or misinterpret, but my sensors picked up readings from quite a distance. That means those emissions are much stronger than any I've seen before. It's one big son of a bitch."

"Then you need to find out if this is the HTV you're looking for and, if it is, whether what Barbas is doing will damage it. We can both get what we want."

"Okay, I do have a sub, *Pegasus*, and I am going to make a reconnaissance dive. I'm not doing this for money like Barbas. All I care about is science. If my theories about this hydrothermal vent are correct, they will start a revolution in how we view this planet. There are only a handful of people who know as much about HTVs as I do." He tucked his chin and looked up at Jack from beneath thick eyebrows. "You're not one of them."

Jack saw an opening. "Is Dr. Renatus Roux one of those people?"

"Renatus! How did you hear about that weirdo?"

"I didn't just hear about him. I've talked with him. He's chief scientist on Barbas's platform."

He sensed a firestorm inside Drake's brain as he processed the meaning of Renatus working so close to the HTV. He looked as grim as Ahab hearing that some stranger was about to kill Moby Dick.

"Barbas and Renatus," Drake said in a pensive tone. "That has to be one of the oddest couples in history. Tell me this. Was all of the equipment you saw on that platform mining stuff, or was any of it different, out of place?"

He was fishing for something that might be related to the HTV. "Give me an example."

"Like a miniature submarine, for Christ's sake."

That gave him another edge. "Not sure, but my friend secretly took photos as we toured the platform. But they might not show you anything helpful, so forget it."

He knew Drake wouldn't forget it. Renatus was one of the "handful of people." He also had unlimited financing and was after that HTV. Drake would see him as a serious foe.

"Damn it. How soon can I see those photographs?"

He took Gano's camera out of his pocket. "Some of them are in this camera." He opened the smaller folder and showed the first image on the monitor. "Take a look at all ten."

Drake studied them closely.

"What do they tell you?"

"Most of the equipment could be used for mining or processing, but these last three are different. They are tools used in oil drilling. Doesn't make sense. Where are the rest of the photos?"

"There are about forty others. You can see them after we get back from your next dive." He hoped Drake wouldn't have his crew grab the camera and discover the rest.

"Are you saying you won't give me those photos unless I take you with me?"

Jack knew that was meant as a challenge so he didn't answer.

"All right, goddamn it, but I make every decision. No discussion. I have my agenda for this dive. You have a different one. If they conflict while we're down there or after we get back, I still get the photos. And you keep my interest in this site secret, agreed?"

"Of course." Drake might get what he wanted without Jack, but without Drake, Jack would never reach Barbas's operation on the seafloor.

"If I make the discoveries I hope to, I'll be a very big deal in the history books. That means everything to me, and I won't let Renatus beat me out of it. If Barbas is only mining minerals and doesn't bother the HTV itself, he's no threat to me. If he is harming the HTV, I'll make him regret it. Make sure you're not a problem either."

Jack decided to let the threat pass. "We'll just follow the yellow brick road and see where it takes us." He didn't need a prophet to tell him that there was a collision coming up.

"*Challenger* will get underway at noon. Be back here at 1100 hours."

He was going to be totally dependent on this guy while crammed into a tiny sub thousands of feet under the surface of the ocean. What's more, he could already feel the claustrophobia snake crawling in his veins.

Chapter 17

July 23
5:00 a.m.
Northeast Pacific Ocean

JACK FELT *PEGASUS* sway side to side beneath the A-frame as *Challenger*'s winch slowly lowered them to begin their journey to the seabed. First contact with the ocean was gentle. For a few seconds, waves churned around the portholes, and then they entered a new realm. His heart was beating fast. Could be excitement. Could be his old nemesis, claustrophobia.

He'd expected silence inside the sub. Instead, there was a background hum of motors and the whine of the blower forcing exhaled air through a filter that absorbed CO_2 and made the air safe to breathe again.

Drake spoke quietly in his raspy voice into a headset microphone. "*Challenger*, checklist complete. Everything A-1 here. Commencing dive now."

As they descended, Jack was surprised by the density of plankton and other minute marine life that surrounded the sub. He didn't recognize most of the fish species he saw, but they were abundant. When light from above grew fainter, he felt a chill and zipped up his fleece vest.

Pegasus's sleek titanium-carbon fiber hull and tight cockpit made him feel like he was sitting in a Formula 1 McLaren-Mercedes race car, except that *Pegasus* had an elongated quartz dome and four short wings instead of wheels. The design was so futuristic, *Pegasus* could have brought an extraterrestrial visitor to Earth.

He and Drake sat inside separate loops of the M-shaped instrument panel with a console between them. The space was barely adequate for Drake's small frame, so Jack's right shoulder was pressed hard against the fuselage, his knees halfway to his chest. The tight quarters gave him a feeling of profound unease, but he would put up with that and more. He had to. This dive was his only way of answering two questions. Was Barbas's mining creating an ecological disaster on the seabed? And what was he doing in addition to mining that justified the size and expense of the Chaos Project?

The only interior lights were red and extremely dim to maintain night vision. Drake seemed unaffected by the darkness as he played the backlit touchscreen in front of him like Ray Charles at his keyboard. He tapped in adjustments almost continuously. The screen was so complex that if something happened to Drake, say a heart attack, neither of them would ever reach the surface.

"Computer," Drake said, "what is our depth?"

"Two thousand one hundred and seven feet," came the answer from beneath the screen.

"Good voice recognition," Jack said, impressed.

"Saves time and prevents mistakes if things get hairy," Drake said. "Jack, look to your right."

Out of the darkness, a wall materialized yards away. Then he saw an unblinking eye gliding beside the sub. It took several seconds to realize it was imbedded in a massive, block-shaped head. The creature was more than three times the length of the sub.

"Sperm whale," Drake whispered. "Computer. Outside audio," and they heard bursts of staccato clicking sounds.

Is that a greeting or is it threatening trespassers?

"Don't worry about him, Jack. They've flipped many a whaleboat and sometimes ram small ships until they sink, but I think this one's just curious."

The whale symbolized the new world they'd entered, where he and Drake were no longer at the top of the food chain.

"But if something attacked *Pegasus*, do you have any weapons?"

"Two torpedo launch tubes, six torpedoes. They pack a hell of a punch, but I can't guide them after the launch. Two are ready to go, and the others reload automatically in seconds, so make damn sure you don't touch this firing mechanism." He pointed to two red-tipped buttons on a small pedestal on the console between them.

Jack made a mental note of that warning. The idea of having to use torpedoes to defend the sub reminded him of how alien this environment was. He had no experience to rely on. Even worse, he had no control of the sub. He was completely in Drake's hands.

"How long before we reach the seabed?"

"Depends on several variables. Because *Challenger* had to stay far away from Barbas's platform, it will take quite a while to cover the horizontal distance. If we find what I hope when we get there, I guarantee time will pass like super fast-forward. An hour on the bottom should be enough for this dive."

"I guess you had plenty of time to test *Pegasus*, I mean for safety."

"I keep her in a secluded waterfront hangar in the Strait of Juan de Fuca near Seattle, and every time I slip her out for sea trials, something new goes wrong. Real pain in the ass."

"But you fixed everything."

"No guarantees in this business. If anything goes wrong, no rescue team could reach us in time, so I wouldn't be here if I didn't think she was seaworthy. Mathematically, she's designed to withstand the pressure to at least forty thousand feet down. Today, we'll bottom out at around seventy-two hundred. Of course, even at that depth a microscopic failure in hull integrity would crush us in an instant." He offered what seemed to be a smile. "No suffering at all."

That was definitely not reassuring. He sensed there were more mechanical uncertainties than Drake was admitting.

When the sub's powerful searchlights were off, they were immersed in absolute blackness. Then suddenly they entered a haze of lights, bioluminescence from unseen creatures.

Long minutes later, Drake said, "This is where the treasure hunt begins. We're hovering sixty feet above the seabed, more or less under Barbas's platform. Put on the glasses I gave you. I'm going to turn on the globe lights and see what's out there. I assume Barbas's operations are monitored by external cameras, but they have very limited range down here. They'll be on the seafloor, so I'm staying above them and out of sight . . . I hope."

The exterior lights came on silently, flooding 360 degrees around them.

"I'll be damned!" Drake exclaimed. Both hands went to the touchscreen, maybe to retreat, but when he recognized what he saw, he paused.

The seabed in front of them was alive with *machines*. Some were only a couple of feet tall, several at least eight feet. They'd been operating in the pitch black and paid no attention to the light or to the sub. Their methodical movements explained everything.

"My God, they're all robots," Drake said.

"Those small tractor-like things have sensors that identify different types of metallic nodules," Jack replied. "The tall ones are pile drivers. The crawlers send them a signal to come over and smash up the seafloor. Then those backhoes drag the rocks to a suction tube—there's one over there—that leads to a grinder. It will break them up, separate out the worthless rock and wash it away. What's left will be suctioned to the surface."

Drake's head snapped in his direction. "How do you know all that? Have you been conning me?"

"I learned a lot when I was on Barbas's platform, including how this part of his system works."

The robots moved in programmed patterns that evolved and adapted as they progressed relentlessly into new areas of the seabed. He saw them as a cross between locusts and whirling dervishes, or maybe weird ballet dancers.

"Can you maneuver in that direction to follow the tubes?"

"Huh! I can make *Pegasus* dance the tango."

"There it is." The grinder plant emerged from the darkness, a steel box about thirty by fifty feet that resembled a storage container for a cargo ship. Tubes running along the seafloor entered its side, and another set of tubes left its front end and rose toward the surface. From its rear, a steady jet of water flushed crushed rock, sand, and mud back to the seabed. A plume of muck rose about twenty feet and then spread out, forming a canopy thicker than Los Angeles smog.

"It took world-class engineers to create all this," Drake said. "Every bit of this was put into place from the platform, and orders to the machines come from there. It's like a space station."

"Look at where the robots have already mined." Jack pointed to their left. "It looks like the Mojave Desert. And the grinder is leaving behind a huge ridge of tailings. No living organism could survive there." This was part of what he'd come to see, proof that Barbas's mining wasn't ecologically benign.

While they hovered, watching the tireless robots perform their tasks, Jack got an eerie feeling. "I wonder if Barbas knows we're here."

"No lights were triggered when *Pegasus* showed up, but he could have other kinds of sensors reporting our presence back to the surface. I'm more worried he might have some sort of weapons that attack trespassers."

That's great. And here we are crammed inside an eggshell.

"Steve, this mining operation is much more sophisticated than I expected, but I knew it was here. Let's move on and see if we can find something I hope *isn't* here."

"Which is what?"

"Evidence that Barbas is doing more down here than what we've seen."

"What kind of evidence?"

"Don't know."

"In other words, a wild goose chase when you don't know what a goose looks like," Drake scoffed. "Well, I *do* know what an HTV looks like, and finding mine is the only reason I'm here. One thing for sure, it took an HTV to produce the metals Barbas is mining. Judging from the number of robots, there must be megatons of the stuff. That means it's one hell of a big HTV."

Drake eased *Pegasus* slowly forward, pausing every fifteen seconds to turn on the lights and look around. By the fourth pause, each dark interval seemed like five minutes to Jack.

When the lights flooded the area around them, Drake said, "Something there." He put the sub in reverse briefly, then climbed about fifty feet. "Staying out of camera range."

Jack saw something he'd seen diagrammed in a research paper. It was what he'd feared he would find. "That has to be what I'm looking for."

Lying flat on the seafloor ahead of them was a grid like a great waffle made of poles connecting five boxes. He recognized it as a template lowered into position from the platform. Each box represented a separate location for drilling below the seabed. As the drills went deeper, they would diverge to serve sites far apart. On top of each box was a blowout preventer that, in theory, would enable a technician on the platform to cut off the upward flow if the system started to run wild. From the center of each preventer rose a flexible marine riser, a tube that held a drill bit, and the drill string that connected the template to Chaos. There were no robots here. This had nothing to do with mining minerals.

"You know what that is?" he asked Drake.

"It looks like the kind of oil drilling rig used by ExxonMobil and the others." Then he pointed to the right. "But I have no idea what that thing is."

"That thing" was a metal cylinder lying on its side. It was about twenty feet long, six feet in diameter. Cables ran from the cylinder to each of the marine risers. A larger cable rose up out of sight above the cylinder. Could be cables for transmitting electricity, but for what purpose?

"Can you tell from that equipment whether Barbas is after oil?" Jack asked.

"No oil drilling rig I've heard of has anything like that cylinder and all those cables. Take a last look. I've wasted too much time here already. There's a monster HTV around here. I can smell it."

While Drake studied the readings that he hoped would lead him to the HTV, Jack sat back, overwhelmed. His belief that Barbas had a project more important than mining had been based on a little reasoning and a lot of speculation. Seeing the reality changed everything. It was the proof he'd come after. Now he knew for sure that Barbas was seeking something that justified the mammoth expenditures he'd made. Something worth keeping top secret and protecting with attack helicopters. He'd find out what that was. And if it had to be stopped? That was a mountain so high he'd take it a step at a time.

A soft *bump* on the hull behind his right shoulder interrupted his thoughts, then a *bump* on the dome above. He looked up. Some kind of creature that resembled a three-foot long lobster with a fat belly seemed to be sitting on the dome. "What's that?"

Drake looked up and immediately said, "Uh oh." He pointed out two more of the creatures moving in their direction. Their most prominent features were eyes whose large lenses had hundreds of facets. They had overlapping scales, seven pairs of legs, and four sets of jaws. Their quivering antennae were stretching out to experience *Pegasus*.

"Those are giant isopods," Drake said grimly.

"As giants go, they're not much."

"It's one of the most dangerous life forms down here. They're carnivores that gorge until they can't move."

"They don't look big enough to make a scratch on *Pegasus*."

Drake shot him a pained look. "Forget about scratches. They're like cock-roaches. When you see one isopod, there are hundreds or thousands not far away." Drake swung the searchlights in all directions. They were there, converging on what they thought was their next big feast. "Those two have attached themselves to our hull with an underwater adhesive stronger than anything we have on land. If enough of them get to us, their weight will keep *Pegasus* from rising to the surface . . . *ever*."

"What can we do?"

"I don't know how fast they can move, but I'll try to outrun them."

As Drake got *Pegasus* moving, Jack felt two more *bumps*, one directly over his head. The creature looked like it was sitting in a pool of mucus. He realized he was gripping the console with both hands, senses vibrating in anticipation of feeling more bumps. As the entire swarm of isopods turned to face *Pegasus*, Drake steered away from them, but they sped up and moved in fast.

Chapter 18

July 23
3:00 p.m.
Northeast Pacific Ocean

BUMB, BUMP. MORE isopods struck the dome—*bump*—but *Pegasus* was moving too fast for them to attach themselves to the hull. Jack saw dozens fall back. In less than a minute, they, except for the ones still locked on to the hull, had disappeared behind the sub.

"Close call," he said. He tried to sound casual, but he felt even more compressed by the cramped space. They'd come damned close to being pinned to the seabed, and he'd been powerless to prevent it. Having no control was stressing him out.

Drake made more adjustments with his fingertips. "When I got serious about discovering HTVs, that meant I'd have to go to them, whether that was three thousand feet or twenty-three thousand feet. If something bad happens, I'll die. So a close call counts for nothing."

Fine for Drake, but the isopod attack still seemed like a damned close call.

Drake went on. "The sunken ships and the gold trinkets I've located don't mean shit in the long run. My real contribution will be based on what I learn from exploring hydrothermal vents. That's why I'll take big risks and run over anyone in my way."

"Does that include Barbas?" He knew it did and said it to provoke Drake.

"Damn straight. To me, this HTV is a shrine. It generates life forms that I think will transform the world. If Barbas's robot wrecking balls damage this HTV, I'll stop him or die trying."

"What about Renatus?"

"He worries me for a different reason. He must have found this HTV for Barbas. My interest is in the HTV for itself. His interest in it may be only as it relates to the mining operation. If it's more than that, we're going to lock horns. I know he's aboard the platform and, because they spotted *Challenger*, he knows I'm in the vicinity, but he doesn't know why—yet. I'm ready to get it on."

Drake sounded combative but, despite his big talk, he had no chance against the Barbas-Renatus juggernaut. Besides, Drake was worried about small potatoes compared to the danger that drill rig, or whatever it was, could mean. And Jack had no more chance than Drake unless he could figure out what was going on.

That meant he and Gano had to get onto Ironbound Island and see what they could uncover. Barbas had a powerful reason for choosing such a remote place and protecting it with concertina wire. He needed to know what that reason was.

Suddenly the cockpit was filled with repeated *beeps.* Jack saw bars spiking on one of the displays. "What the hell is it this time?"

"My 'sniffer' is going crazy. I set it to tell me when there's a high level of methane in the seawater, because that's one sign there might be an HTV nearby." He leaned forward to examine a different display. "The seawater temperature right here is definitely warmer than normal."

"How much?"

"Three degrees Fahrenheit. Not much, but it's significant. Fluids pour out of the HTV at nearly seven hundred degrees and diffuse into seawater that's just above freezing. Readings I've taken before near the mouths of small vents have been less than one half a degree warmer than normal seawater at the same depth." Drake craned his head to peer through the dome. "I'm going to start a search pattern and watch for an increase in temperature."

Jack felt something—the hull shuddering. It wasn't more *bumps.* It felt like *Pegasus* was being blasted with a pressure washer. He strained to see beyond the lights into the darkness. The strength of the vibrations increased.

Drake looked up from his instruments. "Earthquake."

"Good God. Where?"

"Could be right under us."

We have seventy-two hundred feet of water overhead and an earthquake under our butts.

He'd spent most of his life around San Francisco, so he knew the primal fear that welled up each time the earth shook, even after years have passed since the last time. Those had only lasted seconds, and he knew how to try to protect himself. This felt very different, partly because *Pegasus* seemed as fragile as a soap bubble.

Suddenly, the sub was knocked on its side, and he was staring down at the gravelly seabed. *Pegasus* hung for seconds at its tipping point but couldn't hold and rolled farther, both wings on her starboard side stabbing into the seafloor.

"I'll be damned," Drake said almost inaudibly. "If those wings get stuck, *Pegasus* can't free herself." He leaned toward the screen. "Computer. Reverse engine." The sub did not move.

There was a slight rise in the level of mechanical noise in the cockpit, but it didn't drown out the sound Jack dreaded. *Bump.* Then another, two more. Within a few seconds, most of the surface of the dome became opaque. Looking up, countless wide-open jaws blocked his view. The isopod swarm had caught up with them. This time, *Pegasus* was helpless.

Drake's lips were tight as he poked the control panel. "Our lights don't scare those bastards a bit. The only chance we have is in the ultra-low frequency vibrations I'm pumping out. If that doesn't drive them away, we're finished."

These isopods weren't computer-generated giant octopuses out of Hollywood. They were a pack of scavengers whose weight pinned *Pegasus* to the bottom. He watched the creatures completely cover the dome. Countless jaws clattered against the quartz, trying to break through to gnaw on the succulent soft parts of their quarry inside. Sweat broke out. He'd never before been the prey.

In the dim cockpit, Drake's blue eyes glowed intensely against his tan skin. Jack couldn't tell if he was still trying to think of some way to escape or if he'd given up. Then Drake turned and slowly shook his head.

Until that moment, Jack hadn't believed it would end here. His mind filled with Debra, her image, her voice, her passion. She filled him with a rush of energy. He wouldn't let their relationship end.

He beat on the dome with both fists. The scraping and groping of the isopods intensified as though he'd angered them. The ultra-low frequency blasts weren't working, but . . . what if?

"Steve, turn those vibrations off, then on, then off. Alternate. Make the intervals and volume erratic."

"I don't see why"—but he did it.

Nothing happened. He stopped.

"Unless you have something else, keep doing it."

Plop. A sound so indistinct he wasn't sure he'd heard anything. *Plop.* There it was again, but nothing changed overhead on the dome. Then the sounds came more often as isopods dissolved the adhesive binding them to *Pegasus* and drifted away.

Were they fleeing? Had the erratic vibrations confused them? Had they collectively decided they'd wasted enough time? He'd never know.

"Unbelievable," Drake said calmly. "Smart call."

Jack sucked in deep breaths of the oxygen-enriched air. He felt *Pegasus*, with the great weight off her back, wobble and lift slightly.

"Computer, turn port," Drake ordered. After five seconds, "Computer, turn starboard." Another five seconds. "Computer, turn port." Drake kept reversing the rudders until they heard the unmistakable scraping of the hull along the bottom. He coached *Pegasus* into stability and then into forward motion. Visibility returned. He leveled her out fifty feet above the floor.

"I guess that wasn't a close call either," Jack said.

"Couldn't be closer, that one. Between here and the west coast, there's a lot of seismic activity, swarms of earthquakes, even some minor tectonic plate movements. The small quake we just felt shook part of the seabed loose and started a landslide. That's called a 'slump.' It displaced the wall of water that knocked us over. But there's a bright side. It must have played hell with Barbas's robot Tinkertoys."

Damn little comfort.

He wasn't going to let Drake know about his deep-rooted fear of getting trapped underwater. He'd been ten years old when his sea kayak was flipped by a speeding power boat. His paddle had been torn away, so he couldn't execute an Eskimo Roll to right the boat. Then the spray skirt snagged, trapping him in the cockpit. About to suck in seawater, he finally kicked his way out and thrust to the surface, gagging.

To try to erase the fear, he'd made water a second home by swimming, scuba diving, rowing for the Stanford crew, and racing his sailboat. He'd suppressed the fear but couldn't get rid of it. Years later he'd figured out why. After he'd gotten home from being trapped in his kayak, his father had ridiculed him for having been frightened. That nailed the fear deep in his emotions.

"Let's hope there aren't any aftershocks," Drake said, "and I can find what I'm after." He looked to his left. "Oops, I spoke too soon. Look over there. That's a methane eruption coming from beneath the seabed. Must have been set off by that quake." At the outer edge of their lights, a column of water was violently disturbed.

"Is that what's called a 'methane burp'?"

"Yep. If more methane cuts loose, the force will probably toss us up for a few hundred feet and . . . hell, I don't know what will happen. I hope I haven't used up all my luck."

As quickly as champagne that's blown its cork, it quieted down.

"My luck held," Drake said. "Time to get back to business. I'm starting the search pattern."

Jack tried to shift his shoulders and legs, but there was less room than in a seat in economy class. More than ever he felt the unseen squeeze of thousands of pounds pressing on every square inch of the dome. His brainstem was screaming to head up, but Drake would never turn back now.

Drake cut the lights and turned on a different array. "Instead of a globe of light, I've focused all lights in a wedge ahead of our port bow toward where the water temperature is warmest. I'll look at the lighted sector. You watch the right side, just in case."

Pegasus cruised forward slowly, minute after minute. With nothing to do but stare into pitch blackness, Jack felt like a dope.

"It can't be," Drake breathed. He directed one powerful light back and forth in an arc. "This isn't possible."

Through the dome on Drake's side, Jack saw they were passing what looked like a steep wall rising beyond the range of the lights.

Drake feverishly made data entries on the touchscreen as *Pegasus* slid forward. When the wall finally fell behind them into the darkness, Drake turned *Pegasus* to starboard and into a wide circle that brought him back alongside the wall.

"Now we'll see," Drake said, putting *Pegasus* into an ascending course for another pass.

At three hundred, six hundred, then nine hundred feet above the seabed, the stony slope continued upward, narrowing slowly. The temperature inside the little capsule kept rising.

"Do you have any idea what you're seeing?" Drake's hoarse voice was near a shout. "The tallest HTV chimney ever discovered, named Godzilla, is 150 feet tall. This one is almost exactly a thousand feet. This is it, *my* hydrothermal vent." Years had dropped from Drake's leathery features. He looked gleeful. "This baby has been pumping for millennia."

Drake slowly circled the HTV, regularly entering coordinates and dimensions into the digital log.

During the fourth trip around the HTV, Jack thought of Devil's Tower, the core of a volcano exposed by erosion and made famous in *Close Encounters of the Third Kind.* That tower was the site of vision quests for the Kiowa. Maybe Drake felt that way about this one.

"Are you going to take Pegasus across the top of it?"

"Hell, no. I haven't survived this long by being stupid. We've been circling the cone, but the vent at the top is where the action is. Picture a perpetual eruption blasting a screaming hot concoction into icy seawater. In that instant, the precious metals and valuable minerals precipitate out, spread like a fan, and settle on the seabed. That's what Barbas is mining. Before I take *Pegasus* close to that, I have to measure the velocity and density and temperature of what's shooting up from the guts of the Earth. As soon as I know what's a relatively safe distance, I'll start takings samples for my own research."

Jack nodded and recalled fiery craters of active land-based volcanoes he'd looked down into from the rim or a plane. He guessed Drake would be doing his research much closer and wasn't tempted to join him.

He thought he had the big picture now, but had to make sure. "So what's going on inside this HTV," he said, "has nothing to do with the forces that cause methane burps, right?"

"Of course not." Drake shook his head in disgust. "One last swing around the base," Drake said, "and I'm done."

"Did you get all you need?"

Drake guffawed. "I'll be back here many, many times."

Soon after Drake had guided *Pegasus* down to just above the seafloor, Jack thought he saw a shadowy form close to the sub on his side.

"Steve, you almost hit something, but it was too dark over here to see what. It's behind us now. Put *Pegasus* in reverse and give me more light."

"I told you this was my trip, my decisions. No more detours after this." He shifted into reverse.

Seconds later, Jack saw a ghost from the Iraq War. "It looks like an M1 Abrams on steroids, twice the size of a regulation tank. It's on rolling tracks and has a long snout like a 120mm cannon barrel. There's no way that thing is used for mining metals."

Drake used thrusters to maneuver *Pegasus* so he could see it too. "Damn!" he said. "It does look like a tank, but that makes no sense."

"Shoot some pictures."

"Yeah and then we're out of here." He angled Pegasus to point at the tank-thing and touched the screen in front of him. There was a soft whirring sound. He touched the screen again, and then several more times. "I'll be damned."

"What's wrong? Isn't the camera working?"

"Working fine, but we're not getting any images. Something must be—I know what the problem is. The glue from those isopods has coated the lens. The camera can't see anything. You'll have to remember what you saw. I still say—" He was interrupted by an urgent series of *pings*. He jerked his head around and scanned his gauges. The sound changed to a low *whoop—whoop—whoop*. "I have to start for the surface. You'll hear scraping sounds when I release the baskets."

"Baskets?"

"*Pegasus* carries ballast that looks like lead washers in four wire mesh baskets. Ballast makes it easier to descend. Releasing it saves a lot of energy going back up."

As the baskets fell free, *Pegasus* leapt upward.

"Feels good. I guess we're home free."

"We're all right as long as neither of the starboard wings that got stuck in the gravel break away and rip the fuselage. As we get closer to the surface, we have to watch out for lines and nets dumped by fishing fleets, and floating islands of plastic and other crap."

Drake was exhilarated with his discovery, chattering away about trivia. Twice, Jack tried to break in and start a conversation about the sort-of drill rig, but Drake had no interest in anything other than the HTV. As they continued the long trip back to the surface, Jack blocked out Drake's rambling. His mind was racing, trying to set priorities, make decisions.

Barbas had already declared war on Strider & Vanderberg and would order Stan Simms to escalate his attacks. As a result of this dive, Drake now considered Barbas and Renatus to be his enemies. And he'd gone from being suspicious to being committed to going after Barbas. Waiting was not an option. The battle was on.

He turned to Drake. "Could Barbas be doing anything that caused the methane burp we think sank *Aleutian*? And the methane burp we just saw?"

"Don't see how. Those burps, and the shock wave that hit us, are probably all related to methane hydrate under the seafloor that contains extremely compressed methane gas. That gas escapes when pressure is reduced and the methane hydrate destabilizes. Imagine an earthquake under the seabed that lifts millions of tons of rock off a huge deposit of methane hydrate. The pressure drop would destabilize it. Another way to do that is to heat the stuff and—b*ang*!—it releases the compressed gas. But that would be way too dangerous for Barbas or anyone else to do on purpose. In fact, I don't think anyone even knows how. I'm afraid you can't pin those things on Barbas."

Drake was an expert, so he was probably right. Now that he'd made contact with *his* HTV that's all he would care about. He didn't need Jack and would dump him as soon as they got back to the surface. But Jack needed Drake and his resources badly. That meant he had to goad Drake into forming an alliance.

"I see what you mean," he said. "What's your opinion of that tank-like thing we saw?"

"Damned mystery."

"Maybe not. It has no hatches and no crew, so it must be remotely controlled from the platform. Here's the most important part. To me, what looks like the barrel of a cannon is actually a drill."

Drake looked pensive. "A horizontal drill. Yeah, that's possible."

"And since it's positioned right next to the HTV, it's logical that it's there to drill into it. What would happen if it did?" He waited for the concept to hit Drake's hot button.

"They'd be out of their minds to do something that might release the forces inside. They could even cause a blowout vent in the side that could collapse the whole thing." His face was stern. "Barbas's platform is in international waters, so I'll report him to the International Seabed Authority. They'll stop him."

"The ISA can't touch Barbas."

"Bullshit. Just wait until—" He stopped and rubbed the stubble on his cheek. "I get it. It's because the U.S. has refused to ratify the Law of the Sea treaty."

"Steve, I showed you photographs of equipment on the platform that have nothing to do with mining. You've just seen a big drill butted up against the side of the HTV. You know that Renatus is an expert on HTVs, and Barbas will stop at nothing to get to the gold. Add it up before it's too late. You say you want to protect that HTV, but you're outmanned and outgunned. So am I. The only chance we have is to fight them together."

After a long silence, Drake said, "Just sitting in that seat is going to put your name in the history books, because I've just discovered a geological Rosetta Stone. Before I let Barbas and Renatus turn it into a pile of gravel, I'll shoot them down like rabid dogs—with or without you."

Chapter 19

July 23
6:00 p.m.
Northeast Pacific Ocean

PEGASUS BROKE THE surface as gracefully as a seal, and the cockpit flooded with natural light. For the first time in hours, Jack relaxed a little. That lasted for about three heartbeats.

The sea was angry. Eight-foot waves jerked *Pegasus* up and down like she was riding a barroom bull. Shouting a raucous string of seafarer's curses, Drake tried to wrestle her into the sling hanging from the A-frame on *Challenger*'s deck. Every time he got close, the sea threatened to smash her into *Challenger*'s steel hull.

During each emergency at the seabed, Drake had been calm, even fatalistic. Here on the surface, he was in a rage. Finally, by force of will, Drake drove the sub roughly into position, and two crewmen in a Zodiac muscled the sling into the right spot. As *Pegasus* came out of the water and her full weight shifted to the sling, she slipped forward, about to take a twenty-foot nosedive into the ocean. Jack's stomach lurched. The lift stopped, leaving the sub dangling just above the waves.

Jack noticed one crewmember pointing skyward. The outside receivers were on, so he heard the man shouting to his mates. Two more crewmen arrived at the ship's railing, carrying handguns. A shadow swept across the surface of the sea ahead of the ship, immediately replaced by a black shape swooping like a hawk. Jack recognized Barbas's Kamov Ka-52 helicopter, so close that its mission had to be more than surveillance.

The sub's cockpit filled with the *whoomp—whoomp—whoomp* of the rotors and then the hammering racket of two machine guns firing long bursts. Hanging in midair, the sub was nakedly vulnerable. If the helo had come to punish rather than intimidate, he and Drake were about to be shredded.

In seconds, the helo was on the other side of the ship, out of his sight. The sounds grew fainter and then vanished.

The crew scrambled into action, getting more lines attached to *Pegasus*. Finally, they hauled the sub up in its tilted position, leveled it, and secured it to the davits.

When they opened the hatch, Jack was edgy, impatient to get out, but the crew helped Drake down first. Drake immediately checked *Pegasus's* two starboard wings that had been driven into the gravel. "Lou, I see small cracks. Get your instruments on both of these. They've taken much more torque than they were designed to withstand. Must have been close to snapping off. I want experts waiting on the wharf back in Astoria to make repairs. Get on the horn." He looked into the sub's cockpit. "Someone get Jack out of there."

As soon as he had both feet on deck, Alex handed him a cold beer. The expression "rode hard and put up wet" was exactly how he felt.

He joined several crew members on the aft deck near the helicopter pad. They were wound up, talking excitedly, shocked by the warplane that had materialized like something out of *Apocalypse Now.*

Drake walked up. "Damn, we're lucky. Don't see how they missed us at that range."

"Those dumb bastards couldn't hit the Dodger's scoreboard," Jeff scoffed, waving a revolver. "If I'd been up in that whirlybird, I could have shot off the top of that antenna over there with my ol' squirrel rifle."

Yeah, right, like you guys weren't scared shitless. Jack knew how they'd missed. Gano had taught him the answer. If men who know how to use weapons miss at close range, it's because they intend to miss. Barbas had sent his bullies to deliver a final warning to *Challenger* to get out. If they came back, they'd shoot to kill.

Chapter 20

July 24
8:00 a.m.
Astoria/San Francisco

WHILE *CHALLENGER* plowed eastward through the Pacific, Drake and his tech crew stayed busy in the main cabin analyzing the data he'd collected around the hydrothermal vent. Their excitement filled the room like static electricity. Jack sat with them as they laid out a strategy for the next dive. He didn't say so, but, if his alliance with Drake held, he intended to be on that dive too. Drake had made it clear that he'd avoid Barbas if he could, but confront him if he had to.

Eager to get to work, he disembarked as soon as *Challenger* tied up at the Astoria wharf and caught a ride to the airport.

Gano sent him a greeting by waggling the wings of his Cessna Skylane just before he began final approach to the Astoria—or as Gano had begun to call it, "Hysteria"—airport.

"Greetings, Poseidon, God of the Sea," Gano said as Jack climbed into the idling aircraft. "You'll find this baby more to your liking than being cooped up in a tin can."

Before taking off, they went through their usual greeting ritual, like orangutans playfully cuffing each other. Then Gano said, "Okay, I bet you've made up some damn good lies about summer camp in the big pond. Let's hear what you got."

They'd be in the air for three hours or more, so he gave Gano a blow-by-blow of *Pegasus*'s journey.

Gano was fascinated by the sub, Barbas's high-tech mining operation, the mysterious oil drilling rig that really wasn't one, and what they'd seen of the HTV. "But what you said about that thing that looked like a giant tank just rang a bell. When I told you what I saw when I flew over Ironbound, I forgot to mention something. Didn't seem important then. Now I think it is."

"Tell me."

"Not far from the lodge there's what looks like a big shed. Coming out of the shed, two narrow-gauge metal tracks run across a clearing and stop on the far side. A small version of what you just described was parked at the end of the tracks."

"Maybe you saw a toy train."

"No. It was a miniature tank, but why would Barbas take that thing out to a remote island?"

"I don't think he did. Workmen had to come to the island to build those three metal buildings, install the big generators, and more we don't know about. They could have built it as a prototype of what they needed seventy-two hundred feet underwater. I don't know what that is yet, but it has nothing to do with mining gold. The important thing is that it ties Ironbound to Chaos. I have to get to that island as soon as I can."

Gano said with a huge smile, "You're right, and I must admit that your adventure trumps anything I've done."

Jack let the conversation lapse so he could think.

Every hour he spent on Barbas was an hour not spent on the Armstrong lawsuit. And the problem was more than time pressure. He was facing more opposition than he'd expected from businessmen, lawyers, politicians, the massive military establishment, even from ordinary citizens who felt that requiring the military to obey laws that govern everyone else would be outrageous. That disapproval could damage his firm and the reputation he'd worked hard to rebuild. But the principles were worth fighting for.

Too many people at Armstrong—civilian and military personnel, family members, and neighbors—had suffered or died from poisonous emissions. That was plenty of motivation, but there was more behind the intensity he felt. Winning for the plaintiffs would also be a big step toward paying a debt owed by his father. *The bastard.*

If he took any more time away from the Armstrong case, he couldn't possibly be ready when the trial began in twelve days. The only way out was to get a continuance. The judge should grant it automatically.

It came down to setting priorities. To do that, he had to figure out what Barbas was doing. If the potential damage was serious and immediate, stopping him had to be number one. If the risks were tolerable or distant, he could give the Armstrong case top priority. He'd gotten himself into a serious bind. Whichever choice he made, something important wasn't going to get done.

He looked at Gano. "I have a different kind of adventure coming up, one that may be even more dangerous than the sub."

"You're going to jump out without a parachute?"

"I may wish I had. I have to tell Debra about all of this." He picked up his cell phone.

Gano grinned. "I see what you mean. So let me tell her the part about flying over Ironbound."

"If we were in the same room, had all night, and a bottle of rum, you'd do a great job. Since none of those is the case, I'll handle it."

Debra's tone was noncommittal. When the moment seemed right, he jumped into it. "I didn't tell you much about what I intended to do in the last day or two, so I'm calling to catch you up."

"Actually, you told me nothing at all, and it's been three days."

"I'm sorry. I've been out of circulation. It started with Gano tracking Barbas to see what he did when he came ashore."

That part of the tale went well, except that when he finished she said, "So after all that, you don't know any more about what Barbas does or even if that's really his island."

"Technically, that's true, but after that we went to a place called the Bridgewater Tavern and we did get some useful information." He told her about Molly McCoy, and the tight security Barbas imposed on the platform, on "the mill", and on the mouths of his workers.

Gano started making motions like a fighter throwing punches. He wanted Jack to tell her about that part. Instead, Jack said, "Since we wound up spending the night in Astoria, I talked with Steve Drake the next morning. He agreed to take me with him to inspect Barbas's mining site."

"Why? What could you tell from Challenger about anything seventy-two hundred feet underwater?" Now she sounded exasperated.

"Drake had a submarine, a very small one, so we used that." He heard her quick intake of breath, but she didn't interrupt. He rushed through a description of the scale and complexity of the mining operation and the damage it was doing to the seabed. Then he dropped out of chronological order and told her about finding the incredible hydrothermal vent and Drake's excitement about that. He used a brief description of the mystifying tank-like machine as background to say how hostile Drake was now toward Barbas and Renatus.

He left out mention of the shock wave and the swarm of isopods, partly because she'd flare up at his recklessness, partly because his emotions about those events were still so raw.

When he paused, she said, "You've been a very busy boy."

You have no idea. "Here's the problem: Barbas is doing a lot more than tearing up the seabed." He told her about the equipment that looked like an oil drilling rig but wasn't. "No oil has ever been found in that region, and that's not what Barbas is after."

Her long silence made him glad he was delivering all this from the plane.

"That's perplexing, but you still don't know what he is doing or if there's anything illegal about it. Anyway, you've given me a lot to think about, and I'm not talking just about Petros Barbas. I also mean about the future of our relationship, which I'd rather discuss in person."

Future of our relationship? Those words would sound an alarm in any male—and they did. "We'll do that, but I want you to know right now that—"

"Remember that I told two of our associate lawyers to research whether there is enough methane in the area where *Aleutian* went down to make the 'methane burp' explanation plausible. They're set to report to us tomorrow at eight."

HE, DEBRA, AND two lawyers in their late twenties sat in canvas chairs on the balcony outside Jack's office overlooking San Francisco Bay. Pale sunshine was barely chasing away the morning chill. Shouts from longshoremen rang out on nearby cargo wharves.

Sam Cooper, the older of the two associates, was from Miami. His father had been the first African-American to graduate from the University of Miami School of Law and had gone on to become a wealthy tax attorney. Sam had been president of the Yale Law Journal before joining the firm two years earlier. His face showed he was eager to share what he'd learned. As soon as Jack nodded at him, he started talking at a fast clip.

"Seabed conditions off the Oregon-Washington-British Columbia coasts, including where *Aleutian* was, have been studied by marine geologists and by the U.S. Navy. Based on data they collected about the underwater mountain ridges and tectonic plates grinding into one another, they concluded that there are likely to be massive quantities of methane hydrate present out there in the upper levels of the Earth's crust. Bottom line, there's plenty of methane hydrate in the region to have produced a methane burp fatal to *Aleutian*."

With that issue finally closed, Jack was about to thank them and get back to work. Instead, he asked an open-ended question that often paid off in unexpected ways: "Do you have anything else to tell us?"

Sam looked at Tammy Glenn, who had only recently moved from Seattle to join the firm.

"Yes, sir," she said. "Once we knew there was lots of methane hydrate up there, I decided to learn more about it."

"I only took one chemistry class," Debra said, "so please spell out what it is."

Tammy beamed, pleased to show off in front of her bosses. "Picture a tiny cage made of ice. That's called a 'clathrate.' Molecules of greatly compressed methane gas are trapped inside that cage. When they bring it from under the seabed up to the surface, it's like an intensely cold, hard-packed snowball. If they touch it with a flame, it burns, producing carbon dioxide and water. As soon as it escapes from the immense pressure in the deep ocean, one cubic meter of methane gas expands into 164 cubic meters." She looked at each of them as if making sure they appreciated what a big deal that was.

'Is methane hydrate only found in the seabed?" Debra asked.

"Some is also found in permafrost, mostly in the Arctic, but the vast majority is beneath the ocean floor in various concentrations in layers several hundred feet thick. Most people have never heard of methane hydrate, but the so-called 'natural gas' that's piped into homes for domestic heating and cooking is about ninety percent methane. Right now, most of that methane comes from deposits known as natural gas fields on land. A small amount comes from the fermentation of organic matter like manure, wastewater sludge, and municipal solid waste in landfills. As farmers know, cattle, chickens, and pigs also generate a lot of methane gas. Methane isn't toxic but it blows up once in a while. Also, in an enclosed space, it can displace oxygen and asphyxiate a human. Anyway, now that you have an idea what it is, I'll tell you the fascinating part."

She checked her notes and continued. 'I found an article in a scientific journal that said, I quote, 'natural gas locked up in methane hydrate could be the world's next great energy source if anyone can figure out how to extract it safely.'"

As soon as he was satisfied that their research made the methane burp explanation credible, Jack had been only half-listening, thinking more about what he'd say to Hank. What Tammy had just said yanked him back into the present.

Tammy continued. "Late last night, I turned up an article in the *Straits Times* about a big trader on the Singapore Stock Exchange who called methane hydrate 'a windfall profit bonanza without equal in the history of human civilization.' He said there's far more methane in methane hydrate than in natural gas fields like the ones where all that fracking is going on. I know traders love to hype stocks they want to push, but this guy doesn't have a product to sell. Besides, he's not the only one. The Department of Energy, DOE, estimates there are ten *billion billion* cubic meters of gas in hydrates. Evidently the amount of energy locked up in methane hydrate is mind-blowing."

"'Mind-blowing' meaning . . ."

"Enough to satisfy worldwide demand for four thousand *years*. The U.S. Geological Survey, USGS, puts the number of years even higher. If that's confirmed by more tests, exploiting the seabed for hydrates could dwarf the energy we get from drilling for oil. The DOE Strategic Center has predicted that . . . just a minute while I find the quote. . . ." She referred to her notes. "'There is more energy potential locked up in methane hydrate formations than in all other fossil energy resources combined.' If it can be extracted safely, that would mean no more worrying about running out of oil. It would mean total energy security for the U.S."

Her words launched a rocket in Jack's brain. Methane hydrate could be a bigger payoff than winning a galactic lottery. The next step took only a nanosecond. That's why Barbas was spending all that money. That's why he was fixated on getting a monopoly. And that's why he had a stable of attack helicopters.

It all fit together. What Barbas had said, what he'd concealed, and the size of the platform. The mysterious equipment he and Drake had seen on the bottom. *Aleutian*. Deepwater Horizon. All of it was about methane hydrate.

"Mr. Strider?" Tammy said, sounding dismayed that she'd lost his attention.

"Sorry. Go on."

"Today, almost twenty-five percent of all the energy we use in the U.S. is natural gas. In terms of global warming, it's the least carbon-intensive of the fossil fuels. Some industries, especially public utilities and transportation, are already converting to use it."

"But there are problems with natural gas," Sam put in.

"Big ones," Tammy said. "Multinational producers drilling on land rely more and more on fracking. Their TV ads insist they're doing no harm, but a lot of scientific research shows the opposite. For example, fracking consumes vast amounts of water, including in areas where water is scarce. They add toxic chemicals to the water and inject the solution at very high pressure into crevices deep underground to break up rocks to release oil and methane gas. As a result, fracking often causes small earthquakes and can trigger large ones. And fracking produces huge quantities of toxic, even radioactive, wastewater that has, in some documented cases, contaminated drinking water and groundwater."

She pulled a page from her notes. "If the majority of scientific evidence is correct, the costs of damage done could be huge. Obviously, the companies that profit from fracking should pay those costs. Instead, the industry is lobbying to be held harmless on grounds that the U.S. needs the energy. That amounts to a huge subsidy for highly profitable multinationals. Also, fracking on land won't produce enough natural gas to solve global energy problems, but it *does* cut investment in alternative, renewable energy."

"Which would be where methane hydrate from beneath the oceans comes in," Debra said. "Would they drill for it the same way they drill for oil?"

"No. That won't work, but the alternatives they've come up with haven't been tested much. Exploring for offshore deposits hasn't gone far either. They don't even have a reliable theory about where to search, and marine tests are very expensive."

"But given the potential, aren't a lot of people working on this already?" Debra asked.

"Some, but they're in very early stages. Japan, China, India, and South Korea are ahead of the U.S. in government-supported R&D. So far, Japan is the leader in offshore testing. Chinese scientists have discovered a reserve in the frozen tundra on the Tibetan Plateau they think could last them for ninety years."

"President Clinton," Sam said, "signed the Methane Hydrate Research & Development Act in 2000. It directed Energy, Defense, Interior, and Commerce to research use of methane hydrate. For some reason, Congress authorized expenditure of less than fifty million dollars spread over five years. Given the stakes, that was peanuts. Think how much conflict and pollution might have been avoided if that had been a full-out effort."

"Sir." Mei stood in the door to the balcony. "Your 8:45 appointment is here. Ms. Vanderberg, your 8:30 has been waiting."

"I'll be right there, Mei. Sam, Tammy, good work."

After the other three left the balcony, Jack stayed behind to reflect. Sam and Tammy had erased any doubt about what sank *Aleutian*. That had been important, but was dwarfed by the ah-ha moment their research into methane hydrate had generated. That information had brought together all the scraps he'd picked up over the past three weeks about the Chaos Project.

On the face of it, a section of the northeast Pacific might be an immensely valuable source of cleaner, less-expensive energy. And Petros Barbas was going to exploit it however he wanted. He remembered that Tammy had referred to the difficulties of getting methane to the surface safely. If Barbas had solved the problem no one else had, it could be a boon to mankind. He'd be a hero. But Barbas wasn't acting like a hero. Why the secrecy, the denials, the guns? Why the fierce determination that his operation not be inspected or regulated?

If Barbas hadn't solved that safety problem, would he stop? No way. To get what he wanted, Barbas would ignore the damage he might cause. But what did "safely" mean? And if Barbas bulled ahead, how dangerous would it be? Jack didn't know. He had a bad feeling that researching "safely" was going to uncover a nest of scorpions that would drive him further away from being ready for the Armstrong case.

The inescapable facts were that Barbas was a billionaire holed up on a floating fortress protected by a squad of mercenaries. What chance did Jack Strider have of stopping him?

Chapter 21

July 25
5:00 p.m.
San Francisco

GANO TOOK A swig from a mug bearing the red and white logo of the San Francisco 49ers. He was pretending it was coffee, but Jack guessed he'd found the liquor cabinet and laced the coffee with dark rum.

Gano saw him watching and said, "What?" He took another drink. "Hell, it's already way after sundown . . . somewhere."

Mei opened his office door and stuck her head in. "I'm leaving for the day. Ms. Vanderberg said she'll be here in a minute."

"Thanks, Mei. Have a good time at the concert."

Seconds after Mei left, Debra came in and sat at the conference table next to Gano. Jack looked across the table at her and thought, *I'm a lucky man.* She hadn't said a word to him about his call to her from the plane, but he imagined she thought he was a damn fool for having gone down in the sub. If he'd told her the whole story she would have started firing lightning bolts. He'd asked them to meet him here so he could tell them about the research he'd done on methane hydrate since the morning meeting.

"Okay," he said, "let's get started. I've been running my brain overtime to figure out why Barbas has been spending so much money. Thanks to Tammy's research, I have the answer. Capturing methane from the massive methane hydrate deposit under his platform is Barbas's primary objective. In fact, I think he's already trying to do it."

He saw Debra's face slip into the slightly vacant look she wore when seriously evaluating what's just been said. Finally, she nodded. "I think you may be right, but that's not illegal. If it reduces U.S. dependence on oil and reduces global warming, maybe you should cut him some slack. At least he's thinking bigger than getting rid of incandescent light bulbs."

That burned him. "Barbas isn't known for doing anything in the public interest. He probably claims global warming is a sham cooked up by Democrats. When you hear what I'm about to tell you, you'll see why I will never cut Barbas any slack. For most of the day, I've been power reading about methane hydrate. The number of people who have studied the subject is very small, but leading scientists agree that destabilization of methane hydrate in the seabed can cause catastrophic consequences, possibly including runaway global warming. Have you heard of the Clathrate Gun Hypothesis?"

"Of course I have," Gano said. "Clathrate is a social disease."

"Nice try. Actually, Tammy referred to clathrate this morning. It's another way of referring to methane hydrate. The Clathrate Gun Hypothesis says that even a small increase in the temperature of methane hydrate, or decrease in the pressure around it, can trigger an abrupt release of methane gas. That means an earthquake or mining or drilling in the seabed can cause that release. If that methane escapes into the atmosphere, it's a disaster because it's a greenhouse gas *twenty-five times* worse than carbon dioxide."

"How much is a 'small increase' in temperature?" Gano asked.

"About 250 million years ago, the global temperature increased ten degrees Fahrenheit, and that was enough to drive ninety-six percent of all marine species into extinction. A higher temperature causing a massive methane release could exterminate all life on earth. Picture this: Methane loaded with water molecules is heavier than air, so it would spread across land masses as a deadly fog. It could be ignited by lightning, fires, even a match. Fires would generate roaring winds that would carry dust and smoke into the upper atmosphere and speed up global warming. A major destabilization of methane hydrate in the seabed would cause landslides that would launch giant tsunamis." He thought for a moment about Sam from Miami and Tammy from Seattle, both now living in San Francisco. All three cities could be wiped out by major tsunamis.

"I'll be a damned rodeo clown." Gano said softly. "So Barbas might cause that destabilization. Do you think he gets that?"

"He *intends* to cause destabilization to free the methane gas. The unknown is whether he can control it, or it escalates and gets away from him. Scientists say that if BP had drilled into a much bigger reservoir of methane hydrate in the Gulf of Mexico a few years ago, it could have ruptured miles of the seafloor. That would have sunk every ship and drilling platform around and created a tsunami that would have buried Florida under one hundred feet of seawater. It would also have wiped out the coasts of Alabama, Mississippi, Louisiana, and Texas, and killed millions in minutes."

"The greedy bastards knew methane hydrate was a threat, and they drilled anyway," Gano growled. "So you're telling us about all this because you want us riding shotgun for you when you go after the Jolly Greek Giant. Is that about right?"

"Well, are you on board?"

"I'll string along a while, ol' stud, but remember that I've got my own traps to run down Mexico way."

"How about you, Debra? Are you with me?"

"It's not that easy. If we went to a grand jury with what you just told us and asked them to indict Barbas for some crime, they'd laugh us out of the room."

"You're right, and that's why I have to move fast."

"I'm completely with you that messing with methane hydrate would be a crazy risk," she said, "but all you have is a theory about what Barbas is doing. Since you and this firm are pretty much my life, there's only one thing I can do."

He mentally braced himself for the ultimatum he sensed was coming.

"Right now," she said, "you're not getting the job done on the Armstrong case, and it makes me feel bad to keep pushing you on it. It's also driving a wedge between us. I won't let that happen. She put her hands on the table in front of her and looked him straight in the eyes. "I'm taking over the lead on the case. I don't know yet how we're going to win it, but I'm a damned good lawyer. I'll come up with something."

The set of her chin told him she was ready to go to war with him on this. But that war wasn't going to happen. She'd come up with the only solution that could defuse the tension between them and soften the conflict he felt about his priorities. It was also best for the client and, selfishly, a huge load off his shoulders. He was proud of her for having the guts to confront him with her decision. He looked back at her. It felt like their first days together.

"You've got it, partner," he said. "If I can't handle this Barbas thing within a week, I can't handle it at all. Either way, I'll be back on Armstrong full-time by then."

"I hope so, but you'll be second chair. I intend to be ready for the hearing with winning arguments."

Gano set down the 49ers cup. His gaze had been going back and forth between them, with his mouth slightly open. Now he was smiling like a kid relieved that his parents were making up.

Jack's office door swung open hard. Fat and red-faced, Stan Simms filled the doorway, his expression twisted into a sneer.

"Simms." Jack threw the name across the room like a stiletto.

Simms tossed a piece of paper ahead of him onto the floor. "Eviction notice. First one I've ever delivered personally. You're served."

Gano jumped to his feet. "What say I help fatso lose his lunch, boss?"

Simms's bravado faded instantly. He backed out and fast-waddled away.

"Hey," Gano said, "let me go after him. I'll kick his ass so far into the Bay he'll leave a wake all the way to San Jose."

"Right, and then I'd have to bail you out after assault and battery charges."

Debra's face looked like flint. Barbas's attack on the firm she'd help build had just become much more real.

"You think Simms showed up because Barbas found out about your sightseeing tour on the sub?" Gano asked.

"No. Barbas's chopper pilot brought back *Challenger's* hull number, but that would lead to Drake, not to me. The questions we asked at the Bridgewater Tavern must have been reported to Barbas by one of his flunkies, along with physical descriptions that fit us. That told him I hadn't backed down, so he unleashed Simms."

Mei rushed into the room. "Mr. Strider, our receptionist just called. Two of our associates, Walt Wikramaniaka and Peggy Simone, just walked out behind Mr.

Simms. They must have known he was coming. They were carrying laptop computers and heavy briefcases. She wants to know what to do."

Jack and Gano sprinted past her and through the main entrance of Strider & Vanderberg onto the wharf. The two young lawyers had already reached The Embarcadero a hundred yards away. Seeing Jack and Gano racing toward them, they threw their stuff into the back seat of a black Mercedes waiting at the curb. Jack, well ahead of Gano, grabbed the door and jerked it open before they could lock it. Simone was screaming as the Mercedes peeled away and tore the door from Jack's grasp. Gano arrived beside him as the car sped in the direction of Fisherman's Wharf.

Gano pulled out his iPhone. "Call 911?"

"No point. That Mercedes will be holed up in a garage very quickly. Anyway, I saw the license plate. It will trace that car to Simms or his firm. Now I need to get back inside and deal with this."

"How bad do you think this will get? Will Barbas send real muscle?"

"He might when his eviction doesn't work."

"It's not going to work?"

"Over my dead body. So far, it's just been words. Now we fight out in the open."

Debra was coming toward them in the hall. "Those two spread the word that the firm is being evicted. This place is in an uproar."

"We need to circle the wagons," Jack said, "and fast."

"While you two were playing cowboys and Indians outside," Debra replied, "I asked Mei to hire a security guard service to be on duty around the clock. I also told her to have locks and passwords changed and to find an expert to encrypt important files."

"Quick thinking," Jack said. "Simms will try to use all his people and money to win a war of attrition, so we have to go on the offensive. We have to assume that Simone and Wikramaniaka took our client list and other inside information. Debra, please question every relevant member of our staff. Find out if those defectors said anything incriminating."

"Okay, and what about filing a lawsuit against them and Simms personally, and Sinclair & Simms? That will make them think twice about using what they stole."

"I'd rather use what they stole as bait. If we find out they used any of it, I'll file a complaint with the Committee on Professional Responsibility of the California Bar. We'll nail Simms for soliciting them to steal confidential documents for financial gain. And before I leave tonight, I'll draft a request for an injunction against enforcement of the eviction. That will throw sand in their gears."

"You know this is just the beginning," Debra said. "They'll also try to ruin your reputation and the firm's."

For three years he'd worked his ass off to rebuild his good reputation. His recurring dream was of making some mistake that reflected badly on him and the firm. More than he would admit, the possibility that attacks on his character would be coming from Simms gnawed at his gut. Simms was a coward made bold by Barbas's powerful backing. But Simms thought he was dealing with the same man who had left Sinclair & Simms three years ago. That mistake was going to cost him dearly.

Chapter 22

July 25
1:00 p.m.
Chaos platform

THEY HAVE ME *by the balls.*

Petros Barbas fired his half-full snifter of brandy into the floor-to-ceiling window of his Chaos penthouse and watched the liquor slide down the bulletproof glass.

He was a big-time deal maker, but he was getting his brains beaten out by the Chinese and Koreans. His tanker ships were half empty. Like everyone else during the boom years, he'd deferred maintenance on his whole cargo fleet. He'd have been a fool to take his ships out of action when the money was rolling in. Now they were breaking down around the world. Yesterday, one had gotten hung up in Punta Arenas, Chile, because it didn't have the basic parts on board to repair the main engine. His biggest oil tanker had been turned away from Singapore because of safety violations.

Occupancy in some of his ultra-luxe resorts was so low they couldn't even afford decent entertainment. One of them was featuring has-been pop stars performing for guests who had known Frank Sinatra personally.

None of that was going to turn around any time soon. If word got out about this financial squeeze, he'd be ruined overnight. His holding company would go bankrupt. The second his enemies smelled his blood, they'd be on him like starving alligators. He would be a goddamn international laughingstock. He scratched his jaw hard where his beard had started itching all the time.

He detested having his future depend on Renatus. The scientist marched to his own drumbeat, and there seemed to be no way to push him. Bullying was meaningless when Moebius Syndrome was turning him to stone. If Renatus collapsed before he solved the problem, the Chaos dream would be over. But even Renatus had an Achilles heel. Every man did. He had to find and exploit it.

Renatus had been right about everything except what was most important: how to solve the problem that had brought the Chaos Project to a dead stop. Of course there was danger. There were always risks when billions of dollars were the prize. So far, he'd been cautious, but caution was killing him. If Renatus didn't come up with the solution after his next field test, the methane hydrate extraction would go into full-scale operation whether Renatus objected or not.

Every time he thought about Strider refusing his demand, it pissed him off again. He'd gotten so used to people falling over themselves to do what he wanted that he'd misread the guy. What had motivated Strider to fight him? Was he playing hardball to get a bigger piece of the action? Was he helping some other tycoon to compete against him? If it was because Strider had a thing for Debra Vanderberg, they could have worked that out. He'd only wanted to borrow her for a while.

Warning Strider should have backed him off, but he'd come back to poke around Astoria. That was stupid. No outsider could set foot in that pissant town without being reported to his security staff. Now he'd pay. Before long, lawyers in Strider's firm would be interviewing clients in the back seat of a car. And after Stan Simms got done, Strider would be lucky to get a job doing public defense work in Petaluma. But that didn't solve the problem.

He had to face the fact that he could punish Strider, but there was no way *he* could force Strider to line up President Gorton to help him in the Senate. But he knew someone who might be able to talk him into it.

He picked up the phone.

Chapter 23

July 26
8:00 a.m.
San Francisco

"I'VE JUST ADDED 125 lawyers to our staff," Debra said as she walked into Jack's office.

"Since you can't mean what it sounds like you mean," Jack said, "what *do* you mean?"

"You said we had to go on the offensive against Simms, so I did. As you know, J. Keating Sterling is managing partner of Graham & Sterling, the corporate securities law firm. I met him years ago when his son was in the martial arts class I teach. When the son found out I'd quit working for Sinclair & Simms, he said his father's firm often competed with S & S and that his father detested Stan Simms. So this morning, I went to see Sterling.

"After some chit-chat, during which he made it excruciatingly clear he had recently divorced, I told him Simms had threatened us with a lot of things, including trying to ruin your reputation and that of our firm. I said we were fighting back and asked him to let me know if he heard anything coming from Simms. He said he would spread the word in his firm. Then he grabbed the phone and talked with Jim Carlton, who runs Hollingsworth, Banker—they have over a hundred lawyers—and explained the situation. He told me to get over there right away before Carlton caught a flight for China. Just before I left, he said, 'Give me a call sometime when you're free for lunch.'"

Looking across the room at her long, glossy black hair, liquid dark eyes, and exceptionally feminine physique, he understood why she got hit on all the time. He knew she resented it, but she just brushed it off except when someone persisted. Then she verbally flattened him.

"Did you get to Carlton's office before he left?"

"I did, and he said that if anything negative about us touched his web, he'd let me know. It seems he has a personal beef with Stan Simms. He said that after Justin Sinclair died three years ago—yes, he said 'died'—Simms showed his true nasty temperament."

He admired her more every day. Even though she was mad at him right now, she never wavered in doing what was best for the firm.

"You lined up allies and set traps. Very impressive."

"That's because my name is on the sign outside our door. It's part of my job as a partner."

They walked together into a meeting with all their lawyers and staff to explain what had happened and what they were doing about it, leaving out sensitive details in case there were more defectors in the group. This was eating up their time just as Barbas had intended.

Following the meeting, he asked Mei to put a virtual "Do Not Disturb" sign on his office. For the next two fourteen-hour days, he worked on the portions of the Armstrong arguments Debra had asked him to complete. When he finished, he knew what he had to do next. He picked up the phone and placed a call. "Hey, Gano."

JACK EASED THE rented Zodiac inflatable out of the mouth of the Powell River into the Strait of Georgia at eight knots, ridiculously slow given the powerful Honda 70 horsepower, four-stroke motor mounted on the frame behind him.

"Want to kick it up a bit?" Gano prompted. "For God's sake, let's not look like a Social Security tour boat. Think like Tony Toll racing at Monte Carlo."

Jack wound it up to forty knots.

Before long, Gano pointed at an island on his left. "That's Texada where I rented the ultralight. You remember—"

"That I'll have to pay for it? Yeah, I remember."

"Worth every penny. Now keep your eyes sharp. There are lots of killer whales in the strait. Slam into one of those babies and you'll be paying for this Zodiac too." After they passed Texada, he pointed at the silhouette of a very small island ahead. "Ironbound."

Jack circled the island's perimeter and saw no lights, no movement, but they were more than a hundred yards offshore. Damn little to go on. "Use the binoculars. I don't want to get in close looking for a way through the rocks and find myself on the wrong end of a Winchester 12 gauge."

After a couple of minutes, Gano, without taking his eyes from the binoculars, said, "No signs of life, but I think I see a channel leading to an inlet. Take us past that row of boulders ahead then cut in toward the shore."

Jack used the big motor to fight the current that was trying to drive the Zodiac into the jagged rocks. No more banter. The channel was narrow and shallow, and the surge was so strong from behind that Jack had to jam the Honda 70 into reverse to keep forward motion down to one knot. When he reached the inlet and turned in, the current drove the Zodiac into the far bank. After it scraped past, it moved into calm water. Overhanging branches topping the granite cliffs turned the inlet into a dark tunnel.

At the end of the cul-de-sac, a road paved in rough stones rose and curved out of sight on the left. On the right side, two fifteen-foot-tall steel panels were built into the cliff face. He killed the motor, let the Zodiac drift forward, and gestured at the panels. "There's probably a cave behind those big doors where Barbas hides his boat. Could even be a tunnel cut from inside the cave all the way to the lodge to give him real security."

"Well, I'm not feeling secure," Gano replied in a hushed voice. "Barbas could be up in those trees sighting at us through a scope." He looked up, waved his hand back and forth, and dodged to his right. Nothing happened. Then he reached inside his jacket and withdrew his Glock 23. He checked the chamber and stuck the gun back in his shoulder holster. He bent over, pulled up his right cuff, and released a .38 Special snub nose from its calf holster. "Carry this with you."

"No thanks. Every time you get out your guns, someone winds up dead."

"Great overstatement, but at least it hasn't been us. And, by the way, every time you refuse a gun, you wind up with your ass in a crack—or my life on the line. So take the damn thing, or you can play this out on your own."

"Give it to me." He stuffed it in his pocket.

"No, no, no, Mr. Earp. Look at it before you stash it. See which end the bullets come out of. Find the little thing you squeeze to make it go 'bang.'"

While a Navy officer, Jack had qualified as an Expert Marksman with a rifle and .45, and Gano knew that, but he was right about familiarizing himself with *this* weapon. He pulled the .38 back out, examined it, and tucked it away.

"Let's get started."

"That's a problem," Gano said. "Either that rocky road is blocked farther up by a gate, probably remotely controlled, or Barbas is tempting visitors to use it and be sitting ducks."

Jack pointed up the cliff face. "Don't worry, we're going that way."

"Not me, Spider-Man. I can't climb that."

"I'll show you how. The first ten feet of the wall next to the road will be easy. Then we'll traverse above the metal plates. Past that, we zigzag the rest of the way up."

"I told you, I can't do it. When I was a kid, I fell out of a tree. Then off a roof. Next—hell, point is, I just stopped climbing up things."

"I'll use that rope in the boat to make a safety line. If you fall, I'll have the other end around a tree trunk to stop you. No problem." He knew Gano wouldn't stay in the boat and miss whatever action there might be up there.

"All right, damn it."

Jack studied every detail of the rock surface and identified the holds he would string together. It was steep but had no overhangs. All in all, it was nothing compared to the climb he'd made in Tikal. "Okay, watch where I put my hands and feet." He knew Gano didn't have a climber's memory, so it would be tough for him. "I'm starting up."

Moss and lichen forced him to alter his route twice, but the climb was so short that fatigue wasn't a factor. He hauled himself over the top and sat, bracing his feet against the trunks of two spruce trees. He tied one end of the rope around one of the trees, tossed the other end to Gano, and waved for him to start up.

Gano was completely out of his element, so his progress was painfully slow. Each time he moved closer, Jack hauled in on the lifeline.

Then the inevitable happened. Gano tried to move his right foot up too far, putting all his weight on his left foot, which promptly slid off a narrow outcrop. He grabbed for a handhold that wasn't there and fell. The safety rope caught him after a few feet, and he didn't flip upside down. "Son of a bitch," Gano snarled, trying to keep his voice low.

"Do exactly what I tell you," Jack called down.

Ten stressful minutes later, Gano pulled himself over the edge and collapsed against a tree. After his heart rate had slowed closer to normal, Gano said, "I hate to admit it, but that little hee-haw up this cliff took a lot out of me. I'm not built for hanging my whole weight off my fingernails."

"It gets easier," Jack replied, "after about five years of practice."

"Maybe if you have spider blood in your veins. You're like that Alex Honnold guy I read about who solo climbs Half Dome in Yosemite before breakfast."

They each had separate strengths and weaknesses, so Jack didn't needle Gano about the climb. "Just in case we have to make a fast exit, I'll leave the rope here so we can get back down."

"How the hell would we do that?"

"Easy. Just grab the rope, lean back over the edge, and walk down the cliff."

Chapter 24

July 26
3:00 p.m.
Ironbound Island, British Columbia, Canada

THEY'D MADE THE steep climb through the woods without encountering any sign of human presence. "This place feels as deserted as a tomb after the grave robbers have left," Gano said.

Jack stopped at the edge of the woods and looked into the clearing. Fifty yards ahead stood the sprawling two-story, half-timber lodge and, beyond it, three metal buildings. He was finally about to find out what Barbas used this place for and how it was connected to methane hydrate. He and Gano stood silently, still concealed, watching and listening. Nothing except conversation among birds.

"No concertina wire on this side," Jack said. "Barbas must think no one can get here from the direction we did."

A dozen steps away, backed up to the trees, was a big shed made of heavy timbers. They edged out of the woods and looked around one corner of the shed.

"There are the tracks I saw from the air," Gano said quietly, "and there"—his eyes followed the tracks across the wide clearing—"is the contraption I told you about. It looks like a tank with a long barrel but about one-quarter size."

Jack's breath quickened. Right in front of them was the smoking gun, the link between Ironbound and the seabed. He wished he knew what it was for.

"Let's take a look in the shed." The ten-foot-wide door was secured by a heavy new padlock, but its jaws were open. He pulled and they ducked in. To his left were a Bobcat backhoe, a compact Caterpillar excavator, and racks of power yard tools, coils of rope and wire, and other gear needed to make the place self-sustaining. To the right was a very well-equipped machine shop.

"Must have something to do with the mystery tank," Gano said.

Jack wanted to examine the machine shop more closely but was worried about time. "Let's move on."

They turned back to the doorway, and Gano pointed to their left. "Over there on the ground. A body, small one. I hope it's only a coyote. Hard to tell because it's so chewed up, like it was used for target practice. Someone with a weapon was here."

"Or *is* here. Barbas probably has more defenses than just concertina wire."

"Not dogs, or they'd be bitin' our butts by now, but he might have cameras that sweep the house and buildings. Could even be monitored on Chaos. Or maybe there's a guard inside the lodge. Just in case, I'll stick this rake around the corner like in the old Westerns and see if someone shoots at it."

He did. Nothing happened, so he pulled it back. "Hmmm. Don't know if that means all clear, or someone just knows a rake when he sees it."

"Listen," Jack whispered. "Sounds like tires rolling across dry leaves—and some kind of whirring."

"I'll try the rake again."

A split second after the rake went out a red circle appeared on the tines. "I'll be damned," Gano exclaimed. "If that's what I think it is we're in deep—"

A hail of bullets ripped the rake out of Gano's hands. They dove deeper into the shed and hit the floor. The second volley sewed a stream of bullets horizontally across the shed, including hundreds through the half-open door before it moved on.

The salvoes stopped. So did the whirring and sound of tires rolling.

"Could be an automatic rifle with a laser sight, motion detector, and heat sensor," Gano whispered. "If the heat sensor leads the shooter in here, we're in deep bat guano." The Glock in his hand seemed pathetic.

Jack grabbed an ax leaning against the wall. "Gano, get that shovel and stand on the far side of the door. When he comes in, we'll attack from both directions."

"You been smokin' some crazy shit, Chief, but I got nothing better to keep us from winding up like that coyote."

"Gentlemen, throw out your guns." The voice was soft, but authoritative.

"That was no machine," Gano whispered.

"Not Barbas's voice either."

"Whoever it is, I noticed he didn't say the part about 'and you won't be harmed.'"

"Maybe we can sucker him into a cease fire," Jack said. From behind the Bobcat, he called out, "Come in here with your arms up."

"Throw out your guns . . . *now*."

Gano looked at Jack. "Might as well. We ain't going to win a shootout with what we're packin'." He skidded his Glock out the door. Jack followed with the .38.

Hands at his sides, apparently at ease, Dr. Renatus Roux stepped into the doorway. "I will explain," he said.

"Renatus, for God's sake, what are you doing here?" Jack was struck by how calm the man was. He'd just caught two trespassers with guns, but he wasn't angry, not even excited. "And why aren't you amazed to see us?"

"When I motored into the inlet, I was surprised to see another boat there. I have security cameras placed around the property, so I used my iPhone to call up saved images on the boat landing camera. There you were. But the camera on the road showed nothing. That meant you'd climbed the cliff, and that shows me I need barbed wire and cameras there. Anyway, I walked up the road and easily got here ahead of you."

"You walked into this shed without a weapon. Weren't you afraid?"

"Of course not. You're not killers."

"So now that we're all here," Gano said, "shall we dance?"

"Clarify."

"We came to see what Barbas is doing here," Jack said. "Are you going to show us?"

"You do pose a problem. If I force you off my island, you'll try to come back. If I confine or kill you, that might draw attention to Ironbound. So . . . follow me."

Jack noticed he had used the phrase "my island" and had made no reference to Barbas. My God, maybe his assumptions had been wrong from the beginning. Gano hadn't actually seen Barbas on the helo. Whatever was going on here might be about Renatus, not Barbas.

As they walked out of the shed, Gano scooped up both guns and tucked them away. Renatus noticed but didn't object.

When they turned the shattered corner of the shed, Gano stopped abruptly. "That's a goddamn robot."

He was looking at a cart with four fat tires for stability and a half-dozen antennae and cameras to collect data. An automatic rifle mounted in its center rested on a battery pack.

"If I hadn't been here," Renatus said, "my guard robot would have killed you."

"It would have tried," Gano said, but his bluster sounded hollow. "What's that contraption at the end of these tracks that looks like a baby tank?"

"It's a model of something I use to collect biological specimens. I had the parts made in Seattle and shipped to me in Powell River to be assembled here. I needed to perfect it before I had the full-size one built."

Jack knew the full-size one now rested against the HTV. Its components, too, must have been built in Seattle, but were delivered to Chaos. That could only have been done with Barbas's consent.

Renatus walked on to a building marked with a large red number 1. He manipulated an electronic lock, opened the door, and they stepped into a small, chilly room that served as an airlock with a large triple pane window with a view into the space beyond. Renatus flicked a row of switches that bathed the interior room in a ghostly blue light.

"This lab is a sterile space. Only I go in, and I always wear protective clothing."

A long, waist-high counter supported a row of what looked like tabletop copying machines. To its left were a desk, work table, freezers and refrigerators, racks of glass laboratory slide plates, and pieces of equipment he didn't recognize.

"Those are DNA sequencing machines," Renatus said.

"Like the machines Craig Venter used at Celera to map the human genome?" Jack asked.

"Hardly. He needed fifty times more machines than I do, and they were bigger, slower, and ran much hotter. Mine combine robotics, chemistry, and optics and use nanopore sequencing to read strands of DNA as they're pulled through a microscopic hole. Just a few years ago it took supercomputers and months of lab work to disassemble and reassemble a genome. I do it in hours and have also cut costs dramatically. Soon, the cost of sequencing an entire human genome will be less than $1,000."

"Everyone's heard of DNA," Gano said, "but I don't know, well, exactly what it is."

The several seconds Renatus let pass before responding clearly expressed his contempt. "DNA molecules in every living organism are like a set of blueprints, or a recipe, that store information needed to build other components of cells and tell them how to function. The DNA segments that carry this genetic information are called genes. The DNA in a single cell in your body contains about three billion pairs of chemical building blocks. My sequencing machines let me understand the DNA and its code. That's just the starting point for my work here."

Jack didn't want to get sidetracked into a lecture on DNA. "What's in the other buildings?"

"My computers are in Building 2. Come."

He unlocked the door into another airlock. Pointing through the view window, he said, "Those are computers stacked five high in racks. Technology has advanced so far since Venter's work that now hundreds of computers and data storage devices fit inside a few cabinets instead of requiring thousands of square feet."

They backed out of the airlock and turned toward Building 3. Beyond it, dozens of rectangular stainless steel containers stood in rows, raised from the ground on stubby legs. Since each had a locking bar but none were locked, he thought they must be empty. He read the marking on one, Triton, but that told him nothing.

In the Building 3 airlock Renatus pointed and said, "That's ultra-high speed biotechnical equipment for preparing DNA samples, same as they use at the Human Genome Project at Lawrence Livermore National Laboratory in California. We're after the same thing, the gold mine of information contained in the structure of genes. That information is the key to curing genetic diseases, but—" He looked away from them for a few seconds, took a deep breath, and composed himself. "Over there," he pointed toward the far end of the room, "is where DNA is loaded onto glass plates. I've even learned how to use unique microbes to dissect strands of DNA in the preparation process."

Jack heard no pride or boasting in his voice, just flat statements of fact. He recalled other Renatus creations he'd seen—robots scurrying around the seabed carrying out the mining operation. He shook his head in admiration. "What does Barbas get out of this?"

Renatus snorted softly. "He's not interested in DNA sequencing. This is my own scientific work for my own reasons. He's paying for it, but when I solve one remaining problem for him he'll become the richest man on Earth."

Jack knew what that problem was and that no one else had been able to solve it.

You better do it fast because I'm going to try to put Chaos out of business.

Leaving Building 3, Gano said, "Might as well take a look-see at the lodge while we're here, right?"

Renatus nodded curtly. "Remember that curiosity killed the cat."

The lodge had the creepy feel of a haunted house with rooms full of bulky Adirondack-inspired furniture under covers. A large roll-top desk in the den was furry with dust. The kitchen, large enough to prepare meals for dozens of guests, appeared barely used. One small bedroom off the kitchen had probably been a housekeeper's quarters. Its spartan furnishings included a bed, chair, wardrobe, desk, and a chalkboard covered with large, scrawled numbers. A second bedroom, also downstairs, was larger, with an adjoining bathroom. They walked quickly through the empty rooms upstairs. Other than being creepy, there was nothing unusual.

Petros Barbas would not stay in this place for even one night.

Back at the entrance, Jack stopped the procession out the door and turned to Renatus. "You've made a big commitment to DNA sequencing at a time when you have other priorities. Do you mind telling me why?" He was aware of the irony since he was making such a hash of dealing with conflicting priorities himself.

"I'm a scientist indulging my obsession. I work here in obscurity, because I don't need input from anyone, and I detest being interrupted. I have a great deal of work to do before I return to Chaos, so it's time for you to leave. Please don't mistake my civility for hospitality. You are not welcome here. My robot has face recognition capability and *will* kill you." He walked back into Building 3 and closed the door behind him.

"That was a cheery send-off," Gano said. "I doubt he was bluffing about face recognition, so I hope he neutered that robot until we get out of here."

The road was steep, so the walk back down took only a few minutes.

"I respect that guy," Gano said as they climbed into the Zodiac, "for accomplishing so much despite that weird frozen face."

"I noticed that his left arm didn't swing freely," Jack said. "That wasn't true a couple of weeks ago. He's getting worse."

After Jack started the engine and was cautiously backing out of the inlet, Gano said, "Despite the robot gunslinger, tank-thing, DNA sequencing, and haunted house—and no Barbas—I doubt you got what you came here for."

"Absolutely not. I thought we'd find files, schematics, technology, something I could use to stop Barbas. Instead, we found out nothing except that Renatus has an obsession with DNA that has nothing to do with the Chaos Project."

"So I guess we can forget about Ironbound."

"Not yet. I'm pretty sure that Dr. Renatus Roux just played us for fools."

Chapter 25

July 26
7:00 p.m.
Astoria

"LOOK ALIVE, LINDBERGH," Gano said. "I'm about to make a right turn and follow the Columbia River west. That should put us over Barbas's processing plant pretty quick. From there, it's less than ten minutes to Astoria."

"There it is." Jack pointed ahead to the left.

The site was a barren rectangle clear-cut into a dense pine forest. One long side was bounded by the river, and all of it was surrounded by a tall chain-link fence with light towers. It made him think of a prison. Most of the big structures looked like leftovers from the original plant, but there were several new buildings, a couple of them belching columns of oily black smoke. An aged cargo ship was being unloaded by cranes at the wharf. The grounds were alive with workmen, forklifts, dump trucks, and open-bed trucks with six-foot-high tires.

Three vehicles that looked like armored trucks were backed up to cargo bays at one of the buildings.

"Want to go around again?" Gano asked.

"No point in spooking the workmen."

Then he noticed that downriver from the wharf the water was stained by a thick stream of coffee-colored runoff from the plant.

"Look at that. Underwater discharge pipes." As they flew over, he saw something ominous. The discharge was laced with streaks of green and greasy red. "Barbas is dumping chemicals. The stuff they use to process minerals is toxic. That's what he wanted me to defend."

Suddenly, the Cessna was in the midst of a madly swirling cloud of small birds. A few thudded into the windscreen. Some flew into the propellers and became a mist of blood and feathers. Then they were through the cloud.

"Good God," Gano shouted. "Look dead ahead."

A wall of water raced up the Columbia, ten feet higher than the river ahead of it. The leading edge was ugly, full of river-bottom muck. The roiling surface behind the summit carried several cars, the nose of an RV pointing skyward, two sailboats on their sides.

Jack knew instantly what it was. "Tidal wave."

"Like the one that hit Japan?"

"Not even close. That was over a hundred feet high, caused by one of the biggest earthquakes in recorded history."

"From all the crap in the water, this baby must have beaten up on Astoria."

As they got closer to town, Jack saw devastation at the three commercial piers. Dock lines had been ripped loose, setting ships helplessly adrift. A tour boat was pinned against its pier, listing to port, terrified passengers probably still aboard.

The marina and boat yard had taken major hits. All the boats tied up to floating piers had been torn loose and sucked upstream. Two big motor yachts floated upside down, keels like shark fins. A long rack of kayaks and sailboats in their cradles were scrambled together next to the clubhouse. Several commercial fishing boats in the mooring basin were half-swamped and foundering.

The Oregon half of the span that connected Astoria to Megler, Washington, was a high cantilevered truss bridge that looked unharmed. Jack pointed to the much lower flat stretch of bridge to the north covered with seaweed and mud. "Drivers caught on that half of the bridge probably never saw it coming."

"This ain't Katrina," Gano said, "or Tornado Alley, but these folks have taken a pounding they won't forget."

Gano pressed his headset to his ear and said, "Tower, this is Cessna Skylane 3550. You folks open for business?" He listened and said, "Skylane here. Runway 2 west. Wilco. Coming in." Off mike he said, "They're hysterical at the Hysteria airport."

WHEN JACK WALKED into the Bridgewater Tavern it had the feeling of a refugee camp. Some people, clean and dry, must have watched the wall of water from high ground. Others, wet to the knees, saw or heard it coming and fled. The rest were mud-smeared, sopping wet, and thoroughly shaken. They'd seen it up close.

The place was in an uproar, with everyone telling his or her story and shedding tears over losses. Jack noticed rum on many tables, bottles of it. That was a powerful message.

The bartender looked shell-shocked until he saw Gano in his fancy cowboy outfit. Then his eyes narrowed, and he scowled. Gano glared back at him with his look that said he just didn't give a damn one way or the other if he had to make something happen by force.

Molly McCoy was not in sight. "She must be pretty upset," Jack said. "Maybe she's in her office. Let's ease on out and find the back door."

An open door around the corner led into a short hall. At its end a wood sign read "Chief Cook and Bottle Washer."

Jack had been gaming through how he'd approach Molly, the reason they'd come. He had to persuade her to help him.

He knocked. No response. He knocked again. Nothing, so he opened the door slowly. Molly, behind her desk on the phone, waved them in without taking time to focus on who they were.

"What you need to do, Chief," she said, "is run your butt over here right now and get some facts. There are more than a hundred people here who know who's missing, what's flooded, and everything else you're supposed to be working on." She slammed the handset down and looked at them. "What!" Focusing on them, she opened her mouth and her eyes widened, but she didn't get up or offer her hand. She gave a half-wave that meant they could sit if they really wanted to. Her auburn hair, gathered loosely behind her neck, framed her somber expression.

Gano spoke up. "I'm Gano LeMoyne and this is—"

"Jack Strider. I remember you both . . . very well. The pipefitter you, uh, met last time you were in my place still hasn't straightened up all the way."

"I'm sorry about that. I was trying to—"

"What are you doing here?"

"We had business up north," Gano said. "Just flew in. We saw the tidal wave right after it passed through town."

"I just heard on the radio," she said, "that the Tsunami Warning Center reported an earthquake, epicenter a couple of hundred miles off shore. They say that's what started the tsunami. All I know is that that wave was the biggest anyone here has ever seen. At first we thought it was a rogue wave, but it kept coming. Everyone was screaming and running for higher ground. This joint is packed with guys trying to drink their courage back."

"You have a lot more to worry about," Jack said. "Think what would be left if a tsunami the size of the one that killed nineteen thousand Japanese hit Astoria. It would go all the way upriver to the Hanford Nuclear Project and uncover all those barrels of plutonium waste buried right next to the river."

"That couldn't happen," she said with no conviction.

"I'll give it to you straight. The epicenter of the quake will turn out to be very close to Barbas's platform. An experiment he's conducting was the cause of the quake and the tidal wave. His next experiment could generate a much larger tsunami."

"Nobody can cause an earthquake," she scoffed. "Not even Barbas."

He told her about methane hydrate and destabilization. Her pale skin turned ashen. He could tell she didn't want to accept it, so he kept spelling it out.

She leaned forward, elbows on the desk. "I don't want to believe he'd do that. When Petros Barbas first showed up, we thought of him as a savior. When I was growing up, this town was wonderful. I went away to college and stayed to teach at Oregon State. When my father got sick, I didn't mind coming back. I thought it would be a good sabbatical, but the town had changed. The economy had fallen apart. We had panhandlers for the first time in our history. More than fifty people lined up to apply for a minimum wage job at Custard King. A mother who lost her job at the last cannery abandoned her infant at the library." She wiped away a tear.

"Then Barbas came, spending money and talking big. He hired a lot of people and stopped the slow slide. Things were looking up for a while. Then the ones who were hired got envious of the ones who were paid more. The ones who didn't get jobs resented everyone who did. In hard times, we all used to work together. Now it's dog-eat-dog. Everyone's mean. People don't trust each other. There's a lot of drunkenness, not the Saturday night kind, the *every* night kind. And more violence. The littlest thing sets people at each other's throats. In public we all say Barbas is a great man, but that's because we're afraid to be honest."

"The way you weren't honest about your feelings about him the night we met," Jack said.

"Yeah, for the same reason those guys were about to pound on you two. So what was your reason for lying to me about being some kind of grocers? You hadn't been gone ten minutes before I decided that was BS and I'd never see you again."

"Barbas again," Jack said. "I had to find out more about him and didn't think anyone would answer questions just to satisfy my curiosity. Forgive me?"

"Now that I know what's going on, I guess so. The stress here has gotten unbelievable. Working around the clock at the mill upriver. Swearing oaths of secrecy. Mandatory six-month shifts on that platform. There's no more family life. No one just hangs out anymore. And there's no way to get off the treadmill."

"There is a way," Jack said.

"There isn't. You have no idea."

He glanced at Gano. He was about to put their lives in her hands. "You okay with this, Gano?"

He nodded. "I trust her."

"Molly, to break through Barbas's secrecy I need specific information from aboard the platform, which, by the way, Barbas calls Chaos."

She looked skeptical. "You think you can get workers on the platform to spy on Barbas?"

"If I don't find out what he's about to do, and stop him, Astoria is very likely to get slammed by a much worse tsunami. That one wouldn't just take out the waterfront. It would destroy the entire town and maybe everything else along the Oregon and Washington coasts hundreds of miles in either direction. I can't get local people to do anything, but *you* can." He saw she was about to speak, so he held up his hand to stop her from making an impulsive reply. He had to be sure she realized that it could get very rough. "If Barbas catches you setting up a spy network, he'll retaliate."

Her expression was grim. "What do you want from me?"

He listed the information he needed and the kinds of jobs people who might know it would have. He watched her face, hoping she was attaching individual names to those jobs.

When they'd walked into her office, she'd been badly rattled by the damage but was in fighting-back mode. Now she was overwhelmed by the specter of a monster tsunami and the fact that Barbas could cause it. He couldn't predict what she'd do. Why would she think two men she didn't know, who had lied to her at their first meeting, could stop the all-powerful Barbas?

"This is the most important decision of your life. Consider the people who depend on your answer. Think it over. I'll call you from San Francisco."

Gano offered to stay with her, even insisted.

The sparkle had gone out of her eyes. No more smile. She looked weary. "Right now, that's a bad idea on every level I can think of."

SMOKE FROM MULTIPLE fires stung his eyes as he and Gano walked along a street with small warehouses on both sides on their way to the Hotel Elliott. He planned to find a ride there to shuttle them back to the airport. The street was deserted.

A black Ford F-150 pickup rumbled up from behind them, slowly passed them, and pulled over fifty yards ahead at an angle to the curb. Two men jumped from the cargo bed on opposite sides and stood by the rear bumper. The guy on Jack's right wore a sweatshirt with the hood pulled up. He held a two-foot iron pipe in his right hand, making no effort to conceal it. The one on Jack's left had a heavy-boned face and badly mended nose. He wore grease-stained coveralls over a blue shirt. He lifted a tool Jack had seen around Astoria, a lumberjack's "hookaroon" for grabbing logs. It was a hickory pole about two and a half feet long with a steel spike set at right angles at the end. One well-aimed blow from that spike would be fatal. Coveralls held it at waist level as he glanced back at the driver's window, clearly waiting for a signal to get it on.

The driver's door opened. A tall man with a ginger mustache and wearing a leather bomber jacket swung out. He had an elongated skull, and his small, close-set eyes radiated malice. The left hand he rested on the roof of the truck's cab held a silver switch-blade. Jack heard the *snick* as it opened and locked into place.

The fourth man emerged from the passenger's side. It was the bartender from the Bridgewater Tavern. With a lot of muscle backing him, he looked cocky and mean.

"Great service," Gano said loudly. "The airport shuttle has come to pick us up here." Then, very softly to Jack, "I guess you remember I'm not carrying my heat with me this trip."

"You boys should never have come back," the bartender said, curling his lip.

Jack saw that these guys weren't yahoos who'd staggered out of a bar to harass a couple of out-of-towners. They were dead serious, and they'd brought weapons to do serious harm.

"Look, fellas," he called to them, "we're on our way to the airport. Get back in the truck and tell everyone you ran us out of town. Nobody gets hurt."

"You're from the big city, and your pal with the smart mouth looks like a dude ranch cowboy. Somebody *is* going to get hurt," the driver snarled, "and it's going to be you turds."

Gano looked at Jack and muttered, "Doesn't look like Barbas's You're-Not-Welcome Wagon is going away."

"I'll handle this, Gano." He looked at the bartender. "Let it go, guys."

"You are one big candy ass, mister," the driver said. "It's going to be a pleasure busting you up."

Jack knew more conversation was pointless, except for any that might give him an advantage.

"No need," Jack said, addressing the driver and starting in his direction. "To show we have no hard feelings, I'll kick in a hundred bucks. That's a lot of booze. Have we got a deal?" He took out the money and held it in front of him. As he neared the back of the pickup, Coveralls raised his hookaroon a few inches and hesitated. Jack ignored him, appearing to focus on the driver. "Tell you what," he said, "I'll make it two hundred."

In the next second Jack's right leg coiled up toward his chest, then lashed out sideways in a stomp-kick, driving the sole of his shoe into Coveralls's knee. The crackle of the joint disintegrating was terrible to hear. The man screamed and went down, curled over to grab what was left of his knee. Jack took one step forward and kicked him under the jaw, snapping his head back. As he crashed backward like a slaughtered steer, Jack grabbed the hookaroon off the pavement.

In two long strides, he closed on the driver, who dropped the jacket he'd just pulled off and started his switch blade in a horizontal slice. Jack moved in fast and swung the hookaroon. With his full weight behind it, he clubbed the driver in the side of his neck. The driver's knife-hand dropped, as useless as though it had been unplugged. Jack drove the point of his elbow backward squarely into the driver's right temple. His head jerked sideways, his knees buckled, and he sagged into a heap.

Jack glanced at Gano and saw Hoodie squared off in front of him, weight balanced, hands high, eyes focused. *Uh, oh. That one hasn't lost many fights.* But Gano's bigger problem was the bartender. He'd hung back, probably sure Hoodie would take out Gano with the pipe. Now Jack saw the bartender reach behind his back in a move that meant only one thing: a handgun tucked in his belt.

The bartender, focused on Gano fifteen feet away, raised a silver snub nose pistol. He paused, waiting for a clear shot. Jack threw himself around the hood of the truck. The bartender saw Jack coming at him and snapped off a shot at Gano that missed. He swung his pistol around to face the threat from Jack. The pistol was still in its arc when Jack hurled the hookaroon at the bartender's head. The bartender's gun arm came up reflectively to swat at the spinning spike. That gave Jack the second he needed to close at full speed. He grabbed the back of the bartender's head, pulled it forward and jammed his thumb up along the man's nose into his right eye. The bartender shrieked and clawed at his face. Jack launched his knee into the man's groin with such force it lifted him onto his toes. As the bartender collapsed, Jack grabbed his head again and slammed him face first into the pavement. Jack scooped up his pistol, and then the insults being shouted at each other by Gano and Hoodie penetrated his consciousness.

During the few seconds Jack had been in action, Gano and Hoodie had been circling one another looking for an opening. Hoodie made a couple of fakes with his pipe then launched a roundhouse. Gano tried to block it with his forearm but only deflected it. It slammed his shoulder so hard it staggered him.

Hoodie took a step back, taunting Gano to come at him. Gano stayed put and let his guard drop lower. Hoodie couldn't resist the temptation and cocked his pipe for another swing.

Jack raised the pistol.

Gano stepped inside, and put his full weight into an uppercut to the man's solar plexus. The pipe fell out of his hand and the "*arghh*" sounded like a drunk trying to wretch, but he didn't go down. Blood dripping from his nose and breathing heavily, he was paying a price for long nights in the tavern. Gano popped the guy hard in the face with a straight left, then struck with three more rapid-fire punches, drawing gouts of blood. Hoodie, infuriated, rushed forward to wrestle him to the pavement. Gano was ready and hammered Hoodie on the jaw with an overhand right. The man's momentum carried him in a nose dive to the pavement.

Gano looked at Jack. "What kept you, Joltin' Jack?"

"I was busy." Jack leaned over, hands on his knees, totally winded, body craving oxygen. After sucking in a dozen deep breaths, he made sure Hoodie had no other weapon.

"These guys must have been sent by Barbas, but I want to find out for sure."

"Let's ask the driver." Gano walked around the back of the pickup. "Holeeeeee sheeee-it. It looks like a slaughterhouse over here. These two aren't going to be talking to us."

"I'll explain later. The guy in the hood you were dancing with is still conscious. Ask him."

Gano said, "Petros Barbas paid you guys to ambush us, right?"

"Screw off." The answer came from between the bloody lips of a man beaten but still belligerent. He wiped his mouth. The back of his hand came away red. "This ain't over, buddy."

"You're damn right it ain't," Gano said. "I'm having the cops throw you in the slammer."

"Not our cops, you won't." He spat a bloody mess onto the asphalt.

Gano looked up and down the street, and said, "We better mosey back to my ol' Cessna before a posse shows up."

"Fine with me. My elbow hurts like hell." Coveralls, the driver, and the bartender were completely disabled. Hoodie was making no attempt to get to his feet, but Jack took his cell phone, just in case.

In front of Hotel Elliott, they jerked open the back doors of a cab and climbed in.

"Airport. Fast."

"Waterfront's a wreck, so I'll stay two blocks inland."

But when he reached the bridge that led to the airport, several highway workers stood next to the road holding orange cones, apparently about to close the bridge to inspect for water damage.

Those guys knew we were going to the airport, so they might have sent a gang out there. No time for a long detour.

"Don't stop, driver," Jack ordered. "You get an extra fifty bucks in case you have to take the long way home."

The driver glanced over his shoulder and accelerated, ignoring the workman waving at him to stop. The bridge held. When he dropped them off and had the extra money in hand, he gave Jack a big smile. "You folks come back any time. We know how to treat strangers right."

"So we found out," Gano said. "Listen, give 911 a call. We saw some guys fighting a couple of blocks from the hotel toward the river. Looked pretty bad. Might need an ambulance."

GANO BANKED THE Cessna until it was heading south for San Francisco. After leveling out, he settled back and cleared his throat. "Let me ask you something, old pard. Back on that street, I had my hands full with one guy. You wiped out the other three all by yourself. When did Mr. Peacenik turn into Rambo?"

Jack wasn't surprised by the question. "One night in Juarez, Debra and I were jumped by three men who'd been sent to ambush us. One of them knocked me cold, and they kidnapped Debra. After I came to, facedown on the gravel, I tracked them by following a scream from Debra. When I caught up, I surprised them and went in swinging. I was so nuts I might have killed the leader if Debra hadn't pulled me off him."

"You never talk about that night," Gano said.

"I try not to think about it. It was such a close call that it taught me a lesson. I decided to learn how to fight better, so I took classes at the YMCA."

"You're shitting me." Gano frowned, obviously trying to reconcile the mayhem he'd just seen with a YMCA class.

"Of course I am. I didn't have time to spend years studying one of the martial arts, so I took a few lessons from a guy with a concept he calls 'targeted fighting.' He teaches that you never fight if you can avoid it, but if someone intends to do you serious harm, maybe kill you, you use extreme tactics to disable him before he can react. Back on that street in Astoria, nonviolence wasn't going to cut it, so I used targeted fighting."

Gano gave a low whistle. "Rough stuff. Never seen anything like it."

"I tried to get them to walk away."

"Right now, they're damn sure wishing they had."

"I wish they had too. I'm still against using violence, but when your life is at stake, or the life of someone you love, it may be the only way. My commitment to nonviolence was just an untested principle until Juarez. That forced me to get realistic. I did some serious damage to those guys, and I feel bad about that. Honestly, I worry that using a skill like that successfully will make it too easy to use it the next time." What he wouldn't say to Gano, could barely admit to himself, was how much that fight made him think of his own mortality. If he'd been a fraction of a second slow in disarming the guy with the switch blade, or if the bartender had gotten in a lucky shot, he and Gano would likely be dead in that Astoria back street.

Gano looked bemused by his candor. "So, Jackpot, you're a caveman just like the rest of us. You know, you look pretty much the same as you did three years ago—maybe a little gray in your sideburns, lost a few pounds from working your ass off—but you've changed. You step up to trouble faster, take more risks." Gano gave him an appraising look. He had to be wondering whether, if there were a next time, how far Jack would go.

Chapter 26

July 27
12:30 p.m.
San Francisco

"HERE YOU ARE, Debra, panini sandwiches from Joe DiMaggio's Chop House. Perfect for an al fresco lunch." Jack set the tray, also loaded with cheese, fruit, and two bottles of San Pellegrino mineral water, on the trestle table.

He'd chosen Washington Square because North Beach held good memories for him. He'd come here often as a student for cheap pasta dinners and wine where no one checked IDs. The Beat Generation—Kerouac, Ginsberg, Ferlinghetti, and the rest—were long gone, but the place was still alive with fetching female artists in black leggings. Elderly Italian men in dark suits played bocce ball in the afternoon sun and reminisced about the old country. The way things had been going, he needed the good vibes.

He sat facing Debra and, behind her, Saints Peter and Paul Church. He was ready to tell her about the stress-packed hours he'd just gone through. He started with the trip to Ironbound and the encounter with Renatus and the amazing DNA sequencing system he had assembled.

"Why would he show you his laboratory?"

"Can't tell with Renatus. He wasn't trying to impress. He doesn't care what we think. Maybe he just wanted to get rid of us without having a confrontation." He shrugged. "But he refused to tell us why he'd set up the lab. Anyway, after he let us walk through the spooky old lodge, he kicked us out. When we flew back to Astoria, I wanted to see the processing plant, so we approached from upriver and saw all hell breaking loose."

"You picked a heck of a time. The news said Astoria was hit by a minor tidal wave."

"Not so minor. It was a wall of water at least ten feet high that tore up the waterfront. The epicenter of the quake that caused it was somewhere near Chaos. Given what we know about methane hydrate in the area of the platform and the clathrate bomb hypothesis, and those structures on the seabed we couldn't identify, I'm sure that quake was caused by Renatus and Barbas."

"I want to agree, but I'm not there yet."

"I'll keep at it until I convince you. Anyway, Gano and I flew back to Astoria and met with Molly McCoy, who was badly shaken by the destruction. After I told her why I was sure Barbas had caused the tidal wave, she told us about the tension in Astoria that started building after Barbas took over. I asked her to give me the names of Astoria people who work on the platform and might give me information about Barbas. She's thinking it over. I'll call her later today."

"You're lucky you got in and out of Astoria with no trouble. You told me some of the locals were pretty hostile last time you were there."

"Some still are." He didn't like withholding anything, but telling her about the attack on the way to the airport might cause an eruption that would throw them off track.

"You were both crazy to go back there. Anyway, we need to talk about reality on our own waterfront. I'm fed up with Simms sending phony renters to poke around our office during business hours. They upset our clients and our lawyers. And those 'unexplained' power outages that shut us down twice? That was Simms, too." Her voice was bitter. "With Barbas behind him, Simms thinks he's invincible." She turned away to glance at an ambulance screaming past on Columbus Avenue.

She turned back. "When we agreed to file a lawsuit against Armstrong, we knew it could generate serious push-back, but that's all the hostility we can handle right now. We can't take on Barbas too. You have to ease up, at least for a while."

"There's no time. Besides, as long as I'm after him even a little bit, Barbas will come after me. It's all or nothing. Someone has to stand up to him. I'm that someone."

"You're also the 'someone' who brought in big clients, won big cases, and earned big fees. That's why we took the risk of quadrupling our payroll. But lately, instead of being the rainmaker, you're calling in enemy fire on us. This firm is at a tipping point. You step up, or we go under." She regarded him for a long moment. "Don't you care anymore?"

He didn't miss the subtext in her question. She meant "Don't you care about *me* anymore?"

"Of course I do, but I can't let Barbas go ahead. I just need a few days. After that, I'll get the firm, and us, back on track. I promise." Something in his wiring was driving him forward. At the same time, he felt guilty for not protecting Debra and their team. He had to find a way to get them through this together.

"I know who you are," she said, standing, "so I understand. I honestly do. I'm doing my share to keep our firm afloat. If I have to do your share too, I'll do that. Right now, we don't have anything else to talk about."

He saw sadness in her eyes before she turned and walked away, head up, back stiff. It hurt deeply that she was so disappointed in him.

Let Barbas run loose? Lose the firm? Lose Debra? I won't accept any of that, but I have to make choices.

Seconds later, Gano walked up to the table. "Your assistant told me you were here, but I wasn't about to barge in." He sat where Debra had been. "Couldn't help overhearing. By the way, you ever thought about a Dale Carnegie course?" He pointed to the panini. "Goin' to eat that?" He wolfed down an untouched sandwich and hacked slices off a cylinder of Caciotta cheese, eating fast as though the food might be taken away any moment. "So is your firm still getting flack over taking the Armstrong case?"

"We are, which is why the plaintiffs couldn't find any other law firm that would touch the case. The defense contractors' lobby has greased so many clever exemptions through Congress that interpretation of the law could go either way. I'm not going into it right now, but I have a plan."

"Let's see, you have a secret plan to be revealed later that will keep Strider & Vanderberg from ending up like Custer's Last Stand. Is that it?"

"I don't need your sarcasm. Barbas, Drake, and Renatus have conflicting goals, but they all revolve around one hydrothermal vent. Obviously, Barbas's track record of environmental destruction sets off alarm bells, but what if energy from methane hydrate could end dependence on coal and oil? What if using it could slow or reverse climate change? Drake's goal is to understand the origin of life on Earth. Problem is that he's willing to kill to do that. I don't know why Renatus is so focused on the HTV, but he's as fanatical as the other two. All of them will try to run over me to get what they want."

Gano looked at the Pellegrino with distaste and said, "I'm just a simple Louisiana boy, so I'm wondering what I'm doing here, especially cuz I'm not the guy you need for climbing up or diving down. Maybe it's time for me to head back to Copper Canyon and make some real money. And maybe"—he gave Jack a sharp look—"you should step aside and call in Seal Team 6. Let someone else carry the load of stomping Barbas's ass."

"I can't get Seal Team 6 to suit up because, so far, Barbas has committed no crime I can prove. In fact, he's pumped hundreds of millions into the economy. He's what some politicians love to call a 'job creator.' To the international media, he's a rock star. No one else is going to confront him until it's too late."

"So you're going to mount up all your associate lawyers and form a posse?"

"They didn't sign on for that, but I have other resources. Drake has a ship and a sub and is willing to help me take on Barbas. And Molly McCoy can help . . . if she will."

Gano stopped idly scanning women strolling across the Square. "Molly, yeah, she's a sweetheart. Wouldn't mind seeing her again." His eyes narrowed. "But you picked up on that already, so now you're using her as a hook to keep me in the game."

"Of course, because now that Barbas is more on guard it will be harder to get inside information. That's where Molly comes in."

Gano reluctantly took a swig of Pellegrino. "All you're likely to get in Astoria is your head busted, so I guess I better tag along. You know, YOLO."

"What's that?"

"You need to get out more. It means 'You only live once.' But I have one question, Chief. Deep down, you think you can stop this guy?"

"I don't know." He realized his honesty surprised Gano. "Don't look so damned shocked. No one is ever who you think they are."

Chapter 27

July 27
6:30 p.m.
San Francisco

"SHE *MUST* BE here," Jack said, "I'm looking at our schedule. It shows her in the office all day."

"But she's not here, sir."

Jack wanted to deal with the flare-up in Washington Square. Debra was far too important to him to let it fester between them.

"Do you know where she is?"

"She asked me to book her on the next flight to Portland. There was one leaving in an hour and a half, so she left immediately to pack and head for SFO."

"Do we have a client in Portland?"

"I can look that up, but she's not staying in Portland."

"For God's sake, where is she?"

"I booked her to the regional airport in Astoria."

Astoria? She had no business reason to go there, and she knew he and Gano had left some hostile feelings behind. Then he thought of a reason. That's where she'd go to fly to the Chaos platform. But that would be crazy. Why would she—it didn't matter why. He called her cell phone. Not in service. He waited five minutes and tried again. Same thing. Alarmed, he consulted a file for a different phone number. After a long delay, Petros Barbas answered.

"Before you say a word, Jack, I want you to know I'm sorry our parting was . . . uncomfortable. I overreacted to your interest in my affairs. No hard feelings, I hope."

You're trying to destroy my law firm, and you hope I don't have hard feelings? It was obvious that Barbas's fake apology was another build-up to get him to contact Gorton.

"Forget it. I'm calling about my partner."

"Ms. Vanderberg. Yes, I remember her with great fondness."

He almost flared up but held it back. "She's on her way to Chaos."

"Is she?"

"The only way out there is on your helo, and that requires your permission."

"Question is, Jack, does she have *your* permission?"

"She doesn't need it, but I want to talk with her."

"She's not here."

Is he lying? "If that's true, she must be on the helo. Turn it around and send it back to Astoria."

"I don't see why you're upset. Chaos isn't as luxurious as my mega- yacht, but I can still offer decent hospitality to my special guests."

Jack had a good idea of what Barbas's hospitality was like. He pictured the young women on the schooner. "I'm telling you, send her back right away."

"Or what? You'll come out here on a white horse to rescue her? That wouldn't be wise." Barbas's tone had turned ugly. "Because of certain events that occurred after your first visit here, I've made this place a fortress. Look, Jack, I offered to make all your problems go away if you would just do one simple favor for me."

He waited for Barbas to continue, wishing they were in the same room so he could punch his lights out.

"All you had to do was get President Gorton to make a few calls on my behalf. That would have cost you nothing. Don't bother to figure out what to say, Jack. I won't believe you anyway. So we'll just let this play out. By tomorrow, I think you'll help me in any way I want." Barbas hung up.

He'd seldom been in a situation where someone else held every high card. He tried again to reach Debra on her cell phone. No answer. Either they had confiscated it, or she was refusing to talk with him.

Barbas hadn't admitted she was coming to Chaos. If she did, was he enough of a sociopath to try to rape her? Lock her up? Hold her as a hostage? He couldn't get aboard Chaos on his own. Law enforcement wouldn't butt in even if it had jurisdiction—which it didn't. Protecting Debra was up to him. At least he had one important ally to call on.

"THIS IS JACK STRIDER. I need to talk with Steve Drake. It's urgent." He hoped Drake would have an idea of how to get Debra off Chaos.

"Don Bradley here. I saw you come aboard *Challenger* a week or so ago. Got you coffee. Remember?"

"I do. Is Steve there?"

"He and Lou Potter took *Pegasus* for a deep dive."

"Where did he go?"

"I'm not allowed to say."

"When will he be back?"

"Since you know Steve, I guess it's okay to tell you we lost communications with him two hours ago, and he's overdue. All we can do is maintain our location. If he hasn't lost his guidance equipment, he'll know where to find us. If something more serious went wrong, well, we're all damn worried."

"Are you near Barbas's platform?

"About ten miles south of it, which seems to be okay with those damned hornets he sends to stake us out."

"Don't go any closer. Barbas is in a mood to shoot."

"Thanks for the heads up. We've had enough of that."

Obviously, Drake had made another dive to *his* HTV. He was such a pro he wouldn't make a mistake, so something had gone wrong. Communications equipment failure? Isopods? Or Barbas might have programmed robots to attack *Pegasus.* Then the obvious hit him.

"Don, did *Challenger*'s sensors detect an earthquake in the last few hours?"

"Sure did."

"No tsunami?"

"Nothing. Why?"

"Doesn't matter. Please ask Steve to contact me as soon as he shows up."

"Will do."

When he and Drake had gone down together, *Pegasus* had taken quite a buffeting from a small quake. He'd said later that an underwater quake doesn't send a force radiating in concentric circles from a central point. It's more like a shaped charge that explodes in one direction and doesn't become a wave until miles away. So the quake Don reported might have had no effect on *Pegasus.* But if it had disabled *Pegasus*, her air supply would run out before anyone knew where she was.

Chapter 28

July 27
9:30 p.m.
Chaos platform

PETROS GAZED WITH satisfaction around his private suite three levels above the Chaos platform's main deck. Most of the furnishings were rosewood, walnut, or cherry, but he'd added a tall lattice made of fragrant agarwood from Bhutan and Homeric statues carved from Japanese keyaki. His work table was made from planks of fiddleback maple retrieved from a sunken clipper. There were models of his yacht and fleet of tankers in twenty-four-carat gold. The sound system and the cameras concealed in the corners were highest quality, as was the view through floor-to-ceiling one-way windows along both sides of the main salon. In some ways, he preferred this suite to his private club located between two embassies in the Kolonaki district in Athens.

He looked out the window again, watching for the arrival of the helo bringing Debra Vanderberg to Chaos. Odd that he was so eager. He'd had other women flown out from time to time, but a stunning woman closer to his own status turned him on.

He wondered again why she'd decided to come. Plenty of beautiful women had sought invitations to Chaos. Every one of them had claimed to want him, and everyone wanted something more. So what did Debra want? Sex? Money? A peace treaty? Unfortunately, knowing he was behind the attack on her law firm might make her a little prickly.

Regardless, he'd get a good lay without too much hassle. The fact that Strider was infuriated about her coming made him smile. That was the point. More than the sex, this was about humiliating Strider. He doubted the guy was tough enough to cause him a problem. Very few men were.

Maybe Debra would even turn out to be a good omen, a turning point in his fortunes. An old joke described a yacht as a hole in the water into which its owner poured money. What wasn't funny was that the Chaos Project was a hole the size of the Grand Canyon that was sucking the life out of his empire. The cash flow from the gold and silver deposits was barely keeping it afloat. Only he and Renatus knew that the deposits had begun playing out. Even if another giant HTV existed and Renatus found it, he couldn't afford to move his platform and start over. That meant his gamble on methane hydrate had to pay off fast.

Testing Renatus's extraction schemes had been expensive and futile. His most recent, applying an intermittent heat source directly to the methane hydrate deposits, had been the most promising—except that it still had major drawbacks. The first experiment had released a burst of methane that blew out the capture mechanisms and escaped as a huge "burp." Several more attempts had triggered small earthquakes.

He'd ordered Renatus to increase the scale of the attempt earlier today. The methane captured had been sizable, but the quake that followed had launched a minor tsunami. Another failure.

In the beginning, he'd agreed to finance Renatus's personal project having something to do with the HTV, but Renatus had already far exceeded the estimated cost. If Renatus had been producing, he would have ignored it. Instead, it was one more squeeze on his cash flow, pushing him toward bankruptcy.

Lately, Renatus had acted as though the HTV was untouchable. That was a laugh. What he wouldn't know until it was too late was that the Chaos Project was going to exploit the HTV itself. Fluids driven out of the top of the HTV's chimney at 700° F cooled very quickly in the near-freezing ocean. But, captured in a pressurized environment, that heat would produce steam to drive turbines and create electricity. It would be an eternal source of energy. If necessary to fully exploit the HTV's output, he intended to shatter its chimney and drive equipment deep into its core. If he had to, he'd detonate explosives in its bowels to release its full potential.

If the primitive life forms it nourished were wiped out, that would be an acceptable price of doing business. Nothing new about that. The U.S. military frequently detonated explosives, maybe even nuclear weapons, underwater that they knew would kill all marine life in the area—and they went ahead. Some of the scientists who set off the first atomic bomb feared it might ignite a chain reaction that would destroy the planet—and they went ahead. The people who started up the Hadron supercollider in Switzerland in 2008 might have triggered a runaway reaction—and they went ahead. They all took big risks to achieve big goals. That's what he intended to do.

Thinking of Renatus, he was fed up. The day after Renatus's solution for extracting methane worked, he'd exile him from the platform. If he complained or threatened, well, accidents happened on platforms.

The law of the jungle was in his DNA. He was always the hunter, never the prey. He had learned to fight for everything, and never show weakness. When he felt wronged, he took revenge. Some people prevailed because of formidable physical strength, others because of a brilliant mind. He had both, plus overwhelming will power. He was feared and envied, but never loved.

He recalled the time a woman had asked what he was afraid of. He'd scoffed and sent her away, but he'd never forgotten her question. Very rarely, in the nucleus of his being, he was afraid that if he let down even once, he'd be torn apart. He'd never admit it, but that was his core fear.

He saw on his monitor that the helo was landing. Debra didn't know it yet, but in the next few minutes she would decide Strider's fate—and her own.

Chapter 29

July 27
10:00 p.m.
Chaos platform

HE HEARD HIS Indian steward knock softly on the door. *About damn time.* He had no idea what to expect from Debra, but a lot of women had come through that door. He'd prepared for Debra the same way he had for most of them.

"Send her in."

When Debra walked into the room, he felt the same jolt as when she'd come aboard the schooner in Sausalito. What was so captivating about her? Her green eyes projected intelligence and self-confidence. Her long ebony hair flowed down over a form-fitting leather peacoat. She stopped just inside the door.

"I'm glad you're here, Debra. I haven't had a chance to tell you before, but I see you for who you really are. Not just Strider's law partner. You're incredibly talented in your own right. I get that."

What he'd "gotten" long ago was that a woman wanted a man to see all her strengths as she saw them herself. Playing that tune had worked for him many times. Her eyes told him he'd caught her by surprise.

"Thanks. It's nice to get together without the others around."

When she unzipped the peacoat, he stepped behind her, took it from her shoulders, and laid it across a chair near the door. He appreciated the way the fine cashmere of her pale gray cardigan defined her curves. The sweater had eight flowering roses made of coiled ribbons across the front, and the buttons were jeweled.

The fact that she had come to Chaos alone showed courage—or was it some weakness he would exploit as soon as he figured out what it was? He studied her for any sign of hostility but saw none.

He gestured at a small table between two Italian black leather chairs set at right angles to each other with a southerly view across the starlit ocean.

"I had my chef prepare a few *hors d'oeuvres*. But first, I'll get drinks for both of us. I'm having Metaxa brandy. Perhaps you'd like ouzo or retsina?"

"Nothing, thanks."

"Oh, I insist. Maybe a nice Vin Santo from Santorini?" It was a small test of wills. Was she willing to offend him in the first two minutes?

"Vin Santo then—as long as you'll join me and have the same."

"No. I prefer the brandy."

"Then nothing for me," she said, taking a seat and turning to look into the dark night.

"I'm forgetting my Greek hospitality. Of course I'll join you."

He poured the wine, handed her one of the glasses, and sat on her right.

She took it and said, "It's an ancient Scottish custom for us to exchange glasses." She extended hers to him.

The bitch. She suspected him of spiking her drink. He was amused that she thought he'd do something so obvious. They made the exchange and he raised his glass. "Now a Greek custom. We drink the first glass at once and pour the second." He drained his.

She took only a sip, "I hope we can work through the disagreement between us. It started when you pressured Jack to get President Gorton to make sure the Senate does not ratify the Law of the Sea treaty."

"True."

"And he refused."

"Not outright, but he was stringing me along, planning to refuse later. I'll just have to handle it another way. No big deal." *Like hell.*

"It was a big enough deal that you fired our firm, bought our building, and hired Stan Simms to have the offices adjoining ours 'renovated.' Jackhammers and pneumatic nailers pounding away all day long. We can't think, much less deal with clients. That's harassment. Even after we get an injunction, Simms will try something else."

He refilled his glass. She'd be even more steamed if she knew he'd told Simms to do a lot more than harass her firm. "I can see that's a problem all right. Your people must be damned angry at Strider for bringing all that on the firm."

She gave him a hard look. "They're angry all right—at you, especially for having Simms serve us with an eviction notice. You're trying to put us out of business."

Now he knew why she was here. "We'll talk about your firm, maybe come to some agreement, but first let's calm down. Finish your wine and we'll sample these *hors d' oeuvres.* If we don't, my chef will be devastated. This Barbajuan," he pointed, "is better than they make in Monaco. I'm sure you recognize this veal Carpaccio. Here are Thai dumplings stuffed with crab meat, cream cheese, and garlic. Next, Caspian Sea Beluga Caviar. And this last one is Saganaki, a Greek favorite. It's fried cheese, so it's very high calorie."

He popped a Saganaki into his mouth, beamed, and looked at her expectantly. The odds were four to one against her. After being wrong in worrying about a spiked drink, she'd never suspect that he'd ordered the chef to lace every one of the *hors d' oeuvres*—except the Saganaki that he'd steered her away from—with rohypnol, the date-rape drug. She'd lose her inhibitions and quickly become vulnerable to everything he'd planned. Later, she'd be incapacitated. He'd done this many times before, filming it all, and knew she'd wake up thinking she had a hangover, with no memory of what he'd done to her.

She looked at each, chose the Carpaccio on a thin slice of toast and raised it to her lips, then set it on the corner of the silver service plate and took a sip of wine. "You're right. We're all better off if we talk this through. After all, we know much more about your operation than you realize."

Something in her tone made that sound slightly ominous. "What do you mean?"

"When you became our client, I did quite a bit of research to find out about Odyssey Properties, your holding company, and this drilling project—everything we might need to help you. My research included a database that reports contacts with government agencies. A very interesting fact popped out. Quite some time ago, you filed an application with the Department of the Interior to get an exclusive license to exploit a section of the seafloor. That's what I want to talk about."

Holy shit! He hadn't known such a database existed and certainly hadn't expected her to find out about his application. "That application is meaningless."

"No it isn't. What caught my attention was that it applies to an area *inside* the U.S. two-hundred-mile continental boundary. Since Chaos is located well *outside* that limit, your application must not have anything to do with your mining operation." She gave him a bright smile as though she were sharing a funny story. "Not only is that application still alive, meaning you continue to want it granted, but you recently amended it to expand it to twenty miles square. That's four hundred square miles of ocean floor inside the two-hundred-mile limit. Of course the reason you want that license is to exclude competitors but, I kept asking myself, why *that* area?"

He took a deliberately slow sip of wine—now he needed that brandy. No way she could know the answer to her question, but the fact that she'd asked it alarmed him. He'd badly underestimated her, but what he had in mind would shut her up.

"Must have been something my lawyers did without notifying me," he said, trying to sound indifferent.

"Not likely. As of yesterday, your application hadn't been approved or rejected. It's hung up in bureaucratic limbo. Since you didn't ask Jack for help, you must be counting on a political fix. Maybe you have a congressman you think can get to Harry Sneed, Secretary of the Interior. Or maybe you plan to bribe him directly. Either of those strategies can land you in jail. That would be foolish since I know a better way to get what you want. I have a proposal for you." She leaned forward, scanned the *hors d' oeuvres*, and picked up a square of the cheese-filled Saganaki. She swallowed it in two bites, leaned back, and crossed her arms.

She was watching him closely, trying to read his thoughts. That was *his* game. He didn't like her turning it on him.

"Naturally, I'd never do anything illegal, but, out of curiosity, what's your 'better way'?"

This time her smile looked genuine. Of course it was. She'd scored a hit.

"Here's a hypothetical," she said. "Suppose there's a mid-level bureaucrat at Interior who makes licensing recommendations to Secretary Sneed. He knows Sneed is opposed to a certain application, but if the bureaucrat publically recommends granting that application, it would probably force Sneed to go along. Now what would motivate that hypothetical bureaucrat to do that?"

He should have expected this. She was as venal as everyone else.

"The bureaucrat would want a big payoff. So you're here to shake me down for a bribe and probably something for you as well."

She wrinkled her nose. "Don't be ridiculous. Now imagine that bureaucrat had gone to law school with someone he wanted to please. Can you picture that scenario?"

Could she really get his application granted? That would change everything. She had no idea how important that license was to him. Her direct gaze and the set of her mouth made him think she was telling the truth. But that only meant she *could* do it, not that she would.

"Here are my terms," she said, her voice firm. "No harassment. No bad-mouthing Jack, me, or the firm. More than anything, no eviction."

He had been, as she'd guessed, planning to try to bribe Secretary Sneed, but he had a bad feeling it would go wrong. Her offer was by far his best chance. "I accept your terms. I'll call off Simms and have him quash the eviction. Let me know how much hypothetical money it will take."

"You understand this would be illegal, right?"

"I understand it's the way I've succeeded in business all around the world. This investment will be peanuts compared to what I paid in France for—never mind."

"Then we have a deal." She picked up one of the Thai dumplings.

Uh oh. If she swallowed a dose of rohypnol now, the deal would be screwed. He was about to snatch it away when she sniffed it and said, "This smells as if the crab may be a little off. You should warn your chef." She set it down.

"Warn him? I'll fire the bastard."

She picked up a wafer and reached for the Beluga caviar.

He held up a warning hand. "If the crab meat is bad, some of the others might be too. Maybe it's something in the kitchen."

The scornful look she gave him and her tiny smile said it all. She knew exactly what he'd tried to do. That stung more than if she had slapped his face. He'd let his guard down, thinking of her as a piece of ass when she was a cobra all along. She'd made a fool of him.

As if reading his mind, Debra said, "Now that we have a deal, I'm ready to go back."

"Not yet. I want to make sure you understand that doing business with me is very serious. I listened to your hypothetical. Now you listen to a story that took place on the docks of Piraeus, the port near Athens."

She stood. "We're done. I'm leaving."

He slammed his fist on the table. "Sit down. My steward locked that door. You're going nowhere." He realized he was shouting and hated her for provoking him. But, even though she was insulting him, he needed her.

Debra sat but her face was dark.

"Not long ago, a ship owner was using that port on a regular basis. He paid the customary bribes to the old-school Sicilian who controlled the dockworkers. The Sicilian was a brutal man, but away from the docks, his family and appearances meant everything to him. Even tried to dress like a banker. Always had his kids with him."

"What's your point?"

"One day, the Sicilian got too greedy and doubled the vig he demanded. The ship owner offered a reasonable compromise. Instead of taking it, the Sicilian had two of the ship owner's men beaten almost to death. The next day, the Sicilian's right-hand man disappeared. That damned Sicilian still refused to make a deal. Then two of his dockworkers disappeared. He hired more and still wouldn't bend."

Debra wasn't smiling. "Let me guess. The Sicilian disappeared."

"Too obvious. The ship owner went after something so important to the Sicilian that losing it would make him give in."

"And you're going to tell me what it was," she said sarcastically.

"The Sicilian's youngest daughter, the princess of his family, had enrolled at a private college in Rome. The ship owner seduced her. He could have sent somebody, but he did it himself. She broke with her parents and moved onto his yacht. Videos of her having sex started showing up on the Internet."

He could tell Debra was thinking, remembering.

"She's the young blond I saw at the auction," she said, "and on the schooner."

"That's right, so don't miss the point of my story. Killing the law firm you care so much about is a taste of what will happen if you are conning me."

"Just remember to call off your dogs before close of business tomorrow."

"I'll call off my dogs after Secretary Sneed issues that license, not before." Her lips parted slightly. She hadn't expected that.

She frowned. "Do it now, or my hypothetical friend will make sure you never get a license for anything from Interior."

He had a sour taste in his mouth. Time for gloves off. He stood and leaned over her, fists on the arms of her chair. "I can keep you here as long as I want. And don't give me some bullshit story about how you left your itinerary with the coast guard who will come zooming out here to find you." He straightened and glowered at her. "If you're thinking you'll get back to the mainland and tell how you were held captive, forget it. You thought you could con me like I was some dumb dockworker. After you got what you came for, you'd stall and come up with excuses. You and Jack would sit around and mock me. Well, none of that is going to happen. The things I'm about to do to you are things you won't ever want anyone to find out about, especially Jack Strider. Look at the black domes on the ceiling and in the corners. Those are cameras that will record you crawling into my bedroom with your bare ass sticking up. In there, other equipment will capture the restraints, the whip, everything, including every scream and moan you make."

She didn't look frightened, but she soon would. He was getting hot thinking about it.

"Sounds like we'll both have home movies to show," she said. "You've been starring in one ever since I walked in here. I'm wired."

"You're lying. Everyone who comes to this suite is searched. My men would have found a wire if you were wearing one."

"Sure, if it were the kind of wire you see in TV cop shows. Maybe they didn't look close enough after I told them that if they groped me even once you'd have them beaten to a pulp." She tapped one of the coiled roses on her left breast. "This has a micro-receiver. It recorded all your schemes and confessions—and threats. The top rose on this other side has been filming you."

"That's impossible. Those flowers are too small." He shoved her back into the chair, and grabbed the top rose. He felt the wire and metal inside. Tugging at the second rose tore open the front of her cashmere cardigan, exposing her black bra and full breasts. *Son of a bitch.* They *were* electronic devices of some kind.

"You've made a stupid mistake," he said. "After I smash these, you won't have a record of anything—but I will."

"You're such a retro fool. Those transmitters have been streaming to a satellite and then to my office. What's been sent already will make you a laughingstock, a clubhouse punch line. If I'm back on schedule tomorrow, the entire record stays in my office. If I'm not, it will automatically be forwarded to the San Francisco police department and to Jack. You'll be handcuffed the first time you set foot on the mainland, and Jack will find a way to get out here."

Blood roared through his brain. He jerked her to her feet and ripped off the cardigan. If she was lying about the streaming, he'd have the camera and recorder. But he knew she'd told the truth because the recording equipment was her lifeline.

She suddenly grabbed his right wrist. He tried to jerk away, but she got it behind his back, spun him and shoved him into the bulletproof window. His cheekbone hit hard, and his head snapped back. As he tried to turn toward her, his feet got tangled up. He went down on his butt. Before he got his feet under him, he saw the silver tray of *hors d'oeuvres* flying at him. He got his hands up too late and felt the caviar splash into his face and the other food soak his velvet jacket.

Her face was flushed, her eyes narrow. "If you want more," she hissed, "get your ass up. I'll take you out so fast you'll think there were three of me."

Seeing her karate stance, he knew she wasn't lying about this either.

"No?" She straightened and said, "I didn't think so."

She pulled on her leather peacoat and banged on the door. The steward opened it, eyes widening when he saw the wreckage and his master on the floor in a rage. Then he saw the look in Debra's eyes and stepped quickly out of her way.

Chapter 30

July 28
7:00 a.m.
San Francisco

FOR HOURS, FRUSTRATION and anger had chased themselves through Jack's psyche. He paced, unable to concentrate, wanting a stiff scotch but holding off. He'd need all his wits in case bad news broke. Sometime after midnight, he called Barbas again. The call went unanswered. He left yet another message on Debra's phone. If she ever got his messages, she'd know how worried he was and call him immediately. He walked into the den, flipped on HBO, and stretched out on the couch to pass the time with Klaus Kinski and Claudia Cardinale in *Fitzcarraldo*. The story of a man in Brazil obsessively committed to achieving something everyone thought was impossible suited his mood.

He tried to stay awake, but stress had worn him down, and he drifted in and out of sleep for a couple of hours. The sound of the front door closing woke him. He scrambled to his feet.

Debra entered the den, stopped, and dropped her small overnight bag. She looked exhausted. Somewhere in his left brain he wanted to shout at her, but he didn't say a word as he raced across the room and smothered her in a hug. She buried her face in his shoulder and took one deep breath after another, as if coming to the surface after too long under.

"Thank heaven you're safe," he finally said quietly. "I've been so worried."

She said his name and tossed her peacoat onto a chair. He didn't remember seeing the shirt she was wearing before. Maybe something she picked up in the airport. Then she reached behind her back to unhook her bra. In seconds they got him out of his clothes and tumbled onto the couch. She threw herself on him with kisses and passion more fierce than they'd shared in months.

The flood of relief that she was safely home translated into insatiable excitement. They communicated with sounds and touches without words until they fell asleep in each other's arms, exhausted.

WITH EARLY SUN shining through the bedroom's tall east-facing windows, Debra walked toward him, glowing from a hot shower, gloriously naked except for the turban-like wrap around silky hair in a twirl behind her neck. She tossed the turban toward a chair and climbed back into his high king-sized bed. They lay silently together, reveling in each other.

Then the phone started ringing. He ignored the calls, but they broke the magic spell, so he got up and made Jamaican Blue Mountain coffee and returned to bed with two mugs and a handful of ginger snap cookies.

After a few sips, he pushed himself up on the pillows and said, "Let's start at the beginning. You scared the hell out of me by going to Chaos."

"I was mad when I left you yesterday in Washington Square. Back in the office, I got a call from Barbas. He was very sweet and told me we could work out a way to stop the friction between us."

"And you believed that?"

"Of course not. He's always going to do only what he thinks is best for him. But his call gave me an idea, so I accepted. I didn't expect you to be worried, because I didn't think you'd find out before I got back. There was no real downside."

"You mean like him trying to get you in the sack?"

"Are you saying you don't trust me?"

"It's him I don't trust."

"Jack Strider, I believe you're green-eyed jealous. That's sweet. Now get over it. Okay, when I walked into his would-be Playboy Mansion, there was a cloud of testosterone in the air, but I wasn't worried. Besides, I was wearing a micro-camera and transmitter I got from that private detective we hire from time to time. Worked better than a Kevlar chastity belt. Because of what I'd already recorded and transmitted back to the mainland, I knew he wouldn't dare touch me."

"You could have been very wrong. That guy thinks he's all-powerful. He doesn't worry about consequences. You had no right to do something that dangerous without discussing it with me first."

She put her hand on his forearm. "Before you get too righteous, keep in mind that you've taken off on dangerous wild goose chases more than once recently without discussing them with me in advance."

"So what was your plan that was going to persuade him to let the firm alone? And maybe get him to shut down Chaos at the same time?"

"Please don't be sarcastic. I told him I had something to trade that he wants very badly. I'm not sure why, but it probably has to do with methane hydrate."

She filled him in on what she'd learned about Barbas's application for an exclusive license to exploit a vast area of seabed. "I offered to get him that license."

"You can actually do that?" She kept surprising him.

"Of course not, but I gave him such a good story that he agreed to call off Simms."

"But when the license doesn't show up—"

"We won't have to wait until them. When I was about to leave without giving in to his heavy breathing, he refused to ground Simms until *after* Interior grants the license. To be honest, now I'm afraid he'll tell Simms to ratchet up the pressure to give me incentive to do what I said I could."

That thought had occurred to him. He hadn't commented on it because she had just taken a huge risk—whether she thought so or not.

"Actually," he said, "we don't have to worry about that application. If I'm right about what he's doing, I have to stop him before the application is acted on."

She didn't reply, but he knew how disturbed she was. They were at an impasse. He couldn't let go of the fear he'd felt and the humiliation of having to ask Barbas to send her back. And he was right about how dangerous Barbas was. She was equally certain that what she'd done was not only reasonable but essential. What it came down to was that they both thought they were right, and they were both stubborn as mules.

He turned to face her and took her hands in his. "We're both trying our damndest to fix everything. You've been fighting to save our castle, the firm. I've been going far away to try to slay the dragons. But working separately, we're about to fail. And your trip to Chaos reminded me that I care more for you than for anything else on this planet."

"So let's have a do-over. Fresh start. Work together."

He felt a weight lift off his chest. "Exactly, be a team again. So I'll make an offer. One more dive with Drake could give me enough proof to bring the authorities down on Barbas . . . somehow. I need to fight the dragon for four more days. After that I'll be one hundred percent on the Armstrong case and defending and building the firm."

She beamed. "Welcome back, partner. I'll go to court this morning and charge Barbas with breaching his covenant of quiet enjoyment of the premises. Asserting irreparable damage might get us a temporary restraining order. But we don't have to go to the office quite yet, right?" She nuzzled behind his ear.

His cell phone rang. He answered reluctantly. "Yes, Mei, what's up? . . . I can hardly hear you. Please speak up . . . Debra will have it stopped by noon . . . Go ahead . . . I'll call him right now." He turned back to Debra. "Steve Drake just called me at the office. I've been worried about him. When I called his ship last night, he was on a dive in *Pegasus*, and they were out of contact with him. They were afraid something bad had happened. I'll call him and put it on speaker."

Drake answered immediately. "Good news, Jack."

"The good news is that you're back aboard *Challenger*."

"Yeah, my boys got a little worried because I didn't check in. My transmitter went out, that's all. It's already fixed."

"You went back to Barbas's mining site?"

"Hell, no. Watching that damn machinery tear up everything is like watching my child being gnawed on by rats. I approached the HTV from the opposite direction. Then Lou and I spent hours collecting samples."

"What kind of samples?"

"Some of them look vaguely like crabs, shrimp, octopi, and starfish. Others are like patches of mesh and gauze strung together with flexible tubes, not like any marine life I've ever seen before. And we saw three weird species that were too big for *Pegasus* to collect."

"Analyzing all that will keep you busy for a while."

"There's more. I took *Pegasus* up to hover two hundred feet above the top of the cone and off to one side of the vent so I could capture samples of the fluid pouring out. More than ninety-five percent of what I brought back consists of microbes rising from deep inside. These life forms are going to prove my theory about the origin of life on Earth."

Drake was talking fast, still pumped about the results from the dive. Jack felt himself drawn into Drake's excitement. He glanced at Debra. She mouthed the words "origin of life," and her expression was dubious.

"It took longer than I expected because that vent is like a straight pipe from a blast furnace. I had to pull back every few minutes when we couldn't stand the heat. That's why I overstayed my plan."

"So after that, you went straight back to *Challenger*?" He tried to keep disappointment out of his voice.

"I knew you'd want me to take a look at that mutated drill site and that thing you called an 'Abrams tank on steroids.' I thought about going there, but I didn't. I was too eager to get all the life forms to *Challenger.* But don't worry. I'm not finished with Barbas. If I had some armed drones, I'd bomb the crap out of that platform. But I do have torpedoes. He'll find out how badly his platform floats with holes in its pontoons."

"You're still underestimating his defenses, Steve. To get the big-time help we need, I have to get back down there and take pictures of the operations located away from the mining site. As I said before, we need to join forces."

Long pause, then Drake said, "You admit Barbas was your client. You say he isn't now, but I have to ask myself whether you and I are really on the same side."

Chapter 31

July 28
1:00 p.m.
San Francisco

DEBRA KNEW THAT Simms had ordered the hammering, drilling, and sawing next door for the sole purpose of screwing up the work day of every lawyer in her firm. Just after noon, she'd gotten an injunction which Simms was ignoring. She'd been trying to grit it out, because no one in the firm had spare time to go back to court for enforcement.

But when the commotion next door drove swarms of agitated cockroaches into the offices, she had to take action. She called the building management firm and told them to send over whoever did pest control on the double.

For the past two hours, her high-priced, overworked lawyers had been racing from office to office spraying drugstore insecticide on excited hordes. At last, her assistant brought in a man in a lime green uniform that identified him as working for Candlestick Pest Control. He was a round man with slicked-down, thinning black hair, and eyes that looked as if they were permanently stinging from noxious spray.

"Pascal's my name, ma'am," he said, touching his name tag. "This here"—he gestured over his shoulder at a man in a Home Hardware cap who looked to be in his mid-thirties—"is Richard. They sent him to join me as a trainee. I'll have to drill into your walls, do some fumigating. It'll take a while. I'll tell your people when they have to leave a space."

The smell grew foul, and she imagined the air full of chemicals she didn't want to inhale. When she heard Pascal start working in her hallway, she decided to move to Jack's office, since he had already left for Astoria.

She walked into his office with an armful of file folders—and stopped cold. Richard, the trainee, was already there. He'd taken off his cap, and she saw that he was older than she'd thought, actually pretty old for a trainee. His hair was stylishly layered, he was freshly-shaven, and looked as if he'd had a recent manicure, all a sharp contrast with Pascal. Seeing her, he grabbed his cap and put it back on.

"I can do this space later, lady," he said in a gruff voice and picked up a leather satchel he'd set on Jack's desk.

She sensed something about him. "What were you using? I don't see any equipment."

"I was checking it out. Then I was going to tell"—he couldn't come up with Pascal's name—"the other guy what I needed."

That's when she saw the Stanford ring on his right hand. Her first reaction was that he'd bought or stolen it.

"You're wearing a Stanford class ring. What year did you graduate?"

His answer was quick. "Class of 1995."

"Who was the football coach that year?"

"Tyrone Willingham. Played in the Liberty Bowl in Memphis. Lost."

Correct, but maybe he was just a football fan, so she lobbed another question. "Who was Dean of Students?"

"Chris Griffin."

Okay, the guy had been a Stanford student who was now groomed like a banker. Her intuition was sounding a loud alarm. Whoever he was, he *wasn't* an exterminator.

He frowned. "What's this about, lady?" When she didn't answer, he didn't bother to bluff or even feign anger at her distrust. "I see we have a problem I have to take care of," he said softly.

He didn't look like he had a weapon on him, but there could be something in his satchel. He looked at the door behind her. She dropped her armful of file folders.

"All right, smart ass," he said softly, and lunged for her.

She kicked straight ahead into his shinbone. "*Argh.*" He bent to grab the pain with both hands. She swung back with her elbow to the side of his head. The contact made a sound like punching a watermelon. When his hands came up, she kicked him in the groin—but missed. She'd gotten too much thigh.

Instead of going down, he clawed up with his right hand and grabbed her shoulder. She brought her hand across fast and clamped onto his wrist. His arm was a bar when she drove into it with her left forearm and rammed him downward, with a classic karate takedown she'd practiced a thousand times. As he hit the hardwood floor face-first, she heard the ulna in his forearm snap. He screamed and writhed on the floor like a catfish out of water. She planted her knee on the back of his shoulder, stretched for the phone, and called 911.

His reaction to her questions told her she hadn't made a mistake, so she wanted to know why he was there. Keeping him pinned down with her foot, she reached for his satchel and opened it. It was a toolkit full of listening devices. Illegal bugs.

As soon as the cops interrogated him and offered him the traditional implicate-the-bigger-fish deal, she felt sure that Richard, or whatever his real name was, would finger Stan Simms. Then bye-bye baby.

Chapter 32

July 28
2:00 p.m.
Astoria

"SHE'S LIKE A peregrine falcon," Gano said.

"What are you talking about?" Jack asked.

Patting the instrument panel of his Cessna Skylane, Gano said, "This baby is as fast and maneuverable as a peregrine falcon, which she had to be one time in Nicaragua when—"

Jack saw the runway of the Astoria airport coming up fast. "Just concentrate on landing this thing so we can get in to talk with Molly."

"Don't blow your top, Jack-o'-lantern. I could play *Foggy Mountain Breakdown* on the banjo and land her at the same time."

Thirty minutes later, they'd secured the plane. Jack picked up a rental and headed for town. "You're sure she's going through with this?"

"Without a doubt," Gano said, "First, she didn't throw away the business card I left for her the night we met in her tavern. Second, she called me the morning after those four hooligans tried to take us out. Wanted me to know the cops said they had no proof it was set up by Barbas, but nothing like that happened before Barbas took over the town. She believes he turned ordinary locals into would-be assassins. Third, after I gave her a step-by-step on the connection between Barbas and the tsunami, she did her own Internet research. She's one hundred percent on board."

"So the silver-tongued bayou man wins again."

"Wasn't easy. She's asking two men to do something that will make some others call them traitors. She'll have them waiting for us in the tavern."

"Can we trust them?"

"We're trusting Molly."

He parked on the side street near the entrance to Molly's office. When they went in, Molly's face was tense as she stood behind her desk.

"Hey, Gano. Hi, Jack." She nodded to them to seat themselves in chairs to her left, nearest the door. The two men sitting in chairs to her right abruptly stopped talking.

"Jack and Gano are the two I told you guys about," she said. She jerked her thumb at a rangy man wearing a Portland Winterhawks Hockey Club cap and a sleeveless Gold's Gym T-shirt. At the end of his sinewy arms, both hands were lightly closed into fists. His narrow face looked mean, like a guy ready to pick a fight with anyone of any size.

"That's Pete. He's an electrician. I've known him ever since I moved back here." Then she looked at the other man, seated farther from her. "I don't know Heinz, but Pete said he should be here."

Heinz's face was purplish-red and his eyes were a little rheumy as if he'd stared too often into the sun or a bottle of Captain Morgan rum. About fifty years old, he wore black Levi's and a long-sleeved black shirt.

"Heinz is captain of *Palinouros*, one of Barbas's bulk carriers that transports ore from the platform to the mill." She sat and looked at Jack, clearly leaving it to him to make the next move.

"Gentlemen, I have a question. Why are you here?" He looked at Pete. "You, sir?"

"Simple. Molly asked me to be here." The look he gave Molly left no doubt that he had a crush on her. "She looked after her dad when he was dying, and she pours honest drinks. After she told us this shit, sorry Molly, about Barbas maybe killing Astoria with a tidal wave, I'm damn sure ready to hear about putting him out of business. Anyway, she vouched for you two. That's good enough for me."

The ship captain crossed his arms and showed no sign of answering Jack's question. Jack let the silence continue. Finally, the *Palinouros* captain said, "I took this job on a rusty old piece of crap going back and forth like a goddamn school bus because it was supposed to be a big payday. Well, it's not enough. When I told Mr. Barbas I wanted a raise, he just waved me out of his office like I was his room steward. Now Molly tells us you say Mr. Barbas might have caused a tsunami. Makes a good story, but maybe you don't know what you're talking about."

No one moved or spoke until Pete said, "Let's hear what you have to say."

"Barbas claims his platform exists only to mine valuable minerals and precious metals," Jack said. "Have either of you seen evidence he's doing more than that?"

"I've taken tons of equipment out there," Heinz said, "but I don't know what it's used for. All I take off is ore."

"I'm all over that platform doing electrical work," Pete said. "It's like a giant machine shop assembling components from crates of parts. Most of that work is done by Russians and Greeks, not locals. When they finish some contraption, a crane swings it over the side and lowers it to the bottom. Most of that gear is for our mining operation, but I've heard guys say that some of the stuff could be used for drilling or something else. They know better than to ask questions."

"Is anything brought up from the bottom besides the ore slurry?"

"Yeah, about a month ago a separate pipe started bringing up something else that's directed into a red building on the main deck. They put a guard on that building, a Russian with a face like a Kodiak bear. If I get within ten yards, he waves me away with an AA-12 semi-automatic shotgun. Three hundred rounds per minute pointed at me. I don't like that shit but . . ." He shrugged. "I'll see him around here some night when he ain't got that shotgun."

"Have you seen anything come out of that red building and go ashore?"

Pete thought for a few seconds. "In the last few weeks they've been bringing refrigerated containers from the red building and sending them ashore on the helo. Not many, and they're different from anything else we send on the helo."

"What do they look like?"

"Maybe four feet long, stainless steel, not all that heavy. All marked *Caution: frozen carbon monoxide.*"

It took only a second for Jack to make the connection. "Do you remember a brand name?"

"Mostly Thermo King, but some marked Triton."

Triton was the name he'd seen on the containers next to Building 3 on Ironbound Island. That connected the Chaos Project to Ironbound, with Renatus on both ends of that link.

"The other day," Heinz continued, "when the deck hands were loading two of the containers into the helo, I saw Barbas get in the face of his science guy—I never remember his name. Barbas kept pointing at the containers and shouting. Since then, I haven't seen the science guy at all."

"Have you asked anyone about him?"

"No one asks anyone anything out there. We used to get along there, maybe even better than on shore. Not anymore. A lot of people are fed up with their jobs, but we don't talk about that openly, because too many of our mates are what we call 'platform rats.' They're so addicted to the money they'd turn on us in a heartbeat. We also have to watch out for the mercenaries who have worked for Barbas all over the world as personal guards. The Greeks and Russians he brought in as technicians and supervisors never speak English, but some of them seem to understand us pretty good. They're Barbas's eyes and ears." He glanced at Heinz as if maybe he was wondering about him. "A few days ago, I had to go to Command Central, a secure room on the 02 level, to repair a switching station. Three Greeks were watching data flash across monitor screens. While I worked, one got up and stood between me and the monitors, like I might give a shit."

The bits of information seemed disconnected, but they might fit together later on. "Anything else out of the ordinary?"

"One thing I noticed. Getting gold up used to be Barbas's number one priority. Now, the only time I see him on deck is when they're lowering some new piece of equipment to the bottom."

Jack noticed that Heinz kept shifting in his chair, looking around the room, and paying no attention to Pete. Time to change the subject, try to draw him in.

"You men heard that some guys jumped us near Hotel Elliot and got beaten up. Is that a problem for you?"

Pete said, "It's obvious you two didn't start that fight, and those boys never did that shit on their own. Someone sent them to get you. I guess we all got an idea who that was. Makes us think maybe you ain't the greenhorns we took you for right off."

"But," Heinz spoke up, "Barbas has an army on his side. You don't, so why do you think you can make any difference?"

That was the question he'd hoped wouldn't come up. "When it's time to make a move on him, we'll be ready." Fact was, he hadn't figured out the answer himself.

"Damned good," Pete said immediately. "I'm fed up with that whole crowd of foreigners. I'm ready to go back to fixing equipment at the canneries and drinking with men I know I can trust."

Jack looked at Heinz.

"Yeah." He straightened. "I don't have to stand for no man treating me like dirt. I'm a ship's captain, by God."

Molly seemed to sense that the meeting had run its course. "Don't say a word about this meeting. We'd all be in bad trouble if it got back to Barbas."

"No worries about that," Pete said. He looked at Jack. "I guess we're counting on you." He nodded to Heinz, smiled at Molly, and left.

Heinz was about to follow when a realization hit Jack like the trumpet call at a racetrack. Heinz was the key.

"Captain, will you hang around for a minute?"

Heinz looked surprised, then reluctant, but he turned back.

"I have a question for you," Jack said. "Can you transport the two of us on *Palinouros* to the platform and sneak us aboard?"

"Too risky. Too much could go wrong."

"Nope. Your ship is the only way we can get aboard that platform."

Heinz walked across the office and picked a book off a shelf, but didn't look at it. He was probably thinking that Jack and Gano had no chance. And that when they failed, he'd lose his job, or worse. Maybe much worse.

Molly looked at Jack as though he'd lost his mind to suggest he'd sneak aboard the platform. Then she looked longer at Gano. Her concern for the town won out. "Heinz, you can help save Astoria from another tsunami. If anything goes wrong, you can swear you were forced at gunpoint. And after you get back, you drink at the tavern free for the rest of your life."

The sour expression on Heinz's face didn't change.

"And," Molly said, "I'll throw in food and make it the same for your girlfriend."

"You can accept that," Jack said, "or I'll give you $5,000 instead. Which do you want?"

Heinz didn't hesitate. "I'll take both."

They shook on the deal.

"When we get there, how can you get us onto the platform?" Jack asked.

"The platform uses a Frog Personnel Transfer Capsule. It's a stainless steel frame cage that's lowered by a crane to our deck. It has canvas side flaps that roll down for protection in foul weather. But it's dangerous. We've had bones broken when the Frog slammed into the platform, and one rookie fell out and drowned."

"We'll take our chances."

"We have to have men to help us," Gano said quickly, obviously to keep Heinz from changing his mind. "I know a guy who runs one of those so-called security firms. He'll rent us a few of his *pistoleros*. I'll call—"

"No way," Heinz said sharply. "I have the same crew every trip. If a bunch of new faces show up, the crew will know something's wrong. There's a lot of gold on that platform, so everyone's uptight about strangers. I can hide you two, but not a gang of outsiders." His face was set. He wasn't going to be moved.

"But we need more firepower," Gano said.

"You're never going to have enough firepower to take over that platform," Heinz said.

Jack watched Gano's face as he thought about Heinz's refusal of outside guns. Gano put a lot of faith in weapons, so he might push the point. On the other hand, he knew how to listen to the merits of what another man said. He could see it was time to back off and fight another day.

Heinz went on. "I don't want leaks, so I won't say a word about this to my crew until we're out at sea." He frowned and pulled a small notebook from a pocket of his jacket and scanned a couple of pages. "There's another problem. You're in a big rush, but *Palinouros* isn't scheduled to sail until three days from now. Once in a while they get overloaded with ore and call us to come out immediately, but I can't predict that."

"Can you go out early and stand by?"

"I'm going nowhere without orders."

Jack didn't want to sit in Astoria for three days hoping Barbas didn't destroy the rim of the Pacific Ocean in the meantime. But he didn't have a better solution, which meant he had to keep Heinz on the hook.

"Okay, book us for three days from now. Reach us through Molly if you get called out sooner. And Heinz, you're going to save a lot of lives."

Heinz nodded and started out the door again. He looked back and said, "I can help you guys. Trust me."

"Molly," Jack said after Heinz left, "I have no idea what's going to happen next, but it could be another tsunami. Stay connected to the Pacific Tsunami Warning Center on NOAA's National Weather Service website. Quietly make sure everyone in Astoria recognizes the signs of an incoming tsunami. Get people ready to evacuate within five minutes' notice and have a plan to get at least two hundred feet higher than river level."

"I'll start right now. I just hope that making a big deal out of this doesn't make anything bad happen."

Jack shook her hand. Gano gave her a hug. As they left, Jack thought about Heinz's parting words.

As they walked onto the street, Gano asked, "Let's imagine that this pipe-dream, maybe I should call it a nightmare, turns into reality, and we actually wind up back on Chaos. Do you have any plan for what we'd do then, you know, what with being outnumbered a hundred to one? I know your usual thing is to talk until the other guy gives up, but have you got anything better than that?"

"Thanks for the vote of confidence. As it happens, I have the only plan that might work, and I got the idea from Barbas himself when we went there two weeks ago."

"Is this like the Riddle of the Sphinx where I get killed and eaten if I don't figure it out? Or could we do it the easy way where you just tell me?"

Jack did.

"I was hoping for something a little more, I don't know, sane," Gano said. "You better give me the name of your mescaline dealer. He's peddling some good shit."

Chapter 33

July 29
12:30 p.m.
Astoria

THIRTY MINUTES AFTER they left Molly at the tavern, Jack guided a dinghy alongside *Challenger* where she was anchored in the Columbia River, a couple of hundred feet off the battered Astoria wharf. A crew member dropped a line that Gano secured to a cleat on the dinghy.

As Jack used the lifeline and a helping hand to climb onto *Challenger*'s main deck, Drake called, "You handled that dinghy pretty well." He didn't say "for a lawyer" or "for a landlubber," but that was in his tone.

"He ought to," Gano responded as he came aboard. "He won an Olympic gold medal for rowing single shell." Gano's tone had an edge.

Drake shifted his gaze to Gano and cocked one eye but only acknowledged Gano with a nod.

"Steve, this is Gano LeMoyne. He's a friend and a pilot." Jack didn't feel he owed Drake a lengthier bio. "That tsunami cause you any problems?"

"We were a good way offshore, so the waves were small when they passed. Just a bit of a bump. After NOAA placed the epicenter not far from Chaos, I put that together with your claim that Barbas is destabilizing methane hydrate under the seabed. You don't sound so crazy anymore."

"Good. Is there somewhere we can talk in private?"

This was a moment of truth. To persuade Drake to take him to the bottom again, he had to make Drake believe he was better off with Jack Strider's help.

In the chartroom, he said, "Before our first dive, I said I'd give you the rest of the photos Gano took aboard the platform. They're on this memory stick." He handed it to Drake. "And now I have much more information for you."

It took less than five minutes to convey the gist of what the Chaos employees had told him about operations on the platform. "That tells me Barbas must be close to expanding to a full-scale drilling operation. But because those isopods screwed up *Pegasus's* camera lens, I don't have any objective evidence that the drilling template or the 'tank' even exist. With what I have now, I can't persuade anyone in authority to help me go after Barbas."

"If this was my prom," Gano said, "I'd pull Barbas out of his fancy helicopter and put him under my own private house arrest where he couldn't run anything.

That operation would grind to a stop right quick."

Drake's bushy eyebrows went up. Maybe he was seeing Gano in a more favorable light.

"House arrest, otherwise known as kidnapping, might be justified," Jack said, "but until methane is flowing in high volume, Barbas won't leave that platform."

"We could buy a cheap fishing boat," Drake said, "load it with explosives, and set up an impact trigger. We tow it out to that damned platform and lash the wheel on a course that will blow the shit out of two or three of the vertical supports."

"I'm usually in favor of blowing the shit out of things," Gano said, "but that's not a great idea this time. Those Ka-52 puppies are armed with rockets, air-to-surface missiles, and machine gun pods. Oh, and a few thousand pound bombs to drop down *Challenger*'s smokestack. Your ship would be an oil slick before she got anywhere close to the platform. Speaking for myself, I'm not booking any suicide missions."

"Then suppose I use *Pegasus* to take out all of his seabed installations. No more mining and no more tearing into that hydrothermal vent. My on-board torpedoes can do the job."

Barbas's threat to the HTV had set Drake off. He sounded like a wartime commander, not a scientist.

"Can't do that," Jack said. "Blowing up the drilling equipment could destabilize the entire methane hydrate field and launch a mega-tsunami. You could make the worst-case scenario happen all by yourself."

"The risk is worth taking if that's the only way to save my hydrothermal vent."

That HTV was an irresistible magnet that had attracted three brilliant minds—Renatus, Barbas, and Drake—and made them nuts. Each wanted something different from it so badly that he minimized the risk to justify getting his way.

"The risk is too great," Jack said.

"Who's going to stop me? You?"

Gano glanced at Jack with a tight smile, an expression that meant Gano was ready to tell Drake who was going to stop him.

Jack shook his head slightly to back Gano off. He felt sweat break out. He couldn't let anything interfere with getting another trip to the bottom.

"I'm not going to stop you," he said. "We're going down together."

"Suddenly you're okay with my plan?" Drake looked wary.

"No. I have a better one. We get more information on what he's doing. Back that up with plenty of photos. Then I'll go to President Gorton and get his help. It's the only way." He was sure that if Drake dove without him, he'd attack Barbas's seabed installations. "But you have to swear you won't torpedo anything."

"Gorton? How about Superman?" Drake scoffed. "Get real."

"Listen up, damn it," Gano shouted in Drake's face. He pointed at Jack. "I've watched Gorton kiss this man's ass."

Drake's small frame seemed to compress under Gano's intensity. "That true?" he asked Jack.

"Let's just say I might be able to get his help to take Barbas down."

"So call him right now."

"This isn't amateur hour. I need solid proof. Barbas is a world figure. Even with photographs, I'll have to do a lot of convincing."

He saw in Drake's closed face that he hated relying on anyone else, especially someone from outside his own tribe of scientists.

Drake finally said, "I have a feeling I'm going to regret it, but I'll take a chance on you."

"You left something out."

"And I won't use my torpedoes." His rough voice was grudging.

"Now that that's settled," Jack said, "tell me why you'd risk causing a tsunami to protect this hydrothermal vent. What is that about?"

"I intend to prove my hypothesis that this hydrothermal vent is where life on Earth began."

"Damn," Gano interrupted, "that's—"

Drake silenced him with a hard look. "Hydrothermal vents nourish an incredible variety of life forms that survive in scalding temperatures, tremendous pressure, total darkness, and chemicals we thought were fatal to life. And yet they thrive."

He pulled open the door of an Isotherm marine refrigerator, took out three beers, and handed them out. After taking a swig, he went on.

"The genetic material of microbes in and around this HTV indicates they are the most primitive organisms ever identified. Think about that. And every second, these microbes are colonizing and changing the surface of the part of the Earth's crust we call the seabed. We know that life on Earth has gone through many cycles, so it could have originated and evolved differently at different times, not just all at once as taught by most religions. I believe *this* HTV was the crucible where microbes originated and evolved into every other form of life."

Jack *got* it. Drake saw himself as a twenty-first century Darwin who could understand and explain life. The difference was that Drake thought he heard the whole symphony while Darwin had heard only one instrument. No wonder he was driven.

Gano rubbed his forehead. "You're making my hair hurt. So this HTV is like some Garden of Eden?"

"Don't be a fool. No voices, no lightning, no ribs involved. Through these microbes, I'll prove that life originated spontaneously from non-living matter. That will set off an explosion of critical thought in the scientific world."

Life from non-life. Jack imagined how that would turn the teachings of some religions upside down. There would be howling and gnashing of teeth—and rejection.

"I'm not alone," Drake said. "A few other scientists have similar views."

"For example?"

"Günter Wächtershäuser, a German chemist, says the earliest forms of life were based on chemical processes that produce energy. We call that metabolism. I plan to show how that works inside an HTV. Extremely hot water rises and flows over metallic solids like iron sulfide and nickel sulfide. That causes chemical reactions that produce a molecule that replicates itself. It gradually evolves to become a simple cell on which natural selection operates to produce stronger survivors. I had long talks about this with Wächtershäuser at the University of North Carolina where he taught."

Gano looked skeptical. "But Wächtershäuser's ideas are just theory, right?"

"Much more than theory. In 1977, scientists in a submersible named *Alvin* found the first HTV ever discovered, a very small one near the Galapagos Islands. An entire community of creatures was living around it in extreme conditions of pressure, temperature, toxic chemicals, and darkness that should have made life impossible. But those scientists were so unprepared to find life that they took only a few samples and had to preserve them in Russian vodka. Much later, I learned that the density of organisms near an HTV can be a hundred thousand times greater than in seawater farther away. That's one of the most important discoveries of the past one hundred years." His usually hoarse voice had risen; his leathery face creased in a smile. He was in his own private zone.

Jack got the big picture. If Drake was wrong, old beliefs would go on unchanged. If he was right, turmoil, denial, and resentment would follow. What Drake was saying right now revealed how obsessed he was about his mission. That would have consequences for all of them.

"What do all those critters eat?" Gano asked, fully engaged by Drake's narrative.

Drake gave Gano a look suggesting he was a lower life form himself. "Animals—humans, marine life, and the rest—get energy from eating. Plants get energy from sunlight. But life forms around an HTV get their energy from bacteria in the vent fluids. What fascinates me is that those bacteria are chemosynthetic, meaning they were created by the chemical reactions I just told you about that go on inside the HTV. So that's how life is created from non-life. The bacteria use sulfur compounds in the HTV 'juice' to produce organic material through chemosynthesis. Then that organic material is eaten by snails, shrimp, eels, tube worms, fish, and so on right up the food chain."

"And the HTV," Jack said, "is the primary source of energy."

"That's why I'll do whatever it takes to stop Barbas from damaging it and causing its entire ecosystem to collapse." Drake's blue eyes were burning. Then he seemed to realize how intense he'd become, and let his fists unclench.

"We know the early days on our planet were extremely hot, with volcanoes erupting everywhere. As it slowly cooled, land masses and oceans formed, but they weren't shaped anything like what we see today. Does it make sense that life would suddenly spring into existence all over the planet? Of course not. It began as a very local event. I'm convinced that took place at *this* HTV."

"On your second dive," Jack said, "did you see anything that supports your theory?"

"The red-tipped tube worms there are twenty feet tall, triple the height anywhere else. Most of what I collected are microbes, and I haven't examined them yet. In fact, the vast majority of species on Earth are microbes. Even though we've analyzed and classified only a tiny fraction, we've learned that microbes differ from each other as much as they differ from humans. Think what we can learn from them. When I'm successful, you'll see biotech companies using HTV microbes to understand genetic diseases, maybe cure what we consider incurable."

"Or maybe," Gano said, "some of the bacteria and viruses will turn out to be deadly to humans. And what about terrorists getting hold of them?"

"That's absurd. Besides, no scientific progress is risk-free."

Jack broke in. "Nothing we're doing is risk-free. Listen, I know you need to get *Challenger* underway pretty soon. We'll line up a helo and pilot to bring us out for a rendezvous with you tomorrow."

They agreed on coordinates, he and Gano lowered themselves back into the dinghy, and he rowed ashore.

He was worried by hearing Drake being as dismissive of catastrophic risk as Barbas was. On the other hand, he admired the guy because he was fueled by the same source of energy he drew on—curiosity. At least he'd gotten what he'd come for—another ride to the bottom. And he'd learned more about what made Drake tick. Drake was a "true believer," obsessed and, therefore, unpredictable and potentially dangerous. Neither one of them trusted the other, and that would be a problem down the road.

LATER THAT NIGHT in his hotel room, after Gano had left to take Molly for a drive, Jack sat quietly and thought about what was ahead. On his team, he had a handful of people and a half-formed plan that depended on an ore carrier captain he didn't know. On the other side, Barbas was a monarch who commanded a legion of well-armed knights in a castle surrounded by a two-hundred-mile-wide moat.

Jack needed help badly, and only President Gorton could deploy enough force fast enough to stop Barbas. In case he had trouble getting through to Gorton, he decided to call right away. He'd make the best case he could and give him a heads up that his help would be needed. He'd follow up tomorrow with more evidence, including photographs of the drill site.

Years ago, when both he and Gorton had been under great stress, Gorton had given him a secret phone number he said would always reach him. He'd never had any interest in trying it out until now. After the fifth ring, the phone was answered. "Mr. Strider. It's been three years and ten days. How can I help you, sir?"

The deep bass voice belonged to Corte, a tall African-American who reported directly to the National Security Advisor. The day he and Corte had met aboard Air Force One, Corte had drawn an S & W .45 and pointed it at Jack's heart, ready to squeeze the trigger.

"Mr. Corte, please put me through to President Gorton. This matter is as urgent as the one the President and I were involved in before." He paused to let

Corte remember what had been at stake that time.

"I hear you, sir, but I can't reach him."

"Then get the National Security Advisor. She can always reach him."

"She's at Camp David with the President."

"Contact her."

"The President left clear instructions. No one is to interrupt them." The tone of Corte's voice had dropped even lower, like distant thunder.

"Mr. Corte, I'm going to outline this situation. Please take notes and see that they reach the President's eyes."

"Sir, your phone is not encrypted. Our security protocol prohibits—"

"For God's sake, tell the President that by tomorrow night I'll have the facts to prove there's high potential for a catastrophe on the west coast. Make sure I can get through to him then."

"And in what time frame might this catastrophe occur, sir?" Corte's voice was unruffled.

"I don't know, damn it. That's my problem—and his."

"I will do what I can, Mr. Strider. In fairness, I have to tell you that the office of the President is contacted an average of three times a week with claims of disasters that will occur unless the President does or does not do something. And nothing happens. As a result, we—"

"And they say Roosevelt's people ignored advance warnings that the Japanese were going to bomb Pearl Harbor. Remember that, Corte."

Chapter 34

July 30
8:30 a.m.
Aboard Challenger

JACK LOOKED DOWN and saw Drake on *Challenger*'s deck waving imperiously for the pilot to bring the helo in.

"No way I'm landing," the pilot declared. "Damn wind is gusting all over the compass. Besides, I've seen pizzas bigger than that landing pad."

Gano, sitting next to the pilot, took off his headphones and shouted, "Don't be a pussy. My grandmother could put us down here, and she's blind as a mole."

The pilot hovered just above the pad, still wary. Then a wave lifted the ship's stern, banging the pad into the helo's skids. The pilot instantly cut power and settled. Drake's men rushed up and secured it to the frame with chain tie-downs.

Drake ran to the pilot's door. "Go get some coffee in the galley. You're on the clock until I say you can go."

The pilot shook his head. "Nobody said this was a layover. I'm heading back right now."

"Then unfasten those tie-downs yourself, and see if you can take off before this bird slides over the side. Might be even harder if my ship happens to make a sharp turn and heel over about that time. Up to you."

That was the end of that argument.

Jack and Gano jumped to the deck and walked to Drake's side. As soon as Drake saw the third person climb out of the helo he turned to Jack. "I didn't say you could bring a woman. This is no damn cruise ship."

"This is Molly McCoy from Astoria."

"I don't care if she's Annie Oakley. I don't want—"

"She put herself in danger by getting the information I gave you about Chaos. We owe her." He didn't intend to debate her presence with Drake. She was a fact on the ground.

She'd showed up first thing in the morning and demanded to come along. Both he and Gano had tried hard to talk her out of it. She'd stayed in their faces, insisting she had the right, reminding them that she'd come through when they needed her, and the future of her hometown was at stake. She'd made it clear that if they ever wanted help from her again, they'd let her on the helo. They'd given in.

Drake grunted. "This dive is going to take a few hours," he said to Molly.

"Stay out of the way of my crew."

Events had moved fast since yesterday when Drake had laid out his remarkable theory that this hydrothermal vent had been the site of the origin of life on Earth. Two hours after that conversation, *Challenger* had hauled anchor and gotten underway for a point fifteen miles east of the Chaos platform.

Jack had stayed behind because the Armstrong Air Force Base lawsuit had reached another critical point. That meant he and Debra would have to work late into the night. Since phone and email could be iffy on *Challenger*, he'd stayed in Astoria.

When they'd finished the work, he brought her current on the information he'd gotten from the guys Molly had delivered, and about his conversation with Drake. He'd waited until the end to tell her that he'd hired a helicopter to take him and Gano to *Challenger*.

"Drake and I will dive to Barbas's operations on the seabed and take photographs as proof of what he's doing."

Instead of the objection he expected, she'd said, "Make sure that helicopter has room for me."

The thought of her being on *Challenger* so close to Barbas and his attack helicopters gave him a knot in his stomach. The same had been true with Molly, but she'd been right in front of them, hands on her hips. But if he raised his fears with Debra, she'd say she felt the same about him. So he took the easy way out.

"We go airborne just after dawn. You can't get here by then. Even if you could, there would be nothing for you to do aboard *Challenger*." He started to say that the Armstrong case needed her, but bit his tongue before he ate sand on that one.

"Look at it this way," he said. "There's no one else I'd rather have at my side, but the President and the Vice President never fly on the same plane. We shouldn't be on *Challenger* at the same time."

The silence on the other end of the line stretched out. "Reminding me you're going to be in danger is a really crappy analogy. Good thing you do better in court. Okay, since I can't get there in time, be in touch as soon as you're back."

Late as it had been, he'd had a hard time getting to sleep.

Hearing his name called by Lou Potter brought him back to the present. He saw *Pegasus* hanging above the starboard deck amidships with a ladder leaning against her. She looked ready to go. As he and Steve approached the sub, Lou held up a digital Canon camera.

"I want a few photos of you two in front of *Pegasus*," he said and snapped several shots.

Drake climbed the ladder and swung himself into *Pegasus's* cabin. Jack was about to follow Drake when Lou put his hand on his shoulder and spoke softly. "Keep a close eye on Steve while you're down there. One minute he's on an unbelievable high because of the life-form samples we've collected. The next minute, he's cursing Petros Barbas for threatening the hydrothermal vent. He's not himself, so watch the gauges, especially time underwater and air supply. One mistake will kill you."

Not what he needed to hear. He respected Drake as a scientist, but he choked a little at descending seventy-two feet in a carbon fiber coffin with a captain who was "not himself."

He climbed into the cramped cabin beside Drake and listened to various systems powering up. The quartz dome sealed itself with a hydraulic hiss before the davits swung the craft out over the ocean swells. It hit the surface with a thump and swayed sharply as it washed up and down waves. Then salt water swept up the sides of the dome, and they were under. To his psyche, it felt less like a controlled descent and more like they were sinking.

Schools of fish parted to let *Pegasus* pass, seemingly indifferent to the strange creature in their midst. He had the impression he was inside the world's largest aquarium. Remembering the eerie experience of looking into the eye of a sperm whale on their first dive, he kept a sharp watch. When they dropped below the sun's penetration, the environment felt more threatening.

Because of his disagreement with Drake about Molly, he decided to start a conversation on a topic Drake would like.

"I want to follow up on what you said yesterday about this"—he was tempted to say *your*—"hydrothermal vent. You said the microbes there might tell us about life on other planets. Gano interrupted and cut you off."

Drake, focused on the flickering screen, didn't look at him. "It's basic. I want to prove that we have to define 'life' much more broadly and consider that it can exist in a wider range of conditions than we believe now. We need to break away from what we think we know and open our minds. Evidence is all around us. Here's an example. In 1998, a Princeton geoscientist discovered that bacteria could thrive in pockets of hot water miles underground, much deeper than anyone thought possible. Then he discovered roundworms, more complex than bacteria, that lived in the same environment. That was a game-changer. It meant we should start searching for deep subsurface life, not just here but on other planets. When it was bacteria, I was interested. Now that its multicellular life, I'm hooked."

"But when we speculate about life elsewhere in our solar system," Jack said, "we're thinking about whether conditions exist that would support life forms we're familiar with here."

"And that's a mistake. In the past, Mars had huge active volcanoes and, perhaps, HTVs. Water once flowed on the surface. There may still be water deep in the interior in high temperature, low-oxygen conditions. So if we search deep beneath the surface, I would expect to find life on Mars in the form of bacteria thriving on chemical energy." He paused to touch the screen, inputting new instructions.

"When I identify other forms of life and demonstrate the transition from non-life to life, we'll have to stop believing that life can only thrive in environments like the surface of the Earth and a mile or two above or below it. We'll recognize that life is a truly cosmic phenomenon. My hydrothermal vent is going to teach us about life throughout the galaxies. I'll bet my life on that."

Drake's word "obsessed" seemed on target. Time to bring him back from outer space.

"Are there other HTVs like this one?"

"Ever since the big mining companies learned there are deposits of valuable metals and minerals around HTVs, they've been on the hunt. No one has found anything like this one." His eyes scanned the screen. "We just passed six thousand feet. Won't be long now."

Jack watched the numbers flash past until they slowed and then stopped at 7,180 feet.

"All right, Barbas, you son of a bitch, we'll see how much more damage you've done. Computer. Globe lights on." The sub became the center of a 360-degree circle of light, hovering maybe three hundred yards from the mining operation. The section of devastated seabed seemed twice the size it had been a week ago, a raw and ugly sight. Jackhammers and pile drivers pounded away. Small tractor-like robots hunting for metallic nodules moved along invisible lines like disciplined beetles. Beams from tiny spotlights on their "heads" swung across the debris, creating a bizarre patchwork. He half expected the robots to turn in unison and focus on *Pegasus.*

The crusher, five hundred yards or more away, squatted in the middle of the machines like the head of a giant octopus waving its arms. As it crept forward, jets of refuse poured out its rear and disappeared into the dark.

"Time to start filming," Jack said.

Drake touched three circles on the left border of the screen. "Done."

The place was so depressing that Jack wanted to move on to film the methane hydrate site and the place where the "tank" was drilling into the HTV. He turned to make that suggestion and saw that Drake's face was flushed, his expression grim. He was barely breathing.

Drake shook his head. In a quiet voice he said, "Time to go to work."

His right hand dropped to the console between them and pushed one of the two red-tipped buttons. A *whoosh* followed immediately. Jack saw a torpedo speeding through the water toward a dozen backhoes. Seconds later, the relatively small explosion turned them into twisted scrap. Then the percussion wave slammed into the sub, driving her bow up thirty degrees. His ears rang. As soon as the bow dropped, Drake guided *Pegasus* a few degrees to starboard and pushed the other button. That torpedo smashed into the side of the crusher toward its front. Again, the bow jerked up and fell. The sound was even louder.

"Computer. Stop," Jack shouted. "Computer. Stop firing." When nothing happened, he realized it must be programmed to respond only to Drake's voice.

Another touch on the first button, and the third torpedo was on its way to the back half of the crusher. This time he heard the sub's hull groan when the percussion wave added to the already crushing pressure of the great depth. He saw the steel shell of the crusher peel outward, revealing a tangle of ruined motors and pulleys.

Drake looked around the site, apparently satisfied there were no more targets worthy of destruction. He also seemed indifferent to the stress he'd put *Pegasus* through or how close he'd come to killing both of them. His rage at Barbas for threatening his origin-of-life quest had turned him into a vengeance machine.

Since this site was monitored, Barbas would know that Drake and his sub had slaughtered his cash cow. He'd go nuts. Then a much worse thought struck Jack. Barbas would also deduce that the sub had to return to a base, and that that base was *Challenger*. That's where he'd strike. That's where Molly and Gano were waiting.

Chapter 35

July 30
5:00 p.m.
Aboard Pegasus

"YOU CRAZY BASTARD!" Jack shouted at Drake. "Now Barbas will send those Russian helos to sink *Challenger.*"

"Bullshit. *Challenger* is in U.S. territorial waters. Barbas didn't dare touch us before, and he won't this time. Besides, I have four RPG launchers aboard now, and my men know how to use them. If those helos get close enough, we'll blow them out of the sky. If he even breaks a window on *Challenger*, I'll attach mines to the supports of his goddamn monstrosity and send it to the bottom. That madman asked for this."

"You have to warn your crew. Tell them to get weapons ready and take cover."

Drake made contact and gave instructions, saying nothing about the destruction he'd just caused.

"You didn't tell them to head for shore at flank speed."

'No point. *Challenger* can't outrun a helicopter, but if she left now we'd never catch her. We'd run out of air and power. That's not an option."

"You're sacrificing your crew and my friends to save your own skin."

"I'm telling you they're safe. You'd do the same thing if you were in charge, which you aren't." He slowly cruised the length of the ruined mining site for a closer look. Satisfied, he said, "Now we'll visit that drilling site, or whatever it is, and collect some more photos. Computer. Globe lights off." He must have logged in the coordinates of the methane hydrate drilling site, because he directed *Pegasus* ahead without hesitation.

Jack thought about Barbas. He'd be in a murderous rage. With income from gold and minerals cut off, he'd throw everything into extracting methane, and he wouldn't wait. Without turning his head, he glanced at Drake and tried to get a reading. Drake's eyes were intensely focused on the screen and—*holy shit*, he'd started breathing slower again.

Jack knew what was coming. Drake's lust for revenge still burned. Despite the danger of attacking the methane hydrate drilling rigs, that's exactly what Drake intended.

In the pitch darkness, Jack felt *Pegasus* slow. The cabin seemed unbearably hot.

He had to do something—and fast. He tried to remember the sequence in which Drake had fired the three torpedoes at the mining site. Which red-tipped button had he pushed first?

Pegasus stopped. "Computer. Globe lights on."

The multiple drill rigs were less than fifty yards away, about forty-five degrees off the starboard bow.

Jack thought that the first *whoosh* had come from his left. Drake had fired twice more, alternating tubes. The torpedo cued up to be fired next should be controlled by the right button.

Drake directed *Pegasus* into a slow turn to starboard. His hand started down.

Jack couldn't block both buttons, but if he was wrong . . . he covered the button on the right.

Drake's hand dropped on top of his. Jack knocked it away hard.

"What the hell—"

Jack punched the right button. *Whoosh.* Without waiting, he pushed the left button. Another immediate *whoosh.*

"Stop!" It was a screech.

Jack knew there was one live torpedo remaining so he depressed the right button. Nothing happened. He pushed harder. Nothing. Drake's fingers clawed at Jack's wrist, but Jack depressed the button again as hard as he could. *Whoosh.*

Drake screamed in anger and grabbed awkwardly for Jack's throat. Jack drove his left elbow backward into Drake's face but not with full force. Drake blocked it. They faced each other, panting, stalemated.

In the bright lights, he saw that the multiple drill rigs were intact, the three torpedoes speeding farther away in the frigid ocean. Then he saw what had changed in the past week. Two shiny, twenty-foot long cylinders had been added to the system, and the flexible marine riser that ran up toward Chaos had been replaced with one double its size. The outflow of methane must be increasing. Previous failures hadn't stopped Barbas from moving ahead. The drill site appeared lifeless, but Jack knew the action was taking place far below.

Maybe he'd just made a terrible mistake by preventing Drake from destroying this equipment. Maybe it could have been knocked out of commission for a while without destabilizing the methane hydrate. *Get real!* That was wishful thinking. Using the torpedoes had been too big a risk for a possible short-term gain. The only way to stop Barbas's machines was to stop Barbas himself. Mutual hostility was thick in the cabin. Each of them had done what he thought he had to do. And, even though the torpedoes were gone, this dive wasn't finished.

"Take some photographs of this site," Jack said, "then direct *Pegasus* to the place where they're drilling into the HTV. We both need to see that." He tried to sound commanding, because if Drake refused, he couldn't do a damn thing about it.

Drake, seeming shocked by the turn of events, touched several points on the screen and took the photos. Jack used his cell phone to take some of his own even though quality would be bad. *Pegasus* turned to port and speeded up.

When they reached the third site, Jack saw that the long barrel-like snout of the "tank" was butted solidly against the HTV. Something was connected to it that hadn't been there last week. It looked like a small chem lab inside a glass sphere.

"They're extracting bacteria and microbes from inside the HTV," Drake said in a weak voice that had lost its usual gruffness. "That sphere is on a tether so it can detach and be hauled up. I'd like to ram it, but I can't risk it under this pressure. I *will* get him for this." With that, Drake inclined *Pegasus* upward.

After both of them withdrew into themselves, Jack had another insight. Drake must still be worried that Jack was secretly working for Barbas. That's why he had Lou photograph them together about to get aboard *Pegasus* on the way to torpedo Barbas's operations. He could use those photos to convince Barbas that he and Jack were in it together. That would make sure Jack had to fight with him against Barbas. Well, he'd never doubted that Drake knew how to play hardball. In fact, he admired him for it.

Now they had to worry about the Ka-52 gunship that would blast *Pegasus* the second she broke the surface.

Chapter 36

July 30
5:00 p.m.
Chaos platform

THE ADMIRAL'S BRIDGE was Petros's favorite space on Chaos. From his pivoting chair he had a panoramic view, but he wasn't enjoying the view today. Bad news poured in from all sides. Managers had been forced to cut rates over and over at his resorts. One of his cargo ships had been looted in Dar es Salaam. And he'd just had to let his beloved mega-yacht go at a $35 million loss. Worst of all, the line of credit he'd drawn down was being called. If the merciless buzz started against him in Manhattan and Athens, his enemies would start carving him to pieces

He might hold on until world economies improved, but only if he made this methane hydrate deposit pay off. Nothing else mattered.

"Mr. Barbas, this is Watch Officer Sardelis in the Information Center. Please answer, sir." The voice was a wail coming through the wall speaker behind him.

"Stop shouting! If you don't have a damn good reason for bothering me, I'll have your ears cut off."

"Please come down here right away, sir. I don't know what to do."

He knew panic when he heard it. "I'm on my way."

In the Information Center on the 02 level, Sardelis was standing wide-eyed in front of a fifty-inch computer monitor. When he saw Barbas, he jumped back and pointed at the monitor. The screen was frozen on a scene Barbas had observed many times—his mining operation on the seafloor. Even in the murky water, the robot work force and the crusher/grinder were visible in the beams from the head lamps.

"Sir, this is the—"

"I know what I'm seeing."

"I ran the recording back for you. I'll start it now." He touched the control in his hand and stepped even farther away.

The robot crew jerked into motion, executing their tasks based on computer programs he'd paid millions to have written.

"There, sir, on the left side."

It was a very small submarine with a sleek design and no identifying markings. An intruder. Then the unthinkable happened. It fired a torpedo that obliterated a line-up of his ore movers that had cost him $1.5 million apiece.

"You bastards," he snarled at the image on the monitor.

The submarine fired a second torpedo that came almost straight at the camera mounted on the crusher. The camera lens couldn't see the impact, but the picture on the monitor wobbled. The torpedo had obviously smashed into the crusher.

If his anger were a weapon, the submarine would explode on the spot. Instead, it fired at the crusher again. Seconds later, the video feed quit. Sardelis melded into a corner of the Information Center.

"Sardelis, is crushed ore still coming up to the platform?"

"No sir, and—"

"What else, for Christ's sake?"

"The robots were controlled from inside the crusher building. We can no longer direct them. So"—he clearly wanted to stop and get away—"the remaining robots will continue in whatever direction they were going until they run out of power."

Petros couldn't get any words out. In less than one minute, his revenue flow from mining had been destroyed. That meant that the methane— A terrible thought hit him.

"Pull up the video feed from cameras at the methane hydrate drill rig."

"Yes, sir, but the lights there are turned on only when we're installing new equipment, so I don't think—"

"Do it anyway."

"It will take a minute to scroll back to approximately the same time period."

Scroll back. What is he talking about?

"I have it, sir."

The camera lens saw the drill rigs and the risers. It also saw the powerful light source, a ring of globes mounted on the same submarine.

He knew what was coming. More torpedoes. The end of his empire. He saw a torpedo exit the sub at high speed and gritted his teeth. Only his anger kept him from looking away. Then the torpedo disappeared into the darkness. The sub still wasn't lined up facing his equipment when a second fired, again into the darkness, and a third. No explosions.

While the sub's lights still illuminated the area, he saw that the drilling template, its tubes and wiring, and his new methane storage tanks were still intact. He scoffed at so-called miracles, but something inexplicable had just happened.

Why hadn't they demolished that site too? Maybe the sub's captain stumbled into this place and didn't understand what he was seeing. His mind turned to Renatus's site next to the HTV. Had they found it? Destroyed it? It had no cameras, so monitors wouldn't answer that. He also didn't care. He had a new priority. Destroy everyone connected with that submarine.

Sardelis edged a little closer. "Do you want me to scroll back for another look at the mining site?"

"Scroll back?" With a cold feeling in the pit of his stomach, he asked, "How old is what we're looking at?"

Sensing another eruption coming, Sardelis's shoulders hunched inward. "Sir, the cameras record nonstop. Nothing ever happens, so the protocol is to review the feed every four hours to make sure the robots are functioning properly."

"The events we just saw, how long ago did they take place?"

Sardelis referred to an instrument and said, "Three hours and thirty- one minutes, sir."

He concentrated his thoughts on the attacker. It was a very small sub and probably slow, so it had to have a mothership not far away. His helicopter scouts had reported a ship named *Challenger* in the area on and off for the past week. In fact, he'd sent one of his helos to intimidate it to keep it away from Chaos. It had gotten the message and left. *Challenger*, he knew from the research he'd had done, was owned by Steve Drake, whose passion for hydrothermal vents was well-known. Conclusion: the sub owned and almost certainly captained by Drake was on its way back to *Challenger* right this minute.

He yanked the phone off the bulkhead clip and punched in a number. "Dravos, this is an emergency. Get one Ka-52 and one transport chopper airborne. Search until you locate *Challenger*. Have the transport chopper do a fly-by to look for a small submarine on the surface. If you see it, sink it. It may also be on *Challenger's* deck. If it's there, sink *Challenger*. If you don't see the sub at all, take no action until you do. Use missiles from over the horizon. I want that sub and its crew eliminated without warning. Keep me informed."

He didn't care about *Challenger* or its crew. It was Steve Drake who had drawn first blood. He would kill him for that. He glanced at Sardelis. When this was over, he'd have him locked in the brig for a month.

Back on his Admiral's Bridge, he stood and stared at the ocean in shock. There was something else he had to do. "Renatus, report to the Admiral's Bridge on the double."

RENATUS STEPPED back after watching the replay on the computer monitor, pupils sliding up and down as he calculated the consequences, immediate and far-reaching, of the destruction of the mining equipment. He clasped his hands so tightly the fingertips turned white. His body trembled. "You must destroy that submarine."

"I've already given that order."

"I have ideas that will improve the mining site when you rebuild it. That will take—"

"Forget it. You've overlooked something obvious. Since there are rich deposits all *around* that HTV, it logically follows that the richest depository of gold and silver must be *in* the HTV itself. That's why I'm going to put all thousand feet of that HTV through a rebuilt crusher. I'm also going to excavate as deep as I can into the vent below the seabed. I might even drop bombs down the son of a bitch's throat to open it up."

Watching Renatus, whose body language he'd come to know well, he had the eerie sensation that Renatus's mind was no longer fully present, that part of it was running background programs in a separate reality. "Renatus, give me a status report on the methane hydrate project."

When Renatus finally said, "I have good news," his voice had as little inflection as one of his robots. "I've devised a new method of delivering focused beams of heat in a rotating pattern directed on each methane hydrate deposit. That should destabilize the methane hydrate just enough to release the methane without causing a violent eruption. I've loaded my algorithms into the computers, and all of the equipment is in place."

"Excellent. Get started."

"I need more lab tests to get temperatures and length of heat stimuli exactly right. My first field test below the seabed produced a major methane burp. The next two started small tremors. The fourth test was larger and produced an earthquake and tidal wave."

"But you've improved the technique with every test. Remember that a few lives lost are nothing compared to the benefits from capturing the energy locked in methane hydrate."

"True, but if you make this operational now, there's a fifty-fifty chance you'll create a massive tsunami. Give me a little more time, and you'll be Midas."

Was success really that close? Or was Renatus jerking him around like that goddamn Strider had tried to do? If he could just get a respectable flow of methane going, he could fight off his creditors until the big strike came in.

That made him think about how close that sub had come to wiping out the methane site. How had Drake found either one of those sites? Why had he attacked them? Whatever the answers, he'd die for what he'd done. Even if sending the big helo to sink *Challenger* led to an investigation, no one would dare challenge him after he got the methane flowing.

He stepped closer to Renatus. "There is no more time. You have two hours to finish your on-board tests. If you're not ready to go after that, I'll use the settings you've programmed into the computers and implement them throughout the entire methane extraction system."

"You can't—"

His temper flared. No one dared tell him he couldn't do whatever he wanted.

"I can, and I'm going to."

He looked at Renatus to see how he was taking the ultimatum. He sensed the last thing he expected. Not anger. Not defiance. He sensed fear.

Chapter 37

July 30
5:30 p.m.
Aboard Challenger

PEGASUS POPPED UP like a dolphin, then buried her bow underwater and surfaced again before stabilizing. Jack immediately scanned the sky. No choppers in sight. The sub slid into its sling and was hauled aboard. The hydraulic lock hissed as it released the quartz dome. Drake stood in the cockpit shouting orders at his crew. Jack understood the compulsion that had made Drake fire those torpedoes. It was almost a mental illness, but the consequences were likely to be horrendous.

As soon as *Pegasus* was secure and he and Drake were on the deck, Gano and Molly joined them. "Tell us about it," Gano said.

"No time for that," Drake barked. Then he yelled to the pilot of the rented helicopter, "Warm up your engines and stand by." His brusque tone broadcast that he was holding back a lot of anger that could easily explode.

"Gano, you and Molly meet me in the cabin," Jack said. He saw Gano's eyes register that something must have gone badly wrong.

He walked over to Drake, who was talking with the helo pilot. "Steve, I'm going to the cabin to talk with Gano and Molly."

"Talk in the helo. All three of you are outbound."

"It has to be now, because you have to be there." Maybe it was his tone, maybe it was curiosity, but Drake scowled and followed him to the cabin.

When they were gathered, Jack said, "Everything has changed. Steve fired three torpedoes and destroyed Barbas's mining operation. The methane hydrate drilling site is still intact."

"You jackass!" Gano said quietly. "Barbas will trace the sub to this ship." He paused. "Then he'll send his attack helicopters to use us for target practice."

"Not in U.S. territorial waters," Drake said, "and I've already given orders to lay in a course for Seattle. Don't worry about it."

Gano stepped forward and looked down at Drake. "Those choppers can fly ten times as fast as *Challenger* can pound through the waves. You've sacrificed all of us because you got a hard-on for Barbas. I ought to throw your ass off the stern."

Drake didn't flinch. On his own turf, he wasn't about to back down. "Not bloody likely," he said, and reached for a short piece of line resting on a table and tied the ends together with a complex knot. He jerked it to make sure it held, but it flew apart, sending his fists wide. He glowered at Gano.

Jack knew how he'd feel if Debra were aboard *Challenger* right now. He'd join Gano in pitching Drake over the side. "Knock it off," he snapped. "Because of those torpedoes, Barbas has lost his mining income, but he still has the methane hydrate operation. Now that he's cornered, he'll go after it like a wild man."

"The last time he tried that," Molly said, "he started a tsunami. He wouldn't risk doing it again."

"He will, because"—Jack looked at Drake—"we've made him even more desperate. Debra had one of our CPAs conduct an investigation of Barbas's financial condition. Major revenue sources are down, and he's been eating up a several-hundred-million-dollar line of credit. As soon as he misses a couple of payments, that line will be called. He has to go after the methane or go under."

"Even if that means sinking Chaos?" Gano asked.

"He's not worried about that," Drake said. "A massive methane burp could threaten the platform, but a tsunami wouldn't form until it was miles away."

"You're missing the point," Jack said. "Barbas *will* risk destroying the platform. He *will* risk triggering a tsunami. So the only way to stop what he intends to do is to take him down personally."

"Kill him," Drake said.

"How are we going to do that?" Gano asked. "Invite him aboard for cocktails?"

"The odds against us are terrible, but we have to board Chaos and take it over," Jack said. The words came out so easily, but that platform was a fortress. Thinking about its size and weapons and guards gave him a knot in his gut and made him doubt his sanity.

He was also telling them they had to launch a preemptive strike, attack Barbas because he was *probably* going to do something that *might* be disastrous. From his years of teaching law, he knew that, between nations, preemptive strikes were condemned. Between individuals, they were almost always illegal. When some politicians had declared preemptive strikes acceptable, he'd opposed them. In this case, he thought it was the only way. Yeah, which was what everyone else claimed in their own situations.

"To do that," he said, "we need the ore carrier *Palinouros* to take us there. Problem is, it won't sail for Chaos for two more days. Molly, Heinz told me that sometimes he's called out to Chaos ahead of schedule. That happen often?"

Molly had been hanging back. Now she stepped into the circle. "Those ore carriers sail past Astoria day and night. Nobody pays attention. They make off-schedule runs, but there's no way to predict whether Heinz might head out early."

"Two days could be too late. I'm going to try again to reach Gorton and get him to get the Navy involved, maybe even an air strike."

"The President?" Molly sounded incredulous.

"I called Gorton last night to warn him about Barbas, but got his assistant instead. He said Gorton wasn't taking calls and doubted he could get a message to him. That's why I have to try again." He placed the call to the private number and waited, throat tight, hoping he'd hear Gorton's voice on the other end.

"Corte here, Mr. Strider."

"Mr. Corte, did you get my message to the President?"

"Negotiations in the conference room went on most of the night. No one not already in the room with President Gorton is going to get in until . . . well, period. However, I wrote down your message and passed it into the room in a sealed envelope. The President hasn't responded."

"Corte, I don't care whether the man is sitting on the crapper or in conference with the Pope. You have to get this call through to him."

"One minute, sir." Silence, then, "I just checked the Pope's schedule, sir. He's in South Africa at this moment. As for the other—"

"Knock it off, Corte. The danger I told you about yesterday has escalated. Now I have photographs that show equipment that can trigger an earthquake and tsunami that could devastate the west coast from San Francisco to Alaska. Give me a secure email address, so you can get those photos to the President." He listened and took it down in his left-handed scrawl.

"I'll have your photos printed," Corte said.

"The photos are a smoking gun, but they won't mean anything to the President unless he understands what the 'gun' is. I have to talk with him immediately. He should have the Secretary of Defense on the line as well."

"If they take a break, I will hand them to him. If he tells me to, I'll call you back." The connection went dead.

Damn. What if Corte knew he couldn't get through but wasn't willing to say so? If he did get through, Gorton might once again exercise his uncanny ability to make the wrong decision in an emergency. Even if Gorton agreed there was a problem, he might refuse to attack a foreign-owned platform in international waters. Gorton always made the choice that was politically safest for him. This time, that could be fatal.

He handed Drake the email address. "Send the photos immediately, and then have someone contact *Palinouros* for me."

"I'll go tell Lou to do both." Drake said. "I'll give you this, Strider, you've got brass balls."

It was good Drake thought so, but he felt more like his balls were in a wringer.

After Drake left, Gano said, "Just in case we get to Chaos before Armageddon, what will we do then?"

"I'll have a better idea after I talk with Heinz."

Gano's mouth tightened, which meant he knew the plan was still very fuzzy.

When Drake returned, Lou was right behind him. "Tell him," Drake said.

"*Palinouros* received orders yesterday. Her present location is about twenty-five nautical miles east of here. Her communications guy sent someone to find the captain for you."

About damn time the dice rolled in my favor.

"How can we get from *Challenger* onto *Palinouros*?" he asked Drake.

"Ship-to-ship transfer using a high line is possible," Drake said, "but it's slow and dangerous. Besides, the platform will be using its Vessel Identification System, VIS, to track both our ships. If they see the ships come together—well, that would be bad."

"Could the helo fly us over there?" Jack asked.

"That ore carrier doesn't have a landing platform," Drake said.

"I hate to mention this," Gano said, "because it's so high on my list of things I don't want to do, but we could rig a sling to lower the two of us from the helo to the deck."

Jack knew he could handle being delivered by sling. What made his mouth dry as ashes was what would happen if they made it aboard *Chaos.*

"That's risky," Drake said, "but it could work. And make that for the *three* of us. The helo can't leave my ship without help from my crew, so that's non-negotiable."

"Make that four," Molly said firmly. "I know a lot of men on the platform. You need help from them, so you need me. And," she said, looking at Drake, "before you say something sexist, I can more than carry my own weight."

Jack didn't want Drake along, because his hatred of Barbas was too intense. Somehow it would backfire against them all. And he didn't want Molly either, but death might rain from the sky on *Challenger* any minute, so that was a toss-up. He nodded his okay.

"I'll check out what kind of gear the helo has," Gano said.

He was back in a couple of minutes. "That thing is the pedi-cab of helicopters. It has no winch to raise or lower anything, but it does have a rope ladder. Climbing down it onto a pitching deck means at least one of us is likely to break a leg or worse. Still up for it?"

No one answered.

"Will the chopper pilot cooperate?" Molly asked.

"I'll tell him we're landing on a platform that's bigger than an aircraft carrier," Gano said. "If I have to put a gun to his temple at the end, he will drop us off on *Palinouros.*"

Lou stuck his head in the cabin. "Captain of *Palinouros* on the line."

"On speaker," Drake said.

"Heinz, it's Jack Strider here, along with Molly, Gano, and Captain Steve Drake. We're on a ship less than twenty-five miles west of you."

Long pause. "That's great. When I got orders to leave early, I tried to find you. I delayed leaving as long as I could, hoping you'd show up."

He'd been worried Heinz might have decided to back out, realizing that this would be more dangerous for him than it had sounded in Molly's office.

"We're coming in a helo and will climb down a rope ladder onto your deck."

Silence.

"Heinz?"

"Come ahead, but, since I wasn't planning on leaving port so soon, I don't have any extra weapons for you."

Jack heard Gano curse about that.

"Too late now. Did you line up any of your crew to help us go after Barbas?"

"I didn't want to give your plan away, so I just put out feelers. Even the ones who are mad at Mr. Barbas care more about keeping their jobs. Sorry."

Now they had a ride, but no weapons and too little manpower. But this was his only chance. He couldn't shake the feeling of foreboding.

"Molly told me you transport replacement workers from Astoria to the platform. Do you have any on board now?"

"Six."

"And you'll use the Frog to get them onto the platform, right?"

"Yeah, and you two as well."

He realized Heinz was expecting only him and Gano. Nothing gained by telling him otherwise. "We'll check in when we're close." He nodded at Drake to break the connection.

Challenger was rolling heavily through troughs, and Gano looked a little green.

"The man has no weapons for us," Gano said, "so this is a BYO party. I have my Glock, Beretta, and .38 Special snubnose, but you guys," looking at Jack and Molly, "are empty-handed. Drake, I hope you have some concealable handguns to pass around. Mahatma Jack, you need to stash one away for a rainy day—like today. This is no time for a Gandhi moment."

Drake disappeared down the passageway. While he was gone, Jack remembered he should call Debra about this change in plans. She knew he'd intended to make another reconnaissance dive with Drake that would involve some risk, but not that he'd signed up for what could be a one-way trip. That was going to be a tough conversation.

Drake returned, tucking a pistol into a shoulder holster inside his jacket. "Sig Sauer P238, my favorite. I don't have a lot of firepower for you, but they're better than nothing." Shaking his head, he handed a compact gun to Molly. "This is a .22 Magnum Black Widow. Lady, try not to shoot one of us."

"If I shoot you, it won't be an accident," she snapped, checking the weapon like an expert.

Drake grunted and handed Jack a Walther PPK. "This is the only other one I have that can be concealed. I don't suppose they taught you how to use one of these in law school."

"You're selling him short again," Gano said. "With that PPK, Jack can slice a playing card in half, edgewise, from thirty yards." He grimaced. "Only problem is getting him to shoot the damn thing in the first place."

Looking doubtful, Drake handed out extra cartridges then said, "I have four rocket-propelled grenade launchers we should take with us."

"That would leave your crew helpless against a helicopter gunship," Jack said.

"Barbas has had three hours to send those bastards, "Drake said. "He's not coming, and my boys are my responsibility, not yours."

"What kind of RPGs?" Gano asked eagerly.

"RPG-7s, high-explosive rounds. Simple to fire. Just drop the grenade down the pipe, and it blasts off. Only one round for each."

"Size?"

"Launcher weighs fifteen pounds. A grenade is nine. Three feet long in a carrying case with a shoulder sling. They'll slow us down, but it's worth having them."

Jack watched Gano weighing pros and cons but knew he'd opt for the escalation in weaponry.

"Yeah, we should take them," Gano said. "Those little cap pistols you just passed out sure won't terrorize anyone. Besides, there's a lot of stuff on that platform begging to eat a grenade."

The group fell silent.

To have any chance against Barbas's armed guards, he and the other three had to be prepared to use these weapons. Whenever there was a situation like this, the decision always came out the same way. He also knew that the more violent it got, the more likely they were to be killed. What was he bringing to a fight on Chaos? Would he kill Barbas if he had the chance? He didn't know.

Because he had a half-assed plan—people, transport, weapons—they were rushing into action. But should they?

He had to choose between terrible options. If they attempted to board Chaos now and neutralize Barbas, they would probably fail—and die. If they didn't try to board and got away from *Challenger* in time, the four of them might survive. But if Gorton then refused to take charge, tens of thousands of people along the coast might die. The worst part was the uncertainty. What if he was wrong about Barbas? Maybe he *wasn't* rushing to destabilize the methane hydrate.

He looked up. They were all watching him. He wanted them to tell him they understood they might not survive an attack on Chaos. He knew Molly was bursting with righteous outrage, but that wouldn't be enough to carry her through. Drake's obsession with protecting the hydrothermal vent would very likely warp his judgment.

Gano was different. Why would he take this kind of risk? Simple answer, he was an adrenaline junkie. At another level, he knew how dangerous Barbas was and wanted to stop him. Those two made sense, but Gano's most compelling reason was one he might not even be aware of, might even deny. Jack knew that Gano had come to admire what he called "Jack's Gandhi complex." Beneath his disguise as an easygoing mercenary, Gano had a vein of suppressed idealism. At this moment, Gano coming along as his protector felt like a heavy burden.

Jack trusted his skill in outsmarting opponents, but that wasn't enough this time. And he couldn't be swayed by what the others thought about an attack. He thought of the mantra that inspired him: one person *can* make a difference. This was his time to step up and lead. There would be no turning back. Before speaking to the others, he centered himself and composed a facial mask—one of his many masks—to conceal his doubts from the others.

"We're going to do this, and we take the RPGs."

They all nodded.

"I have a phone call to make before we leave."

In a vacant stateroom, he placed the call and assured Debra that he'd returned safely to *Challenger* from the dive with Drake. As soon as he finished, she burst out with her news.

"We went to the mattresses on the Armstrong case, but we still couldn't crack it open. I've been carrying around a sick feeling that we were getting ready to lose—"

"We've known from the beginning that—"

"—until I had a breakthrough this morning when I figured out how we might get what we want. I'm going to make my move tomorrow."

'Great. Tell me what you have."

"Not till it's over one way or the other. It's far from a sure thing. I'll just say this. It's going to happen *outside* the courtroom. I'll tell you all about it as soon as you get back here."

She sounded confident.

"Congratulations. It will be a huge relief if you can pull it off." Now came the hard part, but he'd given her his word. He had to be straight with her. "But I won't be back right away." He described the destruction Drake had caused. "Having lost that income, Barbas will go for full methane production right now. I have to leave here in a few minutes, get to the platform, and stop him. My plan is like chess where Barbas is the queen. I'll explain later."

The next few minutes were worse than he'd expected. Fear, anger, denial, all coming from love. Walking away would be so easy. Not one person on *Challenger* would blame him. In fact, they'd be secretly relieved. But in the end, he had to trust himself. He had to do this. Finally, he heard resignation grow in her voice. She knew she couldn't talk him out of it.

"I'll call you when it's over, but don't worry if that's not until tomorrow."

"Don't forget."

They said goodbye. Before hanging up, he said, "I love you," but wasn't sure whether she heard him.

He sat suspended in time, thinking they might never hold each other again. This didn't seem real, more like a war game being fought with keystrokes and electronic scorecards, that would end in a few minutes.

He heard pounding on the door. Gano flung it open. "Corte is calling you back. Maybe Gorton's ready to send in the cavalry."

This call would change everything. The whole mess would be put into the hands of people who fought wars for a living. He was off the hook.

He ran into the main cabin. "Yes, Corte, do you have President Gorton?"

"I got the photos and your message to him. He called two of his advisors and, before he went back into the meeting, gave me a message to convey to you."

"Thank God. Tell me." He imagined calling Debra back with the news.

"He said to tell you his answer was, 'No way I'm going to attack a foreign platform in international waters on Strider's say-so.'"

Chapter 38

July 30
6:00 p.m.
Aboard Palinouros

SHOWTIME.

The wind across *Challenger*'s deck had a bite to it like the forerunner of a nor'easter. Drake had cranked up the big engines to produce top speed. He had to keep believing Barbas wouldn't attack, or he couldn't leave his unarmed crew behind.

When the four of them were next to the helo, Jack turned to Drake. "On *Pegasus* and *Challenger*, you're the captain. When this helo takes off, I'm in charge of this group, including you. To use your words, that's non-negotiable." He wasn't asking Drake to agree. Drake gave no sign either way.

The pilot was trying to overhear, so Jack motioned for the others to move away from the helicopter. Braced against the wind, he said, "It's not too late for anyone to step back." He had to say that, even though he knew they wouldn't. "We have one goal: prevent Barbas, Renatus, or anyone else from destabilizing that methane hydrate and setting off a tsunami. To do that, we have to get to Barbas, most likely in the Command Center on the 02 level."

They nodded, faces grim.

"Gano, take the co-pilot's seat. Molly, you're first in the back, then Steve. I'll get in last and be first down the rope ladder."

"Let's get stormin'," Gano said softly.

They boarded, and the pilot ran the engine up to max RPMs and backed off. Then he powered up again and kept it there, waiting for an order. He looked back. Jack gave him a thumbs-up.

When *Challenger* paused at the crest of one of the fifteen-foot swells, the pilot lifted off. Drake leaned forward, looked out the window, and saluted his crew. The pilot checked his compass and swung the helo east toward Chaos. Then Jack saw Gano talking to the pilot on the headphone and knew he was telling him to steer for *Palinouros* and that they would use the rope ladder to descend. The pilot shook his head vehemently and pointed straight ahead. Gano slid his right hand inside his jacket, pulled out his Glock 23, and held it where the pilot could see it was pointed at him. The pilot looked over his shoulder at Jack, then back at Gano, and changed course. As directed, he kept the helo no more than one hundred feet above the crests of the swells to try to evade radar.

"Look to the left," Molly exclaimed. "Right whales."

"I see them," Gano said. "How do you know what kind they are?"

"A right whale is shaped like a blimp. It's about the same length as the humpback, but at least twice as heavy, maybe a hundred forty thousand pounds. Harpooners called them the 'right' whale because with all that blubber they were the right ones to kill. Now they are endangered, and those whale processing ships may finish them off."

"Speak of the devil," Drake said, pointing to a bulky ship on the horizon. "There's one now waiting for its whaleboats to bring kills back to be processed."

"If we didn't have to get to *Palinouros*, I'd like to shoot holes in that bastard with our RPGs," Jack said sourly. Molly and Gano looked at him, surprised. He went on, "That ship is like the one that fired on *Aleutian* three weeks ago."

He looked away, feelings of loss choking him as he thought about Katie fighting to survive, then sucking seawater into her lungs. When he looked ahead again, he saw they were fast approaching a sea-going barge, maybe 250 feet long, plowing through the waves. *Palinouros.*

He saw immediately why the helicopter couldn't land. The ore carrier had a row of large rectangular hatch covers running down its spine from the bow to the three-story wheelhouse in the stern. The hatch covers had raised centers and weren't designed to support a loaded helo. The deck was also fouled by vents, bollards, and cleats.

To avoid the wheelhouse and the salt water breaking over the bow, the pilot hovered amidships. Keeping his Glock on the pilot, Gano pulled off his headset and leaned back toward Jack.

"I secured the rope ladder. Toss it out the door, and don't miss that first step." He grinned and reached back to shake hands with Jack as they'd done before when about to enter a high-stress situation. "See you at the bottom, Tarzan."

The far end of the rope ladder piled up on *Palinouros*'s deck. The next moment, the ship and helo separated, leaving the bottom of the ladder swinging in the wind twenty feet above the deck. He could be left dangling high in the air or be hammered into the steel deck. This climb down wasn't as crazy as his climb up the cliff in Tikal, but this time, he had to worry about three other people. He turned his back to the door, knelt, and inched one leg out, feeling for the first rung of the ladder. He got it and felt for the next lower step. Then the next. When he let go of the door frame and held onto the ladder, his weight swung it under the helo at a sharp angle, just like rappelling down from an overhang on a cliff.

Wind-whipped spray stung his eyes and made the rope slick. The *whump, whump, whump* of the chopper's blades felt way too close. As he reached the end of the ladder, he stepped off as if he'd been on an escalator. *No sweat.*

Drake stood in the helo's doorway, looking anxious. Jack tried to hold the rope taut, but it jerked out of his hand and swung free. Drake started down, moving from rung to rung quickly, too eager to get it over with. He was five or six body lengths above the deck when his right foot slipped forward off the rope and he flipped backward, jerking both hands loose. He was head down when his right foot caught in a ladder rung. He swung like a stone on a pendulum.

Jack launched himself up onto the ladder, scrambling higher until he got under Drake's shoulders. He pushed upward until Drake gripped the ladder and righted himself.

Jack dropped off the ladder again, but when Drake jumped seconds later, his right knee gave way, and he fell awkwardly on his side. "Shit," he cried when he got to his feet and walked in a circle, limping. Good thing he didn't realize how close he'd come to a face-plant on the steel deck.

Molly came next, moving like a gymnast, sure-footed and fearless.

Gano lay in the doorway and lined down the four RPGs in their carrying cases. He started down, not as gracefully as Molly but moving with confidence. He was near the bottom when the ship surged up. Before it could slam into him, he pulled himself up three rungs and jumped. He hit hard but rolled to his feet with a smile.

"Can't say I blame that pilot for being pissed," Gano said. "I was afraid he might start home while I was still hanging out."

The helo lifted and headed east for Portland.

We're all in now.

Heinz waved and hurried toward them from the wheelhouse. As he got close, he called, "Four of you?"

"Yeah," Gano snapped, "we didn't need the other twenty, so we left them on the helo."

Heinz looked startled, and his eyes shifted toward the departing helo. Then he realized Gano was jerking his chain.

"Everything's ready for you," he said. "By the way, mind if I ask what's in those cases? Machine guns or anything like that?"

"No questions," Drake said roughly.

"Didn't mean no harm," Heinz said, but his camaraderie slipped away. "Let's get up to the bridge out of this damn salt spray."

They climbed steep stairs to the wheelhouse on the top level of the structure at the stern. It ran the width of the ship and had a flying bridge, or outside deck, on each side. As they reached the bridge, Jack dropped back and whispered quick instructions to Gano. Gano nodded.

Most of the equipment on the bridge looked hard-worn, some of it wrapped in canvas hoods, maybe broken beyond repair. *Palinouros* was an over-the-hill workhorse who would make repeated milk runs until one day a load would break loose, split her hull open, and she'd sink to the bottom to rest.

"Go below," Heinz said to the crewman at the helm. "I'll take the watch."

"What's the drill?" Jack said. "What happens after *Palinouros* comes alongside the platform?"

"They open the biggest door on their cargo deck and extend the conveyor belt in sections until it reaches our Number One cargo hold. It's jointed so the swells don't affect it too much. Then a crane lowers the Frog. After we've finished using it, the crane lifts it to the main deck. Sometime after that, they start transferring the ore to us."

"Understood," Jack said. He caught Gano's eye but didn't change expression. "Have three of the replacement workers on hand. We'll all go up on the Frog together."

Heinz looked puzzled. "Sure, okay."

With Heinz concentrating on navigating, they spent the next three-quarters of an hour mostly in silence. Jack badly wanted a cup of coffee, but the big pot secured to a plastic table with duct tape looked disgusting.

As minutes passed, strain showed in the downturned mouths and tense lips of his team. Looking at Molly, he saw a woman fiercely determined to protect her home and her friends. Drake was committed to advancing scientific knowledge in a way that would change societies, but Barbas stood in his way. Gano was there out of friendship and for the sake of the chase. All three were uncommonly brave, yet all of them were trying not to think about what was coming up. His job was to make them think he was calm and confident when the truth was very different. None of them wanted to die, but it felt close to being a no-hope mission. Gano, with his keen aviator's eyes, was first to spot Chaos.

"We'll be alongside pretty quick," Heinz said. "I have foul weather gear for you, so you'll look like the rest of us." He opened a locker full of red trousers with suspenders and red jackets with hoods. They found sets that fit and pulled on the pants, leaving the jackets until they were ready to go.

Palinouros approached the "safety zone" that started five hundred yards away from Chaos. Heinz called the platform and received permission to approach.

"With wind and waves pushing *Palinouros* around," Molly asked, "how can you maintain a stable position next to the platform?"

Heinz pointed to a console in the center of the bridge. "That computer measures wind, waves, and tide, and uses that information to control our propellers and thrusters. It's called dynamic positioning. That kind of system also keeps the platform in a stable position above mining operations on the seafloor."

When he'd arrived at Chaos by helicopter from Astoria, Jack had gotten a good look at how immense it was in a horizontal sense. Now he was impressed by its height as it loomed above *Palinouros.*

Heinz brought the ore carrier alongside Chaos in slow motion. "This is the part I get paid for. A serious scrape can rip a hole in my hull. If I collide with even one of the main supports, the platform might tilt, might even collapse."

A few minutes later, the ship and platform were in a stable relationship. *Palinouros's* red-jacketed deck hands scurried around getting their end of the conveyor belt into place. When that was done, they disappeared back inside the structure to get out of the sloppy weather.

Looking up the vertical wall of Chaos, Jack saw the orange Frog dangling from the arm of a crane. Drake and Molly were also staring up at the Frog. Gano wandered to the far side of the bridge and looked out the window.

"Send the three replacement workers out on deck for pickup by the Frog.

We'll join them in a minute."

Heinz gave the order.

When the replacement workers were gathered in the Frog pickup station, Jack said, "Tell the platform to send the Frog down."

Heinz did so.

"Thanks for your help, Heinz. We wouldn't be here without you. The men on the platform are expecting these replacement workers, right?"

"I told them they'd be coming up. No problem."

"I wouldn't say 'no problem,' because I have bad news for you."

"Bad news?" Maybe it was the tone in Jack's voice, maybe the look in his eyes, but Heinz had apparently heard enough. He whipped a .45 Remington out of a drawer in front of him and aimed it at Jack. "You're a fool." He spat toward a waste can and missed. "You're going down and getting on the Frog. And don't take them carrying cases with you. Get going!"

Without making a sound, Gano had moved in behind Heinz and delivered a solid *whack* to the back of his skull with the butt of the Glock. The Remington banged hard on the table, clattered on the deck, and skidded to a stop at Jack's feet.

Jack grabbed it and said, "Since I'm *not* a fool, I told Gano to watch you every second. I figured you'd betray us to Barbas for a much bigger payoff. He'd agree to pay you, say, $100,000, because he'd make sure you didn't live to collect it. After I called you from *Challenger*, you contacted Barbas and told him Gano and I were on the way. You planned to stuff us into the Frog and deliver us like pigeons in a cage." He watched Heinz's face sag as he realized how much trouble he was in. "That's right, I played along, because *Palinouros* was the only way I could get this close to Barbas without being wiped out by his helicopters. I also wanted Barbas to expect us to arrive without the weapons and extra men you had promised me. I tested you to find out if I was right. You failed."

Heinz pulled himself to his feet, cursing. He took his hand away from the back of his head and wiped blood off on his pants. He looked around at their hostile faces. "You got it all wrong," he said in a whiny voice. "Barbas doesn't suspect a thing. You just go on up there and do . . . whatever you plan to do. I was just doing this for Molly, honest to God. You can trust me."

"I didn't believe you the first time you said I could trust you," Jack answered. "Don't believe you now. So we're not going up on the Frog."

"Hey, your choice. I got no skin in that game."

"You're about to. When Barbas finds out we're not on the Frog, he'll send his men down here after us—and you. Your skin will be in the game, all right."

Color drained out of Heinz's face. His eyes widened and bulged.

"You can't do that to me," he wailed.

"Heinz, you are fifty-seven varieties of bad shit," Gano said. "You knew exactly what was going to happen to us when that cage rose above the railing. I'll bet you expected a bonus for Drake and Molly. That really pisses me off."

"Look at that," Molly called, pointing out the bridge window away from the platform.

Even before he saw it, the hoarse *whoosh, whoosh, whoosh* told Jack it was one of the Ka-52 gunships. It was returning out of the northeast, the direction of *Challenger*.

"Its missile pods are empty," Gano said softly.

After a long silence, Jack said, "Steve, I'm sorry."

Damnation. Barbas had given that pilot orders to destroy *Challenger*, and the pilot wouldn't dare come back without carrying out that command. Jack's heart ached as he thought of Lou and the rest of the crew dead, their ship on the bottom. His motivation to get to Barbas doubled.

Jack knew Drake would blame himself for the death of his crew, and that guilt would inflame his hatred of Barbas. Jack wouldn't say it out loud, but he was grateful he hadn't blocked Molly from getting off *Challenger*. He thought again how thankful he was that Debra was a thousand miles away.

He saw in Heinz's eyes that he'd known all along that Barbas had sent the helicopter on a murderous mission. Drake saw that too and with a full swing of his right leg kicked Heinz squarely in the nuts. Heinz's scream was cut short when he caromed off the bulkhead and onto the cold steel deck.

Chapter 39

July 30
6:30 p.m.
Chaos platform

JACK WATCHED THE Frog dropping toward *Palinouros's* deck. The three replacement workers stood with necks craned upward, ready for transfer, blissfully ignorant about what was really going on around them.

"Get your foul weather jackets on," Jack said. "When the Frog lifts above us, we'll head for the conveyor belt."

"We have to carry this snake onto the Frog," Drake said, nodding at Heinz. "I want him cut to pieces when they get up there."

"He stays here," Jack said. "Gano, stuff that rag in Heinz's mouth. Tie his arms behind his back and tie him to something out of sight."

In a few minutes, the loaded Frog passed *Palinouros's* bridge on the way up. Jack was relieved at how slowly it rose. That would keep the Chaos crew concentrating on its arrival.

"Time to move. We go up the conveyor belt in the same order we got off the helo. Gano, cover our rear." Jack slung an RPG case over his shoulder and checked to be sure that the others did the same. "Let's go."

Three years in the U.S. Navy had taught him how to slide down a steep ladder at top speed with his hands on the side rails and feet not touching the rungs. At the bottom of the third ladder, he sprinted to the conveyor belt with the others trying to catch up.

The steep angle of the belt changed as the ore carrier rose and fell. Horizontal ribs provided slippery footholds, but he worried whether Drake could make it with his injured leg. He started up, but the awkwardness of the RPG on his back slowed him. He quickly learned to surge forward every time the ship rose and the angle of the conveyor decreased. The high sides of the conveyor belt provided good cover from anyone on the main deck who might happen to look its way from above. He kept glancing up, afraid the belt would suddenly start up and tons of ore would cascade down on top of him.

At the top of the belt, he peered cautiously into the cavernous cargo bay searching for workers or guards. All he saw were bulldozers, skip loaders, and dozens of twenty-foot tall hoppers presumably filled with crushed minerals ready for transport to the mainland.

He swung off the conveyor onto the deck and pulled out the Walther PPK in case he'd overlooked someone. Nothing moved, but common sense told him that the crew who supervised offloading would show up any minute.

Drake stepped up beside him, gritting his teeth against pain, but he nodded to show he was good to go. Molly and Gano were close behind.

"Good plan." Gano smiled. "I never thought we'd get back on this platform without some serious bang-bang."

"I haven't heard any gunfire from the main deck," Jack said, "so Barbas didn't have the men on the Frog shot while they were trapped in the cage. As soon as he finds out we aren't there, he'll scream for Heinz."

"When he gets no answer," Drake said, "he'll think we're still on *Palinouros.* One of those lizards there will tell him about us dropping in from a helo. When Barbas orders a search and can't find us, he'll guess we used the conveyor belt to get onto the platform. We have fifteen minutes, max, before his people are swarming all over this place with orders to shoot."

"Get out of this foul weather gear," Jack said quietly. "We need to create a big-time diversion to help at least some of us get to Command Central. When I was here before, I saw a building with a sign on its side that read Chemical Storage. Gano, use an RPG round to set it on fire. That will draw the attention of firefighters and some of Barbas's guards, and maybe freak people out." He used his left forefinger to draw a map on the palm of his hand showing the location of the building. "Steve, cover his back."

"Got it," they both said.

"After the fire starts, Molly and I will head for Command Central on the 02 level. Meet us there. Remember, we need the workers on our side, so don't shoot anyone if you can help it."

HE AND MOLLY climbed the stairs into a small compartment in the bottom level of the superstructure. Jack eased open a door to peer out onto the main deck. To his left, the Frog rested empty. Workers walked among buildings doing their jobs with no sign they thought anything unusual was going on. If Barbas had concluded they were on the platform, he was keeping that secret for now.

Jack looked at Gano and Drake. "Go for it."

Gano winked as he passed. Seemingly paying no attention to the workers, he strolled across the deck, hands in his pockets. Drake followed about ten yards behind. They both walked out of Jack's line-of-sight. After too many seconds, they re-appeared in a narrow space between two sheds where Gano had a clear view of the Chemical Storage building forty yards away. He unsheathed the RPG launcher and knelt on a knee. Drake kept watch, but no one seemed aware of them. Gano squinted through the sight and dropped the grenade down the tube.

A *clang* rang across the deck when the RPG shell penetrated the metal skin of the building. Nothing happened. Then a red-yellow fireball was followed by a blast of searing heat that knocked him backward. Nothing had exploded, but some combination of flammable chemicals was creating one hell of a diversion.

He and Molly started up an open-rung flight of stairs for the 02 level. When they got there, it was crowded with workers streaming out of their workstations, panicked by bedlam on the main deck. Rather than take a chance on being recognized as strangers, Jack pulled Molly up the ladder to the 03 level. The passageway was empty at the top.

Through a window, he saw flame shooting up from the Chemical Storage building. This had turned into far more than he'd planned as a diversion. He looked back down to the 02 level. Everyone had fled. It was deserted.

"We have to get to Command Central," he said. "I hope Barbas's thugs got sucked away by the fireworks, but we can't wait for Gano and Drake."

Molly pulled the Black Widow out of her pocket, tested the feel of the grip, and slid the safety off.

With the Walther PPK in hand, Jack, with Molly right behind him, started back down to the 02 level. A few steps from the bottom, he heard a command from above.

"Halt. Drop guns." The accent was distinctly Russian.

Jack looked up at a man standing at the top of the stairs, feet spread, gun in his right hand pointed straight at them. If Molly tried to turn and fire, or Jack tried to fire around her, the man could get off several lethal shots.

Jack tensed, about to whirl and shoot. No choice.

Suddenly, a figure blindsided the gunman from his left with a flying body block. The gunman cursed as he crashed backward into the bulkhead. His assailant fell to the floor and scrambled to his feet to attack again.

The Russian rolled and raised his gun toward the man coming at him. Point blank range.

Crack. Crack. Molly's Black Widow spat twice. The Russian's knees buckled. He fell backward and landed on his butt. His head hit the steel deck like the tip of a bullwhip.

Molly climbed the steps two at a time and looked down at the Russian, whose blood was already seeping across the steel deck. Only then did she look at the man standing several feet away who had come flying out of nowhere.

"Oh my God! Randy." She stuck her gun away and gave him an enthusiastic hug. She looked him up and down as if not sure he was real.

"Molly, what are you doing here? What the hell is going on? I heard shouting but had to shut down my electronics before I could leave my office space. When I came through the door I saw that guy"—he gestured at the Russian—"looking like he was about to shoot, so I, well, thank God I did."

Molly turned to Jack. "Randy is the man I told you about, my boyfriend."

Jack remembered that she'd actually referred to Randy as "the man who *wants* to be my boyfriend." He didn't blame her for a little editing under the circumstances.

She quickly told Randy about the cause of the tsunami and why they had come. She ended with, "You have to trust me. Barbas will try to kill us. Will you help us?"

He was a round-eyed, open-faced man who looked willing to jump into an inferno for Molly. "Hell, yeah, what do you want me—"

"Are most of the townies who work here loyal to Barbas?" Jack asked.

"They need their jobs. Since they don't know what Molly just told me, most of them would back him against strangers."

"Do any of them have guns?"

"Not supposed to, but a lot do because they got pissed at the Russians waving AK-47s and shotguns at them all the time."

"Okay. Grab that Russian's gun and lead us to Command Central."

"That's where Barbas spends most of his time," Randy said, "which means you're going after him right now."

Jack nodded and went down the ladder ahead of Molly and Randy.

At the bottom, Randy pointed down a long passageway with a door at the end. "That's Command Central where this passageway intersects with another one in a T. Barbas usually has a couple of guards on duty."

They sprinted down the passageway, stopping just before entering the intersection. Because of the racket coming from the main deck it was hard to be sure, but Jack didn't hear any talking or movements in the other passageway. All three of them stepped forward, ready to fire. There were no guards in sight.

"Barbas has to know we started that fire, so he sent his guards down there after us." At least that part of the plan had worked.

Just then, Gano and Drake showed up at one end of the T. Drake aimed his RPG at them and shouted, "Hit the deck."

They dropped. Down the passageway in the opposite direction, four armed guards were coming through the door. The one in the lead must have recognized the RPG tube because he spun and rammed into the man behind them. All four hurled themselves back out the door just as Drake's grenade ripped out the door and part of the sidewall.

"Take that, party-crashers," Gano shouted.

Three men appeared behind Gano. Jack raised his Walther.

"Don't shoot," Molly cried. "Those are my townies."

The men, shocked by the RPG explosion, turned and bolted.

"Randy, we're going into Command Central. Stand your ground. Keep anyone from coming in after us."

Randy stuck out his jaw and raised a clenched fist to show he was ready.

Drake approached Molly. "I'll carry your RPG for you." He reached for the sling on her shoulder. Molly grabbed the strap and looked at Jack.

"Molly, give that to Randy," he said. "He may need it. Steve, make sure your Sig Sauer is ready." He turned to Gano. "In a minute, you're going to show Steve how 'slap shot' works."

Gano's eyes filled with understanding. "Got it," he said.

"This isn't complicated," Jack said. "We go in there and stop whatever anyone is doing—whatever it takes. Everyone set?" No replies. Of course they weren't set for what was on the other side of that door. Neither was he. A few seconds from now, he could be dead. The only way he could keep his body from rebelling was to cut his survival instincts out of the circuit.

Drake crowded forward, gun raised. Gano moved in next to him. "Okay Gano, slap shot *now*," Jack said and stepped quickly to the side.

Gano's left hand slapped hard on the outside of Drake's extended right wrist. Then his right hand swept in from the opposite direction and swatted the barrel of Drake's Sig Sauer. The opposing forces sent the Sig Sauer cartwheeling across the passageway.

"What the hell!" Drake shouted as Gano scooped up the gun.

Gano had demonstrated "slap shot" for Jack a while back as a desperation way to disarm an enemy. It often broke the victim's trigger finger. Good thing it hadn't this time. He needed Drake's help. What he *didn't* need was Drake storming into Command Central and killing everyone inside.

"Calm down, Steve. Barbas killed your crew so you wanted to walk in there and blow him away with the RPG. I understand, but that's not why we're here."

Drake's narrowed eyes and clenched teeth admitted the truth. There had been no point trying to talk sense into him. He would have lied, just like he did about the sub's torpedoes. Drake would still try to strike at Barbas when he got a chance, but it wasn't going to be now.

Jack grabbed the lever on the vault-like steel door and twisted.

Chapter 40

July 30
7:15 p.m.
Chaos platform

HE COULDN'T MOVE it. There was only one other way. "We have to make them want to open up."

"There may be armed guards inside," Molly cautioned.

"Don't think so. Barbas has to let some of his Greek technicians in, but he wouldn't let guards see what goes on. He rapped hard on the door with his gun butt. "You inside," he shouted, "get this door open, or we'll fire RPGs through the wall. Open up in three seconds, or you're toast."

Almost immediately, the lever swung sharply counterclockwise, and the door was jerked open. A bald, middle-aged man, obviously a technician rather than a guard, jumped back and dropped to his knees, his hands raised. Behind rimless glasses, his eyes were filled with panic. Jack stepped into the artificial chill of Command Central.

The bald man scrambled out of his way and backed to a stool in the corner.

In addition to the techie, only Barbas and Renatus were in the room, both seated at a console. LCD screens lining two walls were alive with graphs reporting temperatures, volumes, pressures, and visuals from the seabed and below. Renatus was touching different sensors on the screens and then working a keyboard in front of him. Barbas, next to him, leaned forward, following closely. Neither looked around.

Suddenly, Renatus leaned back. Both hands dropped to his sides. "Done," he said in his whispery voice. Barbas slapped Renatus on the back. Renatus coughed and looked over his shoulder at Jack, face impassive. When Barbas turned, he looked annoyed, not alarmed.

Jack didn't like that. Why wasn't Barbas troubled by their guns?

"Coming back without my invitation was a bad mistake, Jack. I wanted to be at the Frog to give you the welcome you deserve, but it was more important to be here. I'll take care of you later."

Barbas settled back, arms crossed, scanned the monitors, and said, "If you thought you could stop our full-scale extraction of methane, that train, as you Americans say, has left the station. You just saw Renatus lock in the sequence that's heating the methane hydrate in what we call reservoir number one. It is now irreversible. As soon as the critical temperature is reached, the methane hydrate will destabilize. He has already initiated that sequence for three other much larger reservoirs. Very soon, we'll start harvesting a massive volume of methane."

He shifted his gaze to the Glock Gano was pointing at him. "Mr. LeMoyne, put away your weapon. It's useless. I know the fire on deck was a diversion to draw my guards away from here. That was clever, but they'll be back with reinforcements."

Renatus also turned to Gano. "As long as I guide the heating process in each reservoir, I expect this extraction to be successful. If I don't supply ongoing guidance, one or more will overheat, and destabilization will escalate out of control. If there is a problem of any kind, I'm the only one who might find a solution. So shooting me wouldn't stop anything, but could be the last thing you ever do."

Jack noticed, as he had before, that Renatus had no mannerisms, no "tells," no wasted motions. His voice was faint, as though conserving energy.

Gano flicked a glance at Jack, then nodded and stowed the gun under his belt. Jack knew he'd put it where he could pull it out fast with a cross-draw.

"That's better," Barbas said. "Jack, I see you brought playmates. Molly McCoy, I'm disappointed you're here. I had better things in mind for you." He pointed to Drake standing just inside the door. "And you are?"

"Steve Drake, you murdering scumbag."

Barbas straightened in recognition. "Dr. Steven Drake. You're the bastard whose submarine destroyed my mining operation. Were you on board?"

"Of course, Strider too, and for damned good reason. That hydrothermal vent is one of the most important sites in human history, and you're about to destroy it."

"I may or may not, but I *will* send my Ha-52 back to finish sinking your ship *Challenger*."

"What?" Drake exclaimed.

Barbas looked pleased he'd delivered bad news. "As soon as I found out what you'd done, I sent a chopper with orders to obliterate you and your ship. My pilot blew the crap out of your main cabin, antennas, and everything else on deck. Before he could finish it off, another ship showed up from over the horizon. He came back here to wait until there are no witnesses. If your ship is still afloat when he goes back, he'll finish it off. You'll be along so my men can toss your sorry ass out on the oil slick."

Jack caught Drake's deep breath of relief. His crew might be alive, at least for now.

"Don't feel left out, Jack. What I'm going to do to Drake is nothing compared to what I have in mind for you . . . and Debra."

Drake's chopping motion was back, his fingers straight and hard as an ax blade. That wasn't a nervous tic. It was a threat.

"You son of a bitch," Jack said. "I can put a bullet between your eyes, and you're threatening me?"

"You still don't get it, Jack. There's nothing you can do to change the history that I'm about to make. My guards will come back. They won't break in here because I'd wind up dead in a shootout, but if you kill me, nothing will keep them out. And you don't dare harm Renatus because you have no idea how to control the process. Shooting up the control room would solve nothing. All you can do now is wait." He looked pleased with himself.

Clashing with Barbas was pointless and would take his mind off solving the real problem. He looked at Drake. "Lock that door."

The real power lay with the programs that controlled the bank of uncaring computers and, therefore, with Renatus. Somehow, Jack had to make him see reason.

"Renatus, every one of your experiments has failed. You can't justify doing this full-scale now."

"Scientific advances have a price," Renatus said coldly. "The damage so far was acceptable compared to potential rewards, and I've developed new techniques from what you call failures. I think I've solved the problem." He scanned the data flashing past in front of him. "This is a big day for me. In a very short time I will prove I can capture enough cleaner energy to reverse global warming."

"I'll bet you made that pitch to Barbas in the beginning," Jack said, "but you kept a secret from him—the real reason this platform exists."

"What are you talking about?" Barbas asked.

"Renatus played you like a *bouzouki* to get Chaos positioned above this hydrothermal vent. You think Moebius Syndrome is incurable. Renatus disagrees. He's doing everything he can to find a cure before the disease kills him." He turned to Renatus. "From the symptoms I see, you're already on death row. Your experiments with the life forms at this hydrothermal vent are your only chance for a reprieve. If Barbas destroys this HTV, you're a dead man. And if he shuts Chaos down because he's run out of money, you're a dead man. The way you see it, your survival depends on his success no matter what the risk to the rest of the world."

Renatus didn't flinch. "There's more to it than that, because—" He shrugged as if thinking, *why not tell him?* "I have a daughter."

"You?" Barbas's eyes filled with contempt. "You're a eunuch."

"Nine years ago I formed a joint venture with the most intelligent woman I could find. We created a child. The odds were against her inheriting Moebius, but she did."

Ah, another piece of the puzzle. The existence of a daughter explained the chalkboard and the equations in a child's handwriting Jack had seen on Ironbound. And Renatus had been trying to create that perfect orchid for his daughter. That's why he'd named it *Esperanza*, the Spanish word for hope.

Renatus continued. "My genetic experiments have proven that the form of Moebius we have can be cured by a new type of tissue I'm metamorphosing from life forms around this HTV. My daughter is a genius, but her disease is more advanced than mine. If I don't complete my work, she'll die a terrible death."

Jack was impressed by the incredible efforts Renatus had made for his daughter. He thought about how Katie's death had motivated him and felt a tiny bond of understanding. Then he noticed a thin string of drool running from one corner of Renatus's mouth, another sign of advancing Moebius. Renatus caught his eye, wiped his mouth hard, and turned away. He realized that he'd seriously misread Renatus by believing he would act like a rational scientist. In fact, he was so driven by fear that he was unpredictable.

Barbas stared at Renatus with disdain, clearly caring nothing about the fate of Renatus's daughter.

"Sad story," Barbas said, "but what matters is the big picture. When all four deposits are flowing methane, I'll tell the public that dependence on coal and oil is over. I'll be an international hero."

"You're no hero," Jack said. "You're taking insane risks only to save your company."

"And to become the richest man in history," Barbas said. "Don't forget that."

Jack looked at Renatus. "There has to be a better way to get this methane."

"This *is* the better way. I'm heating the methane hydrate at greater depth using higher temperatures through a wider matrix of source points. This should avoid the unfortunate results of my earlier attempts. As a scientist, I'd rather wait and measure the effects on the first reservoir, but Barbas has directed me to go forward with all four in a short sequence."

"Don't call yourself a scientist," Drake rasped from near the door. "You're a madman. Undersea volcanoes all around the Pacific are in natural balance. If you knock over that giant HTV, geysers of methane and carbon dioxide could erupt in hundreds of other places. The last time something like that happened, it produced global warming, drought, and drove ninety- five percent of marine life and most land life into extinction."

"No way," Gano said.

"You could set off earthquakes that unlock the tectonic plate running from California to British Columbia," Drake said. "The ocean floor would rupture. The result would be a tsunami moving at more than six hundred miles an hour, destroying the entire west coast of North America. Or it could go west and wipe out mega-cities from Tokyo to Shanghai."

Molly gasped.

"Renatus," Jack said, "stop heating that first reservoir before it gets out of control."

"You weren't listening. That process is irreversible. In fact, it's already one-half a degree hotter than required to start destabilization."

"Renatus," the bald technician said timidly, emerging a step from his corner, "sensors in the northwest quadrant of Matrix One have stopped reporting. And look at the intermediate range Alpha-wave readings. That means—"

"I know what that means, Christos," Renatus replied. He waved the techie back into his corner.

"I don't care what stopped recording," Barbas interrupted. "Is methane flowing up to the platform or not?"

Renatus nodded. "More than I projected."

"I knew it would work." Barbas slapped his palm on the console and then frowned at Renatus. "For God's sake, why so grim?"

"My calculations said it was eighty-six percent certain there would be no earthquake around the first reservoir, but one has started in the northwest quadrant. The tsunami it produces will be larger than the previous one."

Jack flashed on images of his office on Pier 9 being ripped off its foundations and swept into a tidal wave raging down the Bay toward San Jose. The nightmare had started. This was what he'd come to prevent, and he'd failed. He was filled with rage and hopelessness.

"Screw your calculations," Barbas snarled. "Will it interfere with getting methane into our tanks?"

"If its epicenter is more than two miles from our drilling templates on the seabed, they might survive. Most of the displaced seawater will be driven on a very deep horizontal plane, passing far below this platform."

"So Chaos will be okay," Barbas asserted, as if saying it would make it so.

Renatus hesitated. Then, looking at the screens rather than at Barbas, he said, "The odds are nine to one that there *will* be a methane burp. Without the sensors in the relevant area, I can't compute its magnitude. Given extensive destabilization, the burp could be substantial."

To Jack, Renatus sounded like an economist calmly evaluating the downside risk of an investment, but in the real world, a methane burp had killed Katie.

"Where would it come up?" Gano asked.

"I can't predict that," Renatus admitted.

"If it *is* under us," Gano said, "would it sink this floating death trap?"

All eyes were on Renatus.

"Reduced seawater density would cause the platform to sink deeper. If it sank enough for the cargo deck to fill, the platform could not recover. There are so many variables and so little time, it's not worth trying to calculate. The greater risk is that a burp would strike unevenly, resulting in different stresses on different sections of the platform. That might tear the platform apart."

"You people are all nuts," Drake shouted. "Get this platform underway. Thrusters, DP motors, whatever it takes. Get away from here."

"Shut up," Barbas shouted back. "I'll have you—"

"Gentlemen, please stop shouting." Christos was waving a very large gun he held in his small right hand.

"Wow," Gano said coolly, "didn't see that coming. Been watching Barbas like a barn owl. Never figured the little fella would make a play. And that's a magazine-fed .50 caliber Desert Eagle he's got. Israeli military brass call it the Dezzy."

The muzzle that had been swinging from one to another of them stopped on Gano. "I don't know much about guns," Christos said, "but at this distance I can't miss. Please take that gun out of your belt with two fingers, set it on the deck, and slide it to me with your boot."

Jack watched Gano figure the odds. He was such a risk-taker, it sometimes led to bad judgment. But he wasn't even slightly suicidal, so he did as ordered.

"Now the rest of you," Christos said in an almost inaudible voice.

"Give your Desert Eagle to me," Barbas said to Christos. "I'll cover them while you pick up their guns and put them in the wall safe." Then he examined the Desert Eagle. "Where did you get this beauty, Christos?"

"I know I wasn't supposed to bring a gun on board, Mr. Barbas," he said, cringing, "but since you brought me here from Athens, the guards didn't search me. I don't trust those men from Astoria, so I keep it in a drawer here in my corner. I hoped you don't think—"

"Don't apologize. You just earned a bonus." He looked at Drake. "We're not using thrusters or DP motors. If we moved more than a few hundred meters, we'd rip out the pipes that bring up the methane."

Jack knew that Renatus, too, would refuse to move the platform, because that would also destroy the life forms stored where he had been penetrating the HTV.

Barbas shook his shoulders as if ridding himself of the conflict and leaned toward Renatus.

"Speed up getting the temperature past the critical point in the other three reservoirs." He had the single-minded intensity of a kamikaze pilot.

Renatus checked a chronometer. "At the increased rate, it will take thirty-four more minutes of targeted heat to pass that temperature."

According to Renatus, the first reservoir was certain to cause a tsunami. If the three bigger reservoirs did the same, monster waves would overwhelm the American west coast. Hawaii would be inundated. The onslaught could spread to Japan, the Philippines, Indonesia, New Zealand, Australia, even China. Millions of men, women, and children would be sucked out to sea. Economic losses would exceed world wars, plagues, anything in history. Cities would turn into savage battlegrounds for food and clean water.

Jack grabbed Renatus's scrawny shoulder and shouted, "You can't do this."

"Shut up," Barbas snapped. He kept his gun aimed at Jack but glanced at Renatus's fingers on his keyboard. He nodded, apparently satisfied that Renatus was complying with his order.

Drake was by the door, Molly standing partially in front of him. Gano had eased onto a stool to one side, right ankle resting on his left knee. Barbas carefully stayed beyond the reach of all of them.

Jack felt every second tick past. He was out of strategies, out of time. He had to get the gun from Barbas, and he'd have to take a bullet to do it. He'd rush Barbas the next time he looked over to check on Renatus. He focused every fiber of his being, ready to go into action as if waiting for the sound of the starter's shot.

Out of the corner of his eye, he saw a muzzle flash and heard the *pop* from the .38 Special snubnose Gano kept in his right ankle holster. Barbas groaned and spun toward Gano, but the slug in his shoulder kept him from aiming the heavy Desert Eagle. Gano pounced on him, jerking the big gun away. He glanced at Drake but handed it to Molly.

"Renatus, get away from that console," Jack ordered. Renatus didn't move.

"Get me a doctor, for Christ's sake," Barbas growled, gripping his shoulder, trying to staunch the flow of blood.

"Stick your thumb in it," Gano said. "You're not on our list of priorities."

"Mr. LeMoyne, I remind you that you would regret shooting me," Renatus said calmly, not bothering to turn from the keyboard.

"It's not all or nothing," Gano said. "I've found that a lead slug in the kneecap will convince anyone to do almost anything."

"Your threats of violence won't work with me. If I don't make adjustments at precisely the right times, within a variance of ten seconds, the heat sources will go out of control and guarantee three more full-scale tsunamis. This process is going forward. Do you think it's better off with my guidance or without?"

"You're free now," Jack said. "Barbas can't force you to destabilize the reservoirs."

"It's *already* too late." Renatus nodded at Christos. "He saw the readings too. The heat caused the methane hydrate in the first reservoir to decompress explosively. That caused caverns beneath the seabed to collapse and destroy our nearby sensors. An earthquake and tsunami from that are inevitable. I've also locked in the accelerated sequence for the other three as Mr. Barbas required. All that's left is to modulate the heat to try to control the process."

Already too late. "Cut the heat to all of them."

"That would be illogical for me to do. You told the people in Astoria we caused the first tsunami. After a second tsunami hits, U.S. authorities will make the connection and come here as fast as they can to terminate my experiments. There's only one logical way to prevent that from happening."

With nothing to lose, Renatus was even more dangerous than Barbas. "What is your 'one logical way'?" Jack asked, careful to keep his voice neutral.

"I've switched to one final, very complex pattern for heating the remaining three reservoirs. If that prevents explosive destabilization and they begin to yield methane, the world will support the Chaos Project. The U.S. government will pay for damage along the coast caused by the first reservoir, and I will complete my research. Success is the one logical way out."

Needing success didn't make it happen. Claiming that last-minute tinkering would produce a miracle was his desperate ego talking. And what if he was lying? What if it was still possible to stabilize the other three reservoirs? He couldn't force Renatus, so they were at a stalemate with the clock ticking. That meant he had to find a way to stop it himself.

He had to go down to the main deck and get help from crew members who knew the platform's mechanical and electrical systems. But the realities down there were fire, hostile deckhands, and Barbas's guards. He thought of a way he could improve his odds.

He looked at Gano. "Search Barbas, then put him on the floor against that cabinet. Tie his hands behind him with his belt. Molly, get on the platform's public address system. Explain to the townies what Barbas has done and what will happen if he keeps going. This is where we find out who are Hatfields and who are McCoys on that deck. We have to get most of that crew on our side."

She nodded, walked a few feet away, and closed her eyes. He heard her taking deep breaths.

"Okay, I'm ready." She took the mike and clicked it on. "Listen up, guys." She waited a few seconds. "This is Molly McCoy. Stop what you're doing and listen, damn it. Your lives depend on believing what I'm about to tell you. Three days ago, Barbas conducted an experiment that went wrong and caused the tsunami that wiped out our waterfront. He's doing it again right this minute, only this time he may destroy the entire west coast. Think about all the things Barbas has been keeping secret from you. He doesn't trust you, so you can't trust him. After the armed foreigners he brought in hear this message, they'll try to take over the platform. Don't let them. My friends and I are trying to stop Barbas, but we have no chance unless you keep his guards from killing us. Keep the guards out of Command Central. Your lives and the lives of everyone you love depend on that."

She sounded like Joan of Arc rallying French soldiers to charge into battle. Jack knew she'd just started a civil war between the townies and the Barbas loyalists.

Chapter 41

July 30
7:45 p.m.
Chaos platform

JACK LOOKED AT Christos cowering in the corner. "Christos, are you ready to die?"

Christos recoiled. "No, sir."

"Then set up the communications links. Molly, get out a Mayday. Say a couple of hundred people may go into the water in less than half an hour. Then tell the Astoria police to get everyone to high ground ASAP. I'll get NOAA and the Coast Guard to broadcast warnings the length of the coast and to ships at sea in this region."

The Mayday was easy to get out, but feedback said it would take hours before potential help could reach the site. The Astoria police chief had trouble understanding the shorthand story about Barbas and methane hydrate. But because the recent damage was fresh in his mind, he promised to get everyone moving.

Since Jack had no hard proof, NOAA was a much tougher sale. After he ran a "what-if-you-don't" scenario for them, they agreed to put out a provisional warning despite their skepticism. That was the best he could get. He was out of time.

"Molly, I have to get to the main deck. I'm taking Steve and Gano with me. Stay here and keep the door locked. No one enters or leaves this room while we're gone. Randy will be outside with an RPG. I'm leaving the Dezzy for you."

"If I have to shoot, I'll keep firing until it's over. Count on it."

Gano put his hands on her shoulders. "These guys are rattlesnakes. Stay alert and out of reach. I'll be back as soon as I can."

"I'm not going down there without my Sig Sauer," Drake said calmly.

Jack knew Drake's tone meant nothing. "After we get to the main deck."

Jack slowly opened the door into the passageway and called, "You there, Randy?"

"Right here."

In the passageway, Jack said, "Molly is guarding Barbas and two others in there. Make sure no one gets in or out."

"I'll keep Molly safe," he said with fierce determination.

They went down the inside ladder to the main deck. Jack stuck his head out the door. None of Barbas's guards were in sight. After Molly's speech on the PA, they'd probably holed up, waiting to see who did what.

The highest priority for the crewmen running and shouting among the buildings was fighting the fires, a mortal enemy of any ship or sea platform. The fire in the building where chemicals had been stored was still white-hot, like a phosphorous flare. More ominous, it was spreading. The construction and manufacturing that went on aboard Chaos meant there were petroleum products in many of the spaces, even stored in barrels on the open deck. Some went up as flame leapt to them from nearby, others from the extreme heat alone.

"Steve, if these fires get out of control, they'll drive us off this platform. Take a look down the deck. Come back and tell me how bad it is."

Drake nodded and held out his right hand. Jack handed over the Sig Sauer.

Looking around, he saw anger and fear in many faces. The crew had been told the platform was indestructible. Now they knew they were in grave danger. Their tension made the air more foul.

A fight broke out and quickly became a brawl involving a dozen men using tools as weapons. It must have been between men who believed Molly and those who still backed Barbas. Then a gunshot. They scattered, all but one who lay still on his back. If Barbas's guards got involved, the fighting would become more deadly.

Standing next to the superstructure, using his hand to shield his face from the heat, he needed information from the crew and had to get them organized. He, Gano, and Drake had no credibility with this crowd, so he had to find someone who did—and there he was, the talkative guide from his first visit to Chaos.

"Hey, Jorgenson," Jack called, "Wait up." He knew that the man was a Barbas supporter or he wouldn't have been assigned as his guide. He'd have to handle this carefully.

Jorgenson stopped, looked puzzled, then made the ID and hurried over. "Mr. Strider."

"Jorgenson, I just talked with Mr. Barbas and—"

"Where is he, and what was all that coming over the PA about him?"

"Pure crap. He had a disagreement with Molly, and she was trying to stir up people against him. He's in his Admiral's Bridge, and sent me down here because he's worried about the fire. He wants to get all the life jackets gathered in one place away from the fire. Same for inflatable life rafts, wooden pallets, and anything else that will float."

"Damn! Does he think this platform is going to sink?" He looked over his shoulder at the fires. When he looked back, fear flickered in his eyes. "I can't swim."

"Then you better get this organized."

"Me? That's not my job."

"You're standing in a furnace and arguing about your job description? I'll tell Barbas you refused."

"No, don't tell him that, but why are you here instead of Mr. Barbas?"

"He's dealing with what you heard on the PA. Renatus has gone crazy. He's trying to take over."

"I never trusted that weirdo, but I still wonder—"

"I don't have time to listen to you shovel shit. If you won't do it, I'll just tell him."

"No, I'm on it."

"One more thing. Point out someone who knows about the power connections between the platform and the seabed."

Jorgenson looked up and down the platform before picking out a tall man, one of several holding a hose spraying foam on a burning tractor. "He's the master electrician." Jorgenson glanced up at the Admiral's Bridge and ran off, shouting orders.

Jack checked his watch and said to Gano, "I can feel those three reservoirs getting hotter. All I can think of to do is cut the electric power to the heat source on the seabed."

"Barbas's reasons for not moving the platform don't matter to us. Should we give that a try?"

"Even if we knew how, it would take way too long. Besides, that could release a huge volume of methane." He rubbed his eyes and wished the heat and smoke weren't fogging his brain. "I have to find the power source here on the platform and cut the connection to the bottom."

Gano was already on his way toward the electrician. After a brief conversation, both of them returned to where Jack stood.

"I am master electrician," the man said, mopping sweat off his grimy face. "What you want?"

"Jorgenson said you could help us. Something's wrong with the computer in Command Central. We have to adjust the settings in the electric power system. Take me to the generator that sends electricity to the seabed."

The man's brow wrinkled. He shook his head, looking ready to run, obviously shaken by the turmoil around them. "Top secret space, locked like vault. Only Mr. Barbas knows combination. Unless he gave it to you"—he looked at Jack with suspicion—"which he didn't."

Jack gritted his teeth. "Mr. Barbas is busy. There must be some other place to reach the electricity supply."

"No." Now the man looked sullen.

"This prick's lying," Gano said, "which means there *is* another place. I'll just feed him knuckle sandwiches until he remembers where it is." He grabbed the electrician under his left shoulder, lifting him to his toes and drew back his fist.

"Stop," the man pleaded. "Electric power to mining site is inside Pontoon Two."

"I don't care about that," Jack said. "Where is the power to the methane operation?"

The electrician's eyes widened. Jack guessed methane wasn't supposed to be discussed among the crew.

Gano jerked the man's glasses off his nose. "Spit it out."

"I tell you," he squealed. "Won't do no good. Above waterline on Pontoon Three there is hatch so someone on tender alongside can make repairs. Padlocked. Can't get in."

"That's what they told Luke Skywalker about the Death Star, asshole," Gano said. "Where's Pontoon Three?"

The man pointed toward the north side of the main deck.

"No time to get a boat into the water," Jack said.

"If *Palinouros* is still alongside, maybe we can get access to the hatch from there," Gano said. He ran to the edge of the platform, looked down, and called back, "Still here."

"We left Heinz gagged and tied up," Jack said. "He'll be loose by now and in an ugly mood. I'm not scaling down there like a piñata on a rope for him to knock off."

Heinz must have seen them looking, because he shuffled onto his flying bridge. Clearly, Drake's punt to his balls hadn't worn off. He was shouting up at them, but Jack couldn't make it out over the uproar behind him. Only a few words came through: "Didn't get paid . . . madhouse . . . screw you." Heinz shook his fist and disappeared into the wheelhouse.

Within a few seconds, the gap between *Palinouros* and the platform widened. She turned slowly into the brisk wind, riding high in the choppy waves.

Drake ran up, coughing. "The fires are bad down there." He pointed to the east end. "I didn't go far in the other direction because of those stupid guards. They're taking potshots, but don't seem eager to fight."

"Are they getting the fires under control?"

"They're getting worse. I watched a damage control team give up on the southeast corner of the platform."

"Jorgenson better be getting that abandon-ship flotation gear ready," Gano said. "Did I mention I hate being in the ocean?"

Jack peered over the side. From above, the long length of Pontoon Three looked like the thick leg of a mastodon extending from beneath the cargo deck into the water. The horizontal sections that joined all the pontoons together in a rectangle were filled with seawater. That ballast gave the platform stability, but its weight might drag the platform down if a methane burp hit.

He saw a curved hatch six or seven feet above the waterline. That had to be the emergency access to the power cables that ran down inside the pontoon and out its bottom to the seabed and below. The hatch looked to be at least sixty feet below the main deck. How could he get there? The crane was positioned much too far away. He could rappel, but there was no time to locate a steel figure eight and the other gear he'd need. Then he thought of a way. It would be dangerous, but there was nothing else.

He turned to Gano and Drake. "I'm going down."

"You're no Acapulco cliff diver," Gano said.

"I'm not diving. I'm going to make a rope ladder. Find a rope at least one hundred feet long, maybe half-inch diameter. If you get shorter pieces, I can use a double fisherman's knot to join them. Find several carabiners and some webbing or thicker rope." He looked at Drake. "Get something to break the padlock on that hatch and something else to cut the cables inside without me getting electrocuted."

They took off on the scavenger hunt, but he felt it was pointless. The fire had begun to cause explosions. The heat was creating updrafts but not enough to drive away oily smoke. He looked over the edge again: another cliff he had to descend or die.

He'd risked death before when climbing, but then the contests had been between him and the rock or ice. Here, there would be fire above him, a methane burp below, and only minutes before the biggest eruption in recorded history. He'd never been this tense in his life.

Gano ran up with two long lengths of new rope. "A deckhand told me this will hold the weight of a full-grown jackass, if you get my meaning."

Another deckhand followed behind Gano with a handful of locking carabiners and a knife.

Jack spotted a steel post bolted onto the main deck that would be a solid anchor for one end of a rope. He snapped a pear-shaped carabiner around the post and tied the rope to the carabiner. Then he tied a string of Alpine butterfly loops down the length of the rope, roughly two feet apart. Creating each loop took only a few seconds. Next, he cut a length off the other rope and formed a harness he could sit in while he worked at the hatch. He snapped a small carabiner onto the harness.

"When I get down the ladder, use the other rope to lower the tools."

The odds seemed like a zillion to one against cutting the power source in time. The unknown was a methane burp. If it came up under the already-stricken platform, it would suck him off the side of the pontoon like a lobster off a boulder.

"You're wearin' a life jacket, right?" Gano had one in his hand.

"It would be in the way and if I fall off, our time would run out anyway. Steve, you know ships. What am I going to see inside that pontoon?"

"Probably several tubes. Each has a different function. The one you're looking for will have an insulated, water-tight jacket inside. In that jacket will be three wires twisted together in a spiral. Two are 'hot,' the other is the ground wire."

"So I cut them and that's it?"

"My God, no. Cut all three at once and you'll electrocute yourself and short-circuit the generator that provides power to the platform. You cut one at a time. Don't let them touch each other after you've cut them. If you're grounded when you cut a hot wire, you'll be French-fried."

"What if the wires are different from what you described?"

"Wing it."

Yeah, right. How did someone as unhandy as he was get into this situation? He should have taken that shop class in high school. He tugged hard on the rope secured to the post and tossed the rest of the ladder over the side. The end slapped the water.

He knelt on the edge of the deck and probed with his right foot until he found the loop. He put his weight on it, swung his body over the side, found a loop with his left foot, and began his descent. As soon as he was below the cargo deck of the platform, the makeshift ladder swung inward, banging him into the pontoon. Body canted backward, arms carrying most of his weight, it grew harder to find each step of the ladder. The wind picked up. Swells rolled between the pontoons. His heart was beating hard from exertion and anxiety. Time was slipping away.

Finally he was level with the three-foot-wide hatch. He clipped the carabiner on his harness to the rope above him so it bore his weight and freed his hands. The end of the second rope dropped next to him with the tools.

He carefully unclipped a bolt cutter. If he dropped it, they couldn't get another to him in time. He got the shackle of the big padlock in the bolt cutter's jaws. After two tries, he knew he didn't have enough leverage. He stood up in the loops and threw his body into the cut. Just as the shackle snapped, his right foot slipped out of the loop. His harness caught him, narrow ropes cutting into his thighs. He righted himself and stuffed the bolt cutter in his belt and the padlock in a side pocket. It took all his strength to pull the door of the hatch toward him, leaning back so it wouldn't strike him as it swung past. Suddenly, the wind jerked it wide open and pinned it against the pontoon.

First break he'd gotten. Feeling chilled and overheated at the same time, wiping salt spray out of his eyes, he clutched the ladder as it swayed in the wind.

Nested inside the pontoon were five separate tubes coming from above and running down out of sight into the darkness. Two were a couple of feet in diameter. Must be the suction tubes that brought up gold-laden mineral slurry. The third was too thick for shielding an electrical cable, probably meant to bring methane to the storage tanks. The last two were much smaller and identical in size. Either could contain the cable he had to cut. *But which?*

The tube to his left was nearly out of reach. Working on it would be almost impossible. The one to his right was closer but, since he was left-handed, would be harder to deal with. If he made the wrong choice, time would run out. He chose the closer one.

He looked on the rope for the cable cutter with non-conductive rubber grips. Instead, there were only a small hacksaw, a boson's knife, and a roll of duct tape. That meant there would be no insulation between him and that high voltage.

He stood up in the loops and adjusted his harness to suspend himself a short distance away from the pontoon. He took the roll of duct tape and stuffed it in his other side pocket. Then he used the hacksaw to cut out a section of the protective tube, revealing the cable jacket inside. He returned the hacksaw to the rope. Boson's knife in hand, he reached inside the tube, grabbed the cable jacket, and sliced until he'd made a cut all the way around. Like peeling a banana, he pulled strips of the jacket from the intertwined wires inside until he'd exposed two feet.

He took the cable jacket in one hand and used his other hand to try to separate one wire from the other two. After failing several times, he managed to twist them apart and expose a couple of inches of one.

He pulled the duct tape out of his pocket, cut off two strips, and stuck one end of each to his harness. Then he unclipped the hacksaw and held it over the short length of wire, like a bow poised above a fiddle string. The blade barely scratched the wire, but it didn't spark or make him part of its circuit. He bore down harder and hacked through the wire.

His thighs stung from the effort it took to avoid grounding himself against the pontoon. *Faster.* He whipped the strip of duct tape around the end of the wire, but couldn't tell whether it was "hot" or neutral. His fingers were on the threshold of mutiny.

Dealing with the second wire was even more stressful. There could only be a few seconds left. He kept hacking. The line parted, and he wrapped its end.

Drake had said a bundle contained two hot wires and one ground. Therefore, one of the two wires he'd cut must have been hot. He'd broken the circuit. Instead of feeling triumphant, he felt bone weary. What if he he'd made the cuts too late? What if he'd chosen the wrong tube? Then he'd failed, and the devastating process had started deep in the Earth's crust and nothing could stop it. He thought about Debra working at her desk. If he'd failed, would she get enough warning to save herself?

He remembered the methane burp rushing up from deep below. He had to get higher, but didn't know if he had enough strength to climb up fast enough. He was about to shout for someone to haul him up when he focused on the wide-open hatch in front of him. If the semi-submersible platform sank even a dozen feet, seawater would rush through the hatch and flood the pontoon. The additional tons of weight could wrench the entire skeleton.

It took all his power to swing the hatch cover closed against the wind. Because he'd cut the shackle, the padlock was useless. *Unless.* He cut off a loop of rope, hooked the shackle of the padlock through the hasp, and tied the two together. The improvised fix might blow apart under pressure, but it was the best he could do.

He tugged on the tool rope, the signal for men on deck to haul up the rope ladder. Nothing happened. He tugged again, then shouted, "Haul me up." No response. "Damn it! Get me out of here." It wasn't going to happen. Something had gotten worse up there.

Climbing up was torture. Over and over, his wet foot slipped off a rung, and he had to hang on until he could shove it back onto a loop. With a last dreg of energy, he pulled himself level with the deck and poked his head up for a look.

Molly was racing toward him. She dropped to her knees, reached over his shoulders, and grabbed the back of his shirt. He gave a push with his exhausted legs as she dragged him onto the deck. *No time to think, not even to feel.* Stumbling together, they took shelter behind a shed.

"Oh my God," she said, "I was so worried about you. I saw Gano a minute ago. He said two of Barbas's guards had showed up here. He was afraid they'd look over the side and pick you off, so he chased them up that way." She pointed west.

They both had to turn away as a wave of heat swept across the deck with a popping, crackling roar. Molly looked roughed-up, long hair in disarray, a red welt on her cheek. Then he realized she shouldn't be here.

"You should be in Command Central. What happened?"

"Renatus was quiet, just watching his monitors, when suddenly he started hammering on the console with his fists. Barbas shouted, 'What's wrong?' Renatus said the temperature in the other three reservoirs was within one-quarter of a degree of destabilization when it stopped rising. The power supply in the primary electric cable to the heat source had failed."

He'd done it. "The Gods are smiling. I cut the right cable."

"But," she said, "Renatus told Barbas there's another electric cable from the generator to the heat source. It's controlled by a panel in the methane storage building. It runs to the seabed right next to the primary cable."

Son of a bitch. A back-up system. He'd cut the right power cable, but he should have cut both.

"What did Barbas do?"

"I don't know. Barbas was cursing and Renatus stood up, so I backed farther out of reach, almost to the door. I heard automatic weapons fire in the passageway, then an explosion outside. Something slammed me in the back and knocked me out. Barbas's guards must have hit the door with a grenade. When I came to, the room was hazy with smoke. I guess they thought I was dead, so they just grabbed my gun and took off. Barbas was gone, Christos too."

That explained the red swelling on her cheek. "Renatus?"

"Sitting in front of the monitor screen but not really watching. Maybe Barbas told him to wait there for instructions. He looked at me with those strange eyes and didn't say a word."

"And Randy?"

"Gone. There was blood on the floor." She closed her eyes.

"You did everything you could. I'm damned glad you're alive." He felt more strength back in his legs and stood. Barbas was on his way to get the electric power started again. He had to get to that methane storage building and stop him.

A regular stream of gunshots was progressing eastward toward them. Barbas must have organized his mercenaries into a sweep to get control back.

About thirty yards away, he saw Drake sneaking up on the helicopter they'd seen return from attacking *Challenger.* The pilot had hunkered down next to his craft, looking the other way. Drake raised his Sig Sauer and took aim. Jack waited for the crack of the pistol.

Instead of shooting, Drake shouted words Jack couldn't hear. Startled, the pilot looked in his direction. Fear flooded his face as he connected Drake's words with the missiles he'd fired at *Challenger.* Drake kept shouting and stood up. The pilot held up a hand, palm out, apparently pleading. Suddenly, he swung his other hand up and fired at Drake. In the same split second, Jack heard the sharp report from Drake's gun.

The pilot bounced off the side of his Ka-52 and slumped to the deck, writhing, then fell inert.

Drake turned and stumbled slowly toward Jack.

Chapter 42

July 30
8:00 p.m.
Chaos platform

MOLLY, HAND OVER her mouth, stared at Drake in shock. She'd just been knocked cold by a grenade blast, and now she'd seen Drake execute a man.

Jack wanted to get her mind on something else. "I told a guy named Jorgenson to pile up all the lifesaving gear somewhere over there." He pointed. "Find him, and make sure he's doing that. I have urgent business with Barbas."

"I know Jorgenson. I'll make sure he's on it. Be careful, Jack."

"Yeah," he said. He was so far out of his comfort zone he'd passed "careful" miles back.

She touched his arm and took off in a run.

Barbas and his mercenaries were like a deadly snake. If he couldn't cut its head off, it would kill him. Now that Barbas knew the methane wasn't coming up, he'd be spitting venom. If he got into the methane storage building and started power flowing back to the heat sources, destabilization of the reservoirs would occur in minutes.

He raced across the deck, dodging a stack of smoldering tires and flames belching out a shed window. He stopped about forty yards from the only door into the red building, unsure how he could get closer without being completely in the open. To his right, a solidly-built man above average height stepped through a door in the superstructure and onto the deck. He wore a knee-length foul weather jacket, and a wide-brimmed rain hat cast a shadow over his eyes. Jack's gaze moved past him, and then the curly black beard registered. It was Barbas heading for the red building. Almost there, he pulled keys from his pocket.

"Behind you."

Jack spun around at the shout and saw one of Barbas's Russian guards walking toward him cradling a shotgun at waist level, finger on the trigger. He'd heard the shout too, raised the shotgun, and pitched forward. The shotgun was knocked from his grasp a split second before his face smashed into the deck.

Drake stood behind him like a specter, smoking Sig Sauer still held in firing position.

Drake was halfway through giving him a mocking salute when someone fired at him, and he lunged for cover.

Jack turned back to the red building. Barbas was already inside, and the door was closing. He fired a quick shot into the door to drive Barbas away before he could lock it. He fired again, jerked the door open, dove inside, rolled to his right and came to a stop behind a tall metal cylinder. Barbas was nowhere in sight.

The well-lighted building, about the size of a basketball court, was filled with rows of fifteen-foot tall shiny steel casks, certainly methane storage tanks. Motors hummed. Compressors chugged.

Barbas knew someone was inside and roughly where. He could also guess it was Jack Strider hunting for him.

Jack was about halfway along the south wall of the building. The control panel Barbas was after must be on the west wall, not far from the door. That's where Barbas would be restoring the heat source to the three reservoirs. *Damn it.* After all he'd gone through in Pontoon Three.

His sharp hearing picked up a continuous low hissing somewhere to his right, farther from the door. Discharge from an overflow valve? Methane leak? Methane wasn't toxic, but a methane build up in an enclosed space could displace enough oxygen to suffocate them. Or it could explode and blow them to hell, as it did when a spark detonated a methane buildup in a coal mine. That gave him an idea.

"Barbas," he called. "I want to be sure you know I was the one who cut the power. That was payback." He wanted to piss Barbas off, goad him into making a mistake. No reply. No sound of movement. "Listen to me. A methane burp is going to hit the platform. If you get out of here now and get a life jacket, you might survive."

He'd just revealed his position, so he moved several feet to his right and edged along the east wall away from the door. Two or three minutes had passed since Barbas had started sending electricity to the bottom.

He scraped his boot and lightly tapped a tank to "accidentally" advertise his movement. In less than a minute he was almost to the corner farthest from the door. "Barbas, your time is running out." No response. Now Barbas again knew where he was and would do the reasonable thing—move along the wall to get between Jack and the door, cut off his escape. Jack had to keep him moving in that direction. To do that, he had to offer himself as bait, not a strategy they'd taught in law school.

He heard the faint sound of Barbas's shoes sliding along the rough deck until Barbas reached the position between Jack and the door, close to where Jack had hidden when he entered the building. Jack picked up a wrench off a bench and skidded it in Barbas's direction. "That's my gun." Still nothing. He moved closer and took off his shirt. "We have to get out of here. I'm coming out." He tossed the shirt ahead of him and dropped to the floor.

Barbas fired a volley. The muzzle blasts of hot gases ignited the hissing methane leak, and a brilliant fireball lit the space like a flash grenade. *Exactly as planned.* For several seconds, Jack's vision consisted of ghostly fractured black and white images. Barbas's shrieks filled the building as he stumbled toward the door, clawing at his eyes, skin boiling off his face.

Jack ran to find the power control. The clearly marked, two-foot long electrical power bypass lever was in the "On" position. He used both hands to pull it down to "Off." If he was too late, the whole world would know soon. He headed for the door.

Outside, Barbas was running as though possessed, crashing into obstacles he couldn't see. He veered toward the edge of the deck where the lifeline had been torn away. Within a few yards of the edge, Barbas looked back over his shoulder at Jack through burning eyes. A deep survival instinct must have warned him, because he tried to slow, but the platform sloped down in front of him. With a wailing scream, he launched himself over the edge into space above the black ocean waiting below. The force of will, money and ambition that had caused all this . . . gone.

Jack had no time to feel victorious, because he heard bolts popping and welds fracturing all along the deck. He heard the voice of the sea grow louder. *It's here*—the methane beast that had swallowed *Aleutian*, gobbled ships in the Bermuda Triangle, and taken down Deepwater Horizon. Now it had come for them, and would destroy Chaos and its crew with total indifference.

Some of the townies and Barbas's imports had seen Barbas run past, waving his arms wildly. All of them had felt the platform shift, something it had never done in the biggest storm. They sensed their mighty platform was in mortal danger. Fighters stopped, hands dropping to their sides. Animosities gave way to fear. They couldn't give it a name yet, but they knew something terrifying had started.

Suddenly, four mercenaries burst out of a welding shop firing rounds from automatic rifles. They weren't aiming at anyone, but were clearing a path for themselves to the helo. Before he could start in that direction, he felt a firm grip on his shoulder.

"Take it easy," Gano said. "They won't get away. While I was on that end of the deck, I checked out the helos. The Ka-52s are in the middle of a bonfire, and the two little fellows are shot to pieces. They're not going anywhere. Just between us, I wouldn't mind staying onboard, ride it out like it was some tired ol' bull. Whatcha think?"

Jack saw a very different Gano—soot-smeared, somber, and apprehensive. No more bravado. He must be close to his limit.

Jack put his hand on Gano's shoulder. "The platform is already lower, and we don't know how far it will go. Besides, we can't ride out these fires. As soon as something really big explodes, there will be nowhere to hide. We have to get off this thing before that happens."

They both looked over the edge of the deck into the bubbling water.

"Don't look good," Gano said. "In a few minutes, we'll have a full- scale panic to deal with. We ought to get some lifeboats ready to go. I saw a few stored down on the cargo deck."

"If we open hatches down to shove them out, we could take on tons of water. Besides, the crew is already freaked. None of them will go below now."

He knew something no one else did. Water pressure on the jury-rigged lock on the Pontoon Three hatch was increasing every second. When that lock failed and water rushed in, the generator would short out, killing electric power. The pontoon would fill with salt water and put immense stresses on the platform. He rubbed his eyes, emotionally and physically drained.

Chapter 43

July 30
9:00 p.m.
Chaos platform

THE MAIN DECK looked like Hades the way it's pictured in some religious pamphlets. Most of the crew was huddled near the edge opposite the superstructure, the only area not yet swept by flame. They were about to be driven into the sea, but seemed to be clinging to denial. He had to shake them out of their lethargy, or they wouldn't even try to save themselves.

He turned to Gano. "Go back to that rope locker and get every long length of rope you can find. Tie each one to anything strong enough to hold a man's weight."

Molly stopped beside him, breathing hard. He put his arm around her shoulders. "We have to get everyone into the water, but these guys are acting like they've given up. Try to snap them out of it." He saw her noticing that the deck was getting more uneven. "Get a couple of dozen men to scavenge for anything that will help us stay afloat in the water. Take it all to where Jorgenson has the lifejackets."

She took off, calling men by name as she ran. Within seconds, she was working her magic and had them collecting flotation.

Glass showered down as window frames in the superstructure were wrenched out of shape. Cable tie-downs holding the remaining heavy equipment in place snapped and whipped dangerously around the deck.

He ran to the assembly area where Gano and his helpers were at work. They were tying the end of each long length of rope to a separate bollard, about a dozen of them, and tossing the other end over the side. He tested each knot around each bollard and re-tied the ones that wouldn't have held.

Molly's troops were already arriving with wood pallets, Styrofoam containers, chairs, coolers, office furniture, and some other stuff that would probably sink immediately.

"Molly, try to get their attention."

She gave a shrill whistle. "All right everyone." She pointed at him. "This is Jack Strider. If you want to survive, listen to him."

"We sent out a Mayday, but don't know when help might get here," Jack told them. "We have no choice. We're going into the water." The reaction was a sound like an enraged beehive. "Shut up, damn it. If you want to stay aboard, that's up to you. If you're going into the water, get into a lifejacket." He pointed to the pile of flotation. "Hanging onto something in the water could save your life. Toss that stuff over the side." He hoped wave action wouldn't take it out of reach before they got to it. Everyone started moving at once, getting in one another's way, but they got it done.

"Now break into groups and line up behind the bollards. Go down hand over hand. As soon as you hit the water, get away from the line or the next guy will land on your head. Good swimmers go down first and help the others. Get to flotation and raft up." He knew some of them didn't have the strength to hang on to the rope all the way down and would land hard in an unforgiving ocean.

"Don't look like we're sinking no more," said a deck hand. "You sure about this?"

"I'm sure the fire is out of control, and I'm sure I'm getting off."

One man broke out of his group, rushed forward, and grabbed the line above where it hung over the side. He turned his back to the rail, got a grip on the rope, and slid out of sight. A few seconds later they heard him cry "Goddamn" and then a distant splash. The next few men in line looked at one another with dread in their eyes. They could easily balk.

Jack shouted, "You"—he pointed to a heavy-jawed man at the head of the first group—"get moving. You next two, help him over."

The evacuation was painfully slow, but began moving faster as people helped one another. Some reluctant ones hung back, almost paralyzed, and had to be prodded over the side.

What he saw reminded him of troops descending from a landing craft to storm a beach. Rope burns and exhaustion were making many get partway down and then drop like cannonballs.

He kept a constant eye out for Renatus, but he was still a no-show. Must still be in his laboratory with his priceless data. Jack raced to the lab and found the far end of it ablaze and the entrance wide open. Smoke swirled inside. Alarmed, he held his breath and edged in. Empty.

He called to a few of the dwindling number of crew still aboard. "Have you seen Renatus?" He got blank stares or quick head shakes until a tall Greek pointed to a building about fifty feet from them. Its formerly translucent walls were fire-blackened and slumped as if melted. Of course, the greenhouse. He should have guessed.

The door was hanging from one hinge. He kicked it open. Inside, heat had shattered glass. Flame had scorched every living organism. Renatus's precious orchid sprouts were blackened waste floating in a slurry of muddy soil on the floor. Renatus sat on a stool swinging a flashlight beam around the wreckage. Nothing could be salvaged. His quest for the perfect orchid for his daughter was over. This was a funeral.

Jack heard strung-out metallic groans and felt the deck tremble. "Renatus, we have to get out."

Staring at his right palm full of soil, Renatus ignored him.

"Where is that shoulder holster of yours with your data?"

Renatus touched his right chest. He seemed to be in a daze. "I have it."

"I'm not going to die here because of you," Jack said, "and I'm not leaving without your data." Without Renatus, the data probably wouldn't be enough. He drew back his left hand, planning a chop that would knock Renatus cold so he could drag him to the ropes. When Renatus turned, his face reminded Jack that a blow strong enough to stun him might kill him.

"You have only once chance to save your daughter, or was all that bullshit?"

Renatus didn't answer.

Jack walked to the door and then looked back. That shoulder holster was too important to leave behind. If he had to, he'd take it, and Renatus would have to decide whether to come along or stay and roast.

Chapter 44

July 30
9:30 p.m.
In the Pacific Ocean

A SPARK CAME back into Renatus's eyes. Without cleaning the mud from his hands, he walked past Jack onto the deck. Jack raced ahead and pulled up one of the ropes dangling over the side. He'd finished tying two Alpine butterfly loops into place by the time Renatus and the Greek reached him.

Renatus looked at the rope. "I can't—"

"You *will*, but first give me that shoulder holster." He'd planned this moment as soon as Renatus told him about the samples.

Renatus had probably known this moment was coming too. He unbuckled the holster and handed it to Jack. Maybe at some deep level he wanted the best chance for his discoveries to benefit humanity. Then he reached out for a life jacket and got it buckled across his chest.

Jack didn't thank Renatus. Each had done what he thought was best for himself. "Put your feet in these loops," he said, "Now wrap both arms around the rope, and we'll lower you. Don't think about it. Just do it."

Jack looked down at the heaving sea where a man clawed at an upended table already claimed by two other men. As it sank under his weight, the others forced him off. Then he saw Gano looking up, one arm hooked around a hunk of Styrofoam. Jack pointed to Renatus and gestured for Gano to grab him when he reached the water. When they lowered him, he would have dropped free had it not been for the foot loops. A swell caught him at the bottom, and he went under. When he popped up, Gano grabbed his shirt and tugged him clear of the platform.

Jack looked at the Greek. "Go."

The Greek grabbed the rope and went over the side. Almost down, he let go and dog-paddled away.

Jack looked across the burning deck. He'd first visited the place as Barbas's unwanted guest and had returned to play David. Goliath had fallen, but so had too many others. He saw none of the dead, but they were there—burned, suffocated, or gunned down. He looked up at the top level of the superstructure and saw flames flickering behind the windows of the fake Admiral's Bridge. He hoped the men who'd refused to leave had made it to Barbas's palatial suite for a final belt of rum.

The sheer mass of Chaos was overwhelming. Even now, it felt too big to fail. Looking up from below, many in the water might be wishing they'd stayed aboard.

He swung over the side and within a few seconds felt the cold sea rise, soak him to his waist, and fall away. He dropped the rope, sank, and came up shaking his head, wiping salt water out of his eyes. He'd passed the point of no return. He was in a new world. Now all of his attention had to be on their survival.

Gano, Molly, and Drake had made an X out of two pallets and pushed Renatus up onto the center, mostly out of the water. Better than nothing, but the gusts that whipped spray off the wave tops would quickly chill his thin frame.

The water here was around fifty degrees, plenty cold enough to cause body temperature to fall. When body temperature dropped as little as four degrees below its usual of about ninety-nine degrees, hypothermia would kick in. That's when their bodies would start to malfunction.

When Jack swam up to his group, Gano said, "Last man off the sinking ship. Grand old tradition—if you're nuts." He was trying to be humorous, but his face gave away how much he despised being in the ocean. He was a desert man to the core.

"I wasn't the last. A few refused to leave."

In a very short time, they'd all know who had made the right decision. Or maybe there had been no right choice. As he rose and fell on the swells and wind whipped spray in his face, he flashed back to when he'd paddled a sea kayak in Paradise Bay, Antarctica. An ice cliff had collapsed, sending a towering slab in slow motion toward his boat. He'd reversed course and paddled furiously, but a powerful wave produced by the slab had flipped his boat and dumped him into near-freezing water. He'd have died within a few minutes, but a motorized Zodiac from a tour ship had moved in fast and fished him out. Was anyone on the way to fish them out?

At the temperature here, they had an hour at most before they'd drown from bodily failures due to hypothermia. Their life jackets would keep them afloat but not alive. Every one of them might be a corpse by the time rescuers arrived.

"Listen," he said to Drake, "the platform could roll over on us. Let's get these people at least a couple of hundred yards away."

They swam from group to group. Some resisted, as if staying close to the place they'd worked was somehow reassuring. Others bobbed helplessly in their life jackets, already exhausted by the struggle. When they'd passed the word, they swam back to Molly, Gano, and Renatus.

Hearing a tearing sound, he turned and saw the pontoon supporting the northwest corner of the platform buckle inward. A horizontal fracture the length of a football field tore open the cargo deck. Huge containers holding thousands of tons of valuable minerals, including gold and silver, ripped loose when the platform listed. One after another they tumbled into the sea and sank. Chaos was surrendering the treasure it had sucked up from the seabed. As the last load slid into the water, the main deck slowly folded down and crushed the gap closed. In its death throes, the inanimate platform had become a living thing. Looking around, he saw shock etched into watching eyes.

Without warning, the smoking skeleton of a Ka-52 pitched over the side, jerking in the air as on-board weapons exploded, until the sea extinguished it with a prolonged *hiss.*

The platform was floating lower than normal, but the methane burp must not have been centered directly under it because it seemed to have stopped sinking. His eyes went to Pontoon Three, where he'd opened the hatch to cut the power. The hatch door was still visible, meaning his jury-rigged repair hadn't been tested. Maybe the platform could survive after all, if only as a smoldering hulk.

He was about to turn to speculate on that with Gano when a colossal explosion filled the night sky with the sound and fury of an eruption of Krakatoa in Indonesia. The flame that had been sweeping the main deck like an acetylene torch had burned down into the cargo deck and administered the blow from which there could be no recovery. The platform's spine had been broken. The remaining pontoons nearest to the swimmers distorted and buckled.

Some men paddled weakly away. Others merely craned their necks, mouths gaping, unable to comprehend that the mighty platform was slowly tilting down toward them. But instead of gaining momentum, the platform stopped at a forty-five degree angle to the sea. The edge of the deck was now hanging only twenty feet out of the water while the superstructure towered overhead.

He was afraid to take his eyes off the hulk. By now, the inferno had engulfed it, and he didn't trust it not to reach out and attack them. At the same time, he didn't want to get too far from it for fear any rescuers would miss them.

They watched, helpless, bobbing on the slopes of the waves and spitting out salt water. Each time a piece of flotation became saturated and sank, a struggle broke out as men fought for a handhold on a new piece. Before long it would be every man for himself.

As minutes passed, the cold penetrated deeper. Jack looked at his friends. Molly was trying to look as strong as ever, but her skin was pale blue and puffy.

"Molly, how are you doing?"

It took several moments to control her chattering teeth enough to say, "I can't feel my fingers."

Gano, shivering uncontrollably, managed a weak smile. Drake, looking stoic, was motionless, conserving every bit of core heat. Renatus's head hung down, and he would have drifted away if Drake hadn't held onto his life jacket. Their temperatures had been dropping from the moment they'd hit the water. One by one, they would lose muscle control. Renatus would be the first to die.

They had passed an hour in the water when one of the roustabouts started screaming hysterically. Not *at* anyone, just into the sky. Farther away, a man fumbled the buckles of his life jacket open and shrugged it off his shoulders. He tried to get his shirt off, gave up, and began to paddle away, faster and faster like a frenzied dog. In seconds, his head went under. Jack heard people trying to talk, but slurring their words so badly no one could understand them. Others were babbling or calling out to faraway relatives.

Hypothermia was getting a grip on him too—breathing and pulse rates way down, fingers losing their grip on the pallet. Worse, he couldn't think clearly and caught himself repeating thoughts over and over.

He'd persuaded these people to make a terrible gamble that help would show up before their limbs no longer worked and they sank. But help hadn't shown up. To survive, they had to get out of the water. He looked again at the platform. Far too steep. Far too hot. Chaos had almost killed them—and might yet—but it could never save them.

He looked at Gano, coiled in on himself to preserve what little heat remained. He stared back at Jack with glassy eyes, almost nothing left except raw will to survive.

Then a low-pitched sound swept across the water.

MOAAAAUM—a sound like a giant foghorn.

Seconds passed. *MOAAAAUM.* This time he counted. Five seconds. *MOAAAAUM.* He was so low in the water, with swells blocking his sight, that he was able to see only a few yards away. He blinked rapidly to clear his vision. First he saw dim lights, then, in the flickering light from the fires, the silhouette of a huge ship, barely moving forward. His excitement turned to horror when he realized the ship's course would plow straight through the field of floating crewmen. He tried to call out, but couldn't expand his chest enough to get air, could hardly make his lips move. Some in the water saw the danger and began waving. Most were too deadened to react. When one drifted away from the board he'd been hanging onto, no one reached out for him.

Jack made out men standing at its railing, but they were all pointing at the stricken platform. Several powerful flashlight beams shot across the great hulk. At last, one of the men peered down, swept his light across them, and excitedly pointed them out to the others. Jack heard a new sound—huge props reversing. The engines were backing down, trying to stop the ship before it ran over them. Or maybe the captain just didn't want to get any closer to the platform. The big ship pitched and rolled in the swells as the men at the rail seemed to be in a heated argument.

"Come get us, you bastards," Jack tried to scream, but he made no sound.

Minutes passed. Then he heard creaking of winches and squealing of steel on steel. Two lifeboats inched down from their davits and settled in the water. They were still secured to cables descending from the winches so they couldn't leave the ship's side. The captain wasn't taking any chances. Three men in black foul weather gear stood in each boat, waiting.

Jack didn't want to believe it, but they weren't going to reach out. Anyone who couldn't make it to the boats would not be saved. Feeling like an arthritic Border Collie, he sluggishly swam to groups of crewmen and prodded them toward the lifeboats. When the first man got close, he summoned up a frantic spurt of energy and tried to seize the boat's gunwale with icy fingers. He missed, fell back, and floated up and over the crest of a wave on his back, quickly swept out of reach.

Men on the lifeboats leaned over the side with boathooks to haul swimmers aboard like stunned fish.

Gano had revived himself and was struggling forward with clumsy, ineffective strokes. Molly swam beside him, pulling him along as much as she could. When they reached a lifeboat, Gano got his hand under Molly's arm and lifted her up to grab a boathook. As soon as she was aboard, she helped haul Gano up.

Jack and Drake pushed Renatus, still in the center of the pallet X, next to a lifeboat. His head was lolling side to side as he mumbled quietly. Jack took him in his arms and shouted up, "Careful with him," but his voice sounded like the croak of a bullfrog.

The boat crewman above looked uncomprehending but set down the boathook and used his hands to pull Renatus up. Jack put his arms around Drake's waist from behind, scissor-kicked as hard as he could, and lifted him enough for the same crewman to seize his arms and drag him aboard.

It took all his will power to keep his brain from slipping into idle. He kept going, rounding up stragglers and the ones who had lost hope. He edged each of them into position within reach of a boathook.

The boats slowly cycled upward with their loads. After three or four more rounds, only one boat returned to haul in remaining survivors. Seeing no one else left in the water, Jack pulled himself over the side and collapsed on the floorboards among the others. When the coxswain signaled to be brought up, the winch protested as it tried to lift the lifeboat out of the sea. The boat, whose capacity was probably fifteen, held twenty-three.

Just as it started up, a swell dropped out from under it, causing the boat to tilt sharply. The master electrician lost his grip, pitched forward, and slammed his head into the low side rail. A lifeboat crewman seized the back of his life jacket, but couldn't hold the man who was twice his size. The electrician went over the rail and hit the water face down, neck twisted to one side. The lifeboat was already even with the ship's deck, and Jack could do nothing.

Onboard at last, Jack saw several members of the Chaos crew laid out on deck in rows like dead seals, many curled into fetal positions. They were probably the ones in the worst shape. The rest must have been taken below.

He also saw the big ship's crew clearly for the first time. They were short men with wiry bodies, light brown skin, black hair, and dressed in the rough gear of seamen around the world. It took a moment before he recognized their language as Japanese. To his left, six men dressed in white, thigh-length coats stood apart from the crew, not helping with the rescue. Two looked Japanese. The others were taller, pale-skinned, with facial hair, and wore glasses. When they realized Jack was watching them, they stepped out of sight.

Members of the ship's crew, sometimes three or four of them at once, pulled men to their feet and helped them stagger through a cabin hatch flanked by ROVs that resembled the one Drake used.

Jack was one of the last to be led through the hatch and to the ship's large engine room with its hefty diesel engines. The temperature—it had to be above

110° F—made his skin sting. He stripped off soggy clothing and took a towel from a stack to wrap up in. He took a second towel and draped it to hide the shoulder holster Renatus had given him. In a few minutes, he regained more feeling in his limbs, but still couldn't corral his thoughts.

He watched two of the ship's crew pull a rubbery-legged survivor to his feet and down a passageway, supporting him on both sides. Jack followed them and joined a line waiting to enter the shower room. For the moment, not being in control, not having to make plans or decisions, was a great relief.

After a shower, the last stop was a large rectangular room with aluminum walls, a steel-grate floor, and long rows of empty racks. Even though the temperature was only uncomfortably cool, he could tell they were in a very large walk-in cooler. That meant their rescuer was a seafood processing ship whose catch must have been moved on into freezers. He walked to where Gano was stretched out on the deck beside Molly, both apparently asleep, holding hands. Gano's eyes opened, and he looked up at Jack. "Thanks, mate," he said and closed his eyes. Just beyond him, Renatus lay still. Drake seemed to have emerged stronger than the others, possibly because his body was so compact. He was leaning on one elbow, looking at Renatus with an expression of concern. Maybe the hydrothermal vent had been a magnetic force drawing Drake to Renatus. The five of them were alive, but could have suffered organ damage that wouldn't show up until later, and psychological damage that could last a lifetime.

Some of the crew had died on the platform, and more in the water. No way to know how many, but his rough head count came to about 150 in the giant cooler.

To get back control of his body, Jack did slow exercises. He gestured to others to copy him. After a few minutes, he noticed a middle-aged Japanese man standing near the door and walked up to him.

"*Konbanwa,*" Jack said. "Good evening. Please take me to your captain." He started for the door.

The man, whose head was lower than Jack's shoulders, held out a stiff arm to bar his way. He indicated that Jack should back away. Then he left. Jack hoped he was going to get the captain.

The Japanese in the room had completed their assignments and offered no further aid. While they didn't look hostile, they spoke behind their hands and seemed to glance at the bedraggled crew with suspicion.

When the man he'd spoken to returned, he pointed out Jack to a taller man in his early twenties entering behind him. Jack pushed to his feet and joined them. "I am Tomohiko," the man said.

"*Konbanwa.* I'm Jack Strider." Nothing about the man suggested he was the captain, so Jack said politely, "I'd like to speak to the captain to thank him for rescuing us."

"My uncle prefers not to speak English. He sent me because I graduated from UCLA."

"Glad to meet you." He didn't offer his hand because Tomohiko had not. "These men are in bad shape. Can you have food and water sent in? We will pay for it when we get to port. We also need a doctor."

"No. You will remain in here until the captain decides what to do with you."

"Seattle or Vancouver are the closest ports. Will the captain take us to one of them?"

"No."

What was that about? Could this captain be up to something criminal? If he was, he might be worried about being caught, maybe having his ship impounded. That would explain the lack of hospitality—no food, no water, no medical help, and being confined to this space. The fundamental law of the sea that commands every mariner to rescue another in distress might be all that had kept their lungs from being full of salt water by now.

"Then maybe Kodiak in the Aleutian Islands?"

The other man gave him a scornful look. "Very large U.S. Coast Guard base in Kodiak. Also, all wharfs probably destroyed."

Oh my God. "The tsunami, where did it hit?" He braced himself for the answer.

"Coast of British Columbia but not so much. Alaska Tsunami Warning Center said Sitka, Seward, and Kodiak hit bad. Twelve hundred miles of Aleutian Islands, much damage, even Kamchatka Peninsula in Russia hit hard."

San Francisco, Seattle, Vancouver, all safe this time. Jack was so relieved he felt almost ashamed. But he still had to get the crew to some port. "Wait a minute, please. I'll be right back." He hurried to Gano and Molly. "Can Renatus talk?"

"He's been incoherent."

Jack leaned close to Renatus's ear. "Listen to me. You know Canadian waters." He explained that he had to come up with a port that wouldn't put the Japanese ship at risk. Renatus stopped mumbling and became still for several seconds.

"Port Alberni," he whispered. "About two hundred miles north of Seattle on the west coast of Vancouver Island, British Columbia."

"Any Canadian military there?"

"No."

"Airport?"

"An hour away." He hadn't opened his eyes.

Ironic. Renatus had helped cause the crisis, but the information he'd just provided might save what was left of the Chaos crew.

Jack returned to Tomohiko. "Take us to Port Alberni on Vancouver Island, *kudasai*," he said with a slight bow. He didn't know many Japanese words, but he knew "please." "It's very small and has no military."

Tomohiko's expression didn't change. "I will tell my uncle." His eyes scanned the room full of exhausted people, many only semi-conscious. Just before he left, his nose wrinkled in undisguised distaste.

Ten minutes later, Jack heard the hum of the big engines grow louder, felt the revolutions of the massive screws increase. They were on their way to . . . somewhere. After another fifteen minutes or so, Tomohiko returned.

"Our charts say the water is deep enough at Port Alberni for us to get in. My uncle will take you there. Now I will have barrels of water sent in here. Also bread."

The men were so dehydrated that water would be a lifesaver. "*Arigatou gozaimasu.* Thank you very much," Jack said, feeling a rush of relief.

"Port Alberni is at the end of very long inlet," Tomohiko continued. "If trouble along the way in, we turn around and put all of you overboard."

The young man's tone was so cold Jack guessed that dumping the Chaos crew back in the water had been the default option from the beginning. He was about to ask how long the trip would take when Tomohiko walked out.

"We need doctors in here," he called after him and grabbed the door handle. It was locked.

A few minutes after that, their clothes were brought in on the makeshift stretchers and dumped in a pile for them to paw through. The clothes must have been hung out in the engine room because they were warm and dry. Hours later, the engines cut back slightly. That could mean the ship had entered the long inlet leading to Port Alberni. Another two hours passed before Tomohiko returned.

"Arrive soon. Port struck by small tsunami yesterday. Don't know how much damage. Captain will put you ashore if possible with our lifeboats, four starboard, three port. We make one trip only."

Now he was pissed. "Hold on. That will overload the boats. They could capsize, and these men couldn't make it across a swimming pool." Tomohiko responded as usual. He walked away.

Less than an hour later, Chaos crewmembers were jammed into the lifeboats. Last to be boarded were two more who had succumbed to hypothermia. Seeing their inert bodies and thinking of the others who had drowned made him revisit his decision to abandon ship. Would they all have been better off if they'd ignored his lead and stayed aboard, praying for rescue? No. It had been a tough call, but it was one he could live with in the future.

Just as his lifeboat began to descend, Jack noticed the same six men in white knee-length coats emerging through a hatch onto the deck, watching without expression. Then his attention shifted to a man standing alone on the flying bridge, scanning the landing area with binoculars. That had to be the captain, alert for possible hostility. When he looked down at the departing lifeboat, his eyes seemed to fix on Jack.

The overloaded lifeboats, sluggish and riding low in the water, put them ashore at a commercial pier at the edge of town. As soon as the ship's crew was back aboard, the mothership started a turn to get away. As the bow swung around, Jack saw white letters spelling out the ship's name.

Nikita Maru. That captain had ordered his crew to fire on *Aleutian*, driving it into the killer methane burp. That captain had killed Katie. "You filthy bastard," Jack screamed across the water.

Chapter 45

July 31
5:00 p.m.
Port Alberni, British Columbia, Canada

"THAT'S IT, MAUD. I just brought in the last load of frozen fish."

Jack heard exhaustion in the voice of the hospital driver who had been working nonstop to transport the Chaos crew from the waterfront to the admitting area of West Coast General Hospital in Port Alberni.

"Thank God there are no more," the admitting clerk snapped. "We're already swamped."

The initial reception by the staff had been concerned and professional. As more patients kept pouring in, their attitudes deteriorated. At first, the admitting clerk had tried to dig IDs out of their pockets, but it was slow going. Then she ran out of official forms and took down names on a yellow pad. Finally, overwhelmed and out of patience, she gave up and used a permanent marker to write a number on the back of each left hand and passed the patient along for triage inspection.

Jack had already discovered that while his clothes were being dried aboard *Nikita Maru,* someone had stolen the cash from his wallet, but credit cards and his driver's license with photo ID were still in place and he still had Renatus's shoulder holster.

He saw the clerk come to Renatus, take a quizzical look at his face, check his pulse, and scrawl a number. She moved on without asking a single question. Renatus wasn't entered into the hospital books.

A man with a high forehead, sharp vertical lines between his eyes, and wings of hair over his ears strode into the reception area. He wore a badge that read *Dr. Harper - Chief Administrator.* "Who's in charge of you people?" he called out.

After no one volunteered, Jack held up his hand. Harper and two other docs immediately pulled him aside. Harper frowned. "You people should have given us notice you were coming so we could call in more staff, not that we have near enough for a crowd like this." He sounded irritated that some protocol had been breached. "What happened to you people?"

Jack wasn't in the mood to be hassled. "We were working on an offshore platform. Fire and explosions forced us into the water. A lot of the crew was on their last legs, some had already died, when the Japanese whaling ship showed up."

"I see," the administrator said, clearly uninterested in hearing more details.

"Well, we only have fifty-two beds. Most were already filled up with everything from a coyote bite to a head-on lumber truck crash plus fishermen and dockworkers beaten up by the tsunami. Our emergency disaster procedures require our whole staff to help your people. With no one working the rooms, blood, vomit, and shit are piling up. That's not how we do things here." He rolled his eyes. "And who the hell is going to pay for all of this?"

Jack wanted to tell the guy he had his head up his ass, acting like these half-dead men had been on a goddamn cruise ship where they could have called ahead for a reservation.

A different doc said, "Can't take hypothermia lightly. We need risk assessments on every one of you. There may be cardiac problems, increase in blood viscosity, or pulmonary abnormalities."

"Acidosis, coagulation issues, or ventricle fibrillation," said the third, nodding his head slowly to show how serious he was.

Jack raised both hands to stop the barrage. "Gentlemen, we appreciate what you're doing for us, but please shut up and listen." They weren't used to being told to shut up, but they did. He pointed to one of them. "Start by doing a risk assessment on me and my friend right now"—he pointed to Gano—"so we can get on with what we have to do."

His medical clearance came quickly. The doc wanted to keep Gano for a twenty-four hour observation, but Gano gave him so much grief that he shrugged and signed him out. After that, Jack and Gano shepherded the rest of the crew through the testing procedures and the hospital's paperwork. Many of those who checked out relatively well were still lethargic and confused and needed rest for a day or two. They would have to get whatever sleep they could on blankets on the floor while medical staff rushed around them. Jack was informed that the most serious cases would be transferred to the regional hospital in Nanaimo, an hour's drive away.

He had a request to make of Harper, so as soon as he was no longer needed he stepped into an office with Harper's name on the door. No Harper. He decided to wait. He'd gotten some strength back aboard *Nikita Maru*, but was nearly exhausted again. After he sagged into a cowhide chair, he picked up a remote control on the desk and clicked off the sound on the TV, muting the opinion of a CNN talking head.

His mind drifted back to the stricken platform as it loomed above them, to men slipping under the waves, and to the relief he'd felt when the survivors were dumped on the pier. He also remembered the captain of *Nikita Maru* looking coldly down at him. And those six men in white lab coats, ghostly figures watching as the ship turned away.

Something about those images snapped everything into context. He'd assumed that the captain had been reluctant to rescue the Chaos crew and refused to take them to any major port because he was an illegal whaler. And that he'd kept the Chaos crew locked in the cooler so they'd see no evidence. Now Jack realized he'd been wrong. That captain had been protecting a much bigger secret.

When *Nikita Maru* had attacked *Aleutian*, it had been in the vicinity of Chaos. It appeared she had stayed in the area for weeks after that. The captain wouldn't have done that to catch whales. But he would have done exactly that if those men in white coats were scientists who, like Renatus, were collecting and analyzing data about methane hydrate. That would also explain the presence of the ROVs aboard *Nikita Maru.*

The captain hadn't been motivated to rescue them by the fundamental law of the sea that required trying to rescue mariners in distress. He'd known that the presence of his ship near the platform was a matter of record— satellite, other ships, transmissions—and he'd be liable if he failed to attempt assistance after he and his crew knew there were survivors.

The whaling expedition was likely a front for a secret mission by some Japanese mega-corporation to exploit methane hydrate. Its drilling platform could already be on the way across the Pacific. But those scientists couldn't be as brilliant as Renatus, and were much more likely to blow up that part of the world.

The people on the other side of the office door were dealing with an emergency that would subside within a few days, but the terrible threat of what he'd just figured out would get worse, much worse. He clasped his hands behind his head, leaned back, and willed himself into a semi-trance, letting the millions of synapses in his brain massage the problem. When it was time, he sat up straight.

A foreign company and maybe a foreign government were doing business in international waters where no U.S. laws could restrain them from taking Barbas's place. Nothing could, except . . . the Law of the Sea Treaty. Ratification would put a sledgehammer in the hands of the U.S. government to prevent the destabilization catastrophe that Barbas had come within seconds of causing.

The vote on ratification in the Senate was scheduled to come up three days from now, but the Senate majority leader wouldn't bring it to the floor unless he had the votes to pass it. Right now, he didn't. The fastest way to change that was to persuade President Gorton to use the full force of his office. But Gorton was in bed with lobbyists who detested any regulation, certainly including that treaty. Gorton could have pushed ratification through before, but he hadn't. He wouldn't this time either. Barbas had been certain that Jack could get Gorton's help just by asking for it. But on *Challenger*, when Jack had tried to get Gorton to prevent the tsunami that had just wiped out towns along the Alaskan coast, Gorton had refused to take his call and then turned him down cold. It was ironic that he never could have done what Barbas went to such extreme lengths to force him to do.

The chill of the Pacific Ocean had left him, and his mind was back in high gear. Even if he had enough time to get a few business moguls, editorial pundits, and four-star generals to blitz the Senate in support of ratification, he knew that would rile more senators than it would persuade. They were comfortable with lobbyists they knew, but resented pressure from the outside world.

He had weak contacts with three senators, but two would never vote to ratify the treaty. The third wouldn't even help force the issue to the floor for a vote. There wasn't enough time to walk the halls of the Senate office buildings trying to get cold-call appointments to make the case for ratification. But he had to get to DC and give it a try.

He noticed a woman on the TV screen being interviewed while standing in the midst of the ruins of a small seaport business district, obviously one of the places hit by the tsunami. The banner at the bottom identified her as Senator Susan Fisher from Alaska and the location as Sitka, Alaska. The banner also informed him that she currently served on the Senate Homeland Security and Foreign Relations committees. He clicked the sound on. She was being questioned with near-hysterical intensity by a young man whose microphone bore a KTNL-TV (CBS) logo.

She ended the interrogation with her assurance that federal bucks were on their way. She promised to listen to the needs of as many people as she could before she had to leave for DC later tonight. Jack was impressed by her calm and compassionate answers.

He thought how, when you throw a baseball over a fence and hear the sound of shattering glass, that's abstract. When you climb the fence and see the damage, it becomes real. On Chaos, they hadn't been able to see or feel the tsunami. For Sen. Fisher, surrounded by the wreckage, it had to feel absolutely real.

After walking away, Senator Fisher turned back to the microphone and said, "Two tsunamis within a few days. That's very, very strange. I'm going to have people at DOE figure out what's going on."

Game on. She would hear from Jack Strider exactly what was going on and what she had to do about it. The treaty had never made it to the Senate floor for a vote during the senator's tenure. If she had been counted as a likely "no," he'd have to turn her around. If she was already a "yes" vote, he had to persuade her to find a "no" and convert him or her to a "yes." She might not have much clout, but she had a lot of heart and would be fighting for her constituents. She was his best hope to stop whoever was behind *Nikita Maru.*

She would be in Sitka only until late tonight. Since she didn't know him, he could never persuade her on the phone. He had to get there fast. But first he had an important call to make. He picked up the desk phone again.

"Oh my God," Debra said. "I've been so worried. Are you all right? What happened on Chaos? Why does caller ID display 'WCGH'? What does that mean?"

The sound of Debra's voice was like a shot of adrenaline. It reminded him that after they hung up yesterday he hadn't known whether he'd ever talk with her again.

"I'm mostly all right, but my head feels like this is the morning after a three-day drunk, so I'm only going to give you the short version right now." He repeated what he'd told the docs and added, "Full disclosure: There's a lot more, and I'll tell you all about it when we're together. By the way, WCGH stands for West Coast General Hospital in Port Alberni, British Columbia. That's where we are."

"It's a miracle you're alive. But wait a minute. If you're all right, why are you in the hospital?"

"The Chaos crew is getting medical attention for hypothermia. I was shaky for a while, but I'm over it now."

"Is Gano okay?"

"He was almost out for the count, but he's on his feet again. Molly McCoy was pretty shut down, but she's much better too. Drake is tough as an iguana. No problem there. All he cared about when he got here was finding out whether *Challenger* was still afloat after Barbas's helo attacked it. He talked with his shore crew in Alameda and found out they'd gotten a call by satellite phone from his ship. Some shrapnel wounds but no fatalities. It's badly damaged and is limping home to Alameda with a Coast Guard escort. Renatus is still in bad shape, but they say he'll make it."

"Since Renatus is there, does that mean Barbas is there too?"

"Barbas is dead."

"My God, I'm sure he didn't think he *could* die. I want to hear all about it, but are you telling me the truth? Are you really all right?"

"I swear it." Later, face-to-face, he'd share exactly how close he'd come to death.

"I look forward to you proving to me that you're all right." She chuckled. "You probably don't know that the TV news channels started screaming yesterday about a tsunami warning from an unidentified offshore source. Did that warning come from you?"

"It did."

"They're saying it saved a lot of people in BC and Alaska."

Her words reminded him how close they'd come to not getting that warning out. "That's great news."

"You being safe is the best news there is," she said, "but I have some other important new for you. It's about the Armstrong case. Do you want bad news or good news first?"

"Bad news." Seemed like he'd been dealing with bad news as long as he could remember.

"We won't collect our fee for a while."

His weary brain wasn't tracking what she was talking about. Then he understood. "Did you say 'fee'?"

"Yep. The Air Force caved and agreed to settle. They'll start payments to our clients, and all others affected, immediately. They'll also start a drastic reduction in their emissions of poisons."

"That's fantastic. Our clients will be overjoyed. It's a stupendous win for you. But what's the hang-up on the fee?"

"They insisted that I agree to delay getting it, but it will be huge. Petty payback on their part, but I had to give them that to close the deal."

"You are a genius. If I weren't already in love with someone, I would fall in love with you. Oh, yeah, it's *already* you."

She was quiet. That was good. She was hearing him.

"Thanks, partner."

"I have to know, how did you do it?"

"When I couldn't find a single legal decision on facts similar to ours to cite as precedent in our favor, I finally asked myself the right question. *Why* were there no legal precedents? One explanation was that the Air Force lawyers had made sure they kept out of court. Maybe they played hardball until plaintiffs gave up or died. And if that didn't work, maybe they'd made out-of-court settlements that included a confidentiality provision. Since they were still playing hardball with us, I wondered what would motivate them to settle." She paused. "What am I thinking? After what you've been through, you don't need to hear about this right now."

"Are you kidding? I'm hooked. You *have* to tell me what you did."

"I invited one of their top lawyers to an off-the-record dinner at Boulevard Restaurant. I thought that would be good luck since it's our favorite place. I talked about how important this case was to the public, and said I intended to ensure full media coverage. I reminded him that a trial would drag the Air Force's dirty laundry into the glare of the media, and that I'd stretch it out day after day. He was looking for the server to order another martini when I asked him 'How much do your generals want to bleed in public?' I saw in his eyes that was the question they'd been asking themselves back in his office.

"He looked away and asked, 'What would it take?'"

"I'll be damned," Jack said.

"I told him that if we reached a fair settlement immediately, none of this parade of horrors would happen, and the Air Force could claim credit for solving a serious problem—and for doing the right thing for everyone injured. He tried to push back, but his heart wasn't in it. I was right. Bad publicity was their Achilles heel. I told him to take his phone to one of Boulevard's private rooms and get agreement to a settlement. Otherwise, I'd go public in the morning.

"When he came back, he had their top gun on the phone. We negotiated terms on the spot. He said for me to write it up, and the Secretary of the Air Force and the Commanding Officer at Armstrong would sign. I went back to the office, called in our best people on the case, and we worked straight through into the next morning despite Simms causing a swarm of cockroaches to invade our offices. That led to a bit of a scuffle, but that really is a story for a different time. Anyway, it is a done deal as soon as our clients agree."

"You know, I've been told quite a few times that I'm a pretty fair poker player. After what you just told me, I'm staying out of games with you." He thought about how close his pursuit of Barbas had come to tanking whatever chance they had to win against Armstrong. If Debra hadn't stepped in, the case might have been road kill. He'd make sure the plaintiffs and the media understood that she'd been the lead lawyer.

"By settling, we won't have a precedent to use against them in other jurisdictions," he said, "but we have all our research and witnesses. I think we'll get the Air Force to clean up its act voluntarily."

"I can't wait until you get back here," she said.

"I have to make one more stop before I come home." Before she could protest, he said, "I need you to come here to supervise getting more than 150 people who worked on the platform out of Canada and into the U.S. or wherever they came from. Molly McCoy from Astoria knows a lot of these people, so she'll oversee medical issues. Molly will tell you all she knows about what happened on Chaos. You okay with all that?"

"I'll be there. Where are you going?"

"Sitka, Alaska. I'll stay in touch and explain it all when we're together." That wasn't enough, but he hoped she'd let it go. She did.

As soon as he hung up, Dr. Harper walked in. His face filled with storm clouds when he saw Jack in his chair.

"I have one small request to make before I leave," Jack said, and reached for Renatus's shoulder holster.

HE LEFT HARPER'S office and found Molly. Her face was drawn, but she managed a smile.

"You're looking better," he said. "Has a doctor checked you out?"

"They say I'm their star patient. They told me to eat plenty of their special nutrition bars and stay warm." She looked around. "Speaking of staying warm, I haven't seen Gano. How is he?"

"Last I saw, he was scrounging in a supply room for anything to help people get comfortable." He explained what he wanted her to do and said Debra was coming to Port Alberni right away.

"I can do that," she said, "and I'll contact families in Astoria who don't know that so many townies won't be coming home."

Her would-be boyfriend Randy was among the missing, but neither of them mentioned him. They shared a hug, and he left her to mourn the loss of her friends.

He corralled Gano and told him about Debra's triumph in the Armstrong lawsuit. "Now we're going to hitch a ride on the next vehicle taking people to Nanaimo. From there, we'll fly to Sitka, more than six hundred miles northwest of here."

"I'm having trouble following the bouncing ball again," Gano said. "Debra pulled your hot dog out of the fire, so you don't have to be in Sacramento for your big trial. But instead of going home, you're going to some godforsaken place with a population smaller than Sausalito. That seems insanely illogical, which you aren't, so you must have a reason I don't know about."

"I always have a reason, probably one of my least endearing traits." That made Gano grin, a good sign. He told him that he had to persuade Senator Fisher to save the treaty. "Now, let's find our transport."

A few minutes into the drive from Port Alberni to Nanaimo in a Dodge medical van, Gano said, "Hey, I saw Steve Drake walking around a half hour ago. I'm surprised he's not coming with us."

"You remember that shoulder holster with Renatus's research in it? I got the hospital administrator to lock it in his safe. As soon as Renatus is able to travel,

Drake will make sure he and the holster get to Ironbound safely and without leaving any tracks. Drake will leave here as a bodyguard, but I hope he'll be Renatus's partner by the time they get there."

"You keep right on thinking, man," Gano said. "I'm grabbing some Zs before we get to Nanaimo."

He had the driver drop them at the Nanaimo airport. Before going inside, they looked around the small plane parking area that paralleled the single landing strip. Gano volunteered to steal one. "We might even get it back here before anyone notices," he said.

"And if not, it would be grand theft. Let's go inside and see if we can pay someone to fly us."

"Bartenders always know that kind of stuff." Gano's wolfish smile made it clear that information wasn't the only reason he wanted to visit the bar.

Jack stopped into a small souvenir shop, bought two cheap cell phones, and headed for the bar.

"Right now," the bartender told them, "that old guy over there, the one with his head on the table, is your only chance. Name's Buck. He's got a sweet Beechcraft Bonanza. Won't rent it, but he sometimes hires out."

Jack's glance warned Gano away from ordering rum. He roused the man, who looked to be on the dark side of eighty. As it turned out, Buck had flown to Sitka often and quickly agreed to a charter. He doubled the fee when Jack said they had to leave immediately.

When they got to his plane, Buck nearly lost his grip when he hauled himself into the pilot's seat. As the engine warmed up, Gano said, "Bucko, you're a damned good man to help us out on short notice. Since I'm checked out on this type of aircraft, I'll take the controls and let you just kick back."

"Nobody flies my baby but me. No worries."

"Then I'll just slide into a seat in back with my friend. Give me a shout if you want a break." He got in, leaned close to Jack, and whispered, "If I see that old buzzard start to nod I'll move up fast."

Buck ran his checklist, took off like a pro, and powered the Bonanza up to cruising altitude. Almost immediately after leveling off, it dropped like it was in free-fall.

Jack was thrown hard up against his seat belt. "Son of a bitch." Then it was over.

Gano looked at Jack. "Easy, *compadre.* Just a little hole in the sky. Your basic air pocket. You okay?"

"Fine. Surprised me, that's all."

Like hell he was fine. Clammy sweat. Heart beating like a snare drum. He knew if he held his hands out in front of him they'd shake like an alcoholic's. Every system in his body was shot to hell. He didn't trust himself to speak.

Gano gave him a speculative look. "What you're feeling is coming from what happened on that platform. You understand that, right?"

Jack swallowed hard. "That's behind me."

"Yeah, in about fifty years. What went down out there was rough, even for me. People screaming, scared shitless, blood running through the scuppers. If things had gone a little different, we'd have been dinner for seagulls. With you marching to the beat of the Dalai Lama, of course it got to you."

Jack had tried to ignore what he was feeling right now and then tried to explain it away. Neither worked. He couldn't stop picturing dead people sprawled out on the platform. But it went deeper than that. He'd made decisions on Chaos that meant life or death for hundreds of human beings. He'd never been accountable for the lives of so many others up close. Part of him couldn't believe he'd done it. Part of him understood he couldn't have done otherwise. And he knew he was a better man for it. Then he noticed Gano waiting for his response.

"It gets to me because I was responsible for a lot of what happened."

"Other than you're a guilt-sucking liberal, how do you figure that?"

"It was my decision to attack Chaos. I knew you and Drake wouldn't go if I refused to allow weapons. I had no chance against Barbas without you, so when Drake started handing out handguns and RPGs, I let it pass. That meant there would be blood for sure."

"Sounds like we're singing from the same hymnbook, so to speak?"

"I think violence comes to you more naturally."

"Pretty damn pious, my friend." All at once, Gano's voice wasn't friendly at all. "I didn't pop out of the womb wearing six-guns, but I got into a line of work where I had to defend myself. Always did as little damage as I could. But one night on the outskirts of Guanajuato, a drunk got after the woman who was with me pretty hard. I backed him off a couple of times, but he kept coming on. It got ugly. He started to pull a Saturday night special, cheap .25 junk gun. I got my Glock out much faster. Had him cold, but I took it easy on him. Just whacked him alongside his head with the barrel. Knocked him on his ass. I was trying to grab him when he started shooting. Hit my woman twice. Killed her. I swore never to let that happen again."

"I'm sorry, Gano." His friend had just peeled off another layer.

"I'm saying that facts on the ground can scramble your values," Gano said. "That's what happened to you." He wasn't gloating, just stating what was obvious to him. "As long as you wear the cloak of Mr. Fix-It-Man— which, by the way, is who you are—you can't avoid conflict." He scooted in his seat to face Jack more directly. "What I'm about to say may sound like I'm your big brother—yes, I'm thirty-nine, two years older than you. When your friend at Greenpeace called, you stepped up. You took on Barbas and the U.S. Air Force when the odds against you were off the books. You had the guts to go down to the bottom of the ocean in a tin can, something I could never do. You swung some good punches in Astoria and didn't back down when we were on Ironbound and Renatus's robot had us in its sights. We couldn't be more different, but I respect you more than any man I've ever known. And if that means I'm the one who has to pull a trigger now and then, I'll be there."

"Thanks, man, and I have one piece of advice for you: If you'd learn to be a better marksman, you wouldn't have to fire so many shots."

Gano grinned. "Let me ask you this, Chief Eagle Scout. Shouldn't you whistle up a passel of media types and tell 'em about the monster in the deep and where these big ol' waves came from?"

"No. If I did that, two things could happen. Based on the little hard evidence I have now, they'd ask if I'd also found Moby Dick while I was out there. Or they'd listen to my story, not give a damn whether it was true, and fire off headlines that would panic a few million people. Either way, my credibility would be shot when I am ready to go public. Deep-water drilling companies can get into action fast, but not overnight. Before one of them can set off the next tsunami, I have a little time to line up proof and get some heavy hitters on my side. After that, I'll bring in the media."

"Heavy hitters like who?"

"Credible scientists with relevant specialties."

"And exactly how will you make them into 'true believers'?"

"The quakes and tsunamis are facts. I have to make the case that Barbas's drilling was a scientifically plausible cause. To do that, I plan to use Renatus as a secret weapon."

"You going to blow his cover?"

"Nope. All the data went up in flames, but he has a mass of information in his head that he can feed me. Even if the scientists aren't 100 percent convinced, they can attest to the probability. If we get that treaty ratified, someone will have to enforce compliance with it. So I'll have a couple of jut-jawed admirals standing nearby to talk about national security, their new mission, and the need for some new weapons. They'll love it."

"Shouldn't the folks who live on the coasts be warned against this new threat?"

"Of course, but in ways that don't freak them out or crash property values. So can you think of an organization that would want the chance to protect millions of Americans living on the coast?"

Gano grinned. "I'll bet the Boy Scouts would jump at it."

"Maybe, but I'll give Homeland Security first crack. They'll produce a swarm of upgraded warning systems, new construction projects, training programs; there's no end to it. I hope a breakthrough makes the energy from methane hydrate accessible, but right now, my highest priority is getting that treaty ratified in time to prevent a disaster.

"I'm impressed. You've really thought this through."

"My thinking is only about sixty seconds ahead of my mouth. This will be a lot harder than I just made it sound. Whatever politician leads the charge, the opposition party will start throwing up roadblocks. Multinationals will do everything they can to defeat any drilling regulation. But we can make this happen. We *have* to."

"I've always got your back, but right now you've worn me out," Gano said. He leaned back and closed his eyes. That was fine with Jack. He didn't want to talk anymore, but he couldn't shut out one thought he'd suppressed for the last three hours. The captain of *Nikita Maru* had ordered the attack on *Aleutian*, forcing it to flee into the path of the methane burp that sucked it, and Katie, under. Watching *Nikita Maru* escape around a bend in the inlet had squeezed his heart. If he'd had a gun he knew he would have taken a shot at that captain. And he wouldn't have missed.

As they got close to Sitka, Buck looked back over his shoulder and said, "Glad we made it. Didn't want to mention it earlier, but leaving sudden like we did, I cut it a little close on gas. If we'd hit a headwind, we'd have been in trouble. Now I think we're okay—barely."

He contacted the Sitka Rocky Gutierrez Airport for landing instructions.

"Instructions? Are you shitting me?" the tower operator said. "That damned tsunami left the runway waist deep in trash. Nobody can land here. Our power has been cutting on and off for—"

Sitka tower was dead air.

Chapter 46

July 31
9:00 p.m.
Sitka, Alaska

"HEY, BUCK, SEEING the airport is out of commission and your Bonanza is running on fumes, where do you stash your life jackets?" Gano's tone was nonchalant.

Jack looked out the window at Sitka below. In the dark, it was hard to make out the extent of the damage, but the waterfront and large patches stretching inland were without lights, not even headlights. Very bad sign. He glanced west at the black, forbidding Gulf of Alaska and felt an autonomic shudder at the thought of being back in the water, assuming they survived a crash landing at sea.

"For God's sake," Buck said. "We don't need life jackets. I'll just drop in on my friend Peter Pilafian. He's got a private strip in a ravine around the corner of that bluff up ahead. He usually shoots at trespassers, but he might be more open-minded tonight." His hands seemed steady on the controls, eyes squinting but alert.

A few minutes later, he turned into the ravine. "He don't monitor nothing, so no way to check in." He shed altitude fast and centered on the grass strip lined with small planes and several Army helicopters. "Damn if that ain't the biggest crowd I ever seen here. Guess Peter ain't shooting at anyone tonight." He cackled.

He landed soft, backed off hard, and taxied to the only remaining space to park. As they walked along the strip past an Army helo, Gano flipped a casual salute at a group of enlisted men in camouflage fatigues. "You boys part of an invasion?"

"Naw, we're a ferry service for the FEMA advance team," answered a red-faced corporal.

"Those guys over there flew in from Juneau bringing senator somebody." He turned back to his squad's bull session.

When they got to the end of the strip, Buck said, "Ain't nothing for me in town. I'll just drop in on ol' Peter, see how he's been keeping. You look me up when you want to head back."

Jack hitched a ride in a Jeep FEMA had hired as a shuttle to town. On the ride in, the Jeep driver told them the entire low-lying part of Sitka was so badly damaged it had been cordoned off and was being patrolled by National Guard troops. The rank stench of sewage from ruptured lines was powerful, and Jack saw flames far beyond the ability of the local fire department to fight. He asked the driver about Senator Susan Fisher and learned she'd finished touring the damage. She was at the Sitka Pioneer Home, now an assisted living residence, meeting with constituents who needed immediate help. He asked to be dropped there.

They jumped out of the Jeep as it slowed in front of a V-shaped, four- story building, white with a red roof. Only the center section of the first floor was lighted.

A human chain extended out the door, past the flagpole, and across the lawn. Some in line looked as though they'd been working on fire-fighting or salvage crews. Most were stone-faced, a few sobbed, some dragged a backpack or duffel bag behind them as they inched forward.

Jack walked straight to a card table placed outside the front door and introduced himself to a burly man who looked like a lumberjack. "I've just flown hundreds of miles to meet with Senator Fisher. I'm sure she's busy, but—"

"Please get in line. Drinking water is provided every thirty minutes." He looked behind Jack. "Next."

Jack knew there was no point in yelling at him. He'd been hearing that for hours. He looked at the line. Way too long. It was getting late, and Senator Fisher had to get back on the helo to return to Washington. Not seeing her was not an option, so he'd have to reach her through someone else. There must be staffers around. He leaned across the table and spoke quietly, close to the guard's face.

"I must see Senator Fisher."

"Like I said before, go to the end of the line."

"This can't wait, so I'm going to tell this crowd that another tsunami could hit here and that the senator could prevent it but has refused. You think that's what she wants?"

"Are you nuts? These people are ready to riot as it is. I'll get the cops."

"They'll be too late. I'm going to do it right now unless . . ."

"Unless what?"

"Unless she sends a senior staff person to meet me inside this door. And if I see a cop coming, I'll start yelling."

The guard wiped his forehead. "Like I don't already have enough trouble. This is an old folks' home, so I also got a few dozen cranky, hungry residents doing wheelies up and down the halls. Now you just wait here." He stepped inside.

When he came back, his face was flushed. Still standing, he pointed a finger at Jack. "You are making a big mistake, mister. Rather than let you say nasty things about the senator, or start an uprising, they're sending a guy to hear your BS. I guarantee he's going to be one pissed-off dude. I'll signal you when he gets here. Wait on that bench on the other side of the yard where I can see you."

When they got to the concrete bench in a far corner of the spacious lawn, he sat at one end, Gano at the other, mute acknowledgement that each needed time to process all this.

He stared back across the lawn at the people in line, every one of them hurting. All he could think of was loss. Much of Sitka had been wiped out. A lot of

Astoria townies had died. Survivors had lost friends and jobs.

The line across the lawn grew longer, and there was no signal from the guard, so Gano left to find food.

Jack was half-watching when an elderly woman in line slumped to the ground. An old man next to her dropped his cane, fell to his knees, and lifted her head. Someone handed him a canteen. After a few sips from it, she struggled up and hung on his arm, looking determined to endure until she reached the senator.

That tiny event somehow reminded him that he, too, had to keep fighting, or his law firm would collapse as surely as the platform had. It would lose momentum and its best young lawyers. It would fall from special to ordinary or worse. The Armstrong fee could make a difference at some point, but only if the firm was still in existence.

For the next quarter hour, as if using mental Lego bricks, he built a plan, shaky and ambitious, that depended on two things: speed, and a man he'd never met, Alex Georgiou.

The bars on his cell told him the tsunami hadn't killed service. It only took a few seconds to get the number of Odyssey Properties, Barbas's holding company in Athens. Georgiou was Barbas's second-in-command. Since the time difference between Alaska and Greece was eleven or twelve hours, he might catch Georgiou in the office. He entered the number.

After two transfers, he was connected to Georgiou's secretary. In response to his request she answered, "Mr. Georgiou is in a meeting."

"Please tell him Jack Strider is calling with information on a crisis at his mineral mining operation in the northeast Pacific."

Georgiou came on the line very quickly. "What is it?" His brusque tone couldn't disguise the need to know that forced him to take the call.

Jack didn't take the bait. "I'm sure you know who I am and that my law firm was fired by Petros Barbas. Yesterday, I was with him on your platform."

"I'm very busy, Mr. Strider. You said you have information about our platform . . ." Georgiou managed to sound like Jack had offered to sell him a used toothbrush.

"When was the last time you spoke with Barbas?"

"Yesterday afternoon."

"And you haven't been able to reach anyone since then because late yesterday your platform turned into an inferno and collapsed. Everything on it was destroyed." He spoke slowly, leaving space between sentences. "All the valuable minerals were dumped back to the bottom. The high-tech equipment on the seabed was ruined. There is nothing to salvage. Your multi-billion dollar project is finished."

Take that, you SOB. Jack pictured Georgiou in a plush office, stunned into silence, caught between disbelief and despair.

"When word of this gets out to the public," Jack said, "which I promise you it will, lenders will demand repayment of loans. Your credit will be shot. Odyssey

Properties will be on the fast track to oblivion." He heard Georgiou mumbling under his breath.

Finally, Georgiou said, "Even if what you said is true, which I doubt, our friends in the big banks would stand by us."

"Hard to believe you just used 'friends' and 'big banks' in the same sentence. I don't have time for your bullshit. Dozens of your employees on the platform were killed. Class action lawyers will be on you like piranhas. Plus, there's your liability for the damage Barbas did to the towns of Astoria, Sitka, and—look, this is pointless. I'm going to make you an offer. Then you will accept my offer. It's that simple."

"I will do nothing until I talk with Mr. Barbas." His voice was tight. "How can I reach him?"

That was the question he'd been waiting for. Time to deliver the *coup de grase.* "Barbas was incinerated. If anything was left of him, it's feeding the sharks." He made it gross to shock Georgiou even more.

Gano, who had returned and was devouring a fat sandwich, had been listening closely. He pumped a clenched fist up and down in support.

Jack went into his pitch. He laid out what he wanted, careful to use general terms. Then he stated what he would give in return. He listened to Georgiou's ill-tempered response for almost a full minute and said, "You are hallucinating. Odyssey Properties will never get back into the mineral mining business. Your creditors will freeze your assets down to the paper clips. My offer is good for one hour." He listened to Georgiou's reply and clicked off.

"Wow!" Gano said. "You kicked his ass."

"Not really." He swallowed hard. "After my tirade, he turned me down and hung up."

"From your tone, I thought you had him by the short hairs."

"That's what I wanted him to feel, but those guys have been riding the crest so long he didn't spook."

"Sorry, Chief, you gave it a good shot." He handed Jack a sandwich in a plastic bag. "Got this at a little place down the street. You won't believe some of the things on the menu board. The special was some kind of fermented fish that had a God-awful putrid smell. They call them 'stink heads.'"

Jack looked at his sandwich suspiciously. "What's this?"

"Said it was caribou but I think they were pulling my leg. Not bad." After swallowing another bite, he said, "So what will Georgiou do?"

"After he finds out I told him the truth about their platform, he'll believe Barbas is dead. Then he'll think about what that means for the company. After he runs that past his accountants, he'll be afraid to talk with the banks. That's when he'll open a bottle and lock the door."

"Sounds like you're in his head pretty good."

"Maybe, but I needed to close that deal right now. At least I put him in the same squeeze I'm in. When he sobers up, he'll shop my offer to see if he can get a better deal. I made that tough by not giving him a list of specific assets that might have a market value. If he can get a better offer fast enough, I'll never hear from him again."

"You gonna tell Debra about this?"

"I would have discussed it with her beforehand, but if I had any edge in making a deal with Odyssey Properties, it was before Georgiou could get on top of the situation. There was no time to bring Debra up to speed. Besides, this was such a long shot. I'll tell her later. In the meantime, don't say anything to her about it."

Gano pointed at the guard standing in the entrance waving at them. Jack waved back, and they headed over.

"He's in there," the guard said, "and he's not a happy camper."

The senator's staffer was a lanky man wearing a wrinkled khaki shirt, black pants held in place by suspenders, and a broad tie bearing multiple grizzly bears.

"I'm Trig Trail, the senator's legislative assistant, and I'll tell you straight out I don't like you one bit."

Oh great. "Have we met before?"

"No, and we're not likely to meet again. You threatened my boss. I wouldn't be standing here if she hadn't sent me." He led Jack into a small library. "Two things you need to know. First, the senator has to catch an Army chopper to Juneau to connect with the red-eye back to DC. She's leaving here in"—he checked his watch—"thirty-seven minutes. Second, she gets approached by a lot of crackpots, so I want to hear your credentials. If they don't cut it, you won't be meeting her."

Very aware of how little time he had, Jack gave Trail a high-speed tour of his professional life, using buzz words and dropping names.

After a couple of minutes, Trail held up his hand to stop him. "Okay, tell me your doomsday story."

After eight minutes, Jack finished. "That's the case. Are you really going to keep Senator Fisher from hearing it?"

"What you're talking about is so far above my pay grade it makes my head ache. Wait here while I brief her." Before he went through the door, he turned back and said, "I still don't like the way you got this meeting."

After Trail left, Jack dropped into a slat-back chair. He felt sure Trail would try to poison the senator's mind against him, but there was nothing he could do about that. Relieved to be away from the hectic scene outside, he tried to relax and thought again how grateful he was to Debra for bailing him out on the Armstrong case. He didn't need a shrink to know why winning that case had been so important to him. But the number of people who would be injured or killed by the next tsunami wildly overshadowed Armstrong. So, against what his conscience cried out for him to do, he'd gone after Barbas. Now he had to stop anyone else from destabilizing methane hydrate without regulation. If that had meant losing the Armstrong case, he would never have gotten over it. Debra had saved him from that.

WHEN TRAIL RETURNED, Jack asked him to swing by the main door to pick up Gano.

"Nope, this is a closed meeting," and he headed down the hallway to an area where disheveled constituents were seated at long tables talking intensely with young men and women, probably FEMA workers, who were taking notes. When Trail got a signal, he guided Jack into a dimly lighted office that smelled of sweat.

Senator Fisher sat at the end of a small conference table, a stack of folders by her left hand, another stack toppled over on the floor. She was a sturdy woman with a square face, short iron-gray hair, and half-glasses. Her expression was forbidding, and she didn't rise to meet him. He introduced himself and sat to her left.

"For nine hours I've been helping people get food, shelter, medicine, and find lost relatives. Now, when I have to leave in twenty minutes to get back to the Senate for critical votes, you show up claiming the Alaskan coast is likely to be hit by a huge *man-made* tsunami. That sounds ludicrous. The only reason I'm going to listen is because Alaska has more than sixty-six hundred *miles* of coastline."

A woman in her mid-thirties, face gaunt from strain, entered the office.

"Linda is my chief of staff and has a degree in biology. Trig was a chemical engineer before he got into politics. You have ten minutes to tell me your story. The moment I think you're blowing smoke, you're out of here."

That really was ludicrous. Ten minutes wasn't enough time for a lawyer to order a beer.

"All right, Senator, first the facts and the science, then the solution." He raced through the litany of Petros Barbas, the mammoth platform located not far from Alaska, and the goals of the Chaos Project. When he got to methane hydrate, seabed tests, destabilization, earthquakes, and what he'd seen on the ocean floor, he focused on Linda as most likely to understand. He capped his argument by pointing out that Senator Fisher, in her statement on KTNL-TV had questioned why two tsunamis had hit the west coast within a few days of each other. "Now you understand why that happened."

"But why aren't reporters all over this story?" Trig asked.

"Because their cameras are focused on wreckage that used to be a fish plant and on a dog trapped in a half-submerged truck. Maybe someone may report that both of the earthquakes that caused those tsunamis had epicenters close together. But reporters know nothing about methane hydrate in the seabed and the role it might have in causing an earthquake. Virtually no one even knows those massive reservoirs are out there. And any wild speculation that these earthquakes were initiated by humans would never get past the editor. After the dog is rescued, the reporters will move on."

"You make it sound credible," Fisher said, "but you have no real proof. In fact, you could be lying or just plain delusional. All we have to go on is your word."

"You have more than that. Dr. Steve Drake, the renowned marine scientist and explorer, will back me up. He saw the same things I did on the seabed. Dr. Renatus Roux, the man who designed the entire Chaos system, can also vouch for what I've said." That was pure bluff. Even if Renatus was still alive, no one could find him in time. "Linda can verify with one phone call that the platform is a smoking ruin, and I guarantee that Barbas won't be showing up anywhere. By the way, my word is plenty good in most circles."

"You understand why I might have had doubts," Fisher said. "At least with Barbas dead, it's over." For the first time, her face relaxed a little, and her body language told him she was about to terminate the meeting.

"No. The threat is even greater now. That's why I'm here and why you are essential. As soon as the real goal of the Chaos Project platform leaks, multinational energy companies will descend on the site to dig into huge reservoirs of methane hydrate. None of their engineers and scientists knows as much as Barbas's chief scientist did, and even he couldn't figure out how to extract methane safely. If they are free to go ahead, there *will* be a catastrophe."

A young man opened the door and stuck his head into the office. "Senator, KSCT-TV, the NBC affiliate, is here."

"Tell them to get lost in a nice way." She turned to her aides. "What do you think?"

"You're persuasive, Mr. Strider," Linda said, "but I don't see evidence of cause and effect with those tsunamis."

"The cause was Barbas's chief scientist applying heat that destabilized the methane hydrate. I saw him do it. One effect was the methane burp that followed. I witnessed it tearing up that platform. And we're all seeing the effects of the tsunami Barbas caused."

"I'm still not convinced," she said. "And, Senator, you have to walk out that door in two minutes."

That was a shocker. He'd counted on Linda's support to offset Trail. Then he saw Trail about to speak. He groaned inwardly.

"I respectfully disagree with you, Linda," Trail said. "From an engineering perspective, his description of how the system worked is logical. Even more important, before I briefed you, Senator, I researched what Mr. Strider told me about his credentials. It checked out one hundred percent. He even left out some impressive accomplishments. I say he's neither lying nor delusional. So the real question is what he wants you to do."

"Thanks, Trig," Jack said. "One more thing before I tell you what I want. Senator, since you're on the Homeland Security committee, you understand that this could be a huge threat to national safety. Terrorists could blackmail the U.S. government just by threatening to destabilize methane hydrate. Or they could adapt some basic subsea mining gear and try to do it. Even more likely, a disaster will be caused by corporate crazies trying to get richer quick. There will be hell to pay if the government doesn't stop it from happening again after it has been warned."

She looked down, thinking. "What are you asking me to do?"

"The United Nations Convention on the Law of the Sea, a treaty, defined rights and responsibilities in using the oceans. It also established the International

Seabed Authority with power to grant or withhold mining leases and regulate seabed mining."

"I've heard of that treaty, but I don't know much about it."

"One hundred and sixty-two nations have ratified it, but the U.S. Senate—along with Uzbekistan, South Sudan, Andorra and Israel—hasn't. The treaty was signed by Bill Clinton in 1994, but no president since then has been willing to spend political capital to get it ratified. As you know, ratifying any treaty requires at least sixty-seven 'yes' votes. The last time it was about to be brought up, thirty-six senators indicated they would vote against it, so it was deferred again. The majority leader has put it on the Senate calendar three days from now, but he'll pull it unless he has the votes to pass it." He saw in her sharp look at him that she finally understood where this was going.

"Barbas located his platform just outside U.S. territorial limits," Jack pushed on, "so the U.S. couldn't regulate what he did. If the Senate ratifies the treaty, the U.S. will become a member of the ISA and able to influence whether an applicant gets a license to exploit resources in international waters and on what terms. Ratification means we can protect our coastlines from the next Barbas. And you know as well as I do that five minutes after the next tsunami destroys hundreds of miles of the west coast, the media is going to investigate who opposed ratification of the treaty that could have prevented it."

"But I'm the wrong person, because I'm sure the majority leader has already counted me as a 'yes' vote."

"But you can twist arms and switch 'no' votes to 'yes.' That would get the majority leader to bring it to the floor for a vote."

Trail spoke up. "It's hard to twist an arm when it's holding hands with lobbyists. We don't have enough time to explain this whole mess. Besides, why hasn't President Gorton been twisting arms?"

Jack had anticipated that question. "He's from a state that hasn't been hammered by tsunamis, so he doesn't care as much." He wasn't about to tell them that the U.S. Chamber of Commerce opposed ratification and so did a lot of heavyweight donors to Gorton's campaigns.

She nodded in agreement and fixed her eyes on a ferociously ugly stuffed halibut mounted on the wall. She was probably running her own personal risk-versus-reward calculation.

She sat up straighter. "I hope you come out of this as a hero, Mr. Strider, but the people who have blocked that treaty for so long play for keeps. If they have a chance, they'll do whatever they can to discredit you, ruin your reputation."

She looked at Jack for several seconds. "I can't do it by myself, but I can count on four other senators, all females, from the west coast. If they're already 'yes' votes, they'll help me convert others. Now I have to hightail it to my helo and back to DC. Because of you, this will be my highest priority."

Chapter 47

August 3
6:00 p.m.
Sausalito, California

JACK STEERED HIS racing sloop away from Pier 9 on the San Francisco waterfront and smiled as it leapt into action. He headed north across the Bay, passing Alcatraz to port, then Angel Island to starboard. This was the first time he'd been sailing since the morning aboard the schooner *Excalibur* when Petros Barbas had revealed parts of his Chaos Project and hired their firm to help with it. That had been three weeks ago—or a lifetime.

Zipping across the water sparkling in the sun lifted his mood. He loved reading the wind and the surface of the water and listening to the sounds of the hull slicing through the waves. But even though he was a water guy, until a couple of weeks ago, he'd had no idea how little he knew about the oceans beyond a hundred feet down. He'd paid a high price for that ignorance.

His heart had been lifted even more by the transformation of the Armstrong lawsuit from an albatross into a golden eagle.

If Senator Fisher didn't jump the tracks, and the Law of the Sea treaty was ratified, he'd be on the phone with her an hour later. A treaty was only as good as its enforcement, and special interests would try to pull the treaty's teeth. The scenario that still scared the hell out of him was a rogue Barbas-clone setting off methane hydrate before the new law was implemented. Fisher and the Secretary of State would have to press the ISA to impose an immediate worldwide moratorium on exploiting methane hydrate. The specter of monster tsunamis could get that done.

Leaving Angel Island behind, he glanced to port into Richardson Bay where his father had lived in luxury. His outrage still burned, but what he'd gone through in recent weeks had changed his perspective. Now his father's crimes were just one of the waypoints on a much larger map. From now on, he'd chart his own course.

He sailed into Belvedere Cove where, nearing the small town of Tiburon, he got a good omen. All the berths at the pier of Sam's Anchor Café were usually occupied, but this time there was one open where he could tie up.

Gano had gone to SFO to meet Debra and Molly after their flight back from Port Alberni. The last time he'd talked with Debra was before he'd flown to Sitka, so she'd extract details about that from Gano as they drove, at least about everything but the failed deal he'd offered Georgiou.

He walked through the restaurant and onto Sam's crowded deck where he discovered he'd beaten the others there. Almost as rare as a spot at the pier was a vacant table next to the railing, but it was waiting for him. Across the Bay, the high-rise skyline, Fisherman's Wharf, and the mansions rising from the Marina up to Pacific Heights were glowing in clear summer sunlight.

Pretty damn different from nearly dying of hypothermia in the North Pacific.

The server appeared. "Ramos fizz? Grey Goose Cosmo? Bloody Mary?"—the standard trio offered tourists.

"Glenora scotch. Double."

"Ahoy, Captain Nemo!" Gano's shout came from the doorway leading onto the deck. Debra and Molly were right behind him.

Jack jumped up, zigzagged around tables, and lifted Debra off her feet in a bear hug. Love swept through him and pushed out all the stress. They kissed and diners around them applauded.

Seconds after they were seated, the drinks arrived that they'd ordered as they'd passed the bar inside the restaurant. After the server took their food orders and left, Debra pointed. "Look, a seaplane circling over Angel Island."

Gano snorted. "That's about a million and a half bucks worth of de Havilland Turbo Boss Beaver. And it's not a seaplane. It's an amphibian, able to set down on land or water."

Debra gave him a "like I care" look and said, "Jack, Gano told me how well you handled the treaty. When it's ratified, only one senator will know you made it happen, but at this table, we all know. It's amazing you pulled it off right after coming out the other side of hell." They touched glasses.

They sat silent, letting waves of chatter from other diners wash over them. Jack wished he could make an announcement about the great business deal that would guarantee the future of the firm, but Georgiou's rejection couldn't have been more final. Without that deal as security for a loan, Strider & Vanderberg would have to find a new home for a scaled-down firm. Worse, they'd be forced to cut back on public interest work, the main reason for the existence of the firm. He had to bury that in the back of his mind so it wouldn't spoil their celebration.

"I saw Renatus in the Port Alberni hospital," Debra finally said. "Lying asleep on a cot, he looked like a string doll. I had a lot to ask him, so I came back a couple of hours later. He'd disappeared. I checked the records. He wasn't listed. I spotted Drake's name and looked for him, but he'd vanished too. Not likely a coincidence."

"Steve called me just before I left the office to sail here," Jack said. "He picked up Renatus's shoulder holster holding his research from the hospital safe and sneaked Renatus out of there and all the way to Ironbound. Renatus is very weak, but beginning to recover. Steve said their shared love for the hydrothermal vent makes them allies instead of enemies, so they can work together. His daughter, Esperanza, and her nurse will reach Ironbound in a couple of days."

"You think Renatus will find a cure for Moebius Syndrome using those new life forms?" Gano asked.

"Maybe, if he has enough time left. If I can get help for him from Stanford

Medical School, maybe even NIH, he could win a Nobel Prize."

"Except," Gano said, "if he showed up to collect it, they'd put him in the slammer because of all the damage his experiments caused."

"I'm not so sure of that." Jack took a swallow of scotch. "Right now he knows more than anyone else about extraction of methane from methane hydrate and about the danger that extraction could start a tsunami. He could be the most important scientist in the world. I think the government will grant him amnesty. Whatever happens, Drake will continue his research into the hydrothermal vent to prove that life on Earth began there."

"You really buy that stuff about dead chemicals getting together and producing living creatures where there's no oxygen and no sunlight? That's sci-fi crap," Gano scoffed.

"We'll find out. Renatus and Drake may change the way we think about ourselves."

"I respect Drake," Gano said, "but I hope he's honest enough to feel damned guilty. Firing those torpedoes set off a string of events that almost ended in catastrophe." He looked at the others seated at the table, a dark look in his eyes. "And he damned near got all of us killed, including his own crew."

Jack had thought more than once how devastating Drake's obsession with the HTV could have been. He hadn't spoken about it, because it was over, but he would never think about Drake without remembering.

He hadn't noticed a man approaching their table until he stopped just behind Debra. He was average in height and build, with short black hair and black-rimmed glasses. He carried a double-buckle briefcase bearing the Frye logo. Nothing distinguishing about him except for his dense black moustache whose waxed ends rose and then curled down. *Somewhere inside that man,* Jack thought, *is a frustrated circus ringmaster.*

"Pardon me, please," the man said diffidently. "I believe you are Mr. Strider. I am chief accountant for the American subsidiary of Odyssey Properties. I have the honor of representing Mr. Alex Georgiou." He bowed slightly and took a legal-size manila envelope from his briefcase. "I am handing you an unconditional Letter of Intent pertaining to sale of certain assets of Odyssey Properties. Mr. Georgiou is sure you will find it acceptable."

"Yayzoos," Gano exclaimed, fingering his own Magnum-like 'stache, "just like a speckled trout taking a mayfly out of the air."

Jack was astonished. He'd assumed Georgiou had already found a better deal or was so shell-shocked he'd given up.

"How did you find me?" he asked, a lame question while he got his wits together.

"A woman named Mei at your law firm told me you were here."

"Mr. Georgiou knows his rejection terminated my offer, so you're delivering this in person to see whether you can bring it back to life, right?"

"That is a possibility, sir."

Jack watched puzzlement and suspicion chase each other across Debra's face.

She knew who Georgiou was. Now she knew Jack had made an offer committing them to buy "certain assets." Given their financial bind, she wouldn't take that well. This was going to take big-time diplomacy.

"Tell Mr. Georgiou that if these documents accurately reflect my terms, I will recommend them to my partner for her consideration."

The accountant's shoulders dropped, and he inhaled deeply. "Thank you, Mr. Strider. Mr. Georgiou will expect your call of confirmation. Perhaps some time tomorrow morning if that's convenient?"

The guy knew how to dance. Obviously he'd been told to get a time commitment but knew not to press.

"I'll do better than that. Give us a few minutes alone, and I'll discuss it with my partner right now."

The accountant half-bowed several times and walked away.

"All right," Debra said, "I know you have an explanation." Her voice was cool, controlled.

I know it better be a damned good one.

"The research, technology, equipment design, and computer programs Renatus developed for Barbas are a light-year more advanced than what any competitors have. That's what we're buying. We'll license them for fat fees to everyone who wants to get rich mining minerals from the seabed. It will save each licensee years and millions they'd otherwise have to spend doing their own R&D. We can even get ex-platform workers from Astoria hired to show licensees how to use the equipment."

"But we can't license any of Renatus's work on extracting methane," Debra objected.

"Not until after the process is perfected, if that ever happens. If it does, that windfall will support our practice into the next century." Then he told her the purchase price and a guesstimate of what it would cost to set up the licensing operation.

"The business concept makes sense," Debra said, "but we'd have to hire more people and go into a field we know next to nothing about. We can barely pay Pacific Gas & Electric to keep the lights on, and you're saying we should borrow millions of dollars. Even if we were crazy enough to saddle ourselves with that kind of debt, who would be crazy enough to lend us the money?"

"Any major lender. This deal works because of the purchase price. Odyssey Properties is out of the business of mining minerals or methane, so that technology is worthless to Georgiou. He needs cash immediately. That's why he'll sell to us at one-tenth the real value. With that price, and the guarantee that we'll get the Armstrong fee as additional collateral, we can borrow the money we'll need for the deal, plus"—this was the key—"enough to fund our law firm at current levels until the Armstrong fee arrives."

"We'd be betting the existence of our firm," she said. Her face was grave.

"A good player can sit at a poker table and struggle along all night with bad cards as long as he has the guts to make a big bet if he finally has a winning hand.

What do you say, partner?"

"If we don't do it," she said, "that would be ironic. We beat Barbas, we beat the Air Force, and our firm still goes down. I say . . . we go for it."

Jack squeezed her hand and waved the accountant back to the table.

"Call Georgiou back. The deal he turned down yesterday has changed."

In a flash, the accountant's expression went from smug to stunned. He didn't say "Oh, no," but his face did.

Jack felt sure that in the accountant's experience, Odyssey Properties had always been the party setting the terms for a deal. He also saw surprise in Debra's eyes. She was probably wondering if he was about to add requirements that would screw up the deal.

"But Mr. Strider, it's very early in the morning in Athens."

Jack ignored his objection. "There are two additional terms. First, he will end Barbas's attempt to evict our law firm from our offices. Second, he will grant us a two-year option to buy any or all of the buildings on Pier 9 now owned by Odyssey Properties. The price will be the appraised current fair market value minus twenty percent. He will accept or reject the whole package on the phone right now. If he agrees, you will hand-deliver an unconditional written commitment to our offices. Any questions?"

The accountant looked taken aback, no doubt wondering if delivering the message would get him fired. "No questions."

"Good. I don't need to talk with Mr. Georgiou, so give him a call and let us know his answer before we take our offer back."

The accountant backed away from the table, as though fearing to turn his back.

Jack had something like an out-of-body experience, looking at himself from another table, coolly laying out an ultimatum to an international oligarch. The future of the law firm hung on a knife edge either way the decision went. Yet he felt completely in his groove for the first time in a long time.

"By God, you're ruthless," Gano said under his breath.

"Georgiou insulted me yesterday when he thought he held the whip."

Debra shook her head. "Those last demands will hit him like a brick, but he's too committed to refuse." Then she kissed him. And kissed him again.

The drama of Georgiou's offer to sell and Jack's counterdemands caused an emotional letdown. They turned their attention to scotch, rum, and wine until Gano asked, "Want me to settle the score with that rattlesnake who served you with the eviction notice?"

His question was directed to Jack, but Debra spoke up.

"Simms is mine," she said firmly. "I'm about to file a complaint against him with the Board of Governors of the California State Bar."

"That's a lot more gentle than I had in mind," Gano said. "What do you have on him?"

"I already had proof of slander, harassment, and aiding theft of our confidential files to hijack our clients. Then I got the clincher."

The server eased up to the table. Jack waved for another round. He knew from Debra's pleased smile that she was about to deliver her punch line.

"Simms sent a man to plant listening devices—bugs—in our offices. I caught the guy in the act. Add that to the other offenses, and the Bar will put Simms on a spit and roast him. He'll never practice law again." She sipped her wine. "After he's disbarred, we'll sue him for monetary damages and file a criminal complaint. I just hope Barbas owed Sinclair & Simms a lot of money it will never collect."

"Hold on," Jack said. "What do you mean you 'caught him in the act'?"

She told them.

"Way to go," Gano said. "As the saying goes, 'Cometh the hour, cometh the man,' except in this case it was a woman."

Molly shook her head in admiration. "Looking at you, I never would have thought—"

"You have no idea," Jack said. He'd seen Debra in full karate-warrior mode in Mexico. "That bugger never had a chance."

"Speaking of rattlesnakes," Gano said, "does anyone know what happened to Heinz and *Palinouros*?"

"Sure do," Jack said. "The Coast Guard found *Palinouros* abandoned about ten miles off the northern California coast. They figure that when she ran out of fuel, the crew headed for shore in lifeboats."

"Sooner or later," Gano said, "it may occur to Heinz that he has a beef with you. What if he shows up in San Francisco?"

Jack saw a flicker of concern in Debra's eyes. "He hasn't committed any crimes yet, so it's more likely he'll try for a job in Central America under a fake name." He smiled. "Frankly, I'm more worried about being run into by some tourist in a rental car." He'd already thought about Heinz being somewhere out there nursing a grudge, so he hoped he was right.

The accountant returned to the table. "Mr. Georgiou requires that you wire $1 million to Odyssey Properties immediately as a non-refundable down payment."

"No," Jack said.

The accountant didn't miss a beat. "He said that if you refused, I was to tell you to go to hell"—his back stiffened and his chin went up—"but to go ahead with the transaction."

"And?"

"He will instruct Mr. Stan Simms to drop the eviction."

"What else?"

"He will have an option on the Pier 9 property in your office tomorrow."

"So that's it?"

"There was more, but I'd rather not repeat it. I'll be in your office at nine o'clock tomorrow."

"Actually, we're tied up for the next couple of days. Have the signed documents there tomorrow, and we'll give you a call when we're ready to see you. That's all. Goodbye."

As the accountant walked away, waves of relief washed over Jack. Finding financing to purchase Pier 9 might be tough, but given the below-market terms, it would be feasible when they were ready. He raised his scotch, and they clinked glasses.

"Good news all around," Debra said.

"Gano," Jack said, "I hope you're not heading back to Mexico right away."

Gano cleared his throat. "Funny you'd say that. I asked Molly to come with me to Divisadero, but she couldn't quite see it as paradise."

"That's an understatement," Molly said. "So I invited him to come to Astoria with me. You won't believe what he did, started talking about helping me get my tavern back on its feet and lending a hand around town." She gave him an indignant look.

"Yeah, well, she rattled my cage pretty good. Fact is, Molly and I are going to be a couple." He beamed and rested his hand on her shoulder. His mithril wristband gleamed in the sun.

"The big question," Debra said, "is whether Molly has any idea what a wild man you are."

"Of course she doesn't. If she did, she'd fly away like a nightingale."

"Nothing I can't handle," Molly said. "By the way, I fired my bartender. Seems he and his pals had ganged up on a couple of friends of mine. I told him he'd be better off in some other state."

Half-listening to Debra trying to draw Gano out about his relationship with Molly, Jack thought about his own relationship with Debra. In the past, he'd been satisfied with sequential relationships. None had been shallow, but none had made him consider a long-term future together either. His feelings for Debra were very different.

In Mexico, they'd fought side by side. She'd had his back more than once and taken the lead when needed. After they returned to San Francisco, he thought inviting her to be his partner in the firm implied a level of commitment on his part that went beyond the practice of law. He'd assumed she understood that, but he'd never spelled it out. *Gee, wonder why.*

She was exceptionally smart, beautiful, a wonderful lover, and an ideal law partner who called him out when she thought he was wrong and supported him the rest of the time. He had no trouble listing all the great things she brought to their relationship, but what did he bring? He started to make a mental list and then had an insight. That was the wrong question. The right questions were: what did she want from him, and could he give that to her? He didn't have a clue.

He had to figure out what she needed. *Oh my God, that might even mean asking her.* Then he'd have to do his best to meet those needs. Petros Barbas was one of many men who had tried to tempt her away and failed, but there were more snakes in the grass. Or Debra might walk away, if she wasn't getting what she wanted. He was ready to confess that he adored her and show her that she was his highest priority.

That made him blink. He took a deep swallow of Glenora.

He'd ask her to go back to Tikal with him for a do-over. This time she wouldn't need to stalk away in frustration. And he wouldn't need to risk his life being stupid and hanging off the face of a cliff. But was he kidding himself? Could he put his commitment in words? Maybe he was so hooked on his self-protective image that he *couldn't* change. Could he really bare his feelings to her, or were his old ruts too deep? As long as he kept his feelings inside his head, he felt safe.

He noticed that Debra, Gano, and Molly had stopped talking and were staring at him. He met Debra's eyes and swallowed hard.

She gave him a quizzical look and said, "What?"

"Nothing."

Just then, their attention was diverted into Belvedere Cove. "Look there," she said, pointing at a red plane with a white horizontal stripe taxiing in the water toward them. "It's that seaplane—I mean amphibian—we saw a while ago. Pretty fancy way to come to Sam's for dinner."

"It's not bringing anyone to Sam's for dinner," Jack said. "It's picking up a very lucky couple to take them on a romantic trip."

"How do you know that?" Debra asked. "Do you know them?"

"We *are* them," he said with a big grin.

"You wonderful man."

He stood and retrieved a carry-on bag from between his chair and the railing. "I have everything we need." He looked at Gano. "Tell the manager my sailboat will be tied up at his pier for a few days. And, by the way, for the only time since I met you, I'm sticking you with the bill."

TWO DAYS AFTER Gano paid the bill at Sam's Anchor Café, a U.S. surveillance satellite was tracking a convoy of vessels that had left Korean waters four days earlier and headed east. Intelligence analysts had concluded that the lead ship was a petroleum drill ship, very large but otherwise not remarkable. Three ships trailing in its wake looked like standard commercial support vessels, except that each carried a cylindrical object about thirty feet long tied down under a tarp on its aft deck.

Lieutenant Terry Ross, watching a monitor in El Dorado, Kansas, asked the analyst next to him, "What do you think is under those tarps?"

Major Rocky de Villiers had done this job for twelve years and was far past giving a damn. "Jet skis for all I know. As long as they aren't nuclear-tipped missiles, which they aren't, I don't give a rat's ass."

Ross shrugged. "On its present heading, the convoy will enter U.S. territorial waters in eight hours heading toward Oregon."

"Won't happen. They'll stop short of U.S. waters. Then they'll drill, baby, drill."

"I wonder if they got that Notice to Mariners about the big-ass drilling platform that burned and collapsed out there. Sure wouldn't want to collide with that baby in the middle of the night."

THE SAME SURVEILLANCE satellite had also been reporting data on the USS

Hopper (DDG-70), a high-tech guided missile destroyer out of Pearl Harbor. At the end of her trans-Pacific voyage she would pass under the Golden Gate Bridge, water cannons blasting, to participate in a Parade of Ships culminating in a ceremony at St. Francis Yacht Club. It was a bullshit assignment resented by her captain, a hard-shelled mustang named Banfield.

Eighteen hours before *Hopper* was scheduled to make port, Banfield was in a sour mood as he sat in his elevated captain's chair on the bridge and stared across the vast Pacific. He paid no attention to idle comments from Lt. Ed Gardner, the officer of the deck. Suddenly an unusual movement a quarter mile dead ahead of the ship caught his eye. He set down a mug of black coffee and squinted but couldn't identify what he saw.

"What the hell is that?" he snapped, and snatched his personal Steiner binoculars from beside the GPS.

Gardner was instantly at his side, raising his Navy-issue glasses. He pointed to where the water was growing more agitated. "The way the water's riled up, it could be a sub about to surface, but none of ours is anywhere near here."

"That's no sub," Banfield growled. Now he saw that a patch of water a hundred yards ahead of *Hopper*, wider than several football fields, was sending spouts high into the air. The surface of the patch had transformed from deep blue into silvery froth.

"I've never seen anything like that. I'd swear a hole is opening in the ocean ahead of us. Helmsman, hard right turn. *Now!*"

"Aye, aye, sir."

Hopper heeled hard to starboard as she began a perilous high speed turn. Pounding forward through the swells at twenty six knots, she couldn't turn nearly fast enough to avoid what was ahead.

Banfield knew it was too late.

The End

About the Author

Rob Sangster is an award-winning author, Stanford lawyer, political appointee in Washington, D.C., newspaper columnist, sailor, rock climber, and has traveled in 110 countries so far. He and his mystery-writer wife divide their writing time between Memphis and the wild coast of Nova Scotia.

robsangster.com
Or find him on Facebook

CPSIA information can be obtained
at www.ICGtesting.com
Printed in the USA
LVOW11s1253110517
534153LV00003B/153/P